Four Kings

A Very Secret Garden
Book 2

by Karan K Anders

All characters in this publication
are fictitious and any resemblance
to real persons, living or dead,
is purely coincidental.

Four Kings
© 2022 Andrea K Hösth writing as Karan K Anders.
All rights reserved.
ISBN: 978-1-925188-34-9
www.andreakhost.com
Cover Design: James, GoOnWrite.com

Author's Note

"Four Kings" is a continuation of the story told in "The Book of Firsts" and is best not read alone.

The story is set in a Greenland that sits 1,000 km further south.

Acknowledgements

With thanks to Michele K for much useful commentary, and to Susan B for executive fan support.

ᐸ

One

Early morning over Helios. Peach and pink streaked the glassy spires of the city centre, shifting to deep blue shadow at street level. Soft silvers caressed the surface of water surrounding the city's island heart, traced the paths of rivers, and shimmered upon the vast stretch of northern lake. Tiny artificial embers faded in the dawn, marking the high points of skyscrapers, radio towers, and bridges.

The interior lights of the plane came on, and my view transformed into reflection before I could finish counting the bridges. I blinked, then turned to the practical business of returning my dad to functional humanity.

My dad and I share a sense of humour, but are opposites in almost every other way. By the time I was fifteen I had followed my mother to gain inches over him. My dark brown hair tends to be long and orderly, while my dad's dirty blond locks turn shaggy and disreputable if he gives them a moment's leeway. I'm a perpetual insomniac, while he can sleep anywhere, any time. The problem is waking him up.

Experience had prepared me for overnight flights where the lights come on only a short time before landing. Reaching into the backpack tucked between my feet, I pulled out a thermos I'd had filled at an airport coffee shop, uncapped it beneath his nose, and waited for scent to work its magic.

As soon as my dad's eyelids twitched, I poured black gold into the thermos lid, and watched as his hands automatically rose. Once I was sure he had a steady hold, I let go, and tried to recapture the view as the plane travelled past Helios and swung in a broad arc before descending to Sturluson Airport. By the time we'd landed, my dad had reached the stage where he could easily manage navigating his way through bag collection and customs, but did so in abstract silence. He usually didn't get verbal for a half hour or more after coffee, so I took the lead in chatting to border control and then the car hire staffer. Dad occasionally nodded.

"I think I'll apply for a learner's permit," I said, as I called up navigation directions to the city's eastern suburbs.

"Mm?" Dad responded, but had by then shifted to mostly awake, and added: "You expect to do a lot of driving?"

"No, it's just a convenience thing. I originally wasn't going to bother, since I couldn't think how I'd get the necessary driving hours up, but at least two of my new housemates have cars."

"Okay. If that doesn't work out, perhaps your mother and I could help you at Christmas."

"You decided to attend the book festival?"

"Well, editors being very tied up in sales, Caitlin is very insistent on me making time for more public appearances. I think wanting me to show up in person is directly opposed to her worries about anyone joining the dots about my various noms de plume."

"Given I've been happily reeling off at least half of them at every opportunity, it's only a matter of time," I said. "Will it bother you when they're all connected?"

"I don't see why it matters. Marketing's never been my strong suit, but I think Caitlin's overestimating how many readers I'll lose if my large portfolio of euphemisms for bodily fluids is exposed. And I think Blake especially would gain readers."

My dad's horror pen name has never sold well, and it seemed only logical to me to cross his reader streams and see if anything exploded. But marketing wasn't my strong suit either.

"I've told Caitlin I'll try to keep my racier side under wraps until *A Tranquil Death* is out," Dad continued. "So, no indulging your hobby of dramatic revelations until then, Mika."

"Until when? You've been working on *Tranquil* for an eternity."

Dad gave me a quick, triumphant smile. "I'm on my second read-through of the full draft. It'll be out before the end of the year."

"Really? You mean you finally found a Booker-worthy conclusion?"

He snorted. "No, I stopped fighting my instincts and gave it the ending I wanted, instead. And am much happier about the whole thing. Now to decide on a new project."

"How about another Blake? It's been ages."

"Want me to ritually execute some more of your classmates?"

I laughed. "Not this year. There were a few pests at Corascur, but no-one worth writing about. Besides, it would hit different when it's people I might still meet, even though I will technically be changing schools."

"How's the adjustment to sticking in one city going? More good than bad, I hope?"

"It's great," I said frankly. "Much as I enjoyed country-hopping, I think it's going to suit me to be long-term in Helios. I liked it here so much that I actually applied for architecture, pure physics and pure maths as backup plans so I could continue with the Helios U plan. Those courses have much larger intakes than engineering physics with Professor Tremaine, and I could have converted to engineering later." I sighed. "I'd love to deep-dive into materials physics in particular. There are too many things I want to study. If I didn't want so much to build actual bridges, I'd probably never leave university."

"There's no hurry," Dad said. "Study what you like. I expect you'll manage to work out a way to have it all, in the end."

This made me smile, for multiple reasons.

"Have you ever thought of going back to finish your degree?"

"Hell, no. University was me waffling because I didn't think I was ready to be a writer. When you came along, I simply skipped the degree and went with what I loved. I sometimes try to talk your mother into getting a few accreditations, but formal education has ended up more or less irrelevant to what Sorenson enjoys doing."

The apartment I'd used during my last year of high school had no parking space, but we found a spot only a short walk away, and made quick work of collecting the suitcase and boxes I'd prepacked. I'd cleaned before heading out on holiday, and given notice, cancelled the electricity, and changed mailing addresses as soon as my acceptance had come in, so only had to check quickly for issues before locking the door and leaving this stage of my life behind me.

"This is a little past use," my dad said, struggling with the single working wheel on my second suitcase.

"It didn't seem worth replacing it," I told him. "I won't have to pack everything I own for ages, since I'm going to be living in one place for at least the next five years. Or at least in the same city."

"Worried the share house won't work out?" he asked.

"Well, people are complicated," I said, grimacing. "It's possible to like someone amazingly, and yet find them unbearable when you're stuck in close quarters with them."

"If they push even your tolerance to the limit, there's no need to stay," he said. "Although we'd prefer you not live alone again. That little hospital trip last year scared Sorenson and I enough that we think this offer from your gamer friends a fantastic option, even though the environment may not be the best."

"What's bad about it?" I asked, stowing my boxes in the car's back seat. "Their place is right up close to campus. I'll be able to walk to classes."

"I've seen you when a game gets under your skin. Devoted as I know you are to your goals, a start-up game studio will surely be full of distractions. I only hope...you said they converted an old dance studio, right? I only hope there's sufficient sound insulation so you have a chance of quiet study, not to mention sleeping."

"I got the impression the place has a floor for living, and a floor for working. They've been amusing themselves wanting to surprise me with it, so I don't have more details. Rin did ask what colour I wanted my room painted, and if I had any special requests. I mainly want a place with good light to put a desk, and

he said there was a room that could manage that." I
thought of the relative wealth of the three boys who
were going to rent me a room, and hid my grin. "They
said it's a good area, so I doubt it'll be the worst place
I've ever lived."

"It would have some stiff competition," Dad
admitted, giving up on cramming my large suitcase into
the car boot, and shoving it in the back seat with the
boxes.

The real estate agency was ten minutes away by
foot, and we decided to walk rather than struggle with
parking again. Arriving just as it opened, I handed in
the apartment keys, took a signed receipt in return, and
turned to find my dad talking to an agent.

"...at least three bedrooms, two studies or one very
large one, an acre or two of land, not entirely isolated.
As beautiful a view as can be managed."

"Are you looking for a new build, or a period piece?"
the agent asked.

"Oh, I like a bit of history."

I watched in faint bemusement as my dad gave the
agent an email address to send possibilities to, but
didn't comment until we were walking back.

"Visiting Newport wasn't much fun this time, was
it?"

"I think it's clear that your Aunt Nia means to stop
at your Nan's. Her pointed comments about our boxes
taking up all of the garage is perilously close to
transitioning to an announcement she's helped your
Nan clear it out so she could convert the space into a
teen retreat for Davey. It's better to make arrangements
before that happens."

"You've practically bought that house twice over," I said. "And it was so hard at the time."

"I know, I know." Dad sighed. "I was feeling very combative about it all too, but something Evelyn said made me decide fighting over the family home wouldn't be in anyone's best interests."

"I know Evelyn's approach to accounting is inventive, but did she really tell you to give up on property you've sunk over a million pounds into?"

"Evelyn told me that her clients, particularly the ones who started out without a lot of money, tend to fall into two categories. Those that cling to every penny, particularly when relatives start trying to take advantage. And those that remember that money in itself isn't nearly as fun as fine wine, expensive perfume, and saucy smiles from hopeful strangers. Now that we have a few extra digits to our bank balance, the thing that would make us happiest is a home port in the same place as you. We missed you a hell of a lot this past year, Mika."

"I missed you too," I said, hugging his arm, and then letting go as we reached the car. "And, wow, just think what we might find in those boxes."

"Twenty years of junk, and enough author's copies to build a respectable fort. Not to mention at least two of my wallets, since I can't think what else could have happened to them."

"Shipping your wallet to Wales once might be excusable, but did you really do it twice?"

"Guess we'll find out. Want to house hunt with me tomorrow?"

"Sure," I said, with only a blink for three boys who probably had a lot of plans for me after nearly two months apart.

Of course, they were expecting me to arrive the day after tomorrow, so the sacrifice was arguably never theirs to make.

On cue, my phone mrrp-ed, and while my dad negotiated rush hour traffic, I checked 'Mockingbird', the special group chat Bran had established, which only four people in the world would ever see.

Kyou: *Nothing more annoying than plans falling into a heap.*

Impressed by the coincidence, I messaged back, asking what had happened.

Kyou: *We were supposed to be going through the final handover of the renovations this morning, but instead we've all been summoned out to The Grove.*

Mika: *Has D-Day finally arrived?*

Kyou: *It didn't sound like it's about us. Rin's sisters' birthdays are this weekend and next week, and in order not to disturb them, Rin has been spectacularly dutiful and compliant, while Bran and I have simply tried to pretend we don't exist.*

Mika: *I'm amazed no-one's noticed that Rin didn't apply for the family-ordered degree.*

Kyou: *Oh, he did, in addition to what he actually wants to study. He'll just withdraw when people notice he's signed up for too many degrees, or start chasing him about not turning up to classes.*

Mika: *Will you not do your house handover at all today?*

Kyou: *We've postponed it until this afternoon. How's things going there? Still problems with your aunt?*

Mika: *Mum and Dad cut short their stay, and Mum took a job in Brazil. Tell you about it later.*

Resigned to a delay in our reunion, I settled back to watch the scenery along the tram line. The route took us to the inner west of the city, passing through a cluster of towers and medium-rise buildings centred on Helios University Hospital. This mass of apartment and office blocks did not offer an enticing first impression of the university district, but the height dropped away as we travelled further west, and soon we turned off into a suburb called Hutton Forest, sprawling over gently undulating land, and dominated by upmarket terrace houses. The navigator led us to the lower end of Sycamore Street.

Because Rin, Kyou and Bran so patently wanted to surprise me, I hadn't looked up the street view of their 'dance school', and so gaped a little as it finally came into view. Dad braked when the app announced our destination was directly ahead, and joined me in staring at white concrete rising three and a half stories above a sloping street and taking up roughly four times the width and breadth of the neighbouring buildings.

"Do you think the locals call it the iceberg?" I asked, eyeing the protruding rounded corners of the otherwise square building. "Or the marshmallow?"

"It actually reminds me of a huge bouncy castle, with those towers-like bulges at each corner," Dad added. "Or...wrong shape, but it's so big and separate from everything around it, it makes me feel like it's about to steam out of port. Like the *Titanic*."

"Looks like it might be an early 1900s build. Or a pastiche, or...well, it's an original."

"Nothing in the way of parking in view," Dad said, glancing about.

"I'll just unload, and you can find a park and come back," I suggested.

After shifting my suitcases and boxes to the footpath-merging-with-steps entryway, I gazed through unresponsive sliding glass doors to a sign on the wall of the waiting room beyond: *Kybirn.*

The absence of the boys I'd been expecting to surprise should not be an obstacle, since there'd been extensive discussion of door codes over Mockingbird. I looked around the area under the small awning, spotted a discreet keypad, and grinned triumphantly when the doors slid smoothly open.

Hauling my bags into a spectacularly neutral waiting room, I glanced from couches on the left to an elevator on my right, fetched my boxes in, then crossed to poke at a tablet fixed to the wall near the elevator. It wasn't turned on, so I gave up and turned my attention to a door that led further into the building. A second keypad was by the handle, and I tried out the 'residential' code, received an affirmative beep, and pushed the door open.

Just inside, sitting on a small stool, was a naked girl with a pink ribbon tied around her breasts.

"Hello?" I said, trying to control my expression.

The girl, a curvy redhead, looked entirely blank, but then stood up, half-covering her chest, and saying: "Miss Niles?"

"That's right," I told her, recovering from my initial boggle. "You're not what I thought Rin, Kyou and Bran would go for in terms of décor."

She flushed, and laughed embarrassedly. "This is— ah, well, anyway. I'm Adriana Xenakis, from Cassadine Malway."

"Hi, call me Mika," I said. "I don't know what Cassadine Malway is, though."

"We handled the renovations for Kybirn," Adriana explained. "*From first idea to final touch*," she added, with an air of quotation.

Ribbons included. But despite the outlandish get-up, she seemed a warm and enthusiastic girl, and I couldn't quite dislike her. "Which of them is it for?" I asked, nodding at her 'outfit'.

"Mr Laurent," Adriana said, going even redder.

"That slight French accent," I murmured conspiratorially.

She widened her eyes and nodded. "Sinful! And the way he holds himself! I was convinced he was a model."

"He could definitely work as one. I have to say, though, I doubt this approach is likely to be successful."

"I know," she said, with undiminished cheer. "But I also know I'd always regret not giving my all." She glanced down at the bow hiding parts of her sumptuous breasts. "It's like entering a lottery. The odds are astronomical, but there's always that chance."

"Then—well, I won't wish you luck, but I hope you feel satisfied having done it. But Kyou told me not ten minutes ago that, he, Rin and Bran were called to a family meeting, and won't be back here until this afternoon."

Adriana's smile dimmed, and she crossed to a shoulder bag tucked just inside the door to check her phone.

"Rescheduled to four," she said, and pushed aside obvious disappointment to turn back to me and say briskly: "Well, would you like me to show you your room?"

"Sure. But I should warn you my dad's probably going to be here any minute. I expect he'll like the bow, though."

"Ah!" Adriana only then seemed to remember her lack of clothing. "I'll be back in a moment."

She tidied herself and her stool away, and I went back out into the waiting room. There was a door beside the couches marked with a washroom sign, and I pushed it open just to be nosy, washed my hands, and returned in time to meet Dad peering through the glass. I waved, found a green push button beside the sliding doors, and let him in.

"There's a wonderful bakery back near the tramline," he said, holding up coffees and paper bags. "Found it by scent alone."

I grabbed the coffee and bag he angled toward me, and sat down on the nearest couch to fill my face with apple Danish.

"Your friends aren't up? Are we trapped in the vestibule?"

"They were called away, but there's a person from the renovation company who's going to show me where my room is. Should be just enough time to eat before she gets back."

My dad took out a croissant while I worked on the Danish. "So how filthy rich are your friends? Or are they in danger of eviction at any moment?"

"Their great-grandfather's the founder of L-B Corp, but since game studios aren't on the parental agenda, I don't think there's any family money going into this. They can afford this place because Kyou is so good at finance his family tried to blackmail him into becoming a corporate slave."

"Oh, really?" My dad's face lit up. He loves a good family drama. "Spill."

"I don't know the full story, but it's part of the reason they're willing to rent me a room. I ran into Kyou on a critical day, told him my response to blackmail would be to break the blackmailer's stuff so they never wanted to annoy me again, and Kyou somehow turned an off-hand comment into an epic reverse play, ending up with a bunch of extra money and an excuse to separate from the toxic parts of his family."

"The best conclusion," my dad said. "So, they're good at making money. How do you think they'll go with the games? If I do work on scripting with them, should I prepare myself for it to never go anywhere?"

"I think they'll definitely ship a game in some form, if only because they're able to throw money at it. And it will have beautiful music and stunning art. I think it's likely it will be a good game in other aspects, but I can't guarantee it."

"Well, it'll be an experience. Do you–"

The inner door opened, and he stopped short.

"Sorry to keep you waiting!" Adriana said. "I've activated the elevator, so we can just take your luggage straight up."

Resisting the urge to tell her she looked so different with her clothes on, I silently admired how the girl had managed such a sleek professional look so quickly.

"This is my dad, Gareth Teyrn. Dad, this is Adriana from Cassadine Malway, who handled the renovations here."

"Nice to meet you, Mr Teyrn," Adriana said, shaking his hand. "I see you've found *Pain Au Lait*. Being a minute's walk away from the best bakery in the city has been a super bonus to this project."

"Coffee's not bad, either," my dad said, smiling. "Tell me about home renovation—that's not something I've had much exposure to. Is it fulfilling?"

"Oh, I love it," Adriana said, with a radiant smile, reaching to take one of my boxes. "Particularly when it's unusual projects like this one. Both historical and state-of-the-art, and the opportunity to work on rooms that we've never handled before."

"Do the locals have a nickname for this building?" I asked, as we fitted ourselves and my luggage into a comfortably spacious lift.

"Moby Dick," Adriana said, with an irrepressible giggle.

"Can't deny it's a whale of a place," my dad said. "I take it it's not a recent build."

"Early 1930s. There's quite a few Art Deco features which we've done our best to preserve. The building's even been considered for historical listing, but more because Dauncey Morgan took his first ballet lessons here rather than the structure itself."

"So, it was some kind of ballet boarding school?"

"Yes, once quite prestigious, but after the original owner died it slowly went downhill, and eventually bankrupted."

The elevator doors opened, and Adriana led the way along a corridor with doors to where a balcony overlooked an atrium. My father stopped as it opened up, murmuring in appreciation of a stairway that curled from the ground floor to the level above us, lit by leadlight windows following the upward spiral. A gorgeous period piece.

"I can't help but picture a whole bunch of kids in tutus running up it," my dad said. He stared down, frowning. "Are there any histories of the place? Do you know what happened to the original owner's estate?"

Adriana looked a little startled, but I had recognised this transformation from self-effacing to focused, and explained: "Dad's a writer. This building must have given him an idea."

"Do you have a business card, Adriana?" my dad asked, pulling out his phone and taking a few pictures of the staircase. "I'm very interested in the process of doing a renovation like this one."

"Of course, Mr Teyrn," Adriana said, and once her card had been handed over, we followed the corridor around until we reached a door in the opposite corner of the building to the elevator.

"This is the quietest part of the house," Adriana said, balancing the box so she could push open the door. "Not that any part of this area is noisy, but with a recording studio on the next floor, sound insulation is an issue we've paid a lot of attention to, both for residents and neighbours."

Seeing the room, I stopped listening altogether, and walked forward in amazement.

My first glimpse had been of French doors, but then the bed stole all attention. Even in a room far larger than I'd been expecting, it stood like a monument to sleep: mounded with pillows, and quite possibly needing a ladder to climb.

"I—I seem to recall saying that I'd like some underbed storage," I managed.

Adriana immediately stepped forward to demonstrate the underbed storage, which proved to be drawers that glided out at a touch.

"All the beds are super-king," she explained, seeing we were still stunned. "Having them all the same size makes it easier to manage the linen. The storage does add to the height."

"Looks fun," my dad said, at last. "Nasty fall if you're a restless sleeper, but would certainly add extra impetus to leaping out of bed each morning."

"You've never leapt out of bed in your life," I said, recovering enough to start looking around.

The décor was primarily eggshell white, from the walls to a leather couch opposite the foot of the bed, and a matching leather chair in one corner. Filmy white curtains and natural wood shutters were both drawn back to allow a free view through French doors to a balcony and swaying green leaves. An open doorway to my right led to a walk-in dressing room that could only sneer at my two suitcases, and beyond that a full bathroom, with a free-standing tub, a toilet partially hidden by a glass brick wall, and a shower enclosure rigged to blast the unwary from every direction.

"How many bedrooms does this place have?" my dad asked, while I admired a trio of decorative pots hanging high above the bath, all frothy with maidenhair fern. "And is this the largest?"

"Four suites and two guest rooms," Adriana said. "This is the smallest suite."

"You're right," my dad told me. "It's not going to be the worst place you've lived in."

Adriana laughed, and said: "One thing Mr Laurent was very particular about was that all the residents have space to get away both from the office, and each other. I rented over near the hospital, my first year of study. Eight of us in a three-bedroom apartment. The horror stories I could tell you about share housing..."

The French doors opened easily, and I stepped out onto a slate-tiled balcony with wrought iron railings that did their best not to interrupt the view, although the outlook was mainly tree close to me, tree further away from me. There was grass below and a paved area to my right, but since the balcony didn't run the length of the building, I couldn't move along to get a better look.

I smiled at the small café table and pair of chairs that took up the right half of the balcony, then glanced left, saw windows, and remembered that each of the corners of this building bulged. Quickly heading inside, I folded back what I'd thought was just part of the window shutters.

A desk had been fitted to the circumference of a small round room. A cup-shaped swivel chair sat in the centre, angled toward twin monitors, a keyboard, and a lush graphics tablet. Near the door, a desk-to-ceiling bookcase boasted a solid selection of the most important engineering and physics references.

Dad poked his head in, smiled at me, then took Adriana off to visit the main stairway.

Sitting down, I spun slowly, marvelling.

Last year, on the first day at my last high school, I'd met three very handsome boys, and ended up playing an extended and very intimate game with them. Over the course of the school year, I'd enjoyed a lot of simple friendship, a great deal of lust, and a burgeoning sense of belonging that had made it impossible for me to walk away from them. Because I liked them, and would miss them, and they'd found a way we could go on without destroying my reputation in the process.

None of us had talked about what we had as love. It had only been a year, and we were still getting to know each other, were working out how far we could go, and deep down I still believed it would all turn out to be a pleasant interlude that would eventually pass.

The feeling I experienced, seeing that row of books and understanding the care that had gone into this room, was new, very strong, and a little scary. Joy. Searing joy. So happy for a moment that I hurt.

This year, I would get to know my Kings better, but it looked like I'd end up discovering just as much about myself.

Two

Refusing Adriana's offer of a tour of the rest of the house, I took my dad off to the city's largest shopping mall to apply for my learner's permit, and pick out one or two small things I wanted to add to my room.

"Early lunch?" Dad suggested, as I admired my zombie-like licence photo.

"Sure."

We found a café with lots of tables, ate lightly while checking our phones, and then settled back to decide what next.

"Not often I see you so happy, kiddo. You always wanted your very own study nook?"

"Well, I think I'll thoroughly enjoy that one, but it's more the thought they'd put into it. I stumbled across some really good friends, this past year. Let's hope living with them doesn't screw it all up."

"If that happens, perhaps we could find a two-bedroom apartment for you and Lania to share?"

"In order to test another friendship? I wonder if I could talk Lania into it? I'll keep it in mind as a contingency plan. So, do you want to try for an early check in at your hotel? Or head straight to the university to hunt for local histories about Moby Dick?"

He laughed. "I'll start with internet searches. But I really have to finish that second read-through of *Tranquil*, since both Caitlin and Devine are emailing me approximately every fifteen minutes asking for the manuscript."

"I'd say it's good your editor and agent are keeping you on track, but you write so quickly it seems unnecessary."

"It's because I've been talking about the book for years. They're not used to me not handing things in as soon as I mention them. How about you go shopping while I camp out here?" He finished doing something on his phone. "Check your bank balance, and then try to fill up that dressing room."

"Have you been stimulated by my over-the-top housing arrangements?" I asked, raising my eyebrows but opening my banking app.

"No, this is something your mother and I discussed last year. Given that we've sometimes lived through very straightened circumstances, I don't think it's possible to say we've spoiled you, but we did want you to have some functional experience living to a budget. Which you not only managed, but somehow could afford a trip to Peru."

"Online tutoring earnings add up when I'm not spending every penny I earn on the latest game." Discovering a significant increase in digits, I raised my eyebrows. "You actually want me to spend all this on clothes?"

"I'll respect your whims. Spend it on games, a phone or laptop, or just more fancy chocolate than even you can finish: it's supposed to be fun money, not your living expenses. For that, you'll get twice your previous monthly allowance, which should, I hope, keep you in sundries."

"Twice the allowance when my rent's been halved, and I don't have the daily commute? I should hope it would keep me in sundries." I locked the screen of my four-year-old phone, which was still serviceable, if not up to date. "I can't really get used to it, this having money."

"It's fun, though, isn't it?" my dad said with a quick grin. "The last few years have been a ride, and I'm going to follow Evelyn's advice and properly enjoy it. She recommended property as an indulgence that is also an investment, so I am simply following my brilliant accountant's advice. Now scoot. Go spend money."

I spent.

My usual approach to clothes shopping is mix and match staples, but no longer having to think of optimal packing absolutely meant I could indulge myself. And everything I looked at now came with an added measure of the likely reaction of three boys who had all shown a strong interest in my clothing—or, at least, taking it off me.

A fun few hours later I returned towing two new suitcases, crammed full, and slung about with the fruits of my labour. Including a new phone, though I decided to hold off on the laptop.

"I saw a store filled with little handbags that cost more than what I just spent," I said, sitting down and picking up the menu to review the drink selection. "Which nicely put my world view into a proper frame."

"Just because someone's riding Moby Dick doesn't mean we can't enjoy our luxury minnow," Dad said. "I've sent the manuscript off to Devine, who is very eager to get an idea of what level of advance we can push for."

"Don't forget to send it to me as well," I said. "You're leaving Caitlin hanging?"

"Now that I want to splash on a perfect house, I admit to being a little greedy about the next advance.

Tranquil is different enough from my other books that it doesn't quite fit any of my pen names, and Devine tells me that's a handy bargaining chip, though I do feel sorry for Caitlin, who assumes that anything remotely literary falls under her first refusal option. I told Devine to favour Caitlin unless she lowballs us. You plan to order something, or just memorising the menu?"

I glanced at the time, then put the menu down: I wanted to be back well before my Kings. "Let's go."

Since Dad was driving a rental, I couldn't try out my new learner's permit on the way back, but that was probably just as well, since there was still no parking on Sycamore Street. My dad plainly wanted to hole up in his hotel to start researching ballet schools, so I didn't try to coax him inside, promising to call him later, and repeating my entry into 'Moby Dick'.

My new home. And possibly my strangest. I never thought I'd go in for such a complicated relationship, one so liable for issues and—worse—so sure to draw on my time and energy. As boyfriends go, I'm sure my Kings could be superlative, but I had my doubts about me being girlfriend material. The one thing I'm selfish with is my time, and even one boyfriend seemed like a potential drain on my most precious commodity. Common sense told me three would soon have me at my limit, but I still wanted to give it shot. Or, at least, enjoy it for as long as I could. Me and Three Kings, no longer just playing.

The afternoon was progressing, there'd been no further word from my future housemates, and—since I never sleep on planes—I was starting to feel the length of the day. I solved this by turning on all the jets in my exciting new shower, and blasting myself a new awakening. Then I dried my hair while messing around in my dressing room, picking just the right shirt, and then trying to sort the rest, partially transforming the area into a bomb site by the time four o'clock rolled around.

I went out ten minutes early, and sat at a point on the spiral stair where I could see into the room immediately inside the 'residence' door. This seemed to function as both cloakroom and entry hall and, sure enough, there was a lot of red hair, pink ribbon and white skin just visible to me.

Adriana certainly had to win points for determination.

More than a little curious, I checked my phone, wondering if they'd keep her waiting long. But, no, a distant, muted sound warned me that something had changed. While I hadn't explored the building, I'd guessed there must be some form of parking, and so that muted hum was surely from the garage. A minute later a door in the cloakroom opened, and my three boyfriends arrived, though I couldn't see more than their legs.

I'd wondered what Adriana had planned to say, all wrapped up in a bow, but she only managed 'Mr Laurent' before Rin cut her off.

"I'm sorry," he said, gently. "It's a lovely gift, but I can't accept."

There was a little pause, then Adriana said something not audible to me, and stood up, retreating once again with her stool to wherever it was she'd put her clothes.

As a door closed, Rin, Kyou and Bran walked into the area immediately before the stairway. Bran was scowling, Kyou looked entertained, and Rin seemed mainly weary. They were all dressed in the kind of upmarket casual clothes that I guess is suitable for visiting the family patriarch. Three cousins, with no particular resemblance to each other: Rin very tall, slender, elegant, and Kyou and Bran a few inches shorter than his six three, similar in build but in other ways complete opposites, with Bran's oat-pale hair and grey eyes contrasting nicely to Kyou's black and black.

"A new approach," Kyou was saying, keeping his beautiful voice relatively low. "Has she been flirting all along, and I just didn't notice?"

"No, it's probably a 'might never see again' proposition," Rin said. "Before this, she's been a complete professional."

"Are you going to report her?" Bran asked, glowering in the direction Adriana had gone.

Rin shrugged. "If she hadn't backed off immediately, I probably would have. As it is, not worth spending time on."

"Imagine if Cheshire had walked in on that," Bran said.

I laughed, a helpless little spurt, and watched them all freeze, then pivot to stare up through the railings of the stairway.

"Imagine if Cheshire's dad had walked in on that," I said. "Not that he'd be unappreciative, but it would have given him an odd idea of the people renting me a room."

Kyou recovered enough to smile up at me. "I still maintain minx would be a better name for you. Come down here."

"I'm surprised you're still calling me Cheshire," I said, obeying unhurriedly. "I thought you were going to avoid that."

"We sometimes slip," Rin said, stepping forward to meet me at the bottom of the stair and sweep me into his arms, all the better to kiss me hard.

I hadn't expected that, had thought we would start with a group hug, but with only a moment's thought for how long it would take for Adriana to get dressed, I responded happily, and then turned to Bran and then Kyou.

Kyou did not take advantage of being last, kissing me for not much longer than Rin, and then leaning me back just a little to say: "How can we not call you Cheshire, when you dress for the occasion?"

"Couldn't resist when I saw it," I said, glancing down at my new t-shirt, completely black except for a vivid fanged grin.

"When did you arrive?" Bran asked, taking my hand, and then letting go, glancing back at the entry hall.

"This morning, just as Kyou told me you wouldn't be here. The earlier flight was because my dad is on his way to New York and we travelled together. He's stopping for a couple of days to go house hunting." I didn't give them more than a chance to frown, adding: "Not for me. He and Mum have decided they need somewhere to replace my Nan's house as a place to go between jobs. They're looking for somewhere with views, not inner-city."

"Oh?" Kyou looked relieved. "Would he like an abandoned farmhouse?"

"You want to palm off your failed speculation onto Mika's dad?" Bran asked, looking disgusted.

"Too soon to call it a failure," Kyou said, unperturbed. "Besides, wherever the rail line ends up going, I want to build a house at Noonerry. Having

Mika's family home nearby would be doubly convenient."

"Have they announced the change to the high-speed rail route already?" I asked. "I haven't been following."

"They've accepted it can't go through the Sunneway Pass," Kyou said. "Mainly because the legal challenges you predicted were filed just after you left. Those are going to take years to grind through the courts, and so the government's already made the announcement that the track will be re-routed. The new route isn't official yet, and there's been murmuring that the stop will be in Stratholm, but, as I said, nothing official yet."

"How big is this farmhouse?" I asked. "My dad's looking for something reasonably large."

"It's not small, though the interior's cramped up with too many rooms. The best part is a veranda currently populated with a variety of decrepit couches. The former owners spent a large amount of time entertaining out there."

"Well, if you're serious about selling, Dad and I were going to wander about looking at places tomorrow."

"Noonerry is over three hours' drive away," Rin murmured.

"Oh?" I raised my eyebrows and said to Kyou: "They'd have to be pretty amazing views."

"You think I'd want a house there for anything less than amazing?"

"Fair point," I said, and waved at Adriana as she emerged in her more professional mode. "I got back in time for your tour."

"Glad to see you, Ms Niles," she said, and then handed Rin one of a pair of tablets she was carrying.

"Are you ready for the final alterations check, Mr Laurent?"

"Whenever you are," Rin said, with only the faintest hint of irony.

It was impossible not to admire Adriana's ability to pretend she hadn't just presented herself for easy unwrapping.

"The only change on the ground floor is the rear courtyard," Adriana said, leading us through an excessively large kitchen to the high-walled paved courtyard I'd seen from my balcony. "The basketball hoop is now at the correct height."

My attention was entirely for two sturdy posts beneath the trees. I looked at the gleaming metal hooks at just the perfect height, then turned to Rin, beaming.

"You remembered."

"Remembered what?" Kyou asked.

"That Mika once said she loves hammocks," Rin said, wearing his mildest smile.

"Is that why you wanted them put in?" Kyou said, narrowing his eyes. "I see."

"Them?" I asked, glad that the sudden air of competition seemed amiable rather than unfriendly.

"There's a set of them on the roof as well," Bran explained. "Since this courtyard won't be bearable in winter."

"Excellent! Five points for..." I began, then cocked my head. "What Hogwarts House do you think you'd be, Rin?"

"Ravenclaw," Bran said. "We worked that one out long ago. And I'm Gryffindor."

"Kyou's Hufflepuff," Rin said. "Though he claims to be Ravenclaw."

"Rin would be Slytherin if he didn't fudge the tests," Kyou said. "I'm willing to bet you come up as Ravenclaw as well, Mika."

"In most of the tests, yeah. Sometimes I get other houses. What kind of trees are these, Adriana?"

"They're all flowering ornamentals," Adriana said. "Two magnolias, a cherry, a plum, a crab apple, and the one closest to the building is a hawthorn."

"So, spring here is going to be all petals?"

"I've some photos of it in full flower," Rin said. "The scent alone is unforgettable."

"Do natural perfumes set off your scent allergies?" I asked Bran, as Adriana led us back inside.

"Some of them. I can't deal with hyacinth. These didn't seem a problem, but my bedroom's on the opposite side of the building, just in case."

"No wind chime," I said, looking around.

"It turned out to be too tall," Rin said, wryly. "We'll save it for another space."

I decided to skip my preview of Rin, Kyou and Bran's bedrooms, since I'd prefer a personal tour on a more appropriate occasion, and took time out to message my dad before re-joining the tour as it headed up to the third floor, which would be primarily devoted to Kybirn Games' technical installations.

"My dad isn't bothered by a three-hour distance," I told them, pausing to admire the skylight directly above the staircase. "So long as the view lives up to the hype. If you've time, could we go look at it tomorrow?"

"I'm in," Bran said. "Only Kyou's seen the place so far."

"Why not?" Rin said. "Leave at eight in the morning?"

"Great. Oh, and Dad wants to know if you know of any histories of this house."

"Uh, not off the top of my head," Kyou said. "Why?"

"He wants to write a book about junior ballerinas running up and down this staircase. Or something. No other details as yet, but I guess it must be a historical, since he's gone into deep research mode."

"It's a great staircase, isn't it?" Kyou said. "I should work on my scene skills with some sketches, with or without ballerinas."

"Start a sideline as a cover illustrator," Bran suggested.

"Well, if Mika's dad is short of one," Kyou agreed. "Coming up is another of my favourite parts of the house."

Adriana opened a solid door at the top of the stair to reveal a great sweep of polished wooden floor.

"One of the ballet practice rooms?" I asked, glancing at a grand piano placed midway along the right wall, and then left to a line of tall, retractable glass doors that gave a clear view of balcony, treetops, and neighbouring roofs.

"This is a dual-purpose area," Rin said. "We'll mainly use it ourselves, but occasionally hold company events."

I discovered a bar and an entire wall of alcohol at the far end of the room, and gave my three boyfriends an awed look.

"I guess you like cocktails?"

"I found an interesting recipe book," Kyou said. "We're going to go from A to Z. Friday cocktail nights."

"At least most of the liquor will taste better than the weird teas from that subscription service they signed up for," Bran said.

"When is the barista coming to teach you how to use that outsized coffee machine?" Kyou asked.

"Tuesday at ten," Adriana said smoothly. "And the domestic service has locked in the Monday afternoon slot for you, but you still need to confirm which day you want Mrs Janssen's lessons."

"We need to set our course schedule first," Rin said. "We'll be able to do that..."

"Final schedules are published day after tomorrow," Kyou said, and added to me: "None of us can cook worth a damn, so once a week we're having someone baby us through producing that night's meal."

"Oh? Sounds fun—I'll try to make sure I keep the time free. Does your company arrange all this kind of thing too, Adriana?"

"Cassadine Malway is very sincere in its motto," she said. "*From first idea to final touch!* For one project I stocked a craft room with an endless array of supplies. Embroidery thread, paints, decoupage paper, felting hooks. I learned an enormous amount in the process." She shot me a quick smile. "I think I ended up doing more crafts than the owner, too, judging from the next time I saw that room."

"People make felt as a hobby?" I asked, and was treated to the process involved in producing fuzzy decorative objects, before being taken on a tour of Kybirn's offices, which featured nearly two dozen desks, a fully equipped recording studio, and one big and one small internal room coloured entirely grey, including camera support girders.

"Motion capture," Bran explained. "The smaller one's for performance capture. Nuanced facial expression."

Rin handed his tablet over to Adriana. "That's the last item, I think. Do you need anything else from us?"

"That's everything!" Adriana said cheerfully. "If there are any further issues, be sure to contact our service number."

"I'll take you downstairs," Kyou said, and led Adriana off to the elevator.

"Bring some snacks up to the roof," Rin called after him and then, as soon as the elevator doors closed, pulled me into his arms.

"I'll meet you up there," Bran said, and left.

Rin didn't kiss me, just squeezed me tightly. Since this was a departure from Rin's usually unruffled surface, I could only suppress surprise as I hugged him back, and when he finally relaxed his grip a little, said: "Close to your limit?"

"The door of the cage is open, but somehow the bars feel tighter than ever," he said. Then, in a slightly different tone, he added: "Thank you for coming back early so I can relieve some stress."

I laughed. "I missed you too."

"Us, or being able to get to sleep easily?"

"Both. Adjusting back to my usual sleep routine certainly wasn't fun."

He chuckled, an action I could feel through all of my body. I'm not short, but Rin's height always made me feel like a delicate little thing, which was sometimes fun, and at other times provoked a more complex reaction.

"What's on the roof?" I asked, as he led me back to the piano room, and opened one panel of the sliding glass doors. "Do you have a good view?"

"For most of it, no, just trees and roofs. You can climb up onto a section that lets you see the university, but for a rooftop, most of it is quite private, which is what we wanted."

A large building inevitably had an air-conditioning plant or ducting taking up part of its rooftop, but there was still plenty of free space, mostly on the back half, which had been converted into a combination of entertainment area and garden. An unexpected amount of garden, with raised planter boxes of vegetables, trellises of espaliered apples hiding the machinery, and even a large, glass-walled conservatory that did not resemble, yet strongly reminded me of the summer house that had been very central to my final year of high school.

Perhaps it was the roses, blowsy pink beauties, growing in pots on either side of the door.

The conservatory was spacious enough for a kitchenette, a daybed, and several low chairs set around a coffee table. Kyou and Bran were sitting at a large café table just outside the conservatory, slicing a baguette and brie respectively. Four champagne flutes and a corked bottle waited on the table.

"Celebrating your French heritage?"

"Our reunion," Kyou said. "We were planning something a little more elaborate—cake and a fancy dinner—so you pay the price of indulging your love of surprising people."

"We can still have cake," I said, brightly. "I particularly like a type I had in Switzerland that was at least thirty percent kirsch."

"Plenty of local cake stores we can sample," Bran said, switching from brie to the bottle of champagne. "The nearest bakery is more breads and pastries, but I think there's something two stops down on the tram."

He popped the cork, and poured very seriously.

"Welcome home," Kyou said.

We touched glasses, four together, and drank. Then they glanced at each other, an almost unconscious action. I wrinkled my nose, then began a conversation I'd been thinking through for weeks.

"When I arrived in Peru, I took out my phone to call you, and ran right into the thing that's going to be hardest to manage," I said, steadily. "One of you would become the person I'd called."

"I did notice you always messaged a good time for us to call you, but never actually called," Kyou said, after a pause. "'Firsts' isn't going to be such an amusing concept this time around, is it?"

"Three boyfriends—if we're really being boyfriends and girlfriend—doesn't work at all the same way as fun noncommittal lunch hours. Even if I scrupulously took turns, I think it would still add up in small ways. You'd notice any differences, wouldn't you?"

"Yeah." Bran, blunt and unequivocal.

"I think, for this to have any chance of working, anything that involves a choice between you is going to need to be made by you. I'll have plenty of opinions on anything else, but don't ever ask me to pick which of you my day involves."

Rin leaned back, the champagne flute balanced lightly between two of his long fingers. "Are you just talking about where you spend your nights, or are you completely removing the possibility that you'll wander by and feel the urge to sit on my lap?"

"Well, I'd like to be able to do that. I might only be spontaneous when you're alone, though. We're going to have to work out some things as we go along, I guess."

"Did you walk in on that girl this morning?" Bran asked abruptly.

"Yeah. My dad missed out by a couple of minutes."

"It didn't bother you?" Rin asked.

"If people propositioning you is going to bother me, I won't survive a single month of this. If I thought for a moment that you'd say yes to her, well, I wouldn't be here." I shrugged, and picked a strawberry from a bowl Kyou nudged toward me. "People are going to proposition me too, even if I have an ambiguous overseas friend. And I don't think anything you can do—from claiming to be married to wearing a paper bag over your head—would stop the constant stream of hopefuls taking a chance. I warned Adriana that I didn't think surprise nakedness would work very well, but she was firm on not regretting not trying."

"Once we've got the security system fully activated, there won't be any more surprises at home," Bran said, still clearly annoyed by the whole event. "Other than some physical keys we'll keep as backup in a second location, all access doors will be controlled by a combination of a proximity app on our phones, and passcodes. Access can also be set to specific times. The cleaning service can only get in on Monday afternoon, for instance, and no-one from Kybirn can access the residential areas."

"Living in the same building as our office space brings certain risks," Rin added. "We wouldn't want our privacy interrupted even without the prospect of...spontaneity."

His gaze was very direct, and Kyou and Bran immediately reacted to the change of atmosphere by putting down their glasses and sitting straighter in their chairs.

Suppressing laughter, I said: "Today, I'm not going to be very spontaneous, because I've been awake for nearly twenty-four hours. But I do think we should start on the highest difficulty setting and see if the four of us and a blindfold can manage to be something other than awkward. Meet in my room in, say, twenty minutes?"

"Fifteen," Kyou said, immediately.

"Okay," I said, sampling a wedge of brie. "Do you have any clothing preferences?"

"Easy to take off," Bran said. "And no tying yourself up with a bow."

I laughed, and held my glass out for more champagne.

Three

Discovering the toilet in my lush new bathroom came with a world of bidet options delayed me a little, but I highly appreciated them all given my experiences trying to clean myself up the previous winter. Trysts in a summer house came with practical challenges, even when it wasn't sleeting.

Ignoring the mounds of new clothing, I dressed myself in my usual nightwear: overlong pyjama bottoms, and a *Star Wars*-themed shirt, both of them soft thanks to a couple of years going through the laundry. Then I covered my enormous bed with a light quilt that I'd bought with easy washing in mind, and sat cross-legged on top of it.

They arrived in a group, knocking first, and waiting until I responded before pushing the door open. They'd obviously used the time since we'd finished the champagne to take showers, and were wearing matching bathrobes, with a lot of bare chest on display.

"If we weren't so complicated, we'd probably be sharing a bedroom," I said, eyeing them appreciatively. "So, it seems a little strange to be making you knock."

"If we do all end up sharing the same room, we'll stop knocking," Rin said. "But, particularly when this is all new to us, having a place firmly your own seemed important."

"The room's incredible," I said. "The study made me regret that I'd seen it without you."

"Did it make you feel spontaneous?" Kyou asked, smiling slowly.

"I guess you could say that." I glanced at the French doors. "Really private, too. Will it be more exposed in winter?"

"Doesn't matter," Bran said. "No-one can see in."

"There's a mirror film on the doors, but not on the windows in the study," Rin explained, moving the shutter back over the study entrance. "Even at night, stray cats and passing drones won't be able to see in here, unless you have the study door open."

"I didn't think about drones," I said. "And I had all these thoughts about that rooftop conservatory."

"The conservatory's fitted with switchable glass," Rin said. "It changes opacity depending on whether there's a current running through it. Also good for cutting down on the heat up there in summer." He fished a strip of black fabric from his robe pocket. "We'll go over the house features another day."

Reaching forward, I took the blindfold, and obediently covered my eyes, trying to gauge the level of discomfort in the room. The four of us and a blindfold had been a suggestion of Bran's, and though we'd all reacted positively, this was still new territory. Rin, Kyou and Bran might be as close as it was possible for cousins to be, but I was fairly sure they'd never had sex in each other's company before.

Spending the better part of a year playing naked games with them in a private garden hadn't really prepared me for three of them at once, either, and I had to admit I'd been wondering if this was a bad idea. It was very important to me to not do anything to fracture their friendship, and this was going to be the first real test. Nor did I want my sex life to start being a source of stress for me, a place where I had to balance jealousy and hurt feelings.

Someone tickled my foot. I kicked reflexively, then said: "No tickling. And blindfold means I don't have to apologise if that hit you some place you regret."

Kyou chuckled, but he seemed to be in a position to not be the culprit. Then my ankle was grasped gently, and I was slowly drawn from the centre of the bed to the edge. In the process, someone took my hand, and kissed my fingers lightly before letting go.

"Also, no demonstrations of your excessive endurance," I added, and then stopped speaking because my voice was such a clear mixture of excitement and nerves that I surprised myself.

"This is going to last precisely as long as you want it to," Bran said, and kissed me.

Bran is such an incredible kisser that I would have no problem knowing it was him, even if he hadn't just spoken. I wrapped my arms around his neck and responded, only a little distracted because Rin and Kyou, obviously standing on either side of Bran, had decided to inch my pyjama pants off. Bran let go when they succeeded, and drew my shirt off as well, and then put his hands on my shoulders and guided me to lie back while he kissed his way from my throat to my stomach.

He reached the point just below my bellybutton and began to indulge his weakness for giving me hickies, but before I could draw breath to comment my lips were occupied, and meanwhile a hand and a mouth had found my breasts. Kyou. Almost certainly Kyou sucking my left breast, but probably Rin massaging my right.

Sensory overload. I responded as best I could, but then they changed position, and it was Kyou kissing me, and Rin giving me a hickie, and Bran enjoying my breasts. There'd obviously been considerable discussion about how this was going to go, and they rotated roles seamlessly until all three had managed to leave me breathless. Then, apparently on a signal I couldn't see, they withdrew, and one of them took my hand and drew me upright.

"You've gone remarkably pink," Kyou told me.

"I'm feeling remarkably...remarkable," I said, then added: "Would like you not to stop, though."

The bed shifted, indicating that someone had sat beside me, but meanwhile a pair of hands drew me to my feet. Then an arm wrapped around my waist from behind, and pulled me backward very slowly.

This was a move I recognised, for a position that involved sitting in Rin's lap. Since Rin was sized suitably for his height, getting there involved care and a bit of concentration on my part. Before I could fully adjust, Bran was kissing me, and then began working his way down my body, while Kyou took over my mouth. Rin tangled his fingers through mine, and began to play with my breasts. I was already struggling to control my breathing, but when Bran went past my new hickie collection and straight between my legs, it barely took thirty seconds before I arched in Rin's hold, and let out a tiny, pained gasp.

Three boys immediately stopped what they were doing and made near-identical smug sounds of triumph.

"Possibly a new record," Kyou commented, sounding immensely pleased with himself.

"Definitely," Rin agreed, and I felt his laughter through the whole of my body.

Bran's resumption of activity cut short my response, and I gripped Rin's hands tightly, wondering if this four-way concept would be too much for me, even at the very start. They fortunately had taken to heart my request to not draw things out, and soon after Bran moved away, and Rin gently lay back, then adjusted our position so we were lying on our sides. Kyou joined us, kissing my face and throat as Rin began to thrust, and, as soon as Rin was spent, moved immediately inside me.

I was wondering if Bran would swap into Rin's place, but Rin stayed with his arms tight around my waist, only letting go when Kyou fell back. Then two hands closed around my ankles, and drew me back toward the bottom of the bed. Still lying between Kyou and Rin, I cooperated a little fumblingly as Bran hooked my ankles across his shoulders and firmly hammered me into the mattress.

By this time Rin had recovered, as I discovered when he stood up and flipped me onto my stomach, before beginning a somewhat less forceful imitation of Bran. Then Kyou drew me up the bed, still face down, and began kissing my back and shoulders, resting his weight on me before slowly pushing into me. One of my favourite positions.

I suspect they could easily have gone on indefinitely, but when Kyou ended, he said: "Are you okay? Do you want to stop?"

Since I'd reached a point where I wasn't properly appreciating the experience, I hesitated, then said: "My dad's always telling me not to enjoy myself too much. I don't think this is what he meant, but it seems to fit. Perhaps finish with fun clean up in the shower?"

"Good plan," Bran said, helping me sit up. "Mask on or off?"

"Off, I think," I said, lifting it away. "It's exciting, but it means I don't get to look at any of you."

Their expressions didn't show any hint that they'd been enjoying themselves less than me, or that they weren't comfortable in each other's presence.

Rin, doing a fair imitation of a marble god, was sitting on the corner of my bed, directing a particularly wicked smile my way. "Mika, that was practically a symphony."

It took a moment for me to realise he was talking about the tiny sound I make when I orgasm. Then I grabbed the nearest pillow and threw it at him. "If I hear you practicing that noise on your violin again, I'll go buy a dog house specifically so I can put you in it."

"Better change your ringtone, Kyou," Bran said.

"My ringtone is a very genuine cat," Kyou said.

"This week," Rin murmured, and then stood up. "I'll postpone musical efforts until Mika's looking less exhausted. And as a birthday treat, Bran can enjoy the shower with you alone. I'll go order some dinner for those of us who expect to be conscious in an hour."

"Today's your birthday?" I asked Bran, astonished. "Why didn't you tell me?"

"Didn't want you to change your plans," Bran said. "But you managed to be here anyway."

I stood up and kissed him, and the next time I thought about Kyou and Rin, they were both gone, along with my somewhat stained quilt. Bran and I made our way to my shower, and worked out a setting that involved plenty of warm water spraying below chest height, so I could avoid getting my hair too wet. I found my second wind, and it was at least twenty minutes later that we took a couple of towels back to bed and curled up together.

"Fresh linen feel," I said happily. "What a ridiculous bed this is. Are all the beds in the house really this big?"

"None are as tall. The height's convenient, though."

"No doubt." I brushed a damp blond curl off his forehead. "Happy birthday. I'm glad I could be here for the end of it, especially since the beginning sounded pretty drear. Or was it a positive clan meeting?"

He snorted. "A waste of air. All about a different branch of the family profiteering at the expense of corporate reputation. Kyou and I only went along because Rin has another week of pretending to be compliant. After that—not sure any of us will ever bother again. It was a shitty start to the day, but it's just gotten better and better."

"Next year, shall we go camping for your birthday? Somewhere super remote, so we don't have to worry about people wandering by."

Bran usually looks like a fallen angel, but there are moments when he brings to mind a heavenly chorus. I closed my eyes, thinking not about the complications of my multi-boyfriend situation, but instead of the things we could do together that would make them smile.

oOo

Having fallen asleep at sunset all tangled up with Bran, I adjusted slowly to dawn with my cheek pressed against Rin's back. There was an arm loosely hooked over my waist, but I didn't move immediately to check whose it was. We weren't due to leave until eight, so I had time to examine my feelings, to think that this would be especially nice in winter, but was a little too warm for the last days of summer. And that three is comfortable, but four leaves someone out.

Easing myself from beneath what proved to be Bran's arm, I sat up. And so did Kyou, who had been lying on the window side of the bed, just beyond Bran.

"Need help getting free?" he asked, in an undertone.

"I think I can slide out the bottom," I said, pushing the sheet further down.

"Use Bran as leverage. He won't wake for anything short of five on the Richter Scale. Rin will react to loud noise but less to movement."

"You're obviously the morning person," I murmured, accepting a helping hand.

"I foresee many breakfasts with you," he replied, touched my cheek lightly, then the three overlapping love bites they'd left on my lower stomach. "All sorts of breakfast."

Holding back a snort, I murmured: "Meet in the kitchen?"

"Okay."

Closing the door between the bedroom and my walk-through wardrobe, I took my time in the bathroom. During my summer holiday, my friend Millie had delivered several stern lectures about my habit of just washing my face with soap, so I obediently followed the basic skin care steps she'd dictated. Finishing up with a moisturising sunscreen, I put together an outfit suitable for visiting an abandoned farm—basically the same as yesterday, but with a long-sleeved cotton shirt over my t-shirt—and then went back out to admire the contents of my bed.

Bran had moved across to snuggle against Rin's back, and as I grabbed my phone, I was very tempted to take a photo, but decided that collecting evidence of our relationship continued to be a bad idea. Much as I would like to be with them openly, one girl and three guys would always attract an ocean of negativity.

Leaving Rin and Bran to get more sleep, I strolled down the magnificent staircase and went to investigate the kitchen, which I'd previously only passed through on the way to the rear courtyard. As with the rest of the house, it was light, airy, and very large. That bulging rounded corner had been set up as a breakfast nook, and there were doorways to the right, one leading to a more formal dining room, and the other an enormous walk-in pantry. Kyou was in there, examining a set of twenty or so canisters slotted into pigeonholes.

Sliding my arms around his waist, I stood on tiptoe to peer over his shoulder. "What's this? Starting an apothecary?" I spotted a label, and added: "Is this all tea?"

"The bottom rows are favourites, and the top row is the latest varieties from our sampler subscription. Do you have any preferences?"

"You pick," I said, kissing his shoulder, then letting him go so I could wander around the pantry, picking over the full array of cooking staples. "Was this all set up by that renovation firm?"

"Most of it. Bran and I grew tired of living on take-out, so we're moderately serious about developing our cooking skills, but even Bran only has experience with a microwave. Once we have the basics down, we'll figure out days when we're all likely to be home, and take turns cooking. What would you like for breakfast, Mika?

"I usually cut a couple of pieces of fruit into yoghurt and sprinkle it with toasted muesli."

"We have fruit and yoghurt. Not sure about muesli. I'll show you how to add it to the shopping order in a minute."

"Want some?" I asked, hunting in the refrigerator.

"Sure. My usual is just toast."

I found a tub of Greek yoghurt, and selected some fruit from a countertop bowl that seemed to be themed around 'one of everything'.

"Why didn't you warn me I was going to miss Bran's birthday?"

"He didn't want you to cut short your time with your parents. I think he doesn't want to be too demanding in case it scares you off." Kyou put water on to boil, then came to return my hug, squeezing me with a sigh. "Meanwhile, during all the dreary part of yesterday, Bran's brother was the only one who even seemed to remember what day it was."

"Does Bran get on with his brother?"

"Hard to say. They've never spent much time together. Rowan promised to send Bran a copy of his debut single as his gift, and that's the core of everything that's complicated between them. Rowan can't fathom why Bran didn't embrace the glorious music career their parents planned for him, yet is clearly uncomfortable with the way Bran's been treated as a non-person in the household since he wrecked his voice. It doesn't help that Rowan's voice took a long time to stabilise after breaking. His whole life is focused around being the Next Big Thing in music, not only because he loves performing, but because it's been made clear just how worthless he'll be if he fails."

"Then I can only hope he succeeds. Do you have any sibling replacements?"

"No. My father's been having too much fun auditioning stepmothers to move on to the stage where official children are a factor, and my great-grandfather has always been very firm on children being official, so if I do have any half-sibs, they won't show up until after The Inheritance has been settled." He paused, leaning against my back. "I think there's a good chance I do, but to tell the truth, I try not to think about it."

I put down my knife and turned to hug him properly. I'd had lots of conversations with these three while I was away, and none of them had even hinted at the obvious strain that had been building, even though they were finally on the verge of stepping away from family control.

"Let's talk about fun things instead," I suggested.

"Okay," he said, and promptly nuzzled my throat, dropping his beautiful voice an octave lower to say: "How was it, Mika? Feeling sore? Or feeling hungry?"

Laughing, I shoved him lightly. "Sore, but not unbearably. As for hungry, this morning I'm sticking to my regular breakfast. Will let you know if anything changes. What about you—did you find it just too weird, or have you discovered a new kink?"

"It went better than I'd hoped," Kyou said. "Bran might have been most into the idea, but I was worried he'd also be the one who struggled actually seeing you with us. Turns out he really does like to watch. And something about it very much worked for Rin, judging from the discussion we had afterwards about whether you'd be open to regular threesomes, rather than very rare foursomes. Of course, we're approaching this from the viewpoint of wanting all the sex, all the time, without being so insatiable we send you running."

"I was thinking some nights just one of you, other times mix and match threesomes. Foursomes..." I shrugged. "Last night included a level of stress that one of you would be feeling neglected. And you haven't actually said how you felt."

"Not neglected. Admittedly, unspeakably impatient during part of it, but also harder than I've perhaps ever been. Overall positive. And I now have a better appreciation of why Rin worries about hurting girls." Kyou let me go as the water finished boiling. "I think, though, if all three of us had been in the kitchen today, and you'd come up to Bran and put your arms around him instead of me...that's the kind of thing I'm going to struggle with." He paused, then shook his head. "No, I'm being over-dramatic. If you did that every day, perhaps, but I know you're too smart to get us thoroughly out of balance."

"I'll try not to miss the little things," I said, then blinked as he poured boiling water into two cups, and the complex perfume of masala chai filled the kitchen. "And appreciate it when you remember them."

"We put in a few varieties," he said, smiling. "You like it with milk and sugar, right?"

I nodded, and he headed to the refrigerator, while I took our bowls to the breakfast nook. All but one of the windows looked out over the one-way alley that ran between Moby Dick and the next block of terrace houses, so the view was primarily of red and brown bricks with a small-leafed creeper growing up it.

"Are these windows one-way as well?" I asked.

"Tinted. The local council has some appearance regulations that limited what we could use on the street-facing windows, and we decided on privacy blinds rather than other options." He put down the two cups, and added in a slightly raised voice: "*Castellan*, close blinds in Breakfast."

"Smart home functions?" I asked, as navy-blue blinds descended over each of the windows. "What else can you do?"

"Let's get you logged in and I'll show you," Kyou said, bringing over a thin laptop and a tablet. "The voice controls have limits for security reasons—you can't open the doors by voice, for instance—but all the major rooms have speakers and audio pickup."

While I doctored my chai with a sufficiency of sugar, he brought up an existing account, then pushed the laptop to me to change passwords.

"Give me your phone and I'll install *Castellan*."

"Is *Castellan* original software?" I asked, dropping my voice a little in hopes of avoiding triggering the audio pickup.

"No, it's customised from a package for people who like virtual assistants, but prefer a level of separation from the various corporations behind them. It still fetches external data, you can do your standard searches, ask the weather and so forth, but with an added layer of privacy."

He passed my phone back as I finished changing my password.

"The residential Wi-Fi password is currently all our initials in order of first name, with only the surname initials capitalised, and you already know the door codes. Bran will activate normal entry protocol today, which means you'll need to swipe with your phone, along with entering the door code, to get in. Here's the main interface."

He switched to the tablet, showing me an array of options. "You can link your phone to it with Bluetooth to answer incoming calls, and also view the security feed for the entrances, elevator and foyer. There's a shared calendar, and here's our to-do lists and the shopping list. The domestic service will bring anything we order over on Monday afternoons when they come to clean and return ironing. You can also indicate areas that want extra cleaning care, or that you want them not to disturb."

I gave him a bemused smile. "I'm really not paying you enough rent. Are you going to be able to fund a Triple A game *and* maintain this level of lifestyle?"

"The investments are going well," he said, smiling faintly. "I'm keeping them diverse, so we won't have a repeat of my near crash-and-burn. We've also separated everything into three different companies, and done a lot of formalities to ensure we won't get caught with our taxes out of order. The game and main headquarters is funded, so my focus is now on other projects. What I want to create is a financial support system for our game production which allows us to not be pressed for completion dates—or relying on the success of one game to fund the next. Not that I think our games will fail, but we're definitely going to be favouring artistic rather than economical choices in their production, so there's a good chance they'll barely break even."

"What are the other two companies?" I asked, trying not to dwell too deeply on how much money Kyou seemed capable of making, with or without the support of his obscenely wealthy family.

"Kybirn Music and Kybirn Investments. We all have equal ownership, even with Music, despite my contribution being a lot lower there."

"How do you decide how much to pay yourselves?" I asked curiously. "And how to split expenses?"

"We have a shared account for expenses—one that covers both the household and costs like our university fees and supplies. On top of that, every quarter we get together to review how we're going financially, and split a percentage out for personal spending. It's a little complicated because a lot of the things we're inclined to buy personally tend to be things that could fall into business expense."

"How many guitars does Rin have now?"

He laughed. "Twenty-two. He usually doesn't acquire so many so quickly, but the drama at the end of the school year really did put us far ahead of where we expected to be financially, so we've been splurging. And Rin impulse spends on instruments whenever his parents particularly press him to become The Heir. He spent the entire trip back yesterday on his phone, and announced as I drove in that he'd just bought a new violin, another Stratocaster, and a pair of timpani."

"Timpani's percussion, isn't it? A drum?"

"Kettledrums. Huge. He's already on his way to running out of space to put instruments." Kyou finished his yoghurt, and pecked at a few options on the tablet. "You can use *Castellan* as an intercom to specific rooms or the whole house, play music, alarms, whatever you like, unless the room's been set to mute."

He showed me my room on the house plan, but I shook my head. "I'll go wake them, the way I expect you'd like to be woken."

"Naked?"

"Noted for the future," I said, kissed him, and then took my dish to the sink.

It was still quite early, so I took my time washing up and when I returned to my room first hunted a book out of my backpack, and then investigated *Castellan*, working out how to play a piece of music from my phone into my room. Selecting the winding recorder duet Rin had composed, I sat beside him on the bed and stroked a thumb gently along his jaw.

Rin has enviably long eyelashes, light brown shading to transparency, perfectly matching the pale gold of his irises. His lashes quivered, and he lay still for a long moment, eyes half open. Then, without preamble, he pulled me down and kissed me.

This was pleasant, and perhaps would have become heated if we hadn't been balanced on the edge of the bed, and Rin's attempt to press me beneath him ended with him hastily catching me before I fell to the floor.

"Another morning," I told him, getting my feet under me.

"I'll keep you to that."

"I know it," I said, retrieving the book I'd dropped. "Do you like waking to music?"

"Yes and no," Rin said, discovering Bran and shrugging him away as he sat up. "I'd prefer to, but it sometimes gets inside my head in an awkward way, and

I wake either wanting to spend time composing, or very annoyed at a piece and never wanting to listen to it again. After being late or in a bad mood often enough, I now use the most neutral alarm tone imaginable."

Handing him the book, I watched intently as his mood shifted from relaxed to focused as he paged through a city inspired by his music.

"I've been drawing buildings and bridges for as long as I can remember, and usually have some kind of theme or plan before I start. It's the first time I've done one to music, but that piece really got under my skin. I listen to it whenever I want to calm my thoughts."

"When you want to get to sleep, you mean," he said.

"Sometimes. But also during my plane trips, or whenever things have been hectic. It takes my mind through the city, even when I don't have the book with me." I sat beside him as he reached the sketches I hadn't shown him before, and he slowed down his paging. "There'll be a time, not so far from now, when people all over the world follow your music through cities and oceans, and whole galaxies."

"Hmph." He reached the images of the centre of the city and paused, tracing the edge of a page. "You make me feel transparent, Mika."

"Do I get to claim credit for recognising that someone who creates music wants people to listen to it?" I asked, leaning against his arm. "How do you feel about live performance?"

"I have to be in the mood," he said. "Those few songs we helped out with at the school festival were exhilarating, but regular touring or anything like that isn't for me. I enjoy listening to small scale live performance most, rather than being on stage myself, or being lost in the human sea at festivals. I do look forward to groping you in the dark at every opportunity, though."

"I'll keep that in mind." I reached up to kiss his cheek lightly. "I've finished the journey through the city for now. A gift for you."

He stroked the page lightly. "One day we'll build this into a game," he said. "And travel this path together."

"Okay," I said, a little delighted by the idea.

Rin kissed my cheek in return, but then left, collecting his robe on the way out. I watched him go, trying to decide whether a faint downturn of his mood was my imagination. Rin's mask is very practiced.

Turning my head, I wondered how much effort I'd need to wake Bran, but found that at some point he'd opened his eyes, and now lay quietly looking at me.

"And here I was thinking I'd have to drag you down a flight of stairs to wake you up. You're not nearly so heavy a sleeper as Kyou would have me believe."

Bran's lips curved to an arc that would be impish if he didn't possess an innate smoulder. "Choosing not to leap out of bed at the crack of dawn doesn't mean I don't know when he and Rin are trying to wake me up."

"You're pretending to be a heavy sleeper?"

"I'd sleep to midday every day if I didn't set an alarm. But I let them think I don't hear them."

"How long have you been keeping that up?" I asked, amazed.

"I don't know. Since we were around ten?" He rolled onto his back and rubbed his eyes before looking back at me. "You're a morning person."

"It tends to depend on when I got to sleep, but yes, I often wake up before my alarm. If it's early enough, I'll do yoga or go jogging, and then have breakfast. But for school days I always set my alarm for just enough time to get dressed, grab something to eat, and get to class."

"That didn't change once we started helping you sleep?"

"No, though it was very nice to have the extra time in the morning. Morning exercise is useful in cutting other distractions, letting me plan out the day's schedule and projects. I'll probably jog more now that I'm living in a nicer area. At least while the weather's still good."

"I'll go with you," he said.

"Okay. Though I believe we have a bike trip to enjoy first."

"Saturday," he said. "Rin will be at Marcelline and Evgenie's birthday, and Kyou has interviews with artists." Bran sat up, wrapped his arms around my waist, and drew me further onto the bed. "He shuffled them all off from Friday when you told us you'd be flying in, and now you've turned up two days early."

"But it was so fun to see your expressions," I said, not at all guilty, then tugged a stray lock of his hair. "And I got to be here for your birthday, which would have been important to me if I'd known beforehand. On the whole, I prefer the chance to make my own choices, Bran."

"I just—" he began, then paused, and said: "I'll remember. I'm glad you were here."

"I knew Rin and Kyou's birthdays thanks to the school forums, but for yours they only had guesses. Does this mean you're the oldest?"

"Youngest. I skipped a year at the start, then refused to skip again. Is moving about the reason you didn't jump ahead?"

"Tell the truth, it never occurred to me to try. And then I was nearly caught out by my own complacency when I started looking at different universities and realised I'd missed the chance to build up the shiny academic record needed for early admission. Fortunately, Helios does half their intake through the final exams. But then I started to think about one single set of exams standing between me and my favoured course and it started to seem mountainous rather than something I should be able to comfortably achieve."

"Insomnia's not something I've ever had to deal with." He looked down, and then back up at me. "Do you think you would have gotten involved with us if you didn't want to experiment with whether sex would help you sleep?"

"I don't know." I thought back to the day I'd first met them, talking about comparing kissing—and other things—and then offering me the chance to be the judge. I'd immediately thought them all attractive, but they were far from the only attractive people in the world. "I think I would have at least tried out the kissing, but your sterling attempts to make me regret it might have edged you all into the too much effort category."

Bran grimaced, presumably embarrassed by past mistakes. "You said something like that before," he said. "That boyfriends are work. And now you have three."

"Three times the morning greetings," I said, a little wryly. "Maybe that will feel like work eventually, but right now I'd be lying if I pretended not to be enjoying myself."

"But would you stand around watching us play sport?"

I laughed. "At least occasionally. I value my time, but I find time spent with you valuable."

And I was getting a little addicted to the expression he made when something I said got completely beneath his armour.

Four

The garage proved to have four parking spaces, and currently housed Rin's Hummer, Kyou's low-key electric car, and a gleaming Harley Davidson.

"You really go out of your way to live up to an image," I told Bran.

"Have you ever ridden?" he asked, unbothered by Rin and Kyou's amused reaction.

"On quad bikes," I said, walking to the back wall of the garage to examine racks containing a three-person scull, three single sculls, and a pair of two-person canoes. "What's the best place to go canoeing?"

"I hear it's Lake Jorgmungandr," Bran said. "Long and twisting through a valley between the Dragon's Teeth, over near Eventide. Never been, but the recommendation is to see it when the water's mirror-still."

"At dawn on an unusually warm autumn or spring day, because there'll be hardly anyone there," Kyou added.

"We can overnight," Rin said, opening the door of his Hummer. "There'll probably be cabins to rent."

"Is it silly to say that I'm really looking forward to experiencing the world with you?"

"Not silly, dangerous," Kyou said, immediately. "It makes me want to let you experience the back seat with me, and that's probably not a good idea when we're on the way to meet your father."

"Are you going to tell your parents about us?" Rin asked, after we were all seated.

"Not yet. I'm not even fully adapted to the idea. Maybe at Christmas. Other than them, I expect I'll eventually tell Lania, but I've no plans for more. I've already told Millie. She was very impressed. What about you? Your sisters?"

"They'll need a year or five to get used to you first," Rin said.

"One thing I don't understand," I said to Rin as we drove out. "Your parents each have other children, but pressure you so much. Are they pushing your sisters down the same path?"

"Yes and no. They're a little looser, but there's definite discouragement of 'pointless' career paths. I get full force because I'm the oldest child of the oldest child of the oldest child, the traditional direct heir, and they think that matters to our great-grandfather."

"Do you think it matters to him?"

"Not as much as business sense. I don't know if it's a little light racism that keeps Kyou from being the obvious inheritor, but he's long been the one Great-Grandfather actually has time for."

"My complete disinterest in taking over L-B Corp should have ruled me out long ago," Kyou said, not apparently concerned by the possibility his Japanese heritage was an actual barrier. "There's too many fingers in the L-B Corp pie, too many shareholders focused on maximising profit at the expense of doing anything interesting. And I'd never have enough time for the art and games I actually want to focus on. I've said that multiple times, but no-one seems to believe me."

"With the exception of our parents, we'll be making a lot of people happy this year," Bran said. "And, hopefully, end some of the petty rubbish that gets thrown our way in the scramble for favour."

"Did you get into a lot of trouble for your reverse blackmail?" I asked Kyou.

Bran snorted. "If you ever wanted an example of Great-Grandfather having a soft spot for Kyou..."

"My father and aunt got a lecture, while I was punished with a project to identify weak points in the construction division fulfilment chain," Kyou told me. "Not uninteresting, but it took up more of the summer break than I liked." He glanced at Rin. "You're not the only one looking forward to your sisters' birthdays."

The opening words of *Paperback Writer* emanated from my day bag, so I fished my phone out and answered it. "Hey, Dad. We're on our way over now, between five to ten minutes away. Meet out front?"

There was a vague murmur of assent.

"Talk to you soon," I said, and hung up. "He'll be mostly awake by the time we get there."

"Hasn't had his coffee yet?" Kyou asked.

"He wouldn't be capable of calling me if he hadn't had coffee," I said. "He wakes in phases."

"Sounds like work getting anywhere on time," Rin said.

"So long as he has at least half an hour to wake up, he's fine. It gets a bit difficult if he's travelling alone and has to wake up in a hurry. Before he goes to sleep, he sometimes sweet-talks flight attendants and hotel staff to help him out. Well, usually he just always travels wherever my mother goes, so it's not a common issue."

"Should we avoid talking about starting work on the game?" Bran asked.

"Bran's nervous," Kyou explained, when I looked puzzled. "He wants your father's opinion on *Echoes of Samerkel*, but he also isn't sure he wants to hear it."

"Really?" This was an unexpected side to Bran, who appeared to be effortlessly accomplished at everything he put his mind to.

"I've always been good at music, and programming is just breathing to me, but dialogue is something I struggle with," Bran explained. "The fine detail work we've done so far on *Echoes'* script isn't nearly what I want it to be."

"I think the story is basically good," Kyou said, judiciously. "But this is one of many areas where we need to bring in higher-level expertise. The key to any successful project is the planning stage—including factoring in your own limitations."

"Dad's looking forward to it," I assured them. "And is never grumpy or anything in the morning—he just gives everyone the impression of being zoned out. But he is listening, even if he doesn't talk. If he's still vague when we pick him up, just wait until he starts asking questions and you'll know you're safe."

The hotel wasn't far away, but it was a busy traffic time of day. Fortunately, there was a drop-off area for Rin to draw into. Kyou hopped out and got into the front seat, while I waved for my dad to come over.

"Hi kiddo," Dad murmured, climbing in, and then blinked at Bran on the far side of me. He turned his head and saw Kyou and what he could make out of Rin, and blinked again before carefully pulling the car door shut. "Hello."

"This is Bran, Kyou, and Rin," I said, indicating each of them in turn, and hiding a smile.   A car full of unexpectedly attractive boys seemed to work nearly as well as coffee.

"Gareth Teyrn." My dad recovered a little during the murmured exchange of greetings. "Glad to meet you."

"I'm a big fan of your books," Bran said, leaning across to shake my dad's hand. "Particularly the horror stories."

"My favourite's the travelogues," Kyou put in.   "I keep spotting Mika in them, getting into scrapes."

"Having adventures," I said, firmly.

"Did you ever want to write, Mika?" Rin asked, as he pulled out onto the street.

"I was always more interested in building things," I said. "Fiction's not my strong point."

"Mika's a very organised writer," my dad said, in a tone of gentle sympathy.

I poked my tongue out at him, then grinned. While I was faintly sorry that my stories never seemed to come alive, there were plenty of other things that drew me more than my attempts to follow in my dad's footsteps.

"So, tell me how you three ended up owning a farm," my dad said.

"We need a site for our company headquarters," Kyou explained. "The Hutton Forest building will be fine for our needs for the next six months or so, but at peak production on *Echoes* we're aiming at between six hundred and eight hundred employees, if we factor in part-timers. While working from home and hot-desking options mean we won't need exactly that number of desks, we'll need facilities for at least five hundred on-site at any time."

"Kyou was supposed to be looking for some place to rent for the next few years," Bran added, "Ideally a newly-built office building that hadn't been fully fitted out yet."

"But then he turned around and announced he'd bought an abandoned farm that doesn't meet any of our requirements," Rin said, shaking his head. "And all he would do was wave a report at us and tell us to wait a few months before we made any decisions."

"We were always going to build an ideal headquarters," Kyou said. "Circumstances just brought the option forward about five years."

"Do you have a copy of the report, by the way?" I asked Kyou. "I wanted to read it."

"Sure." He pulled a tablet from the small backpack he had at his feet, and then explained to my dad: "I bought the Noonerry property because a chance remark of Mika's gave me a head start in seizing an opportunity. While Noonerry isn't entirely unsuitable, I don't think we could convince all our staff to move or commute nearly four hours out of the city, but if it's...how long do you think it would take the high-speed rail to actually get to Noonerry, Mika?"

"From the University stop? Presuming there's only that one stop in between, around forty-five minutes. From the city centre, just over fifty minutes. From the airport, maybe an hour and ten. Stopping and boarding chew up a lot of time."

"Oh, I begin to see," my dad said. "But how long's it going to take to build this rail line?"

"It's been ten years so far," Bran said.

"Stage One's due to open early next year," Kyou said, handing me his tablet. "Linking the airport to Gore

Heights—an outer suburb we'll be passing shortly. It will be by far the quickest way to get from the north-east of the city to the south-west. Stage Two was supposed to open middle of the year after that—an inter-city link between Helios and Sunderry. That line's been working its way south to north, but ran into a major hurdle thanks to the discovery of some caverns full of selenite crystal formations in Sunneway Pass. Almost unique, and will probably become a major tourist attraction someday, but not what you want to find under the only route through the Ramparts."

"The Ramparts are the double mountain range nearly three hundred kilometres south of Helios," I told Dad. "They start at the east coast and stretch over halfway to the west coast. I went there with the Nichols to visit Lake Dorsey. They're spectacular."

"The caverns have basically made Sunneway Pass unviable," Kyou went on smoothly. "During the summer break, every scientific organisation you can imagine rushed to file legal challenges to development, or to propose to list the site as world heritage. Mika predicted that outcome the week of the discovery, and when I understood that the rail line would have to go around the west end of the Ramparts, I commissioned an urgent evaluation of the most likely new route. That ended up being Noonerry, rather than through Vitha Valley, which is what everyone else is currently predicting."

"So, he ran up there and bought literally everything that was for sale," Rin said, sighing.

"More than just the farm?" I asked, skimming the report with a growing sense of responsibility.

"Noonerry's been in a decline, so property is cheap there," Kyou said, calmly. "Though it's also small enough that there wasn't a lot for sale. I bought Fox Farm, two houses, an empty corner store, and a big chunk of wasteland just outside the west edge of town. And then some houses and two large tracts of undeveloped land outside the next-most-likely town. The realtors I worked with couldn't understand it, but I told them honestly enough that my company was preparing to build its headquarters on the tableland, and that we'd need extensive housing as well as a main site. The Noonerry realtor was very excited. I nearly ended up having lunch with the mayor."

"He still hasn't admitted exactly how much he spent," Rin murmured.

"You rarely lose money on land," Kyou said airily. "Even if the high-speed rail doesn't end up stopping in Noonerry, I plan to do a little development in the town, along with building a weekend house there. The views would have already made it a destination spot if it was more convenient to get to. Still..." He smiled at me. "I'm more than interested to hear what you think of the report. Do I need to go back to hunting for that rental building?"

I'd had enough time to skim the summary, and was now paging through the supporting evidence.

"They start with a sensible disclaimer that science won't necessarily overcome political factors," I said. "And make the base assumption that the decision-makers will weigh the time factor heavily, given that they're facing at minimum an extra year of construction thanks to the rerouting, even with that second track builder machine."

"Every prediction I've seen says it'll go through Vitha Valley," Bran commented.

"On a pure science basis, absolutely," I said. "The ideal setup for HSR is as straight as possible between your major destinations, with a limited number of stops, and avoiding turns and gradients. Vitha Valley— that's the gap between the Ramparts and the tableland, Dad—definitely meets those criteria if you don't factor in the two large towns and small city clogging up the way. Land acquisition through built up areas is expensive and time consuming. The tableland offers multiple routes crossing only public land and farmland: much cheaper, and a far simpler process to acquire since there's fewer parties involved."

"Even if it runs well west of Noonerry, it will still make the town much more accessible," Kyou said.

"Why would it run further west, though?" Bran asked. "That would just make the track longer."

"Close to the national park, and there's sharp drops both south and north of the town," I said. "Nothing a gradually elevated track couldn't overcome, but there may be a preference to run closer to Moonmere, which has better roads, a far less significant gradient, and a larger population. I take it Moonmere is the other place you bought land? If there's a stop anywhere on the tableland, all the land in both towns will increase in value the moment it's announced. If there's a stop actually in Noonerry...Kyou, I can see why your family wants to bind you up in employment contracts."

My dad was wearing his bemused look, but I could see that he was also a little delighted at this game of junior property speculation.

"If you plan to build your own place there, or an office building, why sell to me?" he asked.

"There's plenty of room for what I want to build," Kyou said. "The farmhouse is on a separate title, and off at the northern tip of the property. It's about a century old, and it seems a pity to tear it down, so passing it to someone who only wants a handful of acres works out well. I warn you it does need a lot of renovation. It's sat empty for quite a while, and is painfully old-fashioned."

"Why was it abandoned?" Dad asked.

"There was an outbreak of foot-and-mouth disease around fifteen years ago. The owners were in their sixties, and their children weren't interested in running an organic dairy farm, so when their herds were slaughtered to prevent the spread of infection, they never restocked. They lived there for a few more years, eventually rented the paddocks to a neighbouring sheep farmer, and later relocated to a nursing home until their deaths. The property's been sitting on the market ever since, thoroughly overpriced for what anyone was willing to offer. The heirs were very happy when I came along."

"I'm looking forward to seeing it," Dad said. "Not to mention this game you're going to create. What kind of RPG is it going to be? Closer to *Dragon Age* or *Skyrim*?"

"Of those, closer to *Dragon Age*," Kyou told us. "But gameplay-wise it'll be somewhere between *Uncharted* and *Baldur's Gate*, with shades of *Magic: The Gathering*, and some *Mass Effect*."

"Oh, *really*?"

"Dad loves the *Uncharted* series to death," I said. "But *Uncharted* and *Baldur's Gate* are not very similar games, let alone *M:TG*."

"From *Uncharted* we're taking aspects of an action movie focused on the protagonist, with a lot of climbing and environmental puzzles," Bran said. "From *Baldur's*

Gate we want the approach of finding multiple solutions to the same problem, while the similarity to *Magic* is in obtaining abilities much as you would rare *Magic* cards—though no need to buy card packs or any loot box nonsense. Just a combination of luck and your approach to certain problems will reward you with abilities. You can miss out on some abilities altogether."

"How does *Mass Effect* fit into it?" I asked.

"Other than getting into the pants of everyone you meet?" Kyou asked. "Mainly because it has a science fiction frame story, and aims to achieve what Bioware fell a little short of, and make player decisions have a tangible impact on the end game."

"That's one of the primary reasons we're trying to set everything up so we have complete financial control over development," Bran said. "Multiple playable endings are expensive, and we don't want a producer pushing for a simpler game. We want far more than just a cut scene before the credits, we want a game where you can alienate the first character you talk to, and destroy the easiest path to reaching your current goal, forcing you to seek out an alternative—and to continue to feel the impact of decisions long after you've forgotten you even made that choice."

"Which is nightmare-level to plan, as you can imagine," Kyou said. "We've been working on plot variables for years, and still find things we've missed."

"You should bring Sorenson on board," Dad said. "She's unbeatable at finding gaps in systems."

"Would she be interested?" Kyou asked. "I gather, from everything Mika's said, that her mother is hard to hire."

"Well, she loves *Mass Effect*. Unless you need it done in the next few weeks, I'm sure she'd make the time. So, the frame's SF, but the main game is fantasy? Can you give me a rundown of the plot?"

"Sure," Bran said, and actually did sound nervous as he went on. "We start on an orbiting spaceship belonging to the Solsheim Assembly, one of three major galactic forces in a far-future Milky Way whose citizens are guaranteed certain standards of living. You are vat-born, a non-citizen."

"Vat-born are a way for the Assembly to circumvent its own laws, and produce a workforce for tasks that can't be performed by robots," Kyou added. "This opening scene is basically the character creation process, as your Handler 'selects' you, and has you and a number of other vat-born shipped from the manufactory."

"Treats you as disposable, and doesn't hide that there's a good chance you'll die, while holding out the possibility of qualifying for citizenship to give you a reason to try," Bran explained.

"Tier Two Citizenship," Rin put in. "Higher than his."

"The reason for your existence revolves around terraforming," Bran went on. "Terraforming has reached the point where you can find a planet suitably close to habitable, drop a few terraforming cores on it, and come back a hundred years later to move in. Samerkel finished the process about twenty years previous to the game's opening, the cores were retrieved, and a settlement established. All as expected except when they checked the progress of the next planet along, and found one of the cores wasn't functioning. That it was a fake."

"Cores can be replaced," Kyou said, "but not easily since their construction involves an exceptionally rare element. The original investigator assumed that it had been stolen in-transit, and began tracing the route back, reporting no results until she reached Samerkel— where she vanished. As did the next two investigators. You're with the fourth effort, and this time the investigator stayed in orbit observing the situation, cooking up vat-born to do surface exploration."

"He doesn't bother to hide that you're not the first vatties he's sent down there," Rin said.

"Was this planet originally named LV-426?" my dad asked.

They laughed, and Kyou said: "No xenomorphs, I promise. Not even stray facehuggers. In fact, everything about the colony appears to be thriving. Communication hasn't been cut, the spaceport operates normally, and settlement is well underway— though more advanced than seems possible after a mere twenty years, and with an apparently permanent cloud cover over the main part of it. Your Handler explains that he's only able to send drones into the edges of the settled area. About a hundred kilometres from the fringes, he loses contact, and most likely it's the core itself that's interfering. Your mission, of course, is to retrieve the core."

"*It's simple*," Kyou suddenly growled, sounding bored and irritable. "*The thing has to be at the centre. Get to the centre. Find the thing. Shut down the thing. Send a signal for pick up.*"

"Are you going to play the investigator?" I asked, mildly impressed.

"Hasn't been decided," Rin said. "The character's supposed to be a soft-hearted antagonist, so the casting fits at least."

"We keep changing his personality," Bran said. "When we first created him, he was cartoonishly evil."

"We were fourteen when we started to build the frame story," Rin said, laughing. "Now the Investigator's someone one step above you in the pecking order, and just sad about life."

"While still having immense power over you," Kyou added. "He at least gives each of you a forcefield and a gun before he sends drones to drop you at various points around the 'circle of influence', as he calls it. An area around the size of Greenland, so even just getting to the centre is going to be a challenge."

"Gun, forcefield, backpack, some rations, a built-in communicator which has basic smartphone functions, and a biocybernetic tattoo on the palm of your hand which is the key to shutting the core down," Bran said. "You step out of your landing pod into a forest by a lake, and just when you're looking at your communicator overlay to work out which direction to go, this kid runs by you, screaming."

"Being chased," Kyou added. "And that's the first divergence point in the game, because you can try to save him or not, and you can succeed or not, and this not only gives you different opening sequences, it directly impacts one of your potential companion relationships, the ability to gain a particular skill, and your easiest route to get to the core's location."

"Can you save scum in this game?" my dad asked. "I'm a ditherer, and being too slow to save the kid would bother me."

"Yes, you can save and reload as much as you like," Bran said. "We're also considering whether to follow the approach of games like *Detroit: Become Human*, and give you a visible decision tree at the end of the game so you can jump back and make different choices, instead of doing a full replay."

"Is the colony all enviro-habitats and solar collectors?" I asked, trying to picture the place.

"Fantasy," Kyou said. "Villages, horses, amazing buildings. Almost a Miyazaki feel, but no airplanes, trains or cars."

"We still have the original book that we used to create Samerkel," Rin added. "Back when we didn't have the frame story, and our imaginations were following well-trodden paths. Other than some of the names, we really haven't kept very much of what we originally came up with."

"It started to change when Kyou did some junior economics class," Bran said, "and ended up obsessed with trying to work out how the world would be if all the magic came from a single point, and the further you got from that point, the less magic there was. The concentrated magic supported all manner of luxury and miracle, while people at the fringes got by on dribs and drabs, and yet those beyond that were able to develop technologies that wouldn't work in the magic field."

"We wrote about that for a couple of years until Rin asked what would happen to it all if someone could come along and pick up the source of the magic and take it away, and that became the story we wanted to share."

Dad began to ask more detailed questions about what happened next, how the transition to fantasy occurred, and what 'echoes' referred to in the game title.

I settled back to listen, and watch everyone's faces. Their enthusiasm was infectious, and so different from the way they usually presented themselves. Would anyone from Corascur recognise the gentle but distant Rin, the lightly mocking Kyou, and the ever-brooding Bran in these three glowing faces?

This game, and all the secrecy about their plan to build it, had kept these three from becoming truly close to many people. And because of another game, one we'd played in school at the risk of being expelled, I became one of the people who they were willing to share secrets with. And that had made them all closer to me.

Recognising this, I had to wonder what would happen to the bond secrecy had created, when the artist, the musician and the programmer were their public personas. Perhaps it would no longer hold us so closely.

I glanced at the scenery out the window, reminding myself that the important thing was to enjoy the ride.

Five

"That's a very tangled expression Mika," Kyou said.

I blinked, then smiled. "I was enjoying how invested you were, and thinking the game sounded super interesting. But then I realised I couldn't play it for maybe five years, and I'll already know the plot twists."

"The downside of making the game you want to play is never getting the full player experience," Bran said. "Do you find that with your books, Mr Teyrn?"

"Not precisely. When I'm finishing up a book, I'm usually sick to death of it because the editing process requires so much re-reading. But give it a few years and I can come to them with fresh eyes. Some of the earlier ones have almost become books written by someone else, because I'm no longer the same person." My dad shrugged, then added: "Those are some impressive mountains ahead. The Ramparts?"

"None other," Kyou said.

"When I came this way with the Nichols, it was amazing to watch them climbing higher and higher on the horizon," I said. "The area around Helios is so flat that it feels like the entire country must be the same way. It's such an unusual topography, with almost the whole inland being at or below sea level, and the coastline genuinely like ramparts made of mountains."

"Theory is that the centre of the island was either ground down or just outright sank under the weight of a massive ice sheet during the middle Eocene," Bran told me. "Greenland was once way further north, under kilometres-deep ice, but by the Miocene it had settled at this latitude. How far are we from the turn-off?"

"Another twenty minutes," Rin said. "The mountains always look closer than they are."

"One of the reasons Noonerry is such a backwater is Strathold Forest," Kyou explained. "It sits east of the Snowshield Tableland, and is protected against development. So, we first head west to Incun, then up on the tableland and south to Moonmere, and then back east to Noonerry. There are a couple of closer roads, but they are narrow and wind about so much they're actually the longer route."

"Is this forest within walking distance of the farmhouse?" my dad asked. "Forest walks are high on the list of preferred family activities."

"Hm, well, it's a good...ten metres or so away," Kyou said, chuckled, then added: "But there's quite a drop from the tableland. There's some rather dangerous-looking stone stairs down that I didn't chance on my visit. I think they'd need to be restored to be usable."

Dad looked pleased, then said: "Do you remember that house in Senegal, Mika, where the stairs between the ground and first floor collapsed overnight?"

"Not likely to forget nearly walking off the landing," I said. "That was a real fixer-upper. Every other house on the street was pristine, beautiful, and ours just looked good from the outside."

"Sorenson and Mika built temporary stairs out of packing cases and cinder blocks," Dad said. "We were only going to be there another week, and we were getting nowhere with the landlord, so it was simpler to make do." He sighed. "That was back when I had far fewer books out, and Sorenson's consulting business helped her reputation more than our wallets. There was a lot of making do."

Dad began to tell anecdotes of the worst houses we'd lived in, which nicely filled our detour up onto the Snowshield Tableland, which had a strong resemblance to a cow-dotted, gently undulating carpet of green. It grew bumpier as we came into Noonerry, with a rim of low hills ahead, and well beyond that the nearest peaks of The Ramparts: two rows of grey mountains, streaked with downward spills of black, white and charcoal.

"Stop to eat before heading to the farm?" Kyou suggested. "There'll be something on the main street."

"What's the population here?" Dad asked.

"Just over two thousand," Kyou said. "A cheese factory on the southwest edge is the biggest industry outside farming."

The main street was wide, with decorative wrought iron railing in the centre, and plenty of empty spaces among the angled parking. There were only a handful of food options, but we settled down for lunch at a diner that had an internal door connecting to a bakery, and I happily finished off a Cornish-style pasty and a good, proper cream bun, and endorsed the expedition as a fine outing for the lunch alone.

"You'll find Mika's opinion of a town depends entirely on whether it owns interesting bridges and buildings, or if the bakery is worth her time," Dad said, as we headed back out.

"A point in Noonerry's favour, then," Kyou said.

"Mr Westhaven!"

We stopped as a burly, red-faced man came hurrying up to us, trailed by a woman in her late thirties, and two teens.

"Richard," Kyou said, with a nod. "Please, call me Kyou. And let me introduce the rest of the Kybirn executive—Rin Laurent and Bran Ashten. And, of course, Mika Niles and Gareth Teyrn, from our art and narrative teams. This is Richard Ackerton, from Noonerry Realty."

"Pleased to meet you all," Richard said, heartily. "And allow me to introduce our Mayor, Sigrid Thornley—and her son and daughter, Arne and Marit."

A round of handshaking followed, and I amused myself watching the stunned expressions of Arne and Marit. Arne, maybe sixteen, was focused on Bran, while Marit, not much more than thirteen, seemed mesmerised by Rin.

But the girl recovered quite quickly, and put in, with a voice of longing: "Are you really going to build a game company here?"

"The main office of one," Kyou said, amiably. "We've just come down for a site inspection."

"Don't hesitate to contact me if there's anything you need," Mayor Thornley said, not completely managing to hold back a similar expression to the bemused look that kept crossing my dad's face. "The council is very supportive of new industry coming into Noonerry."

"Thank you," Kyou said, fishing a business card from his wallet to exchange with hers. "I mean to begin by clearing away the old milking sheds and workers accommodation, and am happy to hire local if there's someone you want to recommend."

"This is fortunate timing," Richard put in. "I was planning on calling to ask if you're interested in sub-dividing Fox Farm at all? I've been contacted by a very interested buyer looking for land in the area."

"Not currently," Kyou said. He smiled blandly, and added: "I don't want to meddle, but if you do have people thinking of selling properties, I'd strongly advise them to wait until the revised high-speed rail route has been announced."

Both Richard and Mayor Thornley went still, but then Mayor Thornley shook her head. "The rail line's unlikely to impact Noonerry, even if it does have a stop in Strathold. The National Parks Service is adamantly opposed to adding a road between Strathold and Noonerry." She smiled wryly. "The reason why can be found in the name of your farm: Strathold Forest houses Greenland's largest colony of endangered vitha foxes."

Kyou glanced at me, so I cleared my throat and said: "I, ah, just recently read a survey report that suggests the rail line will almost certainly cross the tableland, rather than run through Vitha Valley. The only question is whether the stop will be at Moonmere, Noonerry, or somewhere between the two."

"Understandably, we're holding off on settling the site layout until we hear more," Kyou said smoothly, and then grinned and added: "If you do have anyone wanting to sell after the announcement, don't hesitate to call."

Disbelief and hope struggled for supremacy on their faces.

"Are you certain about this?" Mayor Thornley asked. "How reliable is this report?"

"There's no route through Vitha Valley that doesn't cross at minimum two hundred freehold residential properties," I paraphrased. "Even if they run through Strathold Forest, which you've just said isn't very likely. Despite a relatively small amount of extra track length, and the elevation, it's not only going to be quicker to start construction on a route over the tableland, it'll probably be a good deal cheaper."

The mayor exchanged a look with Richard, then said: "Well, you've certainly given us something to think about. I won't rush to call an emergency council meeting, but I'll definitely follow this up."

"I—I need to talk to one of my clients," Richard said, made a farewell gesture, and hurried away.

"How long would it take to get right into Helios if they put a stop here?" asked Marit, almost white with excitement.

"An hour," I told her, with a smile. "I expect you'll get commuters. If the weather up here is any better than Helios is in winter, I might commute myself."

"It snows," the boy, Arne, said, managing to speak for the first time. He glanced at Bran, blushed crimson, then added: "Even though we're south. Elevation."

"Light snows in winter," the mayor clarified. "Far more pleasant than Helios' sleet. Days much like today throughout summer, though occasionally a particularly hot one mixes in. A lot of early morning mist in autumn and spring that sometimes persists until noon, which is actually the origin of the town's name: celebrating the midday sun. The only real downside is the Buster—gale-force winds that hit at least once a month, particularly when a cool change is setting in. The central portion of Fox Farm is reasonably sheltered, though, since it sits in a small depression rimmed by hills. The farmhouse itself has that windbreak for a reason."

We thanked her, and clambered back into Rin's Hummer, heading east toward a sky filled with mountain.

"That was fun," Kyou said.

"I don't think they're going to believe you didn't have any warning when you ran up here and bought everything you could," I told him.

"That was back before the press even started hinting that the Sunneway Pass route was in trouble," Kyou said. "I call that plausible deniability. Not far now," he added, as we passed out of the main section of town. "The fence is just past this reserve."

Beyond the tree-studded reserve, we could see a small valley backed by a cluster of low hills, and beyond them tall mountain peaks. We stopped for Kyou to let us through a gate, crossed a bridge over a high-banked river, and entered a short loop of sealed road leading through a cluster of ugly buildings: two large corrugated iron sheds, several small wooden houses, and a smattering of barns.

"A biggish farm: originally around six hundred head of cattle, and also sheep kept on the southern portion," Kyou said. "The farm's workers lived down here, while the farmhouse itself is at the end of this road to the left. There's nothing much salvageable here, except possibly these old drystone fences, and some stone cattle byres dotted about the place."

"Practically a mini ghost town," my dad said. "Must be eerie on those misty mornings."

The farmhouse was set on the crest of the lowest of the hills, in the very north-east corner of the tableland, with a row of tall conifers leading up to and running beside the building. The road stopped at the remains of a carport most of the way up, and we stretched our legs to climb mossy stone steps to a big, single storey house. There we stopped to look over the valley.

"How big is this place, Kyou?" Bran asked, frowning.

"Around fifteen hundred acres."

I coughed. "He described this to me as a few paddocks."

"Same," Rin said, smiling a little dangerously. "And somehow never got around to showing us the size on the map of Noonerry. Is it all of this part of the tableland inside that fence?"

"This and a section that runs west along the southern ridge."

Kyou fished his tablet out of his bag and showed us the property line. The farm was shaped much like an extra chunky platform boot, with the hills forming a heel and toes angled east-southeast. The farmhouse was situated on the narrow 'toe', and from where we stood, we had a lovely outlook over the lower elevation that made up the bulk of the 'foot', with a small lake glimmering at the centre. A stream took overflow from the lake down to the river we'd crossed, which ran along the top of the foot and turned near the 'toe', running back along the edge of town. The thick leg of the boot also headed back west toward the cheese factory on the far side of Noonerry.

"Where are you planning to put your headquarters?" I asked, surveying a handful of sheep that presumably belonged to the neighbour renting the paddocks.

"That depends on where the rail line runs," he said. "But for us, a house just here." He touched the top of the biggest hill, that one positioned at the 'heel'.

"Well, I have to agree it's a very pretty view," my dad said.

"Oh, that's not the view," Kyou said, putting his tablet away, and beckoning us to the corner of the veranda.

This wrapped around half of the house, and a handful of mouldering couches were located on a section that faced east. Here the hill dropped away, offering an uninterrupted view over a broad expanse of trees, then further to houses, pasture, and cropland all the way across the wide Vitha Valley, and between the twinned ranges of mountains that made up The Ramparts, where the midday sun was reflecting off Dorsey Lake. While the interior valley of Fox Farm was a pastoral idyll, this was unmitigated grandeur.

My dad blinked a few times, then pulled out his phone and video called my mother.

"*About to go into a meeting,*" she said, sounding distracted.

"View from the back porch," Dad said, and turned the phone so she could see what we could.

There was a long silence.

"*Buy it,*" Mum said at last. "*Even if we don't like the house, we can always build something we do.*"

Mum hung up, and Dad looked at Kyou. "Are you sure you want to sell this?"

"The view from the southeast point is even more spectacular," Kyou said, shrugging, and led us back around the front, pointing out where the property line ran. The farmhouse title covered a slice of six acres that included the small hill with the house, a couple of nursing paddocks, and the corner of the river where it turned and ran west.

"What are you planning to do with all the rest of it?" Dad asked. "Housing development?"

"Destination weddings," Kyou said, and paused to enjoy our expressions. "Imagine getting married on a terrace above Vitha Valley. Or standing on a moon bridge over that little lake. Or in a Sakura grove by the river. Or in autumn, for that matter, looking out over the forest in full colour. I do plan some housing, especially so our employees aren't stuck unable to afford to rent here, but for the valley centre...well, I'd vastly prefer to live by a parkland than a housing development. We can bring forest to the tableland, plant all the most stunning trees—Sakura, Greenland blaze, maple, gingko—set up cycling paths, have a sculpture walk, an outdoor auditorium, picnic spots and outdoor dining areas. Develop the area around the lake into world-class gardens that happen to make brilliant backdrops for wedding photographs. On the fringes, art galleries, a concert hall, that kind of thing. Make the buildings features in and of themselves: unique, interesting, and—"

"Worth charging through the nose for every inch?" Bran asked, raising a brow.

"Weddings are big money," Kyou said, inserting a heavy key into the front door. "Locations that are the stuff of fantasy can dictate their own price. Particularly ones that are an easy trip from the airport."

"Can you possibly fit running a resort in with getting a degree and developing a game?" my dad asked.

"I don't plan to manage the thing," Kyou said, struggling with the key. "We finance it, then enjoy the view while people with a tolerance for high-maintenance wedding parties do the rest. Besides, other than planting the trees so that they're not all saplings when it matters, there's no urgency to start construction for anything except our main office, which I'd like to have ready by the time the HSR line opens. We'll probably still need to rent a small to medium site for at least one year after *Echoes* goes into full production. Our current property only has enough staff space for development for the current, much smaller game, and the pre-production for *Echoes*."

The door finally gave, and we went in to explore. Other than a wide hallway featuring some nice decorative wooden arches, the interior was almost suffocating. Small windows, small rooms, old carpet, a kitchen from the sixties, ancient furniture. Dust, dust, dust.

"I do like that enormous bathtub," I told my dad, after we'd run out of corners to explore. "You should keep that, and those hallway features."

"And not much else," he said. "Do you have suggestions for how to handle this? I quite like the way it looks outside, so I'd prefer to not start over."

"Replace the entire east outer wall with glass," I said, promptly. "Take out the ceiling to maximise the outlook, and make the rear quarter of the building into a shared study, with a double-sided fireplace nominally separating yours and Mum's halves. Put a conservatory on the south side of the building. You'll want to completely gut the interior and re-do the wiring and plumbing, not to mention invest in a lot of insulation and underfloor heating. Remove the back half of the veranda and enclose the rest. I'll do you up a general layout."

Dad saluted, which prompted a cough of laughter from Bran.

"What's Mika like when she doesn't get her way?" Kyou asked.

"Depends on how invested she is," Dad said. "When she goes quiet in the middle of a conversation, that's when you worry." He smiled at my expression. "Sorenson and I aren't fond of drama, and fortunately Mika takes after us in that regard."

"More lies," I said, and he grinned.

"*Participating* in drama, I mean. I enjoy watching drama. All source material, after all. Anyway, if it wasn't obvious, this place has a view that's definitely worth taking advantage of my daughter's friends in order to own. I don't see any downside to either of the options—whether it's in a quiet backwater, or includes a daily dose of bridezilla in the distance. Sculpture walks a bonus. Anyone up for a wander about?"

We went on tour, driving back to the milking sheds to explore the rusting equipment, visiting the unexpectedly deep lake, and then trekking all the way to the peak of the big hill where Kyou wanted to build a house, which indeed enjoyed even better views. Forest, mountains, the picturesque and expensive town of Stratholm on the west end of Lake Dorsey, and great swathes of farmland to the south, with the small city of Ridelmere just visible on the horizon.

"You'll be able to see the rail line," I told Kyou, as we rested on a collection of rocks that provided excellent natural seating.

"Is that an advantage?" he asked.

"Oh, definitely. It won't be as spectacular as something like the Millau Viaduct, but I find a lot of beauty in the kind of clean, incrementally rising line that they're likely to construct. Even if the stop ends up in Moonmere, we'll still be able to enjoy it."

"Do you really think a concert hall is viable out here?" Rin asked, abruptly.

"I was mainly thinking of that as a necessary part of recording the big performances for your soundtracks," Kyou said, shrugging. "But if that stop is anywhere near Noonerry, the most likely trajectory for the town is up-market tourism and highest-end commuters. When you consider that when the traffic snarled up, it would take longer for us to get home from Corascur than it would to take the train here, I don't need to explain why. Even the forest that has been a barrier to development is transformed into an advantage because it means that the land immediately east can't be built upon, and will instead function as an attraction. The land west of Noonerry will be all luxury villas and golf courses within ten years, and the residents the sort to be able to afford exclusive performances."

Kyou paused, frowned, then added: "We'd better sponsor some kind of preservation and breeding program for those vitha foxes. Even though an influx of people is inevitable with the rail line, owning a place called Fox Farm next to their habitat means we need to be particularly sensitive to the environmental factors."

"Leave the farmhouse named as Fox Farm and give the rest a related name," Bran suggested. "Make the environmental approach a feature, and live up to it. High-speed rail fits in with that, since it's a lower carbon footprint than cars and air travel."

"I'm open to suggestions," Kyou said.

We played a name game on the hike back, until my dad said "Fox Hollow," and everyone decided it fit.

I'd grown a little distracted because Rin had barely spoken since we arrived, but my concern eased when I caught a snatch of humming.

"I got my learner's permit yesterday," I told him, as we reached the Hummer. "If you trust me with your behemoth of a car, you'll be free to write down whatever it is that's gotten into your head."

He looked startled, then smiled and tossed me the keys.

"Time to learn if he can compose while you grind his gears," Kyou murmured, hopefully low enough for my dad not to hear.

"Kyou's doubting my driving ability, Dad," I said.

"Oh, don't do that," Dad said, pantomiming fear. "It makes her go faster around corners."

"Don't you need L-plates?" Bran asked.

"Brought them with me," I said. "Hijacking Rin's car was my plan all along."

"Do you like driving?" Kyou asked, after the plates were fixed and we'd piled into the Hummer.

"Tell the truth, I'd rather let someone else do the driving while I read or play games," I said, adjusting the seat forward. "And it makes it hard to properly look at the scenery, which is why I didn't suggest I drive on the way down."

I experimented with the gears, then started the trip back, enjoying the height of the vehicle, and only a little distracted when we travelled down the now-lively main street of Noonerry, where a solid portion of the locals seemed to have gathered to discuss the news.

Big changes. I'm not sure how I'd feel if my idyllic country town was on the verge of being swallowed up. It felt very strange to be aligned with the incoming group of wealthy invaders. Kyou had driven down here and practically bought himself a suburb, and it was a clever gamble, and the usual stuff of capitalism. Still, I was glad that, for whatever reason, he'd warned the locals against further selling, and spared a thought for foxes.

Six

Dad declined the offer of dinner in favour of settling in for a preliminary read of the work done so far on *Echoes*, so I dropped him at his hotel and returned home.

After successfully manoeuvring into the garage, I turned off the car, looked at Rin still making edits in a notebook, and said: "Are you lost for the rest of the day, or would you like to see if all of us can fit in my shower?"

"Shower," Rin said immediately, and closed the notebook.

"Not quite ready to start dividing up your nights?" Kyou asked.

"Pretty much," I said, giving Rin back his keys. "My room in quarter of an hour? Or do you want to have dinner first?"

The answer was very clear, and I thoroughly enjoyed the experience of steam, soap and an excess of hands. Then we ordered Mexican takeout, ate nachos while testing out the gaming room, and finished by giving my bed another workout.

I woke between Kyou and Bran, shifted carefully, then groaned.

"Regrets?" Kyou asked, blinking at me.

"No foursomes for a year," I said. "Maybe ever."

He chuckled, low and impossibly sexy. "We were all too worked up," he said. "When 'maybe ever' comes around, we'll have to rethink our approach. Meet you downstairs for breakfast?"

"Mm."

I'd intended on yoga, but postponed it in favour of moving as little as possible, and thoroughly appreciated that Kyou had my usual breakfast waiting for me, along with a few slices of toast. He was deeply engrossed in his laptop, so I browsed my phone as I ate, belatedly letting Lania know I was back in the city, and then exploring more of the functions of *Castellan*, adding a bunch of items to the shopping list, and finding a useful option to flag some of them to give me a total amount after purchase. Even though I'm sure Kyou would pay for all my expenses without blinking, it seemed important to not take too thorough an advantage of my already bargain rate for room and board.

"How badly did we mess up your schedule?" I asked, glancing at his seemingly bottomless inbox.

"Not much—not to mention that getting the story near to final is one of our primary tasks for the rest of the year, and I'm finally confident that it will reach the level we need. Do you want to come to our orientation meeting on Monday morning?"

"Of course. If I'm going to be an employee, treat me like one. How many people do you have starting next week?"

"Eighteen, with interviews for another half-dozen positions. You're on Team Two, which is pre-prod for *Echoes*. Most of the art hires will be Team One for the next few months, finishing *One Step More*."

Before *Echoes* ramped up, Kybirn's focus would be on a smaller game. "How much work is there to be done on *One Step*? You said you were pretty far along: can I play it?"

"Programming is at ninety-five percent, needing only tweaks and adjustments as we bring in more of the art and music. The bigger compositions need to be recorded, and Rin hasn't found the right voice for a couple of pieces. The most work to be done is on the cut scenes and the trailers. Rin doesn't want you to play it until all the music's in. I think he plans to sit and watch your face for every micro-reaction."

"The game's that personal to him, huh?"

"Since it's a barely-disguised narration of the time he spent in a wheelchair, I'm not sure it could be more personal. No dialogue at all, just some vocal snippets and a lot of music. Bran and I were there for him as much as we could be, but it was music that got him through the injury."

"Is there gameplay, or is it more a movie with button clicking?"

"A kind of puzzle-play involving combining snippets of composition to open up paths, where there's not necessarily a 'right' path, but instead different results. It's an extremely music-focused game, but one that hopefully doesn't exclude people who aren't musical." He smiled wryly. "Bran and Rin were recently workshopping how to make it playable to the deaf and partial hearing community, which created a whole extra layer of work for the art team, but the solution they came up with will enhance the game even for hearing players, so it's a double win."

His phone chimed, and he checked it, then said: "Because I wake up so early, I schedule a lot of the awkward time zone meetings around my breakfast. This is a prospective hire currently living in India."

I left him to it, and went to properly tidy my neglected dressing room. Even after my buying spree, my clothes still looked overwhelmed by all the space. Then I kissed some boys until they woke up.

Rin and Bran had barely come down when Dad arrived for an extended tour of the house, happily accepting photos of the building pre-renovation, and setting in motion some purchasing formalities with Kyou. Then both Dad and I became official Kybirn employees, signed non-disclosure agreements, and settled exactly what work we'd be doing.

After lunch, I walked Dad back to where he'd parked his rental, and gave him a goodbye hug.

"You found some interesting kids to play landlord," Dad said. "Are you dating any of them?"

"Well," I said judiciously. "I'd like to."

"That could get complicated, Mika."

"Yeah, I know. I'll talk to you about getting an apartment if I decide I need some distance. So, what do you think of the game writing?"

"Should be a lot of fun. I'm glad they're open to me contributing more than just a sub-plot. Fortunately, the worldbuilding is intriguing and the major plotline quite solid, though you can tell which parts they were more interested in. Some of the actual dialogue written either undercuts the emotional heft of the story they're trying to tell, or is outright wooden, but that's precisely why they're bringing me in."

"It won't interfere with work on the story about the ballet school?"

"Since I'm thinking semi-historical novel there, where I'll need to track down and interview former residents, it's useful to have what is substantially an editing or shared-world job to fill in the time waiting for people to get back to me. Not entirely sure how I'll break news of my career tangent to Devine, but she has *Tranquil* to occupy her at the moment. And Caitlin has already made the kind of offer needed to shore up my failing ego, bruised as it has been by your teen mogul and his over-talented friends. I can officially give you carte blanche in designing our dream home. While it's being renovated, Sorenson and I will kick off the immigration process. Hopefully that won't be too big a hurdle."

"What country wouldn't want Rock Hardison among its literary luminaries?" I asked.

"I shall list *all* my pen names," Dad said, grandly. "Hopefully the form's big enough. Amusingly, working for Kybirn Games might be the necessary addition to my resume to get me over the line."

I rolled my eyes. "Sure Dad."

Not wanting to get caught in school-hour traffic, Dad left after another hug, and I took a meandering route back, admiring the local buildings. These had been built to look like Victorian-era townhouses, but were clearly much more recent, and larger than the typical dwellings of that time. The area was very quiet compared to the main road two short streets away: on the walk to the car and back I only saw a pair of chicly dressed grey-haired women, and later a boy in a hoodie walking a creamy Afghan hound.

The plumy tail and curling ears were beautiful, but the amount of work that must go into that coat was not attractive. Pets. I'd never had even a goldfish. Did I want a goldfish? Kyou had once talked about horses.

Preoccupied, I negotiated my way through the now fully-active security entrance and looked blankly about, wondering how to go about finding anyone in this oversized house. But then I shrugged, decided to catch up on some quality gaming before my life got busy, and headed to the games room, only to find all three of my boyfriends having an impromptu music session.

Settling on one of two main couches, I took out my phone and recorded Rin and Bran, sitting back-to-back on the coffee table as they stop-started through a catchy melody while Kyou, wearing a faintly long-suffering expression, tapped out a beat on a small drum. After a few repetitions, they started again, and Rin added brisk-paced lyrics, his pleasant tenor painting a picture of a boy drunk for the first time, wandering dangerously down a highway until his friends came and took him home. Then, to my faint astonishment, both Kyou and Bran joined him for the chorus.

Bran's parents had railroaded him along a path to becoming a teen pop idol, and he had hated aspects of the stage so much he'd deliberately damaged his throat. Although surgery a few months ago had restored his speaking voice, I hadn't guessed he'd reached the point of being willing to sing.

He was such a natural-born performer: relaxed, handling the guitar almost casually, eyes narrowing as he took on a rap segment. Every action captured the eye, made me want to look twice. His young voice had been pure, angelic, but now he sang with a husky note.

"Your composition from yesterday?" I asked, when Rin finally sighed and put down the guitar.

He nodded. "Needs more work, but it's coming together."

"What did you think?" Bran asked.

"It's an earworm," I said. "Are you planning on forming a boy band?"

Bran gave me a sour look. "We record a demo of the song in order to sell it."

"And then sit back and enjoy the royalties while someone else deals with world touring and screaming fans? Do you want to keep working on it, or play some games? Or, weren't the class schedules supposed to be published today?"

"Schedules," Rin said decisively. "I need more thinking time for the lyrics."

The gaming room boasted two massive wall-mounted screens, with multiple computers and consoles linked to them, so it was simple enough to display a combined schedule from our Kybirn accounts. We first added in our core subjects, then various other commitments, and colour-coded them according to whether they were mandatory or skippable.

Other than Professor Tremaine's lectures—which were only once a month in the first year—all the lectures were flexible for me, since I could watch the online version any time. All labs and tutorials were things I was reluctant to skip: I'd been looking forward to playing with a university-level physics lab for years.

"You've got another internship scheduled for the winter break?" I asked, once we'd added our first wave of commitments.

"In Vancouver," Kyou said. "Want to come along?"

"I mightn't be able to—there was something in the course notes about a shared project the first week of the break. I'm not sure when my parents will be arriving, either, other than that they'll be here for the book festival just before Christmas."

"We'll be back for that," Rin said. "Usually, I take my sisters to it, but I think my failure to turn up to business school will have been noticed by then. Bran, why is it that half your classes are the same as Mika's?"

Bran shrugged, but cocked a corner of his mouth.

"First couple of years of sciences share a lot of maths and physics classes," I said. "Next year, we'll probably have only one or two in common, though."

"Want to team up for the physics labs?" Bran asked.

"Sure. With Lania as well, probably." I paused to send Lania a text, letting her know which lab time slots I'd chosen, before asking Rin and Kyou: "Did you plan to do that C++ course this semester?"

"If you are," Kyou said.

"Now that I'm a game company employee, I feel like I need to know more than basic programming, even if my job is to draw buildings. Did you decide whether you were going to build a game engine from the ground up?"

"No, we'll continue with *Unreal Engine*," Bran said. "For now."

"We asked him if he wanted to build a game engine or a game," Kyou said. "Since he's done so much work with *Unreal* already, hiring a team to create all the modules from scratch didn't make much sense."

"Something we'll consider a few years down the track, for future games," Bran said, on a faintly stubborn note.

"Before we start picking our non-core classes, let's set Wednesday late afternoon for our cooking lesson," Kyou said. "Since it seems to be clear for everyone. Friday cocktails we'll position around nine. We also have a self-defence course once a month that's on a Monday, Mika—do you want to come to that?"

"Sure. I'll probably need it once some of your fans realise I'm living with you."

We added our optional courses, to the limits that the university would allow us to sign up for, and blocked in Kybirn work hours, which for Kyou and Bran would mean a short meeting each morning, and then time to review the day's work each afternoon. Rin, heavily involved in music production, had a fuller schedule this year. Projects, assignments, practice, and *One Step More* would fill almost all his time.

"It's lucky I'm living with you," I said, surveying the few white spaces in our combined calendar. "Otherwise, I'd see you about once a fortnight. Are you going to join any clubs? Rowing?"

"Not rowing," Kyou said. "We looked into the university club, and it's tediously rigid and serious thanks to a rivalry with Lakeshore College. We won't be rowing nearly often enough to satisfy them."

"Do you play tennis, Mika?" Rin asked. "There's courts near the Conservatory, and the club's just an informal notion that allows you access to the facilities. There's an online booking system, so we can reserve a slot whenever we have time and want to get away from our desks."

"That's one I've never had occasion to learn," I said. I glanced at him. "Should I buy myself a short white skirt and cute ankle socks?"

"Absolutely," Rin said.

"It's a good option," Kyou said. "We can play singles or doubles. And I endorse the short white skirt."

"With no set schedule, we won't have as much trouble with audience waiting for us," Bran added.

"There's an indoor swimming pool somewhere, right?" I asked. "I've been missing swimming."

"Far end of the campus," Rin said.

"We did toy with installing a rooftop pool here," Kyou said. "But gave up on the idea. Something for the Noonerry house. Anyway, now that we've dealt with the trivial stuff, it's time to move on to the important scheduling."

"What have we missed?" I asked, surprised.

"More colour coding," Bran said, changing the display to my calendar and adding categories of green, red, and blue to the two previous days. Then, for Saturday, he added blue before glancing at me. "We'll assign people, but it's up to you how you want them assigned. One, two or three."

"Oh." It had taken me a moment to realise the colours meant who would occupy my nights. "Keep it simple: alternate one and two. But three for tonight."

"I thought you were sore," Kyou said.

"I am," I said, watching them all suddenly excited. "But there's plenty of things I can do to the three of you that doesn't involve me getting sore."

They were so easy to please sometimes.

Seven

Waking tangled in boys was becoming less of a novelty, but remained a very pleasant way to start the day. I particularly liked when I was halfway conscious, and increasingly aware of a heartbeat against my cheek, or a soft chorus of breathing. And, admittedly, the odd snore, gurgle of stomach, and once a muted fart. Living together meant being human up close.

The day was Saturday, and Kyou was stuck with interviews, while Rin went to his first set of sisters' birthday party, and Bran and I were scheduled for a long ride. Since we were planning to beat the weekend traffic, I woke Bran before I followed Kyou down for breakfast, and then sketched design ideas for Fox Farm while Bran and Kyou caught up on overnight email.

"Darcy wants to know if we want to cater Monday's induction," Bran said.

"No reason not to," Kyou replied. "Light morning stuff, sandwiches. Juice. The tea and coffee facilities are already set up. The vending machine won't arrive until Thursday."

Kyou was still processing email when Bran and I filled a couple of water bottles and headed for the garage. There were two helmets and a leather jacket hanging on the wall to the left of the stair down to the garage, and Bran picked up the jacket to reveal another hanging beneath it, which he handed to me.

"I think it should fit," he said.

The jacket was new, and had an artificially faded image on the back of a fox, a wolf and a cat holding game controllers. "This is custom?" I asked.

"Yeah. Asked Kyou for the picture."

"I've still seen hardly any of his artwork," I said, slipping on the jacket. It fit perfectly.

"You'll be seeing a lot of the concept work he's done for *Echoes*, since he's keen to get you started on the city designs," Bran said, zipping up his own jacket. "For the physical paintings, he's got most of them in his room, but turned against the wall. Painting things you feel strongly about is a double-edged sword."

I adjusted my backpack straps so it could fit comfortably over the jacket, then tried on the helmet.

"Ready when you are. I've been looking forward to today for a while."

With a slow smile, Bran donned his own helmet, then mounted the bike, triggering the door while I climbed on behind him. I hooked my fingers lightly through the belt loops of his jeans, and settled back for some city watching. It had rained the previous night, and the streets were a little wet, but thankfully still quiet as we made our way through the crowded inner west. The sun had burned off the moisture by the time we reached the expressway, and then Bran opened up the engine and we shot west like an arrow, turning north an hour later.

This was originally meant to be a coastal ride, among the spectacular mountains north of Dawntread, but the distance to be travelled wasn't practical for a day trip, so we were touring the western shore of the great central lake instead. Motorcycles aren't a passion of mine, but Greenland is spectacular, and one of the things I'd regretted not making time for during the previous school year. Snuggling up against Bran's back, I enjoyed vista after vista, the vast reaches of water a constant shimmering backdrop to flats and hills, farms and boutique towns. We stopped a couple of hours north, bought fish and chips, and then rode up to one of the scenic lookouts: a spot Bran liked where we could sit on natural stone seats to enjoy the distant mountains, lake and sky arrayed before us.

I gazed west at the barely visible peaks that were called the Dragon's Teeth, thinking of how little of this very spectacular country I'd seen. "Some time when the four of us have more than a few days to string together, let's do a big loop. Helios, Dawntread, Morning Star, North Lake, Westering, Eventide and back."

"Okay," Bran said, curling an arm around my waist to pull me closer, clearly pleased by my mood. "Spring after the melt? We have a couple of weeks without anything major."

"Schedule it before something else comes up," I said, and leaned against him. "Does having so much of your time taken up bug you?"

"We've blocked in more time than a lot of shit will really take. Though that's riding on the quality of our staff. We offered higher-than-standard salaries for some of the senior roles because having quality people who've done this before will hopefully save us from our own stupidity. We'll find out in the next few months whether we made the right choices."

"Are you still aiming for December to release *One Step*?"

"January-February," he said. "Came up with a bunch of enhancements, figured they were worth the delay. Since we haven't even announced the game, there's no rush. Besides, Rin is being incredibly picky finding just the right voice."

I looked up at his profile. "While you've become more comfortable with your own singing?"

"No. Yes and no. Helping Rin fine-tune has never bothered me. And whenever I can look at it without any other factors, I do like music. Not nearly to the same level as Rin, and not enough that I'd make it my career, but playing relaxes me. Performance, putting myself on a stage in front of a horde of gawkers, I'm always going to hate that. I got through that concert at school, and in a way I'm glad I did it just to say goodbye to Corascur, but I don't want to repeat it. I especially don't want to sing for strangers. When I'm on a stage I always feel like everyone wants to tear me into strips, and singing was always doubly awful because the reaction from the audience is more intense, and there were times I couldn't keep how I was feeling out of my voice. And I'd get punished for that."

"Punished?" I said, stiffening.

"By taking away my consoles and computer," Bran explained, tightening his arm around my waist. "My parents weren't stupid enough to hit me. They're more into low-voiced, scathing comments. Kyou's dad's a yeller, but only behind closed doors. His aunt throws things. Rin's parents are the worst: they're inexhaustibly reasonable. They make it so tiring to do anything but what they tell him to, and insist that it's all for his own good. Only very occasionally will they lose their tempers. He's going to go complete non-contact with them, which is part of the reason he knows it's going to be hard to see his sisters."

"Are you and Kyou going to follow suit with your own parents?"

"I haven't existed for my parents for years. Toby—that's my mother's secretary—took care of anything I needed, and now that I've finished high school, I'm officially cut off and expected to face the consequences of my defiance. They've completely missed that I've never been interested in playing starving dog, chasing after a bone of inheritance. I haven't needed their money for years."

"Kyou makes that easier than it otherwise might be," I pointed out.

Bran snorted, and nodded. "Kyou is god-tier. Rin and I have earned a solid sum composing music, and we have enough of an understanding of the stock market that we could have increased it, but Kyou has a true instinct. The only time I've ever seen him take a wrong step was walking into that trap his father and aunt set, and even there the opportunity was genuine."

"Is his family willing to let him go his own way now?"

"If his father sees a way to get a hold over Kyou, he'll definitely think about it, but since Kyou's shown he's capable of kicking where it hurts, he'll at least second-guess himself. We've spent a lot of time with a lawyer making sure we're as safe as we can be from interference, but there's no guarantee they won't come up with something we haven't anticipated. This is a mess-with-your-head topic."

"It is," I agreed. "Let's go back down to that village and take a walk about, then head back."

Much of Lake Helios' shoreline is rocky rather than sandy, but there was a pebbly stretch we could wander along. Since we were officially housemates rather than boyfriend-girlfriend, we didn't hold hands, but this kind of quiet, companionable walk is a favourite thing of mine.

"Having only ventured out once while I was at Corascur, I'm looking forward to seeing a lot more than the road between school and home this year," I said, as we returned to the bike. "Do you have a favourite place?"

"Miklok," he said, after a pause. "Up in Avannaata, rather than Southern Greenland. I like watching the auroras."

"I've never been lucky on aurora-spotting trips," I said, considering the practicalities of a visit to the Danish-Inuit territory encompassing the partially ice-locked north of the island.

"The four of us will see them together," he said, with calm certainty, then put on his helmet.

I pondered that promise on the ride back. Bran had broken up with his first girlfriend, someone he'd thought he'd spend his life with, because she'd insisted he choose between her and Rin and Kyou. The three boys planned completely interwoven lives: working together, playing together, and living together, and it was hardly surprising that Meggan had felt like she wasn't high enough on Bran's list of priorities.

Last night I'd blindfolded the three of them, arranged them on a corner of my bed with their arms lightly bound together, and indulged myself. It was not a situation that could possibly make me feel left out, and their reactions had increased my confidence that they were comfortable sharing a bed. Whether the Three Kings could somehow be 'the four of us' in a long-term way was something...well, I was willing to give it a shot.

The house was empty when we arrived back, but there was a message from Kyou on Mockingbird letting us know we'd just missed him. He'd gone with Darcy, Kybirn's admin assistant, to do a final cleanout and handover of their old rental office.

"Not much left over there," Bran said. "It mainly housed Rin's instrument collection and a server, and that's already been moved. End of an era. Start of the rest of our lives."

"Excited?"

"Trying not to run wildly. Or get caught up in things that could go wrong."

"Want to show me your room to distract yourself?" I asked, smiled at the change in his expression, and followed him upstairs.

Bran had the north-east corner, across the stairway from my south-east room. He had broken the area up into several rooms: one for his bedroom, another for his computer set-up, and a lounge-gaming room with a kitchenette attached. The bedroom was relatively small, with a similar dressing-room and bathroom arrangement to mine, while the room with his computers—an impressive six-monitor setup—filled the centre of the L-shaped suite. With all the shutters drawn, the space was a little dim, except in the corner nook, which he'd converted into a window seat: a raised, half-moon affair with bookcases beneath it. I spotted a couple of my dad's titles, but didn't linger, following Bran into his half-lit bedroom.

Playing with one boy is a very different experience to trying to manage three. We had time for all the unhurried kissing, the quiet and tender moments that had not so far been possible.

Bran began to doze off, so I left him and headed to my room for a quick shower, and then to try out the complete dream of a graphics tablet they'd given me, working on the renovation plan for my parents.

Around five, Kyou's voice suddenly sounded from the ceiling: "*Where are you two?*"

"Castellan, Intercom," I said, after a pause to remember the command, then replied: "I'm in my room. I think Bran's asleep."

Bran's voice came, then: "*I'm in the gym. We waiting on Rin for dinner?*"

"*He's on his way,*" Kyou said. "*Darcy's visiting, and wants to play restaurant roulette.*"

"I'm not sure I want to know what that is," I said, laughing. "Down in a minute."

Kyou was waiting in the main hall with a person who had briefly become infamous at Corascur, subject of a series of photographs that revealed a close association with all three of the school's most coveted boys. They'd never explained, and there was still forum speculation about the Three Kings' relationship with the fine-boned boy with bobbed black hair.

"Mika, this is Darcy, who is itching to move on from admin support to equipment design," Kyou said, as I came down the winding stair. "Darcy, Mika's a friend from Corascur who is going to work on buildings for us."

"Hi," I said, shaking hands, since this was in part a professional greeting. "So, what's restaurant roulette?"

"Random restaurant, random orders," Darcy said, with a lightning-quick grin. "Barring allergies, you have to eat whatever you order."

"Bran ended up with sheep's brains once," Kyou said. "He didn't like it."

"Mushy," Bran said, coming from the direction of the entry hall. "Let's talk about the time you ended up with the hottest item on the menu."

"He was tears and snot the entire meal," Darcy said, laughing. "Brick red."

"You have to eat the whole thing?" I asked. "What if your random order ends up being a family meal?"

"We made a one-quarter rule to save Rin from a four-person banquet," Kyou said.

"Sounds like a good way to try food you never thought you'd like," I said, then paused as Castellan said: *Garage.*

"Trying out a new setting," Kyou explained. "It'll pop up on the app as well, letting us know when someone has come through the front door, the garage, or via the elevator. It shows which login ID has been used as well."

"Going to be fun at three at the morning," I said.

"The four of us can disable it if we need to sneak in," Kyou promised.

Rin came through the entry hall, and handed me a cake box. "Leftovers," he said.

"Excellent," I said happily, and led the way to the kitchen. "Was it a good party?"

"As tolerable as forty mid-teens are ever likely to be," Rin said, rubbing a hand over his eyes. "Evgenie enjoyed herself a great deal, and Marcelline put out various fires. Anthea and Jessamin were late, and there was a small upset over why, but it all smoothed out. It doesn't help that my parents continue to compete over who can give the Best, Most Unique and Special birthday party, and the handful of days between parties means all ideas can be stolen and topped."

"Chapter Fifty on How to Suck the Fun out of Everything," Bran said. "Let's order—we're playing restaurant roulette."

"Last time, we ended up with four near-identical hamburgers," Rin said, looking less than enthused. "Not particularly good ones, either."

"If we get hamburgers again, we can consider bending the rules," Kyou said, shrugging. "We've got seventeen restaurant categories, Bran."

"Fourteen," Bran said, after consulting a random number generator on his phone.

"South Asian," Kyou said. "Thirty-nine options."

"Twenty-one."

"Something called *Momo Me*," Kyou said. "Oh, Nepalese. Have we ever had Nepalese?"

"No," Bran said. "Probably similar to Indian, though."

"Potential favourite then," Darcy said. "Particularly if Kyou gets the hottest item on the menu again."

Kyou's randomly-selected meal turned out to be mutton choila, which was some kind of tandoori dish, as was Rin's chicken sekuwa. Bran had alu chop—potato croquettes—and Darcy jhol momo, which were dumplings. I had yomari.

"Some kind of dessert," Kyou told me.

"A sweet bonanza today," I said, examining the contents of the cake box. "Can I order extra items, or can I only have dessert?"

"No problem with extras. There's a four-person momo platter, if you want to try them. Varieties of spiced dumplings."

"Sounds good. Do they have lassi? I'll have mango lassi."

Kyou ordered, and then we all pitched in to shift a collection of office miscellanea from Kyou's car. Much of it went into the recycling bin that had its own special nook in the side street, and the rest we took upstairs and distributed around the new office.

"A real step up," Darcy commented, tidying the desk fronting the mini-reception nearest the elevator. "The rental was a single room with a table and a couch."

"The rest of the space being taken up by instruments," Kyou put in.

"How long have you worked for Kybirn, Darcy?" I asked.

"Two years. I started out needing a little extra income while I studied. Taking messages, and then giving support for the little precursor apps worked out well. All this recruitment and setup work helpfully came along during the break, and now I get to train my replacement and move on to concept art while I work on my thesis! I had no idea a random fill-in part time thing would lead me to a unicorn career opportunity."

"What's your degree? Fashion?"

"Art history. While I love playing with clothes, I've never been really keen on trying to get something onto a catwalk. But equipment design in a fantasy setting...?" Darcy squeezed his eyes shut and gave a little wriggle. "I get to do something I love and be paid for it!"

I laughed. "Same. Drawing bridges and buildings is what I do for fun. It never occurred to me that I'd have a place in game design."

"What's your degree?" Darcy asked, as we followed Kyou back to the elevator.

"Engineering science with a primary of civil engineering."

"Ah, science side. There's a thoroughgoing rivalry on campus between Science, which gets all the funding but is so often dull as a career, and Arts, forever scratching for pennies, but full of future luminaries."

"Luminaries?"

"You'd be surprised the number of top tier musicians and writers Helios U produces. And quite a few drama graduates have gone on to become names. They've just added a new building to the drama faculty, thanks to some juicy alumni donations."

"Good source for voice actors, hopefully," Kyou said. "Even putting aside the major roles, there's a ton of voice work to be done for *Echoes*. Incidental characters and their dialogue will need a whole team we've yet to recruit."

"Gives me a headache, just thinking about how much goes into creating a big game," Darcy said. "Glad it also gives me a job."

Dinner arrived and was full of delicious spices. We went up to the rooftop to eat, and Darcy gave us practical tips for dealing with our Helios U schedule, but couldn't linger long, rushing off to a pre-arranged appointment to go clubbing.

"Do you ever go clubbing?" I asked, as we parted ways with Darcy on the ground floor, and took the leftovers to the kitchen.

"Too much body spray," Bran said.

"Too much groping," Rin added.

"Not my kind of music," Kyou finished. "Are you a devotee, Mika?"

"Lania and I tried it out when we were in Québec, and experienced a little of all three of your reasons. I don't regret going, but it's more a ticked-off-the-list item than something to do regularly. Speaking of things to do often, we've colour-coded my nights, but not gone into detail about what exactly that involves. What happens if one of us is out late, or needs to get an assignment done?"

"It represents where we sleep, I think," Kyou said. "You with one of us, or two of us with you. Sometimes that will mean a long night of passion, and other times it will mean the bed is nice and warm when the latecomer finally meanders home."

"Timely communication about where we're likely to be on that scale greatly appreciated," Rin added, lips curving. "If you're not going to show up until two in the morning, tell me now, and I'll find something to occupy myself."

"I want to put in maybe another hour's work on the Fox Farm plan," I said. "Dad's really keen to get the renovations started as soon as the cooling off period is over, so it's ready before he and Mum come back for the book festival. I'm only doing concept stuff to hand over to the architects, but I'm on variant three, since it'll actually be my parents' first house, and I want it to fit them perfectly."

"Question is whether we'll know before the festival if your gamble paid off," Bran said to Kyou. "We were supposed to be drawing up requirements for the fit out of the rental building by now."

"We can still do that," Kyou said. "We'll just do a Plan A and a Plan B. I've actually located a possibility out at Gore Heights which will be an ideal interim location if Noonerry happens, but is too small for our on-going needs."

"How long until we hear one way or the other?" Bran asked.

"I'm surprised it hasn't been announced already. Give it another month and if it's still up in the air we'll decide on a rental. As for now...early ID registration opens on Sunday. Want to head down and get it over with before things get busy next week?"

We all agreed to this, and I started out of the kitchen, paused, then turned back and took a moment to wrap my arms around Kyou's waist.

"Last chance for a kiss today," I said, since my night would not be with Kyou. He laughed, and rectified the lapse, then let me go.

"I have to admit, I've already become accustomed to us all piling in together," he said, and then frowned at Rin. "We decided on the order of solo sleeping with a series of poker games. Rin had a fiendish amount of luck."

"You mean you kept falling for my bluffs," Rin replied calmly. "I hope you're planning to dress appropriately tonight, Mika."

"Wait and see," I told him, then went upstairs to play with floor plans and design sketches. My mother had sent through a list of desirables, and it was fun to try to work them into the available space. I kept the concept of a vaulted ceiling for the back of the house, but added an upper story to the front that could work as a spare bedroom, with a bookcase staircase leading up to it. I began to look up vaulted ceiling insulation options, and found that two hours had vanished while I was distracted.

After a quick shower, I dressed in the outfit I'd picked out for Rin, then crossed to the opposite corner of the building to mine, knocked on the door, and waited a moment before opening it.

In contrast to Bran's shuttered rooms, Rin's apartment was very light and open, only the bathroom separated. The décor primarily featured pale wood tones and white, including cloud-soft rugs and the covering of the bed. Some of the windows were open, and I could hear the faint sounds of the city as the gauzy white curtains drifted in a night breeze, giving the space a sense of being moonlit. I hesitated, then decided the curtains were opaque enough that the people in the terrace houses across the road wouldn't be able to see in.

My attention was caught by a gleaming metal railing suspended from the ceiling, which Rin was using as a display rack for his collection of guitars. It curved around the corner of the interior wall and stopped just short of the bed. Rin was at a desk in the opposite direction, keyboard and monitor pushed aside in favour of work on sheet music. It looked like a final copy, every stave neat and regular.

"You like to write it all out on paper?" I asked, crossing to lean against the back of his chair.

"It's quicker for me," he said. "Both drafting and making a final copy that I can scan for a digital version."

"Want me to come back later?"

"I'm just checking for errors," he said, then turned his chair and raised an eyebrow. "This is not the look I was expecting."

I glanced down at my fluffy hooded dressing gown and bunny slippers, which was much warmer than necessary for a summer evening, even with the cool breeze.

"I figured you'd enjoy taking off the wrapping to enjoy what's underneath," I said. "Say, can I borrow your lap?"

He laughed, then reached out a long arm and pulled me forward. Rin is truly a perfect height for sitting on.

"An earworm, you say," he murmured, turning us both back to face the desk.

I looked down at the sheet music, and softly sang part of the chorus:

"*I got your back, and you got mine*

Not a moment spent with you is wasted time."

"I can see the Tiktok duos already," I continued, then added: "For this song inspired by a concert hall."

"You noticed that?"

"You went so quiet after Kyou said he wanted to build one. At first, I thought you were annoyed at how much land he'd bought. Even if land in the region is relatively cheap, he's sunk...I hate to think how many million into a sudden tangent into property speculation. But then I heard you humming. Didn't connect the dots until I saw the lyrics, though."

"I *was* annoyed at how much land he'd bought. Finally got out of him exactly how much he's spent, and it's way more than we would have easily swallowed, especially after the scare we had, almost losing everything. But the view was enough to make having a big chunk of our working capital tied up in paddocks tolerable, and the idea of a concert hall... Kyou thinks big, and usually ten steps ahead, which is why he's so successful with investment, but he's not actually all that interested in money in and of itself. He cares about what he can do with it, and so we'll end up owning a concert hall, all for my convenience. Incredible."

Rin was someone who habitually wore a gentle smile, but kept his real emotions from the surface. At the moment his eyes had curved with delight, and he looked much younger, less sophisticated. I loved seeing him like that, was a little in awe of the bond that would see Kyou planning a concert hall as a treat, and Rin trying to put their friendship into words in response.

"You finished your house plan?" he asked. "What did it end up like?"

"Not quite. It's on the home network—you can call it up."

He found the plans and sketches easily, and flipped through them.

"I like this one best," he said, bringing up the option that had more living area and smaller bedrooms. "Have you somehow done an architecture degree already? These look very professional."

"Architecture is so much more than just design ideas. It's knowing exactly how far you can build from the fence line in the local area, tons of safety codes. I've watched a lot of online lectures on, well, just about everything I'm interested in, but they only make me aware that for architecture in particular there's a ton of information I've never touched. And a few areas that I'm pretty mediocre at, like colour matching. I love coming up with buildings that are possible from a structural point of view, but they still need an architect to take them further."

"And you prefer bridges over buildings?"

"I think they're beautiful," I said, shrugging. "And the maths involved in really big structures is tremendous fun."

"Is there any subject or career you don't think tremendous fun, Mika?" he asked, pulling down the hood of my dressing gown.

"I wasn't keen on cutting up frogs," I said. "Had to do that three times. Some aspects of biology are interesting, but most of it's pretty low on my list. How do you feel, now that you only have to study the things you're interested in?"

"I don't think it'll be real until the last time I have to pretend otherwise," he said. "Ask me Friday afternoon. Take this thing off now."

I could feel his impatience, and laughed low in my throat, then pushed with a foot so the chair swivelled. Kicking off the bunny slippers, I stood up, took two steps forward, and then let the robe drop in a pile around my feet.

Rin had once expressed a preference for 'white and delicate', and so I'd been unable to resist a white silk camisole set with boy-style underpants that barely covered my behind. I glanced at him, was satisfied with his expression, and then strolled about his room.

"I match your curtains," I said, after a moment. "Not entirely sure that's a good thing."

"It is," Rin said, firmly. His voice had dropped a note, and I knew I wouldn't be wandering about much longer.

"Did you test whether people outside can see through them?" I asked, not daring to go too close.

"If the ceiling lights are on, and you're right beside the windows, you can see silhouettes," he said. "Come back here and strip for me."

I returned to a point just beyond arms' reach and considered him. He'd showered long enough ago that his hair was nearly dry. He'd left it loose and, though finer than mine, it was almost as long, reaching well below his collarbone. Despite the bare chest visible though the half open bathrobe, he looked very feminine, a lazily beautiful elven creature.

I hooked thumbs through the waist of my pants and tugged them down enough so they'd fall to my feet. Then I hooked them on one foot and flicked them forward. Rin caught them easily, and touched the material a moment before putting them on his desk.

"Wait," he said, and stood up.

He put his hands on my hips and slid them upward. I cooperated as he lifted the short camisole over my head, then smiled wryly.

"No keeping any more of my clothes," I said.

"Long term loan," he said. "Not what you should be worried about now, anyway."

"What should I be worried about?"

"Looking this good," he said, and shrugged off his robe.

Eight

Waking curled against Rin's back, I lingered in enjoyable recollection of enthusiasm, and a fortunately soft rug. Perhaps next time I'd wander around in one of his shirts to see whether that worked him up even more.

Leaving him sleeping, I collected my clothes, and gave Kyou a treat by padding along the corridor wearing only my bunny slippers.

"Are you going to come to breakfast like that?" he asked, smiling broadly.

"I'm going to go do yoga," I said. "If you want to admire my yoga outfit, you'll find me on the rooftop."

"I like free entertainment with my toast."

There was a raised block on the rooftop, about the same height as the planters, which made an excellent location to spread my yoga mat. I started with a basic stretch, and marvelled at the difference between yoga with a dawn chorus from the nearby trees compared to wedging my yoga mat between my couch and tv at my former apartment. I liked what you could do with money as well.

Even more attractive was the idea of yoga in the back yard of my parents' newly-purchased house, at a sensible but not over far distance from the drop to the forest.

"Presuming all your grandiose plans work out, will you live more here or at Noonerry?" I asked, when Kyou arrived.

He was carrying a tray, and put it on the café table before responding.

"Here while we're studying. Noonerry afterwards. I might need to close my eyes until you're in a different position," he added. "Unless you're in a mood to be pounced on."

I snorted, but shifted out of downward facing dog.

"I've never had a morning pouncing," I said. "Let's try it on a day we aren't planning to go out early. Is that coffee?"

"I stayed up late, so need the pick up. I made yours with the same amount of sugar and milk as your chai."

Turning, I saw that he'd brought me breakfast as well, and had to smile. "Living with you is going to lead to me being spoiled, Kyou."

"Go back to this morning's previous outfit, and I'll feel thoroughly spoiled in return."

I thought about yoga wearing nothing but a pair of slippers. "Were you serious about the possibility of drones?"

He grimaced. "There's a yearly drone building competition on campus, so they're not uncommon."

"Then I think naked rooftop yoga is definitely never going to happen."

The scent of coffee was too tempting, so I cut my routine short and hopped down from the raised block. I risked drones to kiss Kyou luxuriously, then made quick work of my breakfast and went to shower and finish my design plan before it was time to leave.

During my shopping trip, I'd decided on a change of look to start my university days, and so donned an ankle-skimming skirt made of flower-sprinkled fabric. Except for an elasticised section that hugged me from

Karan K Anders

waist to the top of my thighs, it was enticingly transparent. Sandals and a cropped peasant blouse completed the ensemble, and I crowned the look by releasing my hair from its usual ponytail, brushing it until it shone, and then securing the sides with little bird clips.

Grabbing a small bag containing my wallet and ID documents, I went down, but paused on the stair to enjoy three identical expressions.

"Me this year," I said. "At least for the warm weather."

"Will it be strange if I walk two metres behind you the entire way?" Kyou asked, smiling broadly.

"Probably only for me," I said.

"Turn," Rin commanded, taking out his phone.

I turned, enjoying the way the skirt flared. Not quite as satisfying as the ballgown I'd worn to the Corascur dance, but at least half the reason I'd gone for the look.

Bran remained silent until Rin had finished taking a picture, and I'd walked down the stair. Then he pulled me closer for a morning kiss, and only let me go far enough to frown down at me.

"Don't like it?" I asked, confused.

"Working on my possessive tendencies," he said. "Even in jeans, your legs are unmissable. Making them half-visible is too good. Let us know if anyone pesters you."

"Will do," I said. "Shall we take the tram down and then walk back? I want an exact gauge of how long it takes me to get about."

"Good plan," Kyou said.

It was a strange feeling, walking out the front door with Kyou, Rin and Bran. Although we'd been to

Noonerry together, this was our first public outing in a place where we'd likely be recognised. Openly associating with these three highly coveted boys was something that would have an impact on me even if we weren't quietly dating. No matter how innocent we tried to pretend to be on the surface, there's many who would now mark me down as Competition.

I had to admit, part of me found that entertaining. Like my dad, I don't mind watching drama. But being at the centre of one was sure to cost me time and patience on occasion. I was still adjusting to my unexpected willingness to spend that on these three.

We walked up to the main road, passing the bakery Dad liked, which smelled beautifully of fresh bread, and was already busy, despite being early on a Sunday.

"I was thinking it would be a good place to grab breakfast when I'm in a hurry, but that line tells me otherwise," I said, as we crossed to the tram stop in the centre of the street.

"Their sourdough's very good," Bran said. "Not a place you can rush."

There was a five-minute wait for the next tram. I spent the first minute studying the schedule and notices of upcoming maintenance, and another speculatively eyeing the hoarding hiding the construction of the HSR entrance. The rest of the time I invested in watching two strangers trying to pretend that they weren't taking photos of Bran. Bran always seemed to attract the boys. And girls. Bran was gazing at his feet, listening to Rin and Kyou talk about their upcoming hiring plans, but it was unlikely he hadn't noticed. Bran never seemed to miss much.

"Darcy said the tram gets incredibly crowded on week days," Rin observed, as we glided from *University West* to *University Hub* to *University Hospital*. "I was thinking that scooters might be the best option for urgently getting to the far end of campus."

"Already ordered a few," Kyou said. "Once I saw that Bran and Mika's schedules take them down here half the time. This semester, I think only that C++ course takes you and I past Hub."

"I'm usually organised enough that it just means I'll get a pleasant stroll every day," I said, as we followed a drift of students to the campus gates. "And better still, I have the option of going home for lunches." I glanced at them, walking in a row beside me, then said: "I'd say I'm still hung up on the lack of places to have lunch at Corascur, but I find I don't regret that at all."

"We definitely have to revisit Corascur lunchtimes," Kyou said. "In fact, how does a lunchtime game sound? Care to supply the prize?"

I laughed. "Sure. What's the game?"

"Hide and go deep," Kyou said, immediately.

Bran made a choking noise, Rin missed a step, and I had to struggle with my expression.

"This weakness for puns, Kyou..." I said eventually.

"Of course, we could play Strip Go Bang if you prefer it. We might need to modify the rules a little."

"Hide and seek," Rin said, firmly. "And not only because Mika can beat all of us at Go Bang."

"That house will definitely offer plenty of hiding spaces," I said. "Now I'm thinking of silly games. Strip Chasie in the dark. Or Pass the Parcel, where I'm wearing twenty layers."

"We need to be having this conversation when we're nearly home, not heading for a wait at front office," Bran said.

"Think about cold showers," Kyou advised. "Cold showers on winter mornings after a walk in the rain."

I laughed, but then we reached a vantage point and I stopped to appreciate the scene. I'd visited the campus of Helios University the previous year, so already knew that it was built around a long, narrow lake. The south shore was more open than the north, but the real division of the campus was between the older, arts-focused buildings of the west end, and the crowded east end, with its laboratories and lecture halls, all backed by apartment towers and the bulk of University Hospital. But it wasn't the buildings that had my attention.

"How many universities could give me three whole bridges?" I asked happily. "They're all quite interesting ones, too, from a technical point of view. The Marden Institute designed two of them as test cases."

"Somehow I always end up feeling I'm less exciting than bridges," Rin said, in a mock-gloomy tone. "How lowering."

"I like breathing *and* eating," I said, shooting him a grin.

"Are we the breathing or the eating?" Kyou asked. "No, wait, that's obvious, given the night before last."

"Sleet in winter," Bran said. "Rain down the back of your neck."

"Sooner we get these IDs, the sooner we can play inventive games," I said, and began to walk back toward the Hub, taking note of the various directional signs pointing the way to the lecture theatres, labs and tutorial rooms, verifying them against my mental image of the campus map. I lingered to survey the entrance of the Marden Institute: the government-funded research facility that was a world leader in engineering innovation, and my ultimate goal. From the outside, very boring, but within, some of the leading minds in practical applications of physics and maths.

"We could go take a look, if you want," Rin suggested, brushing lightly against my arm.

"It's a secure building," I said, reaching to take his hand, and catching myself just in time. "I won't get inside without a post-graduate internship. Let's get these IDs."

Since we were now in a light flow of foot traffic toward the centre of the university, I didn't add: "So that I can go home and get you naked," settling for a quick smile at him instead. He was in a very good mood— either because he liked the prospect of more lunchtime games, or because starting full-time study of music was something he'd longed for possibly even more than I did building bridges.

There were several teams of people setting up stands around the Hub, and a couple were far enough along for me to recognise they were for clubs and societies. There were no flyers out for the Greenland Civil Engineering Society, but I made a note of the location.

"Probably simpler to sign up for clubs through the web," Kyou said, as we grabbed queue tickets from a dispenser just inside the door of the Administration building. "If it's busy like this today, Orientation Week is going to be nothing but lines."

"I'll give it a look when I meet Lania for lunch Wednesday," I said, shrugging. "I mainly want to get an idea of the people, to try to decide between it and the United Society of Engineers."

A pair of girls came through the door behind us, grabbed tickets and stopped just short of a collision with Rin. Staring at him, they backed up, only to narrowly miss Bran. The shorter girl almost fell over her own feet, and was steadied by Kyou, who laughed and said: "He's too shocking, isn't he?" then moved out of the way of more incomers.

She stuttered a thank you, but obviously didn't have the courage for more. By the time we were done getting our IDs, Kyou and Rin had both been asked for their numbers, while Bran had had three hopeful requests.

"At Corascur, most people knew that we'd always refuse," Kyou said, as we headed back down the stair. "This year, I think we'll need to glower more. How did your ID photo turn out, Mika?"

"Not bad. A little washed out."

We compared photographs, and I laughed because the camera that had flattened and bleached me had picked up all their best features, especially for Rin.

"You're too photogenic," I said, but then frowned, and glanced around at our IDs. "Wrong colour."

"What colour?" Kyou asked. "Your hair?"

"No, the ID. The stripes represent the faculty, right? Shouldn't Rin's have blue and yellow stripes? What's green and grey?"

Rin stared at his ID, then about-faced and went back up the stair, taking another number. He waited with his head down, turning the ID over and over between restless fingers.

"Green and grey is Business and Economics," Bran said, after consulting his phone.

I glanced at Rin's austere profile, then said to Kyou: "I seem to recall you were aiming for a Masters in both Fine Arts and Economics. You decided on Fine Arts first?"

"That's where I need to grow the most," Kyou said. "I'll do Economics some time down the track for the fun of it."

"Fun," Bran said, shaking his head. "By the time you get around to actually taking an economics degree, you'll probably be someone they want to invite as a guest speaker."

"Also fun, if not very likely. I have wondered how much I can truncate the Masters in Economics. Cherry-pick the courses, then present them with a thesis. I'm in a similar situation to you, Mika, in that I read up on the things I'm interested in, but it's not practical to try to formally study it all."

Rin was called to the counter, and recovered his usual gentle smile as he did so. It was the first time I'd seen him so obviously put it on as a way to get what he wanted, charming the initially unhelpful counter staff, using amiable calm to push past their early response to get them to look into his enrolment properly. It took almost ten minutes and two telephone consultations before he returned with a new ID, and led us back outside.

"'Corrected' by the Dean," he said, evenly. "I don't think my parents were directly involved: the Dean probably thought it a genuine error."

"Will next week be more dramatic than planned?" I asked.

"I don't know." Rin closed his eyes briefly. "Thankfully we caught it before my place at the Conservatory was offered to someone on the waiting list.

The only thing at stake now is Anthea and Jessamin's party."

"Orientation Week should be hectic enough the Dean won't have any time to gossip with your parents," Kyou said.

"Hm," was the whole of Rin's response.

The eager atmosphere had been lost, so we strolled quietly, marking the location of the main eating spots, the student union, the Arts-end lecture halls, the new School of Drama, and then the gracefully-fading Hall of Fine Arts. The Conservatory of Music was the last major building on campus, conveniently next to the tennis courts, and not more than fifty metres from the gate separating the University from our neighbourhood.

"You're really not going to have trouble getting to class on time," I said, eyeing the ornate building.

"Not for practical performance," Rin said. "Music technology and sound design will take me to the Hub." He'd recovered himself a little, and seemed to be eyeing my legs. "We were talking games."

"We were," I agreed. "How about you three stop at *Pain Au Lait* to pick up something for lunch, while I find a place to hide? Do we have a time limit where I win if you don't find me?"

"You win when one of us finds you," Bran said, voice low.

"I'll hold you to that," I said.

There was no need to think overmuch about a hiding place. I curled up in the rear compartment of Rin's Hummer, knowing he'd check it.

Much stress was relieved.

Nine

Sunday night was Bran and Kyou, and a thoroughly satisfying experience. Monday, I woke curled up along Rin's back, with Bran clasping my waist. This pleasant but confusing circumstance occupied my semi-awake mind until my bladder refused to let me think it over further. Extricating myself from the bed, I found Kyou once again on Bran's far side, for once not awake before me, his handsome features only partly visible in the faint pre-dawn light. I pondered the change through my morning routine, preparing tea and toast for Kyou with fairly accurate timing for when he appeared in the kitchen.

"What happened last night?" I asked.

"A couple of hours past midnight, and even through the double glazing I could hear dramatic piano music," Kyou said, with a faint grimace. "Rin playing upstairs with the doors open. By the time I got up there he'd pounded out whatever he hadn't managed with you, so I brought him back to bed. I didn't think you'd mind."

"Do you?" I asked. "You always seem to be the one wedged out."

He chuckled. "Is that how it seems? We're simply rotating the Mika-clutching if and when we get up during the night. Though I also end up on that side of the bed because I enjoy watching the dawn through the trees. Lots of delicate greys and greens." He idly rotated his teacup. "If not for what we're building with you, I doubt it would ever have occurred to us to climb into each other's beds when we're upset. We're close, but I don't think we've slept together since infant school. I'm not sure we'd do so without you being in the middle, but I outright like it when we're all in the same room, beyond whatever exercise is involved."

I considered this. "Well, four in together for the sleeping part is only an issue for me if one of you feels pushed aside. If Rin and Bran are okay with arranging more of our nights so we're all together, go ahead."

"Fine with me, so long as we don't give up the days when we get you alone," put in a tousle-headed Bran, strolling into the kitchen.

Kyou grinned. "That definitely won't happen," he promised. "I hope you're not planning to work late tonight, Mika."

"Only if my boss gives me overtime," I said. "Are you a taskmaster?"

"Well, like most everything this year, today is going to be a learning experience. Ideally, we want to foster a collegiate, friendly atmosphere, where everyone gets their job done with minimal fuss."

"That and other pie in the sky fantasies," Bran muttered, spooning coffee into a French press.

"The more staff we hire, the less likely it'll be," Kyou agreed. "The people who start today will be guinea pigs for the systems we've developed—"

"Stolen from the more successful bits of L-B Corp," Bran said.

"And will hopefully form a protective layer of senior management to shield us from petty office politics, while fostering the corporate culture we want."

"Kyou has been dealing with personnel because neither Rin nor I can stand it," Bran added.

"It's not where I want to spend my time either," Kyou admitted. "We've hired a HR manager with a high reputation to hold our hands through the tricky stuff."

"I'm trying to imagine scaling up to five or six hundred employees within...when do you expect to be fully into production on *Echoes*?"

"Three years to reach our core recruitment goals, and peak numbers in about four. It's not something we can do quickly, even if we had everything else in place, because the people to fill the roles aren't just sitting around waiting for us to advertise." Kyou sipped his tea, looking pensive. "I'm going to go ahead and sign a three-year lease on the two-hundred desk place in Gore Heights. We'll need the space wherever we end up putting the main building, and it may be worthwhile maintaining in the long term."

"Good," Bran said, flatly. "This farm of yours has held us up long enough."

Kyou grinned. "You'll like it when you can go on a walk through the woods at lunch."

Bran snorted, then lifted one shoulder in concession. "Not having to spend an hour riding through city traffic when going out on the bike is another massive bonus," he admitted. "The tableland's got a couple of nice riding roads, too. And it'll be a lot quicker to get to the west coast. I just don't want to waste time thinking about it until it's confirmed." He glanced at my tank top and sweat pants. "Is that for yoga?"

"I figured I'd put in a half hour jogging, since I'm up early enough," I said.

"Hold off for fifteen minutes and I'll come with," Bran said, pouring coffee and taking a pear from the nearly-empty fruit basket.

"I will too," Kyou said. "You're the only exercise I've been getting lately, Mika."

"Happy to contribute to the cause," I said, laughing. "The food delivery comes today, right?"

"Eight-thirty's the cut-off time for adding to the shopping list," Kyou said. "The domestic service arrives at one. I've set an eight am and midday reminder in 'tellan—mainly so we have a chance to make sure Mika's bed isn't the only one that looks slept in."

"And that none of us are currently in it," Bran said, turning up his smoulder fractionally.

We left Rin to get as much sleep as possible, and headed out for our jog in the opposite direction to campus, following a promenade beside the river that fed University Lake. Darcy had told us that on weekends it was usually well-supplied with open-air entertainment and boutique stalls, but at seven in the morning it primarily featured other joggers, delivery drivers wheeling trolley-loads of boxes, and a lone painter valiantly trying to capture the scene before the light changed.

"My probable future," Kyou commented. "Four years of still life, rapid figure sketches, and short studies of the locale. Working quickly is not my strong suit."

"Will you regret it and switch to Finance?"

"Only if the teachers are absolutely intolerable," Kyou said. "I really do need to stretch myself."

"You really need to stop working on the same pictures and let them be 'finished'," Bran said. "Let's head back—Darcy and Gram are due to arrive at eight."

"For longer runs, we can loop all the way down to Ashby Bridge and come back the other side," Kyou said, as we reversed direction. "It's a good route where we don't have to worry about cross-streets and cars."

"It is, though you've made me want to go lunchtime walking in Strathold Forest now," I complained. "I agree with Bran about not talking about the Noonerry office until it's real. Who's Gram?"

"HR Manager," Kyou said. "We head-hunted him, and lucked out because he's a new dad and wants to work only limited hours for the rest of the year. We're offering much greater flexibility than his previous role, and he's got the experience to help us scale up smoothly."

"Let's not keep him waiting around then," I said, and paid for it when Kyou and Bran decided we could race the last section. They could both outpace me, and while I didn't lag too badly, I was red-faced by the time we reached the front door.

"It's a much better area for exercise than my last place," I panted, while Bran swiped the locking sensor with the phone he'd stored in an arm strap. "Which is good, because I clearly haven't been jogging enough lately."

"Add it to the schedule?" Kyou suggested.

"I usually have an as-the-mood-takes-me approach to exercise," I admitted. "But—weather permitting—I'll probably alternate jogging, nothing, and yoga in the mornings. Feel free to join me."

"If I join you, it'll be jogging, something, and yoga," Kyou said.

"Well, that's an option."

"Is something possible this morning?" Bran asked.

I hesitated. "What time is it?"

"Seven forty."

"Something really quick in the shower?" I suggested.

Rin was still asleep, and I paused in our rush to kiss his cheek and murmur: "Twenty minutes until show time—want to make it evaporate in a wet tangle?"

He did. Kyou and Bran were hasty, and had to kiss and run, but Rin ground me into the wall for the better part of half an hour.

"I should have made sure you came out jogging as well so you had less energy," I said, when we'd finally reached the stage of towelling off.

"No, this worked out much better," he said. "Where's your blow dryer? I'll do your hair while you recover."

"You've gotten past the shock of yesterday?" I asked, sitting on my bed.

"A hot wet awakening seems to do wonders for my frame of mind," he said, plugging the dryer into the nearest socket.

"I wasn't sure whether to wake you yesterday morning," I said. "If I haven't stayed up late, I usually wake around the same time as Kyou."

"Kiss me when you get up, and you'll soon find out whether I want to," he said. "While I admittedly usually only get up at dawn for rowing, right now I'm feeling motivated."

We talked about the prospect of rowing along Mornington River, and then jogging routes, and then I admired the messy bun Rin had given me, with exactly the right amount of body, and a few delicate tendrils to give extra interest. It managed to look both effortless and elegant.

"You're good at this."

"With four younger sisters, I've had plenty of practice. You'll know they like you if they start showing you pictures of what they've done to me over the years."

Rin picked out my outfit before he left: skinny jeans and a white, tailored shirt. Overall, informal but classy. I admired it, then reviewed my room for any evidence of multiple occupation before taking the elevator up to Kybirn's reception room. This was small, set up to prevent visitors wandering into the working areas when they were buzzed up from the foyer.

Since there was no-one visible at the reception counter or through the glass walls, I tried my phone pass and code on the door to the right, but the north half of the office was empty. I crossed through the linking passage behind the reception desk into the west section, wandering all the way down to the kitchen before I found anyone. The kitchen was opposite the secure door to the piano room, and I paused to read a sign explaining that the area wasn't accessible to staff.

"We were just discussing whether to hold our welcome address in there," Kyou said, coming out of the kitchen. "The one thing we couldn't manage in the fit-out was a large meeting room. And we were intending to use the piano room for celebrations and things."

"Starting there would make it more a rule than an exception," I said, immediately resistant to the idea. "Just bring the chairs from North to West and put two at every workstation. Mum says people listen better sitting down, anyway."

"Why?" Bran asked, joining us along with a fit man with close-cropped lime-orange hair, and a matching neon artificial leg.

"Not distracted by their sore backs and corns," I explained, and held out a hand to what I presumed was the HR Manager: "Hi, I'm Mika."

"Gram," he replied, with a quick smile. "And I agree that the workstation area will be suitable for a quick welcome. Particularly if you want to emphasise that the residential part of the building is off-limits."

"Let's start moving chairs then," Kyou said.

We rearranged, while I tried not to think about Dad's quip that the building reminded him of the *Titanic*. Hopefully, Kybirn would not be so ill-fated. Starting a business with a dozen or more employees was complex enough. Going from one employee to hundreds in the space of a few years was a mammoth task, even with the wealth of funding Kyou had managed to conjure from stock market sleight-of-hand.

Rin and Darcy arrived with trays of bite-sized edibles pre-ordered from *Pain Au Lait*, and then we each stood in turn before the Kybirn logo in the reception area to have our pictures taken for our employee IDs. My photo turned out well, and I opted to wear it on a lanyard rather than a pocket clip.

"The card works as a key the same way as the phone app," Kyou explained. "Since we're requiring staff to wear their ID all the time while in the office, it'll cut down on the number of times people get locked out because they've left their phone at their desk."

"Speaking of which..." Darcy said, as a muted tone signalled that there was an arrival in the ground floor waiting room.

Kyou had sensibly not scheduled everyone to start at the same time, but most of them appeared to have shown up early, judging from the constant stream of new faces. I took over ID photo duty, while Bran activated the proximity keys, checking off arrivals as he did so. No-one was late, and as soon as the last ID was issued, I joined the crowd filling paper plates with pastry and fruit, and found myself a seat at one of the workstations.

Darcy briefly popped into the centre to explain that he'd be filming, and to email him if anyone wanted their image to be blurred, and then he moved back for our new bosses. Kyou took the centre position, which didn't entirely surprise me. Rin might have been Student Council President at Corascur, but he was far less of a people person than Kyou.

"Welcome to Kybirn," Kyou said, and sounded so genuinely happy to be making that simple statement that it somehow became thrilling. "You will all have spoken to at least one of us during the interview process, but to fill in the blanks, I am Kyou Westhaven. To my left is Bran Ashten, and to my right Rin Laurent. The two games we have under production are, for us, passion projects that we've been planning half our lives. Thank you for joining us in bringing them into being."

This produced a patter of warm applause. Kyou smiled, then laughed lightly.

"Of course, half our lives mightn't seem impressive when your CEO is the youngest person in the room. While we do have a level of experience and expertise, we'd be stupid to pretend we'll always know the best approach to an issue. You'll find that there's several feedback systems built into our processes—and one of the things we particularly want as we bring *One Step More* to completion is feedback on those processes so that we don't trip over our feet too spectacularly when we ramp up for *Echoes*."

"Um..." A woman in her thirties raised her hand, and went on when Kyou nodded at her: "Are all three of you the CEO?"

"Bran is CEO of Kybirn Games. Rin is CEO of Kybirn Music. I'm CEO of Kybirn Investment, which technically makes me the ultimate boss, since it's the parent company. Major decisions go through all three of us." Kyou shrugged. "Most of you will work directly with us in our core areas, but daily supervision will fall to your team leader. Imani—" He indicated a woman whose greying hair was set in bantu knots, "—is leader of Team One, finalising *One Step More*, where the primary work to be done is playtesting, final art, and music. Ahmed is leader of Team Two, prepping for *Echoes of Samerkel*, where the current focus is on concept art and mechanics design, finalising the script, and the basic technical framework.

Imani raised a hand in acknowledgement, while Ahmed, a mid-thirties man with hollow cheeks and a beard clipped stylishly close to his jaw, smiled and feigned bashfulness.

"We're currently in Team One's half of the office," Rin said, after a glance at Kyou. "Team Two—and a number of staff who are cross-team—will be based in the north section. Those of you who are full-time have been assigned permanent desks, as you can see from the name tags, while part-timers will hot desk. This morning, along with signing off on the Code of Conduct and your NDAs, you have some online training to get through that will explain various rules and expectations. You'll find a set of headphones at every desk for listening to the training: hot deskers should put theirs, along with any other personal belongings you want to keep in the office, in the lockers behind reception at the end of each day."

"After lunch—at two-thirty—we'll have a fire safety drill," Bran said, managing to repress his usual impatient note. "And throughout the day your team leader and one of us will be sitting down with each of you to go over what's wanted in the first couple of weeks. You'll also find early tasks assigned to you in Castellan, our management system. Mostly just reading and reviewing today."

"Before we play musical chairs, if you've any questions that aren't about your specific role, now's a good time to ask," Kyou added.

A girl with short black hair raised her hand. "Um, did you—ah, where did the main office end up being?"

"There'll be a mid-sized facility at Gore Heights," Kyou said promptly, quite as if he hadn't only decided to lease there over breakfast. "The location for the main office hasn't been settled yet, beyond that it will be accessible either via the high-speed rail or the Second South tramline, and won't be located in such a high-cost housing area as the university district."

"How broad are the working from home options mentioned?" asked a burly man with a round, freckled face.

"It varies," Rin said. "Some roles simply aren't practical for working from home. Others will have task-based flexibility: coming in for recording sessions, for instance, but able to do post-processing from home. In the early stages, while we fine-tune our systems, we'd expect all staff to be in for the majority of the week, but during the bulk of the development, in some cases it might only be necessary to come in for the monthly reviews."

"And you're really committed to not requiring crunch?" the man asked.

"Crunch is a math equation," Bran said. "Where you've failed to resolve release date and set of tasks with number of staff."

"*One Step* and *Echoes* are fully funded by Kybirn Investment," Kyou continued. "So, we don't have an externally set release date pushing us toward a crisis, and will only get into a mess if we can't get the staff to get *Echoes* done before the game's so dated we're laughable. One way we aim to avoid that is to be an attractive enough employer that we can recruit to the point of not requiring things like crunch. We'd prefer to train up additional staff rather than mandate overtime."

I'm not sure this entirely convinced the crowd, since overtime was ubiquitous in the gaming industry, but everyone at least seemed hopeful as the meeting ended. I dragged my chair to the hotdesking section of North. All the workstations had been set along the windows, while the recording studios and motion capture rooms, none of which benefitted from natural light or exposure to street noise, were arranged along the interior.

Only two of the desks in the area had drawing tablets, so I picked one and logged in smoothly, found my headphones, and glanced at the instruction sheet Darcy had handed out, but didn't immediately launch the new starter training, turning instead to the three people at the closest workstations: "Hi, I'm Mika. Environment artist."

"Pip," said the girl who'd asked about office locations. "I'm your friendly neighbourhood Foley Artist."

"Nehi, Pipeline Tools Programmer," said a woman who looked to be in her late twenties, her plumply pretty looks emphasised by fantastic orange and gold eyeshadow.

"Ion," said a man somewhere in his lower twenties, his pale face half-hidden beneath a shock of black hair. "Graphics Engineer."

Pip plopped down on her chair, and then spun around on it. "I think maybe I need to go run around the block or something, I'm so excited. Dream job, impossible dream job. It's all too surreal."

"Surreal because of our teenaged bosses?" Nehi asked, laughing softly.

"That too!" Pip said. "Are they, like, literally teenagers? They look super young, but..."

"Didn't you google them?" Nehi asked. "There's reams about them on the local forums—a lot of it not exactly safe for work. They're cousins, just graduated from some local private high school, heirs to L-B Corp. People call them the Three Kings."

"O-oh," Pip said, pausing in her spinning. "I've never actually met any of the mega-rich before. Just think of a world where your family will drop a couple of hundred million into a company for you to play around with. And I've always envied a friend of mine who got a car for her twenty-first."

Ion made a choking sound, and I glanced across to see he'd googled Bran and been treated to some of the racy fan art produced by Corascur students over the years. BranxRin art was slightly more numerous than BranxKyou.

"All speculative, so far as I can tell," Nehi said, giving a whips-and-chains scene a critical glance. "Their school seems obsessed with them, and I ended up having to look away not to feel like a middle-aged creeper. Still, have to say that they'll make for great marketing with their background and looks."

"Bishounen Games," I said, unable to resist.

Even the more reserved Ion laughed at that, and then we all settled down to read the Code of Conduct and run through a lot of training modules on company regulations and the office management tools, which were fairly standard, but with an overlay that integrated them with Castellan, which from the office-side looked like a task management and time recording system. I was mildly fascinated to click up through the hierarchy of a few early tasks assigned to me and discover the entire project plan for *Echoes*. Some parts were less detailed than others, but I had to wonder if its accessibility was a deliberate demonstration to new staff that their teen CEOs weren't just fumbling blindly.

I'd already read the plot overview and a chunk of the worldbuilding information, so immediately went to delve into Kyou's concept art. Although many people had told me Kyou was a brilliant artist, I'd seen hardly anything of his work, and began reviewing it as source material very happily.

The first picture was Rin's hand, the palm decorated with blue lines forming organic circuitry. Kyou's preferred style was hyper-realism, and I spent far longer than necessary staring at the picture. Rin has long fingers, calluses thanks to playing various instruments, and a couple of small scars which he'd told me were thanks to snapping strings, when he'd foolishly overtightened them. Refined, interesting hands that had seen a bit of wear. Kyou had turned his left into an object of beauty and consequence.

I finally emailed him a link to it and said: "Box cover art?" then began working my way through the rest. Kyou really was exceptional, though with a primary focus on character studies, usually with bare minimum backgrounds or even none at all. I did find a cache of action-packed images for various major events, but far less environmental detail than I'd expected.

"You look like you've just received a decade's worth of birthday presents," said a familiar voice.

I beamed at Kyou. "I was expecting the general designs for the cities to be more formed by now. Do I really get to start from scratch?"

"Well, from our concepts," Kyou said, laughing. "I've listed the mandatory components against the tasks, but otherwise go wild with initial images. We'll review for anything that doesn't match what we need, and in a couple of months our environments lead will be on board, and will work with you on transforming inspiration into outlines suitable for the specific scenes in the game. That won't begin until script finalisation. Do you have any questions before Ahmed and I move on?"

"Is Falls City built around a single drop waterfall or cascades?"

"Good question. I don't think I've pictured it as a single giant fall, but it should be a relatively steep area."

"Cool—it'll look much better with cascades. If I do the initial art on paper, do I put that in my locker at the end of the day?"

"No, the stores room has a set of secure cupboards. You'll be able to use your pass to access all but the most secure of these."

I hadn't seen the stores room, so thanked Kyou and Ahmed, and went on a wander to find primarily a stockpile of spare mice and keyboards, a much smaller cache of stationery, and a moderate amount of art essentials. Taking a large pad of heavy sketch paper and a stack of pencils, I lost myself in the world we were all going to build.

oOo

An urgent beeping startled me into nearly stabbing the page. I put my pencil down and looked around in confusion.

"Fire drill," Nehi explained, smiling at me.

"Wasn't that after lunch?" I said, then checked my phone and found that it had become two-thirty in an instant. "Oh, whoops."

"You were so into it, we didn't want to interrupt earlier," Pip said.

"I love drawing cities." I looked down at the work I'd done, reluctant to leave it for a drill, but then resolutely closed the sketchbook and picked up my phone. "Is this still the get ready to assemble sound?"

"Uh-huh." Nehi stretched, then crossed to a door a good deal closer than reception. "Apparently this unlocks when the fire alarm is pulled, but Darcy came around to warn us not to go in during the drill. It is incredibly tempting to snoop, though. This is such a weird old building: I'd love to see what the residential part is like."

"Sounds like the quickest way to get fired," Ion muttered.

"There's a really magnificent coiling art deco staircase," I volunteered. "The rest of it's fairly neutral."

I smiled when they looked at me. "I went to high school with the Kings—and now rent a room from them."

I watched their expressions change, primarily to simple surprise.

"You really do call them the Three Kings?" Pip asked.

"Habit picked up from school," I said.

"Dating one?" Nehi asked, frankly.

I laughed. "Well, can't say I'm not tempted, but they're considered pretty unattainable. Beyond that...it's a condition of my lease to not talk about their private lives. No way gossip is worth risking such a great rental in the university district."

The change in alarm cut the conversation at a point convenient to me, and I happily joined the back of the crowd at reception, listening to Gram describe what to do if any staff or visitors had mobility issues, and then taking the short trip down the fire stair that wrapped around the lift shaft and spat us out in the side-street where the garages opened up. From here, Gram directed us to our left, past another row of houses and into the park area that bordered the river.

"For all drills and any actual emergencies, assemble here rather than crowd around the building," he instructed. "Wait for roll call, and don't go back into the building until instructed."

I had by now started to feel my missed lunch, spent roll call wondering how the domestic service's schedule had intersected with the fire drill, and upon release decided to check out *Pain Au Lait*.

"Absconding already?" Kyou asked, catching me up as I left the crowd.

"Forgot to eat. This is an awesome job, Kyou."

"I'm going to have to give you the 'no overtime unless approved' lecture, aren't I?"

"Possibly. Realistically, my hours are going to be limited once my courses start up, so I may as well enjoy...ah, do some serious work this week. How does it feel to finally get underway?"

He didn't answer immediately, and I glanced at him.

"I've been enjoying Rin demonstrating *One Step*," he said at last. "It's so important to him, probably even more than *Echoes*, and he's just..." Kyou shook his head. "He lives to watch people react to his music."

"And how are they reacting?"

"Very positive, so far. Music composition isn't something all that easy to gamify, but we've come up with something that Team One at least seems to be finding fun." He shook his head, then added: "I won't describe it further, since Rin's very keen to watch you blind react to the complete game."

"Will that be soon? I'm not good at being the one who doesn't know what's going on."

"Final graphics will be a while, but the only holdup for a full play-through is Rin settling on a voice for a particular sequence. We've emphasised to Team One that Team Two will be blind testing, and to not discuss *One Step* around your part of the office."

"Okay. Speaking of which, I've told my desk neighbours that not talking about your private lives is a condition of my rental agreement."

That made him laugh. "We probably would make that a condition. You surprise me, though. Given your love of holding out for big revelations, why have you already mentioned you know us?"

"Well, first because someone would inevitably see me going through one of the internal doors. But mainly because surprise fun announcements require the 'fun' component. If you started a new job, you'd not want to spend too long admiring the fan art and discussing the lives of the stupidly rich before discovering the person at the next desk has a direct line to your boss."

"Fair point."

"When people ask me why you owe me a favour, do you want me to skip over the blackmailing dad part?"

"Now there's a question. I've no reason to protect him, but I don't want to draw fire to you. Stick with being vague for a few weeks, until we know what the situation is with Noonerry. If that train stops anywhere on the tableland, we at minimum double the investment, and potentially could earn more from my land grab than I'm ready to estimate. Reason enough to do you a few favours."

Pain au Lait smelled delicious and had an eat-in section that fortunately had tables free after the lunch rush. Kyou and I ordered cappuccinos, to which I added a sourdough sandwich and a friand, and we talked more about what was needed from my concept art. Then I went back and lost myself again, until a hand was waved in my line of sight, and I found that most everyone had gone home.

"What time is it?" I asked, discovering Bran.

"Half six," he said, picking up my sketch book and flipping through the pages. "Has Kyou seen these?"

"Not yet. I couldn't resist starting with Falls City because I can do such interesting things with water-powered lifts, but once I've caught the major features, I might jump back and do that little starting hamlet. It amazes me that Kyou's done so much on character, and yet only has verbal descriptions of most of these locations."

"He hasn't shown you the original book we used creating Samerkel. We decided not to make it part of the direct source material as it's stupid funny embarrassing in parts. We're about to order dinner: I'll find it while we're waiting for the delivery."

Heading back to my room, I spent some quality bathroom time, then changed into a light, thigh-skimming dress. I felt a little strange about the domestic service having been through my room—especially that they'd emptied my dirty clothes hamper—but decided it was a little like living in a hotel, though it was best not to think about what my room and board would cost without Kyou's casual approach to price-setting. My parents had been living well the past few years, but nothing like this.

"Do you think you would have been able to adapt to a low-rent and ramen lifestyle?" I asked as I walked into the kitchen.

"For the short period of time it would have taken us to get past it," Kyou said, making a face at me.

"It would have only pushed release of *One Step* by a few months," Bran commented, paging through the local food delivery options. "*Echoes*...at least two years delayed, with a longer development period."

"And the guilt would have been with me a lot longer," Kyou said, sitting down on the end of the breakfast table bench, and tugging me into his lap. "I still don't like to think about it."

"Your staff think your family is funding your hobbies."

Bran snorted. "Not likely."

"Great-grandfather doesn't entirely dismiss the Arts," Rin said. "But he certainly wouldn't throw significant money into game development."

"The return usually isn't big enough," Kyou explained. "Outside the kind of predatory money-sinks we don't want to go near, there's few games that would equal the time/cost benefit of a well-targeted property development. The idea that, while we'd prefer to make a profit, it isn't the reason we're doing this, will seem senseless to...large portions of our family."

"Who are now happily irrelevant," Bran said, and lifted the tablet. "Italian or Greek?"

We opted for Greek, and ate on the roof, looking over the thick leather-bound journal that was titled *The Book of Samerkel*. Bran had done most of the writing, with occasional contributions from Rin, and Kyou had illustrated their ideas.

"This is so adorable," I said, smiling at the rounded script in the earliest part of the book, and then hunting out Kyou's simple depiction of a waterfall city. "How old were you when you started?"

"Bran's eleventh birthday," Kyou said. "We were very into *The Lord of the Rings* movies at the time. The book was a present for Bran, for him to write a 'There and Back Again' story. I was going to illustrate it, and Rin would add epic ballads. We drew a map, started naming things, and Samerkel slowly grew."

"We'd put it down and pick it up again," Bran added. "Keep the names and change what they stood for. Filled the place with wars, intrigues, dark lords, wandering mages. Replaced them with rogues and assassins. Then merchants and bards. Added spacemen. Looked at the mess we'd made and did a complete revamp when we were around sixteen."

"And now are sensibly hiring professionals," Rin said. "Did you see the email from...it feels odd to call your father by his first name, Mika, but odd not to."

Bran straightened, then grabbed his phone and checked his mail.

"Dad can't have finished any substantive writing yet," I said. "Must just be tweaks to the plot outline."

I checked my own phone, but didn't have any email. Dad, being generally professional about such things, hadn't sent it to me. Rin, Kyou and Bran all lost themselves to the redraft, so I amused myself flipping through the original versions of Samerkel, a little amazed that my own sketches would help shape the final one. Focused as I am on real-world construction, it had never occurred to me to go into game development, but the idea that I could design a city and dozens—hundreds—of people would come together to virtually build it made me incredibly excited.

"Any big changes?" I asked, once they showed signs of coming up for air.

"No," Bran said, smiling. "Some extra flesh to the backstory, minor adjustments to tighten the plot."

"It should add..." Kyou hesitated, then said: "I think resonance is the right word. Some events will be more meaningful, some will really kick the player in the guts. The stronger motivations for some of the characters will completely change how they're viewed."

"While not actually changing the progress of the story we put together, which I'm glad of," Rin said. "I've always been worried about bringing in writers, because I don't want *Echoes* to end up being someone else's story. Though I like this suggested twist for a post-credits scene, instead of the way we were planning to approach setting up a sequel."

"I'll have to ask what name your father wants to be credited by," Bran said. "I've been reading his hard science fiction books, and was wondering if he'd use the Mullahy name."

"I vote for Rock Hardison," Kyou said. "Purely for the advertising potential of his impressive fanbase."

"Does your father have a fantasy pen name?" Rin asked. "That would probably fit best."

I shook my head. "He wrote a big fat fantasy novel when I was around ten, and couldn't sell it, and I don't think he's gone back to fantasy since. At the time, he couldn't afford to spend so much time writing books that didn't bring in income, and I think he's also been sulking about the fact he couldn't sell it. I liked it a lot: it was about people on the edges of the epic plot, getting their quiet scholarly town burned down and fleeing across the border, and then settling down in a place that turned out to be...well, I won't spoil it. He was talking about dusting it off and self-publishing it, but I think he'd use a new pen name for that. Or maybe he'll try to shop it again through Devine—she wasn't his agent when he tried the first time. She's really wants him to focus on his romantic suspense and literary novels, though, so maybe not."

"I'm going to go over this again," Bran said. "Have a deep discuss after breakfast?"

"Sure," Kyou said, glancing at me. He began gathering leftovers. "I'll be working on my review in my room."

They were learning to leave me a bit of space in my schedule, which was only sensible. "See you in a couple of hours," I said, and helped take the dishes downstairs.

I logged into my computer and chatted with my parents for a while, initially about my first day as an Environment Artist, but mainly about the draft design for Fox Farm. We spent some time on a three-way video chat, going over the title plan, discovering that the property boundary was rectangular, and we'd technically just bought part of the forest below the tableland, though I doubted the National Parks Service would be keen on us actually doing anything down there. Still, we decided to restore the stairs down, for ease of forest strolling, briefly discussed issues like access roads, septic tanks, and internet cabling, then moved on to whether we wanted landscaping done.

"For now, I'd like to keep it as is," Dad said at last. "Our very own little hill, drifting in the morning mist. For some reason, I'm very attached to the idea of that mist, perhaps almost as much as the 'real' view. We can put in more trees or other bits of landscaping if we feel the need after living there a while."

"I've ordered a bunch of anemometers because I want to start modelling the impact of this 'Buster' the mayor mentioned. I'm a little worried about that wind break of trees, which doesn't look in great shape. Do you want me to be primary liaison with the renovator?"

"You're best situated," Mum said. "Loop us in if there's any major decisions. You'll know the things we care about."

"Have them rebuild the garage at the foot of the hill first," Dad suggested. "Then we can ship our boxes over for safe storage and stop worrying about losing them."

"Go ahead with that only after we hear about this rail line," Mum added. "That might impact our plans. Nor can we keep driving through the neighbouring site to get to the house, no matter how your friends promise they won't interrupt access." She paused, then smiled at me lightly. "Judging from the course of that small river, we'll need our own little bridge to get to our own little hill."

"I know! I was thinking I could make it a project for my course."

"Mika's first bridge?" Dad smiled at me. "Don't hold back with it. Devine's getting queries about the film rights for *Tranquil*, and is thinking of setting up an auction."

"Already? You only just turned the thing in."

"It's now formally been sold to Caitlin, and she wasted no time kicking off the publicity machine. I have the feeling she's not going to let me squirm out of a promotional tour this time."

We discussed their next move, since Mum's current job had been simply resolved, and then I said goodnight, spent some time doing leg maintenance, dressed in a robe with nothing underneath, and went to find Kyou.

His rooms took up the south-west corner, with the best light, most suitable for painting, and I was entirely unsurprised to open the door onto a studio, spacious and open, with a faint scent of turpentine. There was a long bench with a double sink beside shelving containing various supplies. Several easels sat empty and at least a dozen canvases were set facing the wall.

No sign of Kyou. I explored, found a bedroom/study currently empty, and finally poked my head out through the open French doors.

"Turn the lights off and it'll probably be dark enough for you to safely come out," Kyou said.

I did as suggested, and found him sitting on a café chair in the dark. A little confused by the sudden air of gloom, I hesitated, but then settled into his lap. "Are you in need of a hug?"

He snorted, but tightened his arms around my waist in a satisfactory way. "Brief mood-killing interruption. I've been trying not to completely blow up with the entire extended family until Rin's ready to cut ties, but they make it hard some times."

"Your dad?"

"Him I don't even talk to. No, my aunt's oldest, convinced we're in an epic battle of wits for great-grandfather's favour."

"And you still have a few days of pretending to care?"

"More or less." He took a long, deep breath, then began nuzzling my throat. "Do you have any family members you outright dislike, Mika?"

"Oh, sure. Depending on what degree of dislike we're discussing, basically all of them except my parents."

Kyou chuckled. "Comprehensive."

"One side of the family is complete no-contact. On my dad's side, I probably dislike my Nan—my dad's mother—the least. She thinks my mum ruined my dad's life, but she mainly only shows it by looking sad and sighing occasionally. She still insisted on taking Mum in when Mum's side kicked her out."

"How old was your mother when she had you?"

"Sixteen. She met dad at a rights rally at Edinburgh University. He was struck speechless at the sight of her, thought she was a student there, and took her back to his dorm room. When he found out a couple of weeks later that she was still in high school, they scaled right back to handholding, but that was post latex failure. Mum kept the fact they were dating quiet because she knew what her family's reaction would be, both to the rights march and the pregnancy, and wanted to skip the weeks of attempts to talk her into an abortion. She was nearly five months along before they knew, which was a feat given she's got the same sort of straight up and down build as me."

"Not entirely straight," Kyou said, exploring, and then making a happy noise when he realised I was only wearing the robe and my slippers.

We became a little distracted, then very distracted, and left conversation behind altogether. Kyou's bed was a four-poster, with gauzy drapery, and a very romantic feel. Kyou let the curtains down, and we were shut into our own dreamy little world.

"I'll never in my life forget falling asleep in the summerhouse," he said, toying with a stray wisp of my hair, most of which I'd looped into a topknot. "After the stress of nearly losing everything, it felt so freeing to wake with it all done one way or another, and to have to concentrate on escaping the school."

That little adventure had been a highlight of my entire high school experience, though somewhat dimmed by the fact that Kyou had been very ill afterwards.

"Rin mentioned you get sick in response to stress, but do you get stressed very often?"

Kyou shrugged. "There's times it's hard not to. Neither Rin nor Bran have been in a good place the last couple of years. Bran's doing enormously better now, thankfully. Rin...doesn't hate his parents enough, which is going to make the break even harder. They're good to him so long as he's doing what they want."

"Sounds like a common problem in your family."

"All three of us would be in very different places if we happened to have the same goals as our parents." He turned his head, stifling a yawn, then lay gazing up at the dimly visible gauze surrounding us. "This is the dream, to be in our own home, surrounded by the people we value, able to shut out all the noise while we do the things we love." He found my hand and laced our fingers together. "I'm so glad you decided to be here with us. I hope we're not overwhelming you."

I laughed, and kissed him on the cheek. "I'm enjoying myself enormously."

I'd also discovered I really like the sleeping part of being together, now that sleeping wasn't such a big issue for me. Particularly in a relatively cool place like Helios, where even at the end of summer the nights can bring a chill creeping from the city's myriad lakes and rivers.

Being elbowed in the ribs less so. I woke in confusion, realised Kyou was having a nightmare, and hesitated over whether to try to wake him. He wasn't thrashing about a great deal, just occasional sharp shifts, making some kind of protest too unformed for me to untangle. Ignoring another elbow, I wrapped my arms around him, murmuring until he quieted.

The little problem of my three boyfriends holding in the things that hurt them most was unlikely to be easily overcome. Bran had been driven to self-harm by his hatred of a performance career, and had then melted down rather than tell Rin and Kyou that Meggan had tried to make him choose between them. Rin's mask-wearing was deeply ingrained, not hidden from us, but so exhausting for him. And Kyou, who seemed simpler on the surface, had lost his mother to an overdose of prescription medicine, and loathed his father, who was a 'yeller'.

What had the cousin who called said to him, to bring on this nightmare?

This wasn't something I could force Kyou to talk about, and I wouldn't push it, any more than I'd ask to see the paintings he'd yet to show me. Being a proper girlfriend was very new to me, but I felt that it was something that had to move step by step to work properly.

Kyou had once said he wanted to build a home for me. If so, we needed foundations first.

Ten

"How did your parents go from living with your grandparents to gadding around the world with you?" Kyou asked, when the four of us had gathered in the kitchen the next morning.

"That started a couple months after I was born. Dad had dropped out of uni, and taken Mum to Wales, and though neither of his parents were exactly keen, my Nan insisted that Mum move in, and go to school in Newport."

My expression must have been sour, because Bran asked: "That bad?"

"Good to start with. My Mum actually managed to graduate high school: she skipped ahead, and took her GCSE and A levels in very short order. My mother's family has a big tradition of higher education, which was part of the reason they were so furious my Mum was pregnant, but going nuclear didn't exactly help with her continued studying, so I appreciate that Nan did practical, supportive things for Mum. The plan was that Nan would babysit, Dad would work, Mum would go to uni, transition to some high-powered career, then support Dad as a writer. It was a bit cramped, especially after I was born, and Aunt Nia, who was fourteen, was not exactly keen on the noise, but I think they would have stayed in Newport much longer, except Mum noticed a pinhole of light through the bathroom wall."

They all paused, then Rin said: "Peephole?"

"Yeah. My dad's dad." I sighed helplessly. "Dad had just turned nineteen, Mum wasn't even seventeen, I was two months old, it was winter, and they needed a new place to stay. That ended up being Malaysia, thanks to my maternal great-grandmother. She was in a nursing home at the time, frail, and couldn't help much with money because she'd already passed her assets over to my grandmother, but she knew a lot of people, and landed my parents a house-sitting gig in George Town. No income involved, but it put them somewhere with a low cost of living, where they could get by on what Dad had saved for uni."

"So, your father jumped straight to writing?" Bran asked.

"Yeah. Mum picked up some part-time secretarial work, Dad wrote frantically, and they shared kid-minding duties. They were in Malaysia for two years, then met May Brunsfield just as the housesitting gig came to an end. May was there to film *Last Bastion*, stretched her shoestring budget enough to take Mum on as a production assistant, and my parents followed her around south-east Asia for a while. That was apparently a wild ride, and my Mum came up with so many brilliant work-arounds and pulled so many rabbits out of hats that when production closed, she got a job offer from one of the resorts they'd filmed at, and then another offer a while after that, and built a reputation through pure word of mouth. Dad wrote, did lawn mowing, dishwashing, house cleaning, anything else in between, and sold his first book when I was three. Which earned him practically nothing. It's only been in the last few years that he started out-earning Mum."

"Were there any...consequences for your grandfather?" Kyou asked.

"Nan leaned toward pretending it hadn't happened, which is why my parents had to leave, and why I sometimes struggle to like her. She's very much a 'keeping the peace' person. I'm not sure how she would have behaved if my Aunt Nia had been in my Mum's position, but so far as my parents could tell that wasn't an issue.

"Dad kept in touch with Nan, but we didn't go back there until I was eight, after a heart attack removed the issue. It's been our home address the whole time, though not really home, especially since Aunt Nia's always been kind of half sweet, half sour to us, and we've never been inclined to stay there for long." I smiled at Kyou, handing him a yoghurt bowl. "I had this super fun conversation with Mum and Dad about Fox Farm yesterday. When Dad started calling it 'our own little hill', I could really feel how huge a milestone it is for them. Thank you for finding them such a magical place."

"After hearing that history, I'm glad I had something at hand," Kyou said. "So, you've never had much to do with the other half of the family?"

"I've never met them. For the most part Mum only kept in touch with my great-grandmother, who she was very close to. I was named for her."

"Mikaela or Niles?" Rin asked. "Or did you leave a name off the school register?"

"I usually don't write them all down because people get confused. My full name's Mikaela McAllister Teyrn Niles."

"Why one surname when you can have three?" Kyou said, grinning.

"Exactly. McAllister is my great-grandmother's maiden name."

"Things never got better with your mother's family?" Bran asked.

"They've never tried to contact my Mum. Not even when my great-grandmother died when I was three. Mum found out weeks after the funeral, when a gift she'd sent made its way back to her via returned mail. My Mum's one of the most easy-going people in the universe, but I don't think she'll ever forgive them for that. She changed her email address and has never gone back to Scotland."

I sighed, then glanced at Rin, who was adding sliced apples to cereal. "It was today that was your sisters' birthday, right?"

"Yeah." He was looking relaxed. "Unless someone decides to announce something during the party, I think I'm clear."

"When are you heading out?" Bran asked.

"Midday," Rin said. "It'll probably run until late afternoon. I'm going to try to bring all four back here for dinner afterwards, so don't hold any Bacchanals."

"Chances are, we won't even be able to drag Mika away from her sketch pad," Bran said. But then he smiled and leaned over so he could press a kiss to the corner of my mouth. "Admittedly, you look so happy when you're working that I hate to interrupt you. Do you want to come along when the barista explains my coffee machine?"

"Sure. I usually take a guess-or-read-the-manual approach to appliances, but my dad insists good coffee is an art. And if you come collect me, I mightn't work through lunch."

"Should we incorporate making sure you get to places on time into our schedules?" Rin asked, amused.

"I usually set alarms," I said. "I only rarely stop noticing the time, anyway. Mainly when starting a new city, playing really good games, or afternoons in summer houses."

That last item almost disrupted our morning, but we managed to keep ourselves just to mussed clothing, and hurried off to packed schedules. I immersed myself in Falls City, learned to make a variety of coffees, lunched with Bran, and had a late afternoon meeting with Kyou, who looked carefully through the work I'd done so far, and only asked for a couple of minor changes.

"It's a little eerie. Some of the things you've drawn are exactly what I've pictured," he said, holding up the view of the warehouse area above the falls. "Other parts are nothing like, but fortunately in a way that just demonstrates why we hire experts to do the things we aren't particularly good at."

"I want to go back and do the starter town next," I said. "Is it okay if I make it an odd sort of mix between space colony and rural village? Occasional incorporated pieces that make it look like the place was long ago settled from space?"

"Give me some quick sketches to show the idea, first," he said. "But not today."

"I do need a rest," I admitted. "And maybe some prep time before the descent of Rin's sisters. Do we know yet whether they're coming to dinner?"

"Not yet."

I nodded, and took my work off to scan and store, mildly entertained by the interested glances from my fellow hot-deskers. I'd decided casual and apparently open conversations with my 'high school friends' was the best approach to making it seem I really was just renting a room from them. Kybirn employees would likely accept this more readily than people who had known the Three Kings longer.

Rin's four sisters were probably the most important, since Rin most definitely would care about their opinions, so I spent some thought on how I wanted to appear before them. I've occasionally used clothing to play games with how people perceive me, but in this case, I simply changed back to my default of jeans and a t-shirt: today a faded watermelon and mint stripe. I gave myself half an hour to catch up online, then went downstairs only to find no-one about.

Shrugging, I took myself off to the games room to hurl myself through a newly released platformer, and eventually Bran and then Kyou found me, and we traded off the controller with each death until Castellan announced: *Garage.*

Kyou paused the game and put the controller down with a sigh. "Well, guess he got through it without drama. After this we can await the day of the big blow-up, then block his parents' phones for a year or two until they give up."

"Sure they will?" I asked.

"Probably not until great-grandfather's shares are settled," Bran said. "The power of being majority shareholder is hard to give up."

"But why does that have to involve any of you? Surely, it'd be way more satisfying to inherit directly?"

"Great-Grandfather's made clear that he thinks most of his children and grandchildren are waste material," Bran said, leading the way back into the central atrium. "Current frontrunners are all the most recent generation: Kyou, Rin, Kaden, Stacia, Antoine, and Damasque. Marcelline will probably be up there in five or so years but right now she's too young to be taken seriously."

"You have a cousin called Damasque?"

"She's a piece of work," Kyou said. "But very smart. L-B Corp would flourish under her rule."

"Beautiful and terrible as the dawn," Bran added, then stopped as a younger version of himself came in through the entry hall. After a pause he simply said: "Hey."

"Hey," said the boy, who was around fifteen, with all Bran's angelic beauty, but fewer apparent thorns.

"Koo-Koo!" a girl exclaimed, ran forward, and flung her arms around Kyou's neck, then let him go, cried "Ran-Ran!" and repeated the process with Bran.

"Almost as if you hadn't seen us just a week ago, Genie," Kyou said, and then was lost in a group hug from three more girls.

Two sets, one pair getting close to six feet in height, with Rin's colouring and willowy build. The other pair a little shorter than me, with black-brown hair and delicate frames.

"Mika, meet my sisters," Rin said, then indicated each of them in turn as he continued: "Marcelline and Evgenie, and Anthea and Jessamin. Also, Bran's brother, Rowan. This is Mika, our friend and housemate."

"Hi!" said Evgenie, looking me up and down frankly. "But I don't get it—what happened to the apartment Dad bought?"

"Not enough bedrooms," Rin said, smiling. "And, well, rather more than that. I told you I had big news—come out front and I'll show you what I mean."

He took them out to the foyer, producing only mild confusion until Rowan said: "Wait, are you Kybirn Music?"

"Kybirn Music, Kybirn Games, and Kybirn Investment," Kyou said, watching from the door.

"You started your own companies?" Marcelline asked. She seemed a much more composed girl than her bubbly twin, interested but not so excitable.

"What kind of games?" Jessamin asked. She had opted for a princess style for her birthday, while her twin Anthea matched short-cropped hair with a simple summer dress.

"First release is a music composition game, and then we burn ourselves out on a triple-A RPG," Bran said. "Office is upstairs."

"Ran-Ran, are you actually going to perform?" Evgenie asked, as we went back to the spiral stairs.

"Kybirn Music is Rin's," Kyou explained. "He's been selling compositions for around five years now. Bran workshops them with him, but Bran's more involved in the programming side of things, and has been writing custom apps for small businesses. They hand their money to me, I invest it."

"We bought this building," Rin said. "And are already in a position to fully fund the games."

They'd reached the first landing of the stair, and they all stopped and turned to look at him, drawn by the outright joy in the statement.

Evgenie laughed, and hooked his arm. "Well, that puts into perspective the conversation Dad had with you about being sure to budget your allowance. I couldn't figure out why you were almost visibly biting your lip."

"We're coming up on some drama, aren't we?" Jessamin asked.

"I'm enrolled in a Masters of Music," Rin said.

"*Enormous* drama," Anthea said.

"You always have looked happiest when playing that violin," Marcelline said, and hugged him. After a moment the other three piled on. Lots of hugging with this part of the family, it seemed.

The several puzzled glances they'd already sent my way made it seem advisable to give them a brief break for a 'how good a friend' conversation, so I said to Kyou: "That book's in my room. Want me to bring it upstairs?"

"Good idea," he said.

I slipped past the sibling cluster, took my time collecting the Book of Samerkel, and re-joined them as Bran was explaining why the motion capture rooms were all grey.

"Here's our origin story," Kyou said, as I looked in the door.

"It's mostly lived at Bran's place or our old office, which is why your frequent ransacking of my possessions never showed it up," Rin said, as I handed the book over. "Come on—time to show off one of our obsessions."

"But why have you never told us anything about this?" Anthea asked. "Didn't you trust us?"

"You were all of six when we started this," Rin said, taking the book out to the nearest workstation. "And more recently it's not been a question of trust so much as your ability to stand up to cross-examination. You know how they get when they think you're holding something back."

"Does Great-Grandfather know anything about this?" Jessamin asked.

"Unlikely, from the conversations I've had with him lately," Kyou said. "Last week he gave me a full half-hour of advice on what to concentrate on in my studies. Quite interesting stuff, but hardly relevant for a Fine Arts degree."

This brought a shock perhaps even greater than Rin's determination to study music.

"Not enormous drama," Marcelline said at last. "Complete upheaval of the accepted order. So, you're all stepping away from L-B Corp?"

"None of us have any interest in The Inheritance," Kyou said. "What we've always wanted is freedom to do what interests us, and to never obey a summons out to The Grove again."

Evgenie curled her arms around one of Kyou's.

"Koo-Koo, if we ask very nicely, and give you half our allowance each month, will you turn it into boundless riches for us?"

He laughed. "Not boundless, but I'll invest it for you. Or, if you prefer, give you a monthly video chat with recommendations on how you should invest."

"That sounds like the best idea," Marcelline said. "Presuming we're allowed to talk to you."

"Why—?" Evgenie began, frowned, then said with dimmed cheer: "Well, invest it for us until we're allowed to take lessons." She let go of Kyou's arm and swapped to Rin. "It's probably going to be a bit awful for a while, isn't it? Couldn't you just not tell them?"

"Our enrolments won't stay under the radar much longer," Kyou said.

"There's little they'll be able to do to me except make noise," Rin added. "And the world is too connected for it to be at all feasible for them to cut contact between us completely. But what I want to avoid is a series of escalations where you end up punished for talking to me. So, for a while at least, if they tell you not to talk to me, I want you to do as you're told."

"You won't be taking us to the Book Festival?" Jessamin asked, sounding lost. "You were going to help me be brave enough to talk to my favourite authors."

"I think we can safely happen to encounter each other on the first day of the Book Festival," Rin said. "It's still at the Lakeview Convention Centre, right? We'll meet just inside the south entrance at midday. I think—I hope—the parents will have recovered by the time your birthdays come around again, but if not, we'll make arrangements."

The prospect of drama dragging on to an entire year was understandably upsetting, and it took quite some back and forth before they returned to the subject of game development, and finished the tour of the office, ending up at the recording studios.

Rowan, who had quietly followed along the entire way, finally spoke. "You wrote *Not My Friend*?"

"That's right," Rin said.

"Why wouldn't you sell it to me?" the boy asked, voice small.

Rin tilted his head a fraction, then shrugged. "I sold it to the highest bidder, and didn't even know your agent was a prospect. I don't think it would quite have suited you, though, so perhaps it's for the best. If I write something that fits you, I'll give you first right of refusal. When's your album drop?"

"Beginning December."

"Send me a copy so I can get an idea of how they're positioning you."

"Okay," Rowan said, ducking his head.

He seemed a very quiet boy, and I had to wonder how he'd hold up performing. Bran had said Rowan enjoyed the stage, so perhaps he was only shy socially.

Since it was getting late, we headed back downstairs and ordered a lot of Thai food, while Rin's sisters searched out the performances of the songs he'd written. I'd heard of a few, but there'd been no major hits, though *Not My Friend* had evidently been the subject of a small bidding war, and was now an upcoming release for someone I'd never heard of, but who was considered a rising star.

This topic kept us busy until halfway through dinner, when Evgenie turned her focus to me.

"Koo-Koo said he owes you a debt, Mika, but it must be something special for him to rent you a room. What did you do exactly?"

"From my point of view, I made an off-hand comment," I said, smiling. "It just happened to be a 'for want of a nail' situation."

"The kingdom was definitely nearly lost," Kyou agreed. "Dad was trying to blackmail me into a ten-year employment contract, and Mika inspired me into a response that meant we got to keep all this without me having to deal with him for another decade. Officially, though, Mika simply gave me a tip that I've converted into a nice land development deal."

"Mika...are you the Mikaela that beat these three for Corascur's Dux?" Marcelline asked.

"That's right." I spooned some more green curry onto my rice. "I should probably feel guilty—these three were super helpful settling me into Corascur and prepping for the exams—but since being Dux may have made the difference for me getting into my course at Helios U, I've no regrets."

I could see Kyou struggling to hide a smile at that, because their help had primarily revolved around sex as a sleep aid, but Rin and Bran managed to keep straight faces.

"Only Rin's parents cared about any of us being Dux," Bran said.

"And it doesn't matter at all for what I want to do," Rin added, shrugging. "I did have to sit through a tedious session of 'what happened' when the results came out, but to be honest me being Dux always required Bran to not be on form. And for Kyou to slip up a little. I had to put a lot of work into my grades because my strength has always been music."

"I feel a little like we've never known you at all," Jessamin said, unhappily. "And haven't been helping."

Rin reached across the table to ruffle her hair. "You four are the main reason I've been able to bear going home. You can help by not letting yourselves get caught in the crossfire until everything settles down."

"Well, here's hoping it takes months for the folks to notice," Anthea said, practically. "Mika, give me your phone number. I'm great at obeying the letter but not the word of the law, and they're sure to tell us not to talk to Kyou and Bran either."

I did as asked, and then spent some time explaining my degree, and talking about bridge building, and we ended the evening on a fairly neutral discussion about the girls' own studies, and their plans to all share an apartment. Rin was very quiet after he returned from driving them home and snuggled into bed with us, but his mood overall seemed to be positive.

Eleven

On Wednesday, I put on a casual, ankle-skimming dress, divided my hair into two loose braids, and strolled down after breakfast to meet Lania. Helios U's campus had transformed from orderly preparation into a hive. Even the relatively less-populated western end was swarming: the grassy areas between the wider-spaced buildings set with marquees, rest areas, and information booths, all of them crowded.

The closer I got to Hub, the more difficult it became to make my way through the throng, but fortunately the designated meeting place allowed me to cross the bridge to the south side, to a series of tables outside the library. Here I found familiar faces associated with Art Club—Lania, Sean, Rick, Sue, Anika, Hanni, Natascha—and a few people I recognised as Corascur graduates without ever having spoken to them.

My approach produced a strange mix of expressions. A combination of entertainment and sympathy? My living arrangements surely hadn't spread so far already. But, from what former Corascur students knew of me, I had a suspicion what might have set them off, and smiled blandly as I approached.

"I was thinking this early in the day the crowds wouldn't have built up," I said. "I can't imagine what it'll be like at lunchtime."

"Heaving," said Anika, who had cut her dark hair over the summer break, and now sported a riot of curls.

"How was the tram ride in?" I asked Lania, who was looking tanned after a family-oriented summer.

"Not bad," Lania said. "I'm far enough out that I won't have any problems getting on board during the morning squeeze, and I figure I can do some of my required reading on my phone. I like the new look."

"There were all these end-of-season sales, so I picked up a bunch of options," I said, glancing down at the soft floral fabric. Then I hefted the small bag I was toting and added: "Let me hand out these photos before I forget." I pulled out an envelope containing signed polaroids and started distributing them to those who'd asked for one.

"You're really dating Christophe Barrington?" asked a curvy brunette I didn't know.

"I dated Christophe for a couple of months over a year ago," I said, firmly. "We're just friends now."

"Friends you go on trips to Peru with," Sean said, excitedly reviewing the three candid shots of Christophe standing beneath a waterfall that I'd reserved particularly for him. Christophe's shirt had gone nicely see-through.

"That's right," I said, smiling. "One day I expect he'll be too famous for such a low-key holiday, but he managed to only be recognised a few times. He's been practicing an American accent, and tried to stick to it the entire time, which threw people off nicely."

"Really not dating?" the brunette asked, making me suspect she was here specifically for gossip about rising hot actors.

"Neither of us are particularly good at long-distance relationships," I said.

Hoping this would make people think we'd broken up over the summer, I turned the subject. "I picked up my ID on the weekend, so I'm here to look at the clubs," I said. "Want to wander around, Lania?"

"I've got a ticket for the 10:15 slot for IDs," she said. "Wander after that? What clubs are you interested in?"

"Engineering. Tennis."

"I didn't know you played," she said.

"I don't, but I hear that it's a very relaxed club, and I don't have a lot of time to spare for the next decade or so."

"Not aiming to be Helios U's leggiest party girl?" Rick asked.

"I've put myself down for a very full course load," I said, shrugging. "Between that, playing all the games I absolutely can't resist, and my new part-time job, I'm going to be severely rationing other activities."

"You said your new job came with a great rental?" Lania asked.

"Yeah, the company's office is just outside the western edge of the campus. They don't generally offer accommodation, but I happened to give them a line on a fantastic lead writer, and they like him so much they want to keep in his good books."

"Your dad?" Lania looked confused. "What kind of company needs lead writers?"

"Film production?" Sean asked, attention shifting from his photographs. "Need any extras?"

"Game devs," I said, smiling. "They will need a lot of actors, eventually, but I don't think they're casting until next year. Voice acting, mo-cap, that kind of thing."

"Is it Verdant Games?" Anika asked, perking up.

"No, a new developer, Kybirn. They've got a music-based game slated for release beginning of next year, but I'm doing concept art and modelling for a triple-A RPG. Dad's polishing the script. There's a half-dozen romance lines, so his Rock Hardison work is coming in handy."

"I looked him up," Sean said, sparing a quick grin at Lania. "And even read a couple of his books over the break! I'm totally down for more interactive stories from him."

"How are they as an employer?" Anika asked. "And are they hiring interns? A game dev just outside campus would be fantastic for me."

"Well, I've only done two days' work for them so far, but the higher ups are promising flexible work practices, and seem pretty organised. Massive geeks, of course. They've been working on the game world and story for over a decade, and need to bring a ton more people on board for the RPG, but I don't know about interns. The website will probably have details."

I hadn't spent much time on the website. I'd have to check later to see whether it named the CEOs.

Lania and Anika's ID appointments were close to due, so they headed off to join the crowd at the admin building. I chatted with Sean about his ambition to be an actor, and the courses the Faculty of Performing Arts offered. Sue wanted to be a director, and shrugged wryly about being the person in charge rather than someone helping in the background.

"At least a quarter of my classes seem to be people management techniques," she said. "From the couple of music clips I've worked on so far, I already know that that's the hardest part. Larger productions are...daunting, but I'm keen to try. How are you at acting, Mika?"

"If you need someone for crowd scenes, I'm happy to help out, but I'm no use for bigger parts. I find it odd, since I can lie at the drop of a hat, but I'm told I'm very unconvincing when trying to pretend to be other people. I guess I'll always be better at sciences than Arts."

"Says someone with a job doing concept art," Sue said.

"Oh, anything related to buildings, bridges and cities will always be an exception. If you need me to act like someone who knows bridges, I'm there for it."

"Did I remember to congratulate you on getting into your course?" Sue asked. "I know you were worried, though once you were announced as Dux, I had to wonder where the nerves came from."

"Chronic insomnia—particularly before important events. Did everyone here get their first choice?"

There was a chorus of affirmatives. Rick was heading for a Literature degree, which surprised me a little. Hanni had enrolled in Medicine, and Natascha was studying Fine Arts.

"I'm hoping to be in some classes with Carr," she admitted frankly. "I know he's mostly going to be in the photography stream, but there's sure to be some crossover."

"Not seeing Carr regularly is definitely the worst part of moving on from Art Club," Sean agreed. "Beaten only by the lack of Kings in my life. There hasn't even been a whisper of them for far too long."

I considered volunteering that I'd spotted them getting their IDs on the weekend, but decided to stick with my planned slower reveal of my living arrangements. Unless my Kings and I found a way to be boldly public, I was always going to be lying to people. This didn't necessarily bother me, but I still hadn't fully adjusted to losing the freedom to say anything I wanted, secure in the knowledge I'd be gone from the school before people found out the truth.

Lania was my current preoccupation. I had been lying by omission for a year, of course, but my relationship with the Kings had changed, and I knew I couldn't keep it from her much longer while truly treating her as a friend. Would she feel betrayed? Or perhaps even disgusted?

"Did you hear about Sirocco?" Natascha asked.

Sean perked up. "No? Goss?"

"She's also enrolled in Fine Arts. Sculpture. Pottery, even. Her mother cut her off to try to bring her to heel, but she's got some trust fund from her grandmother, and has moved out on her own."

"And there falls a future industry leader," Rick said, sounding impressed. "Mrs Melville always did seem to want a mini-me, not a daughter."

"Perhaps Sirocco finally heard the big old 'No' Rin has been telling her for years," Hanni said, lightly amused. "And with that piece of the planned out future missing, the rest was easier to put down."

Lania, returning, wrinkled her nose. "Let's not talk about Sirocco." She paused, then smiled helplessly. "Though I really would love to see her at a potter's wheel, all daubed in clay."

"Wearing overalls," Sue added, grinning, but then shook her head. "Not that this would be something I'd laugh at if it wasn't Sirocco. More power to her, I say.

Now show me how your ID photos turned out before I go line up for mine."

After some horror pic comparisons, I left with Anika, Sean and Lania to look over the club stalls, which were clustered more toward the western end of the campus.

"Tennis will be all the way down near the courts, I expect," Sean said. "Why don't we start there and work our way back?"

"Anyone want to play with me?" I asked, as I joined the line of applicants.

"I need to work on my legs more before I run around in shorts," Sean said. "I've been buffing up over the break, but I'm not where I want to be yet."

"I like tennis, but campus sports aren't really practical for me," Lania said.

"I'm going to go with something art-related for my club," Anika said. "There's a few I want to check out: particularly one called Props and Pillars that supports the theatre performances. It sounds very cool, but it's also really popular because of proximity to some of the campus luminaries. I haven't decided on the backup club yet."

"Who are the campus luminaries?" I asked, curious.

"Well, not involved in theatre there's a couple more of the Laurent-Beaulieu clan," Sean said. "Stacia Laurent and Damasque Beaumont. Damasque is an ice queen, but you can't help but want to let her step on you. Stacia is the one I'd really like to meet, though. She was the outgoing Student Council President when we started at Corascur, and she was just the coolest, wittiest person I'd ever seen. Theatre-side there's Iain Flanders, who is finishing up his degree even though he's already considered Greenland's best current-generation actor. Dimitri Tang and Nyssa Larsson are also outstanding theatre-side. And, of course, the resident maths genius everyone drools over—he has a YouTube channel."

"Oh, Yan Eileson," I said. "I've read a few of his papers—he's made some interesting points in quantum theory."

"He also does parkour and has possibly the best shoulders on campus," Sean said, fanning himself. "If I was the least bit mathematical, I'd do every class he offered."

Wondering why Lania seemed subdued, I said to her: "You can keep your sports gear at my place, if you'd like to play tennis. Rather than cart a racket around all day."

"How far away's this office/rental room?" Anika asked.

I peered at the western boundary of the campus, then said: "See that bit of white visible through the top of those sycamore trees? That's the rooftop elevator."

"When you said close you meant it!" Anika said. "What did you say it was called again?"

"Kybirn—K Y B I R N."

"I better put in an expression of interest before word spreads. Even if they're not taking interns right now, I can hope for a high spot on the eligibility list."

"Which part of game development are you most interested in?" I asked.

"I'd have to flip a coin between level design and combat mechanics." Anika was searching on her phone. "Both of which I'm not going to be able to waltz into on a large game, but I'm flexible, will do anything they're offering. Sound, art, programming. My C++

isn't at Lania's level, but I'm way better than the average first year, and I've deep-dived on both Unreal and Unity. Hell, I'd empty bins and make sandwiches, so long as it gives me the opportunity to progress into something juicier."

"Ever thought about going in for the games industry, Lania? Is the AI for robotics suitable for game development?"

Lania shrugged. "Plenty of intersection, but I'm not nearly far enough along to put in an application yet. Not to mention my resume really is mainly making people sandwiches."

Anika and I exchanged glances, and then Anika said firmly: "If they're taking names, both of ours are going down."

"Kybirn's very open to working-from-home arrangements, depending on the job," I added. "You wouldn't be stuck with a ton of extra commutes."

"Well, I guess it can't hurt to try," Lania said, slowly.

"And sign up for tennis too. Even if we only play once a month."

We progressed through the tennis club line, collecting a helpful brochure of rules, then walked over to the Performing Arts Faculty buildings to blink at the crowd for Props and Pillars.

"You weren't kidding about it being popular," I said, perching on the stone edge of a planter. "We'll sit over here and wait."

Sean and Anika lined up, and I took the opportunity to ask Lania: "What's wrong?"

"Wrong—?"

"You've been off all morning."

"Oh. Just period pain. Usually, paracetamol is enough to get me through, but sometimes it's rough." She gave me a half-smile. "I'm willing to admit to being jealous that you never show any signs of a bad period."

"I get back aches," I said. "But my birth control implant stopped my periods altogether, which I am very happy about. I do feel super queasy once a month, but I'll take the trade-off."

Lania went delightfully pink, as she usually did when approaching the subject of sex, but then asked cautiously: "Did—did you and Christophe..."

"Oh, while we were dating, yes." I laughed. "Christophe made a great starter boyfriend: fun, caring, but never pretending to be committed. Were the odd expressions everyone was wearing when I came up related to him?"

"That new post on his Instagram..." Lania said, uncomfortably.

"I don't have an account—show me?"

Christophe had posted a picture of Macchu Piccu that happened to include a rear view of me, sitting on the stones gazing over the mountain tops. The text of: "Enjoy to the fullest those perfect moments that can't be kept," was suitably ambiguous, and just what I'd asked for.

"Forty thousand likes. When I was at school with him, he'd get maybe fifty each picture. He's being bombarded with roles now, even though his first leading part hasn't even been filmed."

"No regrets for the breakup?" Lania asked.

I shook my head. "While star turns at the ball are fun occasionally, I'd never fit in with a celebrity lifestyle. My ideal week involves 50% construction, and the rest of the time drawing cities, playing with maths, and somehow cramming in all the latest games. Christophe is delightful of course, but extremely social, and would never understand an afternoon curled up on a couch together to separately read books, or go head-to-head at *Tyranny*."

"That's a relationship goal I could be on board with."

"Guess we're meant for each other," I said, laughed because there was zero heat in my interactions with Lania, and briefly wondered if there were any women in the world I'd find more attractive than my Kings. Shrugging, I said: "I don't think I mentioned that my parents have gone and bought a house south of Helios."

"Really?"

"Everything's happened very rapidly—not least because we lucked into an old farmhouse with the most gorgeous views. We're working on a complete renovation."

I showed Lania the photos I'd taken—the subset that didn't involve sneak shots of handsome profiles—and then my sketched designs.

"It's going to take plenty of financial grease to get the whole thing done by Christmas, but they've fallen in love with the place, and are willing to spend. It's a little surprising—my parents always seemed so happy wandering about that I think I really underestimated just how much a place of their own means to them."

"Are they just buying property, or immigrating? You too?"

"Most likely me too, but I'll happily let them pave the way for me. With their combined incomes, I think it should be a smooth enough process for them. How are your parents going with the new business?"

"It continues to be fun and scary. Evelyn has completely revised my understanding of accountancy. My parents have been having these wonderful speakerphone training sessions with her, half of which are the most incredible anecdotes, and all of us sit around mesmerised, which is not something I'd ever think I'd do for anything involving international tax law. Not having a regular pay check coming in is daunting, but if Mum and Dad successfully inherit even half of Evelyn's current clientele, they..." Lania shook her head. "I never knew how much money you could make with other people's money."

"Yeah." I shook my head, thinking of Kyou's apparently effortless accrual.

If I dwelled on my family's years of scrimping and saving for basics, and the countless odd jobs I'd had in order to enjoy any luxuries, I could almost resent Kyou's abilities. But, for a long time Lania's family, with their middle income and outer suburbs house, would have also provided an uncomfortable comparison. Perhaps, during those meagre years, my parents had never shown any sign of wanting 'their own little hill' because it was out of their reach. Instead, they'd made our lives an adventurous game, one we'd progressed through until we'd unlocked a housing mini-game.

"I'm in danger of waxing philosophic," I said, laughing at myself. "How nice it is to be here, Lania."

Though crowded, it continued to be a fun day. We toured past Clubs of every variety, then met back up with the rest of Corascur's former Art Club and headed north, crossing the main road and tram line to the bustling shopping and restaurant district that serviced the university. After lunch, I urged Lania to head home to a hot water bottle, and spent some time touring clothes stores. I suspected that one day I might actually fill my generous wardrobe because I kept seeing things I wanted a King to take off me.

Returning in the mid-afternoon, I discovered a neat pile of boxes addressed to me by the base of the main stair, along with Bran, supine upon the steps.

Bran's natural state seemed to involve sprawling, not owning Rin's effortless grace, but still managing to be breathtaking at every turn. I paused to appreciate him, then put down my bags and joined him on the steps, lying back so my head rested beside his on the first landing.

The view this angle afforded up the curving stairwell, and the interplay between the railings and the leadlight windows proved to be especially lovely, so I quietly enjoyed it. A few minutes later I heard the lift doors open, followed by faint footsteps that paused, then approached. Kyou, who wordlessly joined us.

About ten minutes later, a door clicked above us, and we all watched Rin walk slowly down the stair, which mostly involved glimpses of his hand occasionally touching the railing, but sometimes opened up to more of him, until finally he reached our landing and stopped to gaze down at us.

"Am I missing the joke?"

"Great view," I said, smiling up at him along the long length of his body.

His eyes widened, and then he smiled, the slow and entirely wicked smile he never shows outsiders. Then he dropped to his haunches, and leaned all the way down so that those champagne eyes were the only thing I could see.

"Is it?" he asked.

Rarely have I had such a visceral reaction. It must have been clearly apparent to Rin, too, since he drew back slightly, looked triumphant, and then kissed me hard. Kyou laughed, and Bran let out his breath in a little snort, and then they joined in.

Spectacular as it is, the stairwell isn't my idea of a venue, so I took them up to my shower, and we lost a chunk of the afternoon, but remembered in time that we were due a cooking lesson, and came back down a half hour before Mrs Janssen was due to arrive.

"My contribution to this cooking session is going to be limited to quips and unhelpful suggestions," I said, perching on one of the tall stools usually slotted beneath the kitchen island, and then slumping on the counter.

Unlike me, all three of my Kings were looking energised and pleased with themselves. "I've no doubt you're ahead of us on the basics, anyway," Kyou said, adding a couple of neglected dishes to the dishwasher.

"I can cook a few things well, and follow most recipes to at least edible level, but my dad's the real cook of the family," I said, shrugging. "Mum and I aren't usually down for anything that takes more than quarter of an hour to prepare."

"Once we all have some basic competence, we can work out how we want to arrange meals ongoing," Rin said. "Wide as the selection is in this area, I don't want constant takeout."

"If none of us ever have the time or inclination, the domestic service can source daily cooks," Kyou said. "I didn't arrange that because I wanted to minimise the amount of time other people are in the house."

"My preference," Rin agreed. "Even if we weren't, ah, admiring stairs, I don't want any more surprise unwrapping opportunities."

Given that cleaners were already an adjustment for me, a daily cook wasn't my preference either.

"Do you want me to move all those boxes to your room?" Bran asked, offering me a glass of water.

"No, they're the anemometers and some survey equipment I ordered for Noonerry. Let's put them in the garage until we can get down there again."

"This weekend's as good a time as any," Kyou said. "It's the clearest we'll have for a while."

"I want to overnight there, and take a better look at that forest," Bran said. "Are any of the houses you bought habitable?"

We discussed options while packing my anemometers into the back of Rin's Hummer, and decided to leave on Friday afternoon and come back Sunday. I talked possibly a little excitedly about how I planned to map the winds across Fox Farm. Wind physics are one of my favourite fields, but also important if Kyou really did want to develop the place into a resort.

"You don't want to plant a garden and have it stripped to the stalks once a month," I said. "If they're severe, regular gales will alter the kind of structures you build as well."

"Extreme wind would make for interesting weddings," Bran said, contemplatively.

"The occasional airborne bride could be considered a form of advertisement," Kyou said, chuckling. "It's always good to save on promotion costs."

"Given you can't yet afford to build the place..." Bran said.

Kyou shrugged. "One step at a time. The initial focus is going to be the main office anyway, and a wind map will be just as useful there."

"How's the first few days of Kybirn Phase Two been?" I asked. "Everything you hoped for?"

They listed a handful of issues, but smiled while they did so, and I watched their faces light up as mine probably had while I talked about wind load. Kybirn was, in its way, the 'little hill' these three had been anticipating for years. It needed a lot more funding, but was also a home they'd longed to build.

Twelve

Since Corascur's pre-qualification program had allowed me to directly take the examination for a couple of freshman courses, my—and Bran's—first lecture was actually a sophomore calc class at ten on Monday morning. Kyou and Rin's first classes were both at nine-thirty, but because they were at the western end of the campus while Bran and I were heading all the way east, we left home together.

"We'll be able to monitor office emails from our laptops, so no matter where we are on campus we can deal with urgent work," Kyou said, as we headed through the campus gate. "Though Imani, Ahmed and Gram have so far lived up to their reputations, and we don't really need to hover."

"Think you'll be able to not?" I asked, tilting my head so I could better hear what Rin was humming.

"Maybe in a week or fifty," Kyou admitted. "Though going away on the weekend helped me with not checking the reporting function every thirty seconds."

"Only two people have been cleared for weekend overtime," Rin pointed out.

"Overtime, yes, but a sizeable chunk are taking the flexible working time option, and putting in a few standard hours whenever's most convenient for them."

"The weekend should be kept as a proper break," Bran said, shoving his hands into his pockets. He seemed to be in a bad mood, but trying to hide it.

"Let's make a point of going somewhere that keeps us off our devices at least once a week," Rin said. "Not necessarily tramping over every inch of a farm again, but that forest walk cleared my head nicely. Perhaps a movie on Saturday?"

"Sure," Kyou said, and Bran and I nodded.

"What are you going to do with those two houses if the stop is located in Noonerry?" I asked Kyou.

"I've already arranged for the centre town one to be renovated. That kind of old-world classic bungalow should be preserved, and we can continue to stay in it on our no-doubt frequent trips down there this year. The other, well, you saw it."

A tiny house on a large semi-rural lot, where we'd only peered through the windows while adding a token anemometer to the garden. "Tear down?"

"It's actually one of the earliest parts of the project I'd want to start on. A small villa or townhouse complex that will be useful accommodation. Until our staff need to be out there, it'll bring in income as holiday lets." He smiled. "Probably used by railway construction staff for the next couple of years, at a suitably inflated price."

We'd reached the end of the lake that divided the campus, and Rin left with a wave of his hand to the nearby Conservatorium.

"He's so happy," I commented, as Bran, Kyou and I took the less-crowded path to the south bank.

"He's been looking forward to today for a long time," Kyou said. "Dreaming for years of leading a full symphony orchestra to perform some of his pieces. Or even just setting up a quartet. Or fooling around with friends for an afternoon of jazz or blues or whatever's inspiring him at the moment. Bran and I aren't nearly enough for him, in terms of the conversation he wants to have with music."

"Let's hope he gets to enjoy more than a single day before dealing with the fallout," Bran said, flatly.

"It's an achievement to even get one, really," Kyou said. "His parents must have something that's occupying their attention." He paused as we reached the entrance of the Fine Arts building, and looked across the lake to the stream of students on the north bank. "I'd say it's the quiet before the storm, but we get to simply block them now. Ignore their emails. Never answer another summons out to The Grove again."

"Is your great-grandfather that awful?" I asked.

"Oh, he's...himself," Kyou said. "Brilliant, driven, stopped short of actually cutting people's throats on the way to building an empire."

"Just suffering from the effects of half the world trying to crawl up his ass," Bran muttered.

"The problem's more the constant pressure from parents to, ah, crawl," Kyou said. "Entire generations focused on talking their kids up, and kicking everyone else down. I can't remember a time I've been out at The Grove when I haven't wanted to hit someone." He paused, shook his head, then said: "I'll probably go back to the house for lunch break. See you there, if you decide to walk down."

He headed toward the Fine Arts building, and Bran and I continued on.

"Is university something you've looked forward to at all?" I asked. I had no problem guessing why Bran's mood was low: our classes meant that a lot of time he'd be without any of us to help keep admirers away.

Bran shrugged. "Rin's really the only one eager to be here. The things I'm interested in I can self-study. Formal classes will probably fill in some gaps, so it's worth doing, but it's not necessary. And Kyou needs to study finance like a fish needs swimming lessons. For painting...I don't know. Kyou says he wants to push himself out of his comfort zone, which I think might be truer than he realises."

"How so?"

"He's the kid of a soulless shark and an extreme perfectionist, both big on appearances. His mother had a finance background, but she also did things like ikebana and calligraphy, and everything that wasn't up to her standard would go in the trash. Which was almost everything. Nothing could ever show the slightest flaw. She was completely devoted to Kyou, but she's also the reason he can play piano at Grade 6 level when he has no interest in it."

"How old was he when she died?"

"Ten. He didn't find her, but he was in the house."

"And he reserves his perfectionism for painting? Does he ever throw them away?"

"No. But the only one he doesn't have facing the wall at the moment is that piece he did of the school summer house. He might be able to look at it because it's not in his usual style. Or just all the positive associations of chasing you back and forth."

"Well, I'd like to think so," I said, not quite able to smile. "There are times I'm amazed you three are so even-keeled."

"We were never hungry, never hit or abused, had plenty to balance it all out. And you won't get many people who claim I'm even-keeled."

He glanced at me, and I wondered if he was remembering the time I'd told him boyfriends were a lot of work I didn't want. Bran, endlessly moody, fiercely stubborn, and more than a little self-destructive, was possibly the opposite of what I'd consider a good prospect. And, while his state of mind had improved immensely since he'd moved past both his parents and his ex, those personality traits weren't going to simply be erased.

"No-one sails smoothly through a storm," I pointed out, then was distracted by a handful of people going into the Marden Institute ahead of us. I stared unabashedly.

"Are you going to drool at this building every time we pass it?" Bran asked.

"Probably only for the first month or so. Repeated exposure can immunise me to anything. Like how I don't even blink when you wander around without a shirt these days."

"The reaction still seems kind of similar," he said, after a moment. "What happens to your grand plan if this Institute closes down or something?"

"Mika with added sulking." I gave the question more thought, then shrugged. "I want to build interesting, difficult, technical things. Especially but not limited to bridges. Marden is a shortcut to the forefront, to opportunities to do that with large-scale structures. It's not the only way. But if Marden closed, there would definitely be a period where I shut myself up in my room and did nothing but play games with the sound turned up loud."

"Too much of that and Kyou would spend all his time concocting elaborate distractions."

I laughed. "Well, I like it when Kyou distracts me. Speaking of distractions, what do you think are my chances of sneaking into his bed on the morning of his birthday without waking him up?"

"Not likely. Best chance would be if we kept him up really late the night before."

"Do you have any plans for his and Rin's birthdays? Do you prefer it to be just another day, or an event, or in between?"

"Kyou will like it if we do something semi-formal. I'd prefer a quiet night in gaming together. Rin's usually busy with his family on his birthday, but chances are high he'll be in exile this year, and upset about it."

"Maybe I'll let him tie me up. Just a little." Rin had gone way overboard on our first attempt at bondage, but a milder version wasn't likely to bother me, and I knew he'd enjoy it.

"You're even happier than Rin today," Bran said, brows creasing.

I nodded, and bounced a little on my feet.

"Life is good. While we stand on the cusp of family drama, extreme gossip, and possible public scorn, right here and now is just peachy."

He looked at me for a long moment, snorted, but then said: "Yeah," and smiled.

Thirteen

Despite my prediction, our first week at Helios U passed with a distinct lack of drama, let alone scorn. There was gossip, of course, but primarily in the form of a recap of alumni belonging to the extended Laurent-Beaulieu clan, accompanied by photographs of various L-Bs in lecture theatres, or walking down the wide, busy paths by the river, or frowning over books in the library. Somehow, I was never in any of these shots, although I did catch a glimpse of my skirt in one of them.

In part, my being overlooked was due to the settling-in period, with the whole of the freshman year fumbling their way into lectures, tutorials and labs. And because most of the first two years involved courses that crossed dozens of degrees, they were mainly held in the largest auditoriums. Without arriving together and early, Bran and I couldn't even find each other, let alone sit together in the handful of subjects we shared. But even when I literally sat between Rin and Kyou for our C++ course, I somehow managed to not make the gossip radar.

The thing that truly amazed me, though, was that no-one seemed to have noticed Rin and Kyou's enrollment switch.

"Carr thinks I've crammed in a couple of elective subjects," Kyou said on Friday night, as we were drying ourselves in the wake of an enthusiastic four-way shower. "He's sat with me in lectures, and is pleased I 'haven't given up on art altogether'. Because I haven't encountered anyone I know in the much smaller practical classes, it's not entirely obvious that I'm full-timing Fine Arts."

"I've spent almost all my time one-on-one with tutors," Rin said. "And skipped a few lectures because I wanted to work on some of the pointers they gave me. It's been so long since I've had real feedback on anything except violin."

"You being all giddy is fun to watch," I murmured.

He clicked his tongue as Rin and Bran laughed, then pinched me lightly and said: "I'd deny it, but I really have been close to giddy on occasion. Light-headed all over my body, like I've taken off a cast. I was even given a lead today on a potential for the voice I need for *One Step*: a post-graduate student I'll meet up with next week."

"Finally," Bran said. "Can we firm up for a February release then?"

"Wait until after she auditions." Rin took my hairdryer into the bedroom and plugged it in, and I sat obediently on the bed and let him start our small post-shower ritual. He and Bran both liked to play with my hair, which worked well for me, since hair maintenance is boring.

Kyou settled on the couch to continue working on a sketch of Rin doing my hair. Sketches seemed to fall into a grey area for him: he didn't like people to look at them while he was working on them, but had happily shown me the contents of 'my' sketchbook, full of memories of a year playing games in a garden. He'd added a few more pages since then, and no longer framed them so our faces weren't visible. When not being worked on, the sketchbook was kept under greater security than any other item in the building.

"What time tomorrow morning?" Bran asked, setting an alarm on his phone.

"Five-thirty?" Kyou suggested, over the roar of the hairdryer.

"Still not interested, Mika?" Rin asked, separating my hair for easier drying.

"Canoeing trip, yes, but I'll take yoga over early morning rowing. What time do you want to go to the movies?"

"Let's do dinner at one of the lake view restaurants, and then an evening session at North Street Theatre," Kyou said. "Make it an official romantic date."

We talked over the options, and settled on a science fiction prison escape called *Borders of Infinity*.

"Want to try out the tennis situation on Sunday?" Rin asked. "Do you need a racket, Mika?"

"I'm fully outfitted," I said, turning my head to smile at him.

He went still, then said: "I'll book two courts, and we can start off with singles, then switch to a doubles game."

"I'll—" Bran began, but stopped when *Mr Roboto* began to play. He leaned over to snag my phone and then handed it to me.

"Hey Lania," I said.

"*Sorry to call so late, Mika,*" Lania said, sounding like she was somewhere with traffic.

"No problem. What's up?"

"*I did a long session in the Chem lab, and forgot there's night maintenance on the Second South Line. There's a massive backlog on rideshare, and the replacement buses are on the south side and—this is*

*going to sound silly, but can you stay on the line with me
while I cross campus? I had this weird feeling the whole
time I was walking to the tram, and I'd just feel more
comfortable with some virtual company."*

"Wait, are you still at the tram stop?" I asked,
standing up. "Stay there, I'll—"

"I'll go get her," Bran said, who had clearly made out
enough to understand the situation. "Find out the
stop."

"Which stop are you at? My housemate'll go pick
you up. We're only a couple minutes away by bike."

"*Oh, Mika, there's no need—*"

"Every need," I said firmly, as Bran strode out of the
room. "Besides, it's about time you came over to visit.
I've been itching to show off my fabulous bedroom."

Rin and Kyou were removing any signs of shared
habitation, and departed with a wave. I headed into my
dressing room and put the phone on speaker while I put
on a night shirt, dressing gown, and my bunny slippers.
I came out to catch Bran going down the stairs, and told
him "Wicker Street Stop."

"*I hate to do this,*" Lania was saying. "*I didn't want
to worry my parents, but shifting it to you isn't kind, I
know.*"

"I'm less likely to lecture you," I said, heading down
to the kitchen. "Keep an eye out for a Harley rider
wearing a dark green helmet. He's just heading to the
garage."

Even though it was only the beginning of autumn,
Helios nights were already relatively cool, and I figured
Lania wouldn't dislike a hot drink. I put water on to
boil, then asked if she wanted cocoa.

"*What? Maybe, I'm—*" A second voice was partially audible over the rush of traffic, and Lania broke off for a moment, then said: "*Thanks, no, a friend is going to pick me up.*"

More talking, the person's voice low, the tone pleasant.

"*Yeah, it's okay, thank you anyway,*" Lania said. More words, then she added: "*Oh, science.*"

Rin and Kyou had come down to the kitchen, and grimaced listening to Lania's reluctant responses to a series of questions, and then her clear relief as she said: "*My ride's here! Got to go! Bye!*" and added to the phone: "*I'll see you in a minute, Mika.*"

The call ended and I sighed. "I'm glad we live close."

"Campus Security is supposedly competent, but it was a good decision to call you," Kyou said. "That persistent type can turn nasty."

"If you need to walk back late at night, call us," Rin said. "There's too many free-range creeps out there."

I nodded. "The paths are well lit, but I noticed a couple of places where someone could pull you out of sight really easy. I didn't take any night lectures, but labs are a different matter. I'll keep 'tellan updated when experiments look likely to run into the night."

"We'll make the drinks," Kyou said. "I'm in the mood for energy recovery."

Smiling, I left them to it, heading over to the garage. Bran took a little longer returning than it had taken to reach Lania, but it wasn't more than a couple of minutes before the garage door opened and he eased the Harley in. Lania, wearing my helmet to finish off a jeans and t-shirt ensemble, hopped a little awkwardly off the back of the bike, pulled off her helmet and looked at me with clear relief. She turned back to Bran as he dismounted, but then her face changed, and she actually took a step back.

"That—"

"What?" I asked, a little confused.

"Is that Rin's Hummer?"

Bran pulled his helmet off, which was probably answer enough. Lania gaped at him, and I had to laugh, then took the helmet she was holding and hung it back on its hook.

"Yeah, one of my landlords. Come on—did you want that cocoa?"

This was probably too much to land on Lania after her encounter with a creeper. She looked quite pale, so I took her hand and led her upstairs.

She stopped short when she saw Rin and Kyou in the kitchen, then protested: "You said you were renting from that game company."

"I am. They're the CEOs."

"You said the CEOs were massive geeks!"

Kyou and Rin dissolved into laughter at that. "Well, I suppose that's true," Kyou said. "Have a drink, Lania. You look like you need the sugar."

Taking pity on her, I sat her down and explained: "I did Kyou a favour, so he's renting me a room as thanks. Plus, Dad really is doing script work for them."

"I'd rent you a room just for the introduction to your father," Bran said. "He sent through rewritten dialogue for one of the companion quests yesterday, and somehow turned our least interesting character into a stand-out who'll probably end up as the fan favourite."

"I can imagine Sean's fanart already," Kyou said.

Lania had started to recover a little, looked at each of us in turn, and then said: "One of these days I'm going to strangle you, Mika."

"Probably," I agreed. "I haven't even begun to hit you with fun things I failed to mention."

"She does that to us as well," Rin said. "I'm fully expecting to find out she's transmigrated from another world, or something similarly preposterous."

"That Time I Was Reincarnated as a Civil Engineer?" I suggested.

"Are you *really* going into game development?" Lania asked them.

"Is it that hard to believe?" Kyou asked. "It's not like we've ever run around disparaging gaming. Or hidden that we play."

"I always thought you'd all end up in suits running L-B Corp."

"Game development is far more interesting," Kyou said. "I'm art lead, Rin is music, and Bran's programming."

"Is this a secret?"

"Not anymore," Rin said.

"It was, for the sake of avoiding family arguments," Kyou explained. "It won't be once our increasing employee base chat a little more, or someone notices what courses we're actually enrolled in."

"I—I applied for a *job*," Lania said, sounding mortified.

"Yeah, so did Anika," Bran said. "Our programming lead passed you through the first cull, though all that gets you is a place on a list, since we're not taking interns yet. Probably in the new year."

"Most recruitment won't directly involve us," Kyou added, reassuringly. "Nor, given the skills shortage in the game development world, are we going to rule out people because we went to school with them. Our traineeship program isn't in place yet, but once it is, we'll be doing small intakes multiple times each year, because it's very much in our interest to develop local talent rather than try to convince people to move to Greenland. We don't want the majority of the team to be remote-only."

Lania shook her head, took a sip of her cocoa, then pulled herself together to say: "Well, I hope I pass the recruitment, then, because it sounds like an incredible place to work."

"On that note, I simply have to show you my room," I said. "And, if you don't have anything early tomorrow, why not stay the night? My bed's enormous, or there's a couple of guest rooms."

This produced a very doubtful look at three boys known for their standoffishness. Rin, faintly amused, lifted one shoulder. "It's Mika's room. Though, speaking of early starts, I seem to recall a five-thirty alarm, so I'll say my goodnights."

Bran and Kyou followed suit, leaving me with Lania, who was free to turn fulminating eyes on me. "Mika..."

"You took it well," I said, smiling. "I'm impressed."

"Impressed!" she exploded, in a high whisper. "You're living with the Three Kings! The *Three Kings*! What the hell kind of favour did you do for them?"

"The official story's going to be that I helped Kyou make a huge land deal, which is true enough. The actual favour was more an off-hand comment that inspired Kyou out of a trap of his father's, and let him save the funding for Kybirn. We're not spreading that outside the closest of friends, in case of retaliation."

Lania shook her head, stared around the kitchen, back at me, then sighed and took a deep gulp of cocoa. "I suppose I should have expected something like this from you. Do you have anything else to spring on me?"

"Sure, but it's no fun to do it all at once. Did bonus kings at least thoroughly distract you from being unnerved tonight? Do you think you were followed from your lab, or was that guy just someone who happened to be at the tram stop?"

"I don't know. I hate that I feel like I was overreacting. It's not like there was nobody else around when I left the lab. Though I ended up super glad I'd called, since I was running out of ideas to get rid of that guy offering me a lift."

"So, you going to stay the night?"

"I absolutely cannot resist staying the night."

"Fair warning—they're going to go off rowing tomorrow morning, so you won't get to ogle them at breakfast."

"Shame."

Lania called her mother, and then I took her up to my room and watched her gape at the bed.

"Even the guest beds are oversized," I said. "Though mine's the tallest. I'm desperately in love with the study nook.

Sending Lania in to have a shower, I dug out a pair of sweatpants, then contemplated the rest of my wardrobe. Lania was petite, but had all the chest I didn't, so I went and knocked on Rin's door.

"Borrow a shirt?" I asked. "I don't think I've got anything that'd be comfortable for Lania."

Rin, who had been tidying his desk, paused to give me a long, cool look.

"Is that really the thought you want me to sleep on?" he asked.

I considered it, then said: "Borrow two shirts?"

He narrowed his eyes, then walked into his dressing room, made a selection, and returned. I took them, stripped, and then donned the more time-worn of his offerings. It swam on me, and I let it slip so one shoulder was exposed, then checked out his intent response.

"Going to tell her everything?" he asked, hooking a hand around my waist.

"While I doubt I'll ever tell anyone about the challenges, I think it's only fair I tell Lania I have an, um, boyfriends."

"An um boyfriends?" He pulled me closer, but then let go. "Be prepared to be chased around the house tomorrow."

I smiled and stretched up to kiss his cheek, then went back in time to hand over Lania's makeshift pyjamas, and offered up the hairdryer in exchange for her clothes, which I took down to the laundry.

"The washer is one of those ones that dries," I said, on my return. "So, they'll be all ready for you tomorrow. "Do you prefer the left or right side for sleeping?"

Lania had tugged the chest of her new nightwear out, frowning at the size.

"It's Rin's," I said. "He gave me this too."

She stared while I posed, then sighed: "Are you going to subvert all my views today? I've always felt Rin was a completely remote person. Impeccably polite on the surface, but not at all caring."

"He seems to save his caring for a select few," I said. "Really, most of him is so consumed by music that I don't know how much he has to spare for acquaintances." I opted for the right side of the bed, and rearranged pillows. "That's the main reason for the secrecy: Rin's parents are firmly opposed to music as anything but a hobby. A career writing game scores will no doubt seem nonsensical to them when the controlling interest of L-B Corp is at stake."

It's not like me to chicken out of a decision, but after we settled in bed, I spent quite a while telling Lania about the origin and future development of Kybirn, and none at all mentioning naked fun times with unofficial royalty. While Lania was shy, not prudish, it's entirely possible that three might be two Kings too far for her.

On the whole, it was nice to think that Lania's opinion of me had come to matter that much.

Fourteen

"This is a hell of a house," Lania said, after I'd taken her on a pre-breakfast tour and finally settled on the rooftop with juice and yoghurt. "Gorgeous Art Deco touches."

"I know. Dad and I just gaped the whole time we were first going over it. Plus, he fell in love with that staircase and is researching the building for a new book."

"I'd envy you, but I'm not sure I could afford the price you're going to pay," Lania said, with a solemn glance at me. "Just because you're only renting a room doesn't mean your back won't be full of knives. There are people who would give anything to spend an afternoon with the Kings, let alone live with them."

"Yeah." I sipped my juice, grimaced, and said: "Not to mention if someone figures out we're playing purloined letter."

"Letter? What do you mean?"

"Trying to hide something by putting it out in the open. It helps that I really am renting the room, and I really did say things Kyou found useful. But I doubt I would have moved in with them so quickly if we weren't trying to keep quiet that we're dating."

Lania, with a raised spoonful of fruit and yoghurt, looked at me over it, glanced down, ate the yoghurt, and then propped her chin on her fist and considered me. "I'd guess Rin because of the shirt, but I would have thought you and Kyou had more in common. Or...wait. Are you Bran's mysterious girlfriend?"

"Yes, yes, and yes," I said, laughing. "I thought you'd be more surprised."

"After finding you're living with them, nothing's going to surprise me. And it seems kind of inevitable that you'd end up dating...which one does yes, yes, and yes mean?"

"All three. We're having a ménage. Or is that not quite the right word? Poly-something."

That broke her. She drew in such a sharp breath that she started coughing, and knocked her juice into her yoghurt bowl. I barely caught the glass before it rolled off the table, patted Lania's back for a moment, then went into the conservatory to get a sponge and towel from the kitchenette. By the time the table had been restored, Lania had washed her face at the sink and recovered enough composure to simply fold her arms and say: "Talk."

I raised my hands in mock-surrender. "On the first day of school last year I was looking for a place to have lunch. I climbed a tree, and found this cool walled garden with a summerhouse in it. And three very good-looking boys, who were having a debate over which of them was the best kisser because they'd overheard the views of a girl who'd kissed all three. One of the boys spotted me, and I agreed to consider giving them a neutral, outsider's opinion. After that, they let me have lunch in the garden sometimes, one thing led to another, and we ended up doing an extended friends-with-benefits thing because none of us planned to date that year." I wrinkled my nose. "The idea was it would all end when we graduated, but we got way more invested than any of us expected. Being their girlfriend is a huge risk for me, and so we're going to lie through our teeth for as long as we can get away with it. But I wanted to tell you."

She still didn't speak, and I tried to decipher her expression.

"Mika..." she began at last. "Are you're sure they're sincere? It's not just some sort of elaborate game?"

"Game?" Given my history of games with the Kings, it took a moment for me to put the question in the context Lania must be seeing it. "You mean, mega-rich playboys keep commoner as a pet? Inevitably to end up in the doghouse?"

"Kind of," Lania said, embarrassedly, and her already-pink skin flushed complete scarlet as she added: "Are—are they gay? Bi? Using you as a shield?"

"We'd need to be way more public before I was an effective shield. I don't know about gay or bi. Admittedly Bran lights up the radar of every hopeful young man in the vicinity, but he never seems to try to. And Rin, Kyou and Bran don't seem interested in each other. They are cousins after all. Only second cousins, but closer than most brothers."

Lania shook her head, frowned, then smiled a little. "No wonder that bed's so big. Did I—did I displace them?"

"Yeah, actually."

"Will they be annoyed?"

"I doubt it. They knew you'd been spooked. Besides, we have this complicated rotation of sleeping arrangements, so we're not always in the same bed."

"Huh." Lania stared out at the treetops. "Three Kings and a Queen? Hidden Queen. I don't know, Mika. Is there any future in this? A relationship you have to keep secret? Even telling your families would be a bad idea. You'd never be able to get married, always have people questioning you or treating you as a hanger-on..."

"I think I'll see if we can manage to live together for more than a couple of months before worrying about proclaiming myself Queen or whatever," I said, holding my hands up in protest. "Baby steps, no need to rush. The four of us haven't even gone on an official date yet."

"Well...so long as you're enjoying yourself, I guess," Lania said, doubtfully, then shook her head. "Mika, I know it must be incredible, but do you really think it's worth the risk?"

"I wouldn't be here if feelings weren't overriding common sense," I said, quietly relieved that Lania's reaction primarily involved concern. "Okay, enough worrying. If you want to visit *Pain Au Lait* and still get home by nine, we'd better go line up. The ride home will give you time to digest."

She snorted. "Yeah, you've given me a lot to chew over. I'm glad it's the weekend, so I can decide how to face Sean and Anika. And I'm glad you stuck with the rental story last night, because I mightn't have been able to sleep just...imagining."

That kept me chuckling all through the short walk and the wait to buy some of the beautiful sourdough on offer, along with a heaping of pastries, since I knew a few people who'd be hungry and back soon.

"The living arrangements aren't supposed to be secret, right?" Lania asked, as we paused before parting.

"No. I was truly expecting it to be open gossip by now, since I've been wandering around with Bran half the week, and meeting up with Kyou and Rin the rest of the time."

"Okay. I think I'll message Sean and tell him I have the best goss for him on Monday, and arrange to meet up with you and him for lunch, because I know the first thing he'll want to do is find you."

"Sure. I'll meet you at those library tables around twelve?"

"Works for me." Lania paused. "So, which of them?"

"Hm?"

"Is the best kisser?"

I laughed. "Bran. But they all have their highlight talents."

Walking back down to the house, I found an extended Rolls at the entrance. There's only parking on the opposite side of our street, so the Rolls thoroughly blocked the way, though fortunately there was no traffic at the moment. Wondering if this was the beginning of the inevitable confrontation with Rin's parents, I studied the tall, slender man who got out of the front passenger seat. Expensively dressed, wire-rimmed glasses, and not much like Rin, but it could be the stepfather.

Since it was the weekend, the ground reception room was closed, and so the visitor had a choice of two buttons on the intercom, one for "Kybirn" and the other for "Residence". A moment later, my phone sounded with the alert that signalled "Residence Doorbell".

I was still on the opposite corner, but the man heard the alert and turned, so I crossed the road, smiled lightly over the collection of paper bags I was cradling, and said: "Who are you looking for?"

"You are?" he asked, not quite looking down his nose at me, but clearly considering it.

"A resident," I said blandly. I used my phone to trigger the door and walked inside, pausing just beyond the entrance. "So, who are you looking for?"

His attitude became a little more polite, as if he'd decided I wasn't simply being nosy. "I am Dahat Kaftar, Mr Laurent-Beaulieu's secretary. Mr Laurent-Beaulieu wishes to speak to Mr Laurent, Mr Westhaven and Mr Ashten."

Great-Grandfather in person? I glanced at the car, but the windows were too tinted to see the occupant in the rear seat.

"They went rowing at dawn," I said. "They expected to be back in around a quarter of an hour, but could be longer. Would you like to come in and wait?"

"I'll see." He turned and bent to the window of the car, which cracked just enough for him to murmur the details, and then opened the door.

Arinn Laurent-Beaulieu wasn't on the same tier as a Bill Gates or a Jeff Bezos, but he was one of Greenland's wealthiest, so I'd seen some photos in the news. He did vaguely resemble Rin, but in a more leonine cast, without Rin's feminine ambiguities. Although he must be in his eighties, he didn't seem to have significant mobility issues, standing with ease, and walking at a steady pace with the assistance of a cane. I led them past the elevator into a room I'd only glanced into: a small and formal receiving room in the north-west corner.

"I'll send them a message that you're waiting," I said. "But I don't know that they'd see it while rowing. Would you like something to drink or eat?"

"*Who is this girl?*" Mr Laurent-Beaulieu said in French to his secretary.

"*I'm Mikaela Niles,*" I replied evenly, in the same language. "*I went to high school with Rin, Kyou and Bran, and rent a room from them.*"

The old man looked at me for a moment, then turned his head away.

"Thank you, Miss Niles," Mr Kaftar said, smoothly. "If you would show me the kitchen, perhaps we could put together a small morning tea?"

"Sure," I said, and nodded farewell at Mr Laurent-Beaulieu, but didn't say 'nice to meet you', since he seemed to consider me irrelevant. I took Mr Kaftar off to the kitchen and let him select from Rin and Kyou's collection of tea and tea sets, but decided to make myself another coffee, and—when I received a text from Kyou—put one together for Bran, who was not a fan of tea.

"Five minutes away," I told Mr Kaftar, who nodded gracefully, and made polite conversation until the three absentees arrived, thankfully ahead of schedule.

Kyou looked in at us in the kitchen and said: "We'll just go clean up, Dahat, and come straight back down."

"Thank you, Mr Westhaven."

I helped Mr Kaftar bring in the morning tea, then collected my coffee and pastry and went upstairs. Bran met me on the landing.

"Does your great-grandfather always show up without bothering to check ahead first?" I asked.

"Showing up at all is a new one," Bran said. "Must be bigger than Rin playing his own fiddle. Stay quiet on the line, and you can listen in."

He rang me, then stuck his phone in his front pocket and went downstairs. I wrestled briefly with my conscience, successfully tossed it out the window, and settled in my study for Danish, cappuccino, and eavesdropping.

Very formal greetings. Even Bran was courteous, his French slightly less fluid than Rin and Kyou's.

"*Three companies registered under your names*," Mr Laurent-Beaulieu said. "*Not, I presume, simply to practice your hands.*"

"*No.*" Rin was very firm. "*This is our future.*"

"*Music? Well, perhaps that is enough to satisfy you. But you.*" There was a pause, and I could only guess he was giving either Kyou or Bran a long stare. "*You are currently my named heir. Is that something you are ready to walk away from?*"

This confused me, since I thought the whole thing with the Laurent-Beaulieu clan was that everyone was in competition to be named heir. Had there been developments I'd missed?

Kyou, after only a moment's pause, said: "*I'd infinitely prefer to build my own empire than inherit someone else's.*"

Arinn Laurent-Beaulieu made a noise that was two parts disgust, one part resignation: a kind of muted t-chah, but then said: "*Very well. Since you are walking this path, I expect you to do it well.*"

There was a pause in talking then, and some indistinct noises followed that I eventually realized were sounds of departure. Perplexed, I took my snack downstairs in time to see Rin and Bran coming back into the main hall.

"Scarcely enough time for half a Danish," I commented.

"Great-Grandfather's never one to waste words," Rin said. "Though, speaking of Danishes..." He headed back into the receiving room, picked up one of the pieces I'd cut, and swallowed it neatly. "Let's take this back into the kitchen and—did you get the bread?"

"Yep. Smells fantastic." I didn't immediately move, instead putting down my coffee cup so I could touch Bran's hand. "Did it just seem that way because I couldn't see you, or did he ignore you completely?"

Bran snorted. "He hasn't said a word to me in years. I've long been established as waste material."

"Mainly because you started to refuse to jump through hoops well before we dared to," Kyou said, returning. "Great-Grandfather took rebellion better than I expected. But I suspect he has ulterior motives."

"At what point were you named heir?" Rin asked, picking up the tea tray and heading back to the kitchen.

"It's news to me," Kyou said, grabbing the tray of pastries and following. "Must be in his will. I expect he'll change it now, and stir up a storm."

"What hidden motives?" Bran asked.

Kyou smiled as he slid onto the curving seat of the breakfast nook. "Before he got into the car, Great-Grandfather said to send him a proposal if I wanted to cooperate with L-B Corp. Which, given that L-B Corp doesn't have any direct involvement in either games or music, makes me suspect that the reason we had this visitation is that the location of the high-speed rail station is about to come out."

"Finally!" Bran said. "Near Noonerry then?"

Kyou shrugged. "Anywhere on the eastern half of the tableland would make our properties interesting to great-grandfather. Let me try a couple of calls and see if I can get an early look at the announcement."

"Did you tell Lania?" Rin asked, as Kyou skimmed through his address book. "Was she scandalised?"

"One part shocked, two parts worried you're taking advantage of me," I said. "I'd bask in my ability to pick friends, but really, it's all the luck of close surnames putting us at the same desk. How was rowing?"

"Good," Bran said. "River's wide and smooth, and we only encountered real traffic on the way back. We're going to head out semi-regularly before autumn gets cold."

We quieted down during Kyou's amiable conversations with what appeared to be senior staff at L-B Corp.

"There's definitely something going the rounds," he said, putting down his phone. "They'll try to get their hands on it and send me a copy."

"How many of your sources will stop doing you favours once we're officially out of the running?" Rin asked.

"The slower ones. The more sensible will see me as a viable alternate employer."

"Do you regret giving up on the prize, now you know you'd won it?" Bran asked.

"There's a vast difference between a controlling interest, and being in control." Kyou smiled at me then. "Not that I wouldn't have had fun with that much money. With L-B Corp, I could keep you in bridges indefinitely, Mika."

"If I have my way, I'll become the person people come to, cap in hand, pleading for me to design their bridges. Then I'll pick the interesting ones to do." I sighed at the idea. "A long way off, yet. Still the degree, the certification, and reputation-building stages to go."

Rin leaned against the back of the banquette, giving me a curling smile. "I'd call you ambitious, but that's how I'd picture my career as a composer if we weren't self-funding the things I want to write."

"You'll no doubt still get petitioners," I said. "As some of your employees have already pointed out, you represent amazing promotional opportunities."

Kyou laughed. "If we run desperately short of budget, Rin can be the sacrificial spokesperson. Vain a wish as it might be, we're otherwise planning to keep our faces out of Kybirn branding."

"Even for *One Step*?" I asked, surprised. Given it was apparently deeply personal to him, I'd expected Rin to at least do interviews.

"I want *One Step*, as much as possible, to speak on its own," Rin said. "Our marketing will focus on the gameplay rather than the story." He contemplated the tea cup he held. "If the voice audition goes well, I'll soon be able to watch people play it through."

"Music's one of my weaker areas," I said. "Will you be forgiving if I stumble at composition?"

"So long as you don't start cracking jokes at inappropriate moments," Rin said, putting down his cup and curling his arm around my waist. But then he sighed and let go: "I'd do things to you to demonstrate that I'm serious about that, but I have a backlog of homework, so I'm going to go immerse myself for a couple of hours."

"I'm supposed to paint six versions of the same apple," Kyou said, swallowing the last of his tea. "I suppose I should polish that off before the thing rots. How's your homework situation, Mika? You said your courseload would be relatively heavy this term."

"Lots of exercises, but I usually get those out of the way between classes. I do have one major assignment that involves a small mountain of reading."

"Let's have a light lunch on the rooftop around one," Kyou said. "Eat the rest of that watermelon that's been taking up half the refrigerator, and save our stomachs for tonight's dinner."

I borrowed Bran's window seat to do my reading: an excellently designed space that allowed me to watch the street—and Bran—between chapters, and we worked in quiet peace: something we should cherish. Arinn Laurent-Beaulieu's visit meant more family were sure to follow, with whatever pressure they could bring to bear. Even though Rin, Kyou and Bran had carefully planned their freedom, that didn't mean they'd enjoy the next few weeks.

At one, I took my study material back to my room, then knocked on Kyou's door. "Do I get to look at the apples?" I asked, poking my head inside.

"If you find it interesting," he said, busy cleaning brushes.

Rather than multiple canvases, he had divided a single stretcher into six sections with tape, and had made progress on two studies. First a piece that reduced the apple to sections of dominant colour, and then one that was entirely tiny horizontal lines, as if the apple had been through a shredder.

"Is it worthwhile?" I asked, wondering if I, even with my years of practice drawing buildings, could manage something so precise.

"The challenge is. The teacher who assigned it...I won't say plays favourites, but has particular biases. My preference for figurative work has already failed to impress—he's more an Art-as-ideas type. Still, the exercises he gives will be useful for me, and the other two senior tutors have already helped me see a weakness I'd overlooked. I'm definitely not regretting signing up, anyway."

We headed to the roof. Kyou checked his phone, then grabbed the laptop that lived in the conservatory, and I reflected, not for the first time, on the luxury of having a selection of devices scattered around the house so you didn't have to carry them about. Bran and Rin emerged with the lunch, and set it down on the café table.

"My sources came through," Kyou said. "The new station's going to be announced first thing Monday morning."

He looked down at his computer, and then one corner of his mouth ticked up. We, of course, crowded around him. I blinked, then shook my head. The proposed rail line ran along Fox Farm's main boundary, and crossed its boot shape at the ankle.

Bran snorted. "No wonder Great-Grandfather's interested. You've the devil's own luck, Kyou."

"Disgusting," Rin murmured, happily. "So, where do you want to put my concert hall?"

"Let's eat, then we can work out some positioning on a bigger screen," Kyou said. "Then call tonight a celebration for the easiest money we've ever made."

"Are there any projections on when the line's likely to be open?" Rin asked.

Kyou flipped through text. "Two years."

"Optimistic," I commented, then fished out my phone and texted my dad: *A week turned out to be a long time in the property valuation world. Brace yourself for Bridezilla Park.*

"In an ideal world, we'd time opening the main office to just after the opening of the HSR line," Kyou said. "But a lot is going to depend on planning permission. Noonerry Local Council only has limited approval powers, and there will no doubt be upheaval in local politics."

"Cassadine Malway has submitted an application for the farmhouse already," I said.

"You went with Cassadine Malway?" Rin asked, frowning faintly.

"Dad's thinking of writing a story based on their complete renovation service. And I liked Adriana, though hope she won't be tempted to gift-wrap anything in the future. Even though the close inspection turned up some largish issues, they wasted no time converting the design ideas into a full plan and getting it in. Of course, we aren't trying to subdivide or rezone or even significantly change the footprint of the building. You're looking at a completely different challenge."

We ate quickly, and headed to the office, greeting the handful of staff who'd come in for the limited weekend opening hours Kybirn allowed for people wanting to use flexitime. I grabbed the drawing tablet from my desk, and connected it to the pc in the small conference room.

"We can use my wind map as a starting point," I said, bringing up the diagram of Noonerry and environs, with a layer of numbers that indicated all the anemometers I'd set out on Kyou's various properties.

Taking the stylus, I quickly added the details from the purloined announcement. Twin tracks just west of the north-south boundary road, crossing the property's boot shape at its ankle. Ultra-long platforms, starting just south of the farm gate and stretching nearly halfway to the lip of the tableland. A pedestrian bridge along with a block of structures backing each platform: a combination of station buildings and 'retail'. The rest of the reserve that separated the farm from the town was hatched off with a "To be advised" written on it.

"It shows how quickly this has been done, that they haven't settled this already," Kyou said, indicating the hatched area. "A development opportunity that'll be going up for tender soonest, I expect."

"There'll have to be some form of public car park here," I said, gauging the size of the hatched area. "Unless they strictly limit car access and rely on buses, which is worth thinking about since they'll have much of the increasing population of the entire tableland travelling to this end of it."

"Will our headquarters be west or east of the train line?" Bran asked.

"West," Kyou said. "The grounds will start at the edge of the area they've marked for compulsory acquisition, but the building doesn't need to be set up against it. I want something widely-spaced with a lot of trees and places to get out of the office, Mika."

I estimated generously, sectioning off about a third of the 'leg', and drawing a circle in the centre marked 'Kybirn'. "A gloriously short walk from the station," I said. "Through a bunch of shops, then some park-like grounds. I'd recommend a covered walkway. What about the remaining chunk to the west?"

"Residential, for expensive holiday letting, but also an area we can rent control in the long term if it becomes an issue for staff. I was even thinking of having a dormitory-style building, for those inevitable occasions when the whole rail system shuts down and we have hundreds of staff members stranded. There'll need to be a crèche, too, in the company grounds."

Noting these requirements in their relevant areas, I turned my attention to the main area of Fox Farm/Fox Hollow, and drew my parents an access driveway extending from the existing road.

"This could have been complicated by the location of the rail crossing, but they've kindly put everything west of this north-south road. You'll also need an access road to your house that doesn't cut through your wedding resort. How much of this big hill do you want to section off?"

"All of it," Bran said, firmly.

"Most of it," Kyou said. "I was thinking of a row of low-key residences along the northern base. Part of the resort, giving an option for those who want a more home-like accommodation, and forming a border to prevent the majority of visitors from approaching our property."

"Hm."

I drew lines, putting in place an access road that would run behind this border, and service both the main house and the area I marked as 'holiday lets'. I roughly blocked in the location of the house on the crest of the hill, and marvelled at the amount of space they'd have. A considerable estate that they'd be able to keep as grass or cover with trees.

Then I turned my attention to the three remaining hills, which formed a kind of instep for the 'platform boot' shape of the original farm. "How big a hotel are you thinking? Do you want something grand and imposing that's visible for miles around, like the Fairmont in Banff? Or maybe a series of smaller buildings?"

"I don't want an eyesore of a hotel dominating the view," Rin said.

"Just your concert hall," Bran said.

"We haven't established where it's going to be, yet," Rin said. "Perhaps on the nearest of these hills?"

"I mainly want something that's an attraction in itself," Kyou said. Larger rooms, perhaps a thousand beds. If you can do that without it being an eyesore..."

"Since one of the selling points will be the view to the mountains, the most logical place to build is the eastern slopes anyway," I pointed out. "Not something primarily facing into Fox Hollow. You'll also need to include space for wedding halls and function rooms, and some way to accommodate the bigger weddings when the grounds get rained out."

I switched to a photograph I'd taken of the hills. Fox Farm on the left stood quite separate. The hill slated for the Kings' private house, on the right, had gentle slopes that partially disguised its height, and also put its crest at a distance. The three peaks between them were more distinctly cone-shaped, clustered together at the farm's mid-point, like three hats placed in a row. I called up a blank canvas and sketched their shapes as they'd be viewed from the east, then added rising columns, connected together by a smooth line at the top, and then some curves underneath.

"Any excuse for a bridge, Mika?" Kyou asked.

"Well..." I said, pursing my mouth, then grinning. "You have to admit there's few man-made structures more beautiful than the arches of old-time railway viaducts. Joining up all three hills is probably a bit excessive, but would be truly spectacular, and you could functionally have multiple hotels—one for each hilltop—with handy walkways between. Maybe with a clear retractable rooftop awning for the wet days. And a few infinity pools and whatnot. As for the concert hall, I think maybe on the hill closest to Fox Farm. There's a nice hollow in the western face that could be turned into a natural amphitheatre for outdoor performances."

We moved on to smaller buildings, discussed parking, restaurants, a row of galleries and shops along the fence line, places for brides having garden weddings to get ready, a new bridge across the river, and the Sakura walk Kyou wanted along the banks. It was a lot of fun, like drawing one of my fantasy cities, except with the possibility that some of it might happen.

"What do you want in this gap between your hill and the HSR line?" I asked, pointing to a largish empty space. "More residences?"

"Not sure," Kyou said. "While more accommodation equals more income, I don't want to cram in housing at the expense of having interesting attractions. Any suggestions?"

"Winery?" Bran suggested.

"It's not really a grape-growing region," Kyou said. "Could do a brewery? Not that I think there's any local hops. Maybe cider?"

"Are you talking an outlet or a full-on distillery?" I asked, raising an eyebrow, and we paused to do a few Google searches on the practicality of the idea.

"Let's create an artists' retreat," Rin said suddenly. "You need something to put in those galleries. Partially charged through the nose, but we can sponsor suitably talented artists, give them inspirational living quarters and studios, provide the expensive facilities for things like wood and metalwork. Have a forge." His long eyelashes drooped, then he added: "A couple of kilns."

Kyou laughed, then said: "Fairly sure Sirocco can afford her own kilns, but sure, an artists' retreat makes an attraction of its own. And now that we've got a rough idea of where the buildings are, I can look at getting early planting done for all the trees I want to put in."

I shook my head. "No, infrastructure first, then trees. Get the main arteries of your pipes and power and so forth in place, even if you're not going to build half of this for years, so you won't have to uproot all your blazes and maples when its time. Make sure the drainage is properly managed, put in your major paths, and then add your trees. You should also think about how you're going to get sudden influxes of pedestrians from the train station to your hotel. Maybe a ring road with light rail?" I drew one in, running around the base of the hills, then amused myself by adding a diverging line that ran along the top of my fantasy viaduct. Then I added a location for light rail support. "What about this land east of town? Now you know you don't need it for headquarters. And the parcels in the other town."

"Leave it a year or three, until we see the direction of the town's overall development," Kyou said. "If we suddenly need money, it'll be handy. Or perhaps I'll wave it at Great-Grandfather as a potential cooperative project. Headquarters first, along with the west-of-train residential projects, since we can quickly convert them to ongoing income. Mika, if we give you a list of internal requirements, can you give us a few building concepts to take to the architects? As I said, I don't want something run-of-the-mill. I want enough mandatory selfie backdrops to fill half of Instagram."

"You give me all the fun assignments," I said, happily. "Uh, come get me about half an hour before we're supposed to go out so I can get ready."

I spent a very enjoyable afternoon, then allowed Rin to play dress-up with me, ate at a beautiful lake-side restaurant, and even managed to focus on the movie, despite all the design concepts filling my head. Best to fully appreciate the calm before the storm.

Fifteen

Sunday started with snuggling with Bran, and then my first tennis lesson. Rin, Kyou and Bran restrained their competitive impulses enough to teach me well, though it quickly became apparent that I was awarded to Rin as a handicap in our doubles match, to balance his height and arm reach.

The small audience we collected wasn't surprising, since three Kings in tennis whites were eye-catching even among people who didn't know them. Only one particularly brave girl tried to strike up a conversation, the rest restraining themselves to applauding impressive volleys, and taking photos. No more sliding under the radar for me.

"Going to spend the rest of the day playing with building concepts?" Kyou asked, as we walked back.

"Definitely. Though a budget guideline would be helpful, or I'll keep coming up with things that are as stupid-expensive as that viaduct hotel."

He chuckled. "Go wild. Add some very rough costings, and we can review them and pick out concepts we like, and work out what seems worthwhile to spend."

"I liked the viaduct," Rin said. "Would it really be that expensive?"

"Well, not cheap."

"Would it be built in the same way as traditional viaducts?" Bran asked. "Brickwork?"

"A fusion of modern and traditional, I would think. Let's not talk about it, or I'll spend all my thoughts on how to make it possible, and even if you somehow found enough money, it's not what you want to build right now. I'll be ready around dinnertime to show you fun ideas for your headquarters."

"That's definitely priority number one," Kyou agreed. "Given how tortuous I expect planning permission to be, I'll want to start the process off before the end of the year."

Rin, looking up from his phone, said: "It's happened. Anthea says we should expect my parents to descend from the sky within the hour."

"Try to upset them enough they leave before lunchtime," Bran said, bouncing a tennis ball on the path as we walked. "Or we'll have them in the house going on and on for the rest of the day."

"I'd rather try to talk them down," Rin said. "Especially now I know Kyou was named heir. That might be the one thing needed to make them give up the idea of me as next head of L-B Corp."

"You tell yourself that," Bran said, tossing the tennis ball at him.

Rin hit it back, and they made a valiant attempt to sustain a volley on the short walk home.

"What do you think?" I asked Kyou. "Can he talk them round?"

"He'd be happier with the clean break." As we caught up with Rin and Bran at our front door, he added to Rin: "This seems a good time to have a fun call with your sisters before they're banned from talking to you."

Rin evidently agreed, and went upstairs. I headed to my room to shower, then set myself a reminder and lost myself to unlikely buildings for a couple of hours.

To be honest, I was hoping to miss all family confrontations, but when I came down to the kitchen for lunch, it was clear there'd yet to be a visitation.

"...sandwiches every day ad infinitum," Rin was saying. He was wearing the faint, deceptively pleasant smile that I'd learned spelled danger.

"There's salad ingredients," Kyou said, looking over the contents of the refrigerator. "Or we could order something."

"Limp lettuce leaves?" Rin said. "And what happened to your determination not to live on takeout?"

"Come up with an option instead of picking at everything," Bran told him, a distinct snap to his voice.

Instead of getting drawn into the squabble, I simply glanced in the fridge, picked out a block of cheese and then found a grater in the cupboard.

"Can you slice the rest of that sourdough, Bran?" I asked. "Just under an inch thick. Kyou, I swear I saw a case of beer somewhere—can you bring a can? Rin, slice an onion very thin."

I watched Rin hesitate, then decide not to exercise his temper on his new girlfriend, and obediently if somewhat inexpertly cut an onion.

"Why do none of the methods for avoiding the fumes work?" he complained, washing his hands and face afterwards. "What are we making, anyway?"

"Welsh Rarebit," I said. "The onion's an added extra."

"I don't know what a rarebit is," Kyou said, cradling several cans of beer. "Are we drinking in the middle of the day?"

"It's fancy cheese on toast," Bran said.

"The beer's an ingredient," I explained. "But will probably do as an accompaniment as well. Mum and I used to make this for Dad on his birthday. Not that he was particularly attached to Welsh national recipes or anything, but it's tasty, easy and quick, which fits my criteria for cooking. Anyone want to skip the onion layer? And do you know how to use the grill setting in your oven?"

They didn't, since we hadn't had occasion to grill anything before, but it wasn't difficult to figure out, and I had them toast one side of the bread while I made the cheese sauce. Then flip, add the optional layer of onion, pour over the cheese, and toast again.

"Will you make this for my birthday as well?" Bran asked, after devouring several slices.

"If you want." While I'd avoided cooking so it didn't become my default chore, I was happy enough to take my turn, and do occasional extra treats, and I'd really been missing some of the family standards. "I can do some nice mocktails as well. Speaking of which, we don't seem to have gotten around to our cocktail nights at all, yet."

Before he could reply, all our phones chirped in unison, and Castellan joined in. Rin glanced at his screen, and immediately stood up.

"Wish me luck," he said.

"Call us if you need reinforcements," Bran said.

Rin paused, then smiled properly, and went to answer the door.

I finished my juice, then tidied my plate into the dishwasher, and threw away the foil I'd used to protect the grill tray. Bran, who I'd noticed was the tidiest of the three, took care of the rest of the plates, then wiped down the benches, while Kyou put the juice away. Then we stayed where we were, listening to the murmur of voices from the main hall.

Having two sets of parents must be a mixed blessing. It certainly opened up plenty of opportunities to play one against the other, but when they all came at you as a group, it must be overwhelming. The discussion didn't seem to be going well: the long spates of talk had shifted into shorter, sharper words. Not quite angry, but getting there.

Bran shifted uneasily, and I noticed that his gaze was directed at Kyou. Kyou's own face was calm, with a suggestion of long-suffering patience, but there was a weird dissonance to his posture, as if he was deliberately trying to appear relaxed.

Kyou's father, I remembered, was a shouter.

I took two steps and leaned against his side, slipping an arm around his waist. I couldn't remember my parents ever shouting at each other, let alone me, but there'd been the occasional cold war, the worst of which had dragged on for days, until disrupted by a surprise storm that had sent us all running to rescue laundry, fumbling, breathless and flurried, and then laughing. I had been quite young at the time, had felt all squashed and pressured and confused about what was going on, and I remember afterwards watching Mum and Dad smile, and then hold hands, and it felt like I could finally let out a breath.

Kyou, after a moment's stillness, tucked me into his side, but before either of us could relax, a sharp *crack* jolted us. Bran took a step forward, stopped, and then moved again when Rin called out: "Kyou, come here."

We all went. I knew that Rin's mother was from a related part of the Laurent-Beaulieu clan, and wasn't surprised to spot a woman with the same tall, slender build and pale amber colouring as Rin. The watered-down version of Arinn Laurent-Beaulieu must be Rin's father. Ranged beside him was a small, dark-haired woman the spitting image of Anthea and Jessamin. Rin's stepfather, a pace back from this cluster, was stork-tall, and had a slightly disorganised air that reminded me of my own father.

Between the two pairs, Rin stood bolt upright, a red mark discolouring one cheek.

"Kyou, put together whatever these people think it cost them to raise me. I'd hate to owe them something."

"No problem," Kyou said, promptly. "Do we have an estimate? Do you want to split evenly?"

"I take it you're making this folly possible?" Rin's mother said, in a marked French accent. "How convenient, for you."

Kyou looked startled, then smiled, an expression full of edges. "To be honest, Rin's never been my competition in that regard. No matter how hard he studies, no matter how much you push him, his heart isn't in it."

"It never will be," Rin said, his tone absolute. "You can accept that, and support me, or you can get out."

The last words seemed to tear in his throat, and they all looked a little startled.

"Arinn, you need to calm down," said his father, after a moment. "Think—"

"You four need to fuck off," Bran said, crudely. "Unless you'd like to feature in local gossip for having been thrown out for trespassing after a 'family altercation'." He held up his phone with the emergency number ready to dial.

"Don't be ridiculous," Rin's stepmother said. "What an overreaction—"

"Is it?" Bran asked. "All our lives I've listened to you four going on and on, telling Rin to be this, do that, planning out a path for his whole life, and never once caring if he wanted to walk it. Why should you be given the grace to say one more word to him after he's finally in a position to walk in a direction that makes him happy? So, I'm going to count to ten, and you're going to be out that door, or I'm dialling."

"He will," Kyou advised. "And, since I'm technically the owner of the building, I think you'll find the police will take the call seriously. So, save us all an embarrassing scene. And maybe consider being proud that your son is such a brilliant musician that he not only can make a very good living, he's been accepted into the most prestigious school of music in the country."

Rin's mother drew in an angry breath, but her husband stepped forward and put an arm around her shoulders, murmuring softly to her before speaking to us.

"We're clearly not going to get anywhere right now," he said. "Let's let everyone cool down, and then see if we can come to some sort of sensible resolution another day."

Bran muttered something to the tune of 'sticking resolution up your ass', then pointedly went to the foyer door and held it open. Rin's mother glared at Kyou, who had apparently been promoted to the role of grandmaster schemer, then stalked away, trailed by her husband. Rin's father shook his head, gave Rin a look of deep disappointment, then took his wife's hand and followed. Bran couldn't quite manage to slam the door after them, since it had a soft-close mechanism, but it did wheeze rather when he tried.

I took a step closer to Rin, who was still standing rigidly upright, the red mark on his cheek all the more livid because he was so pale. To tell the truth, I hesitated to reach out to him as I had Kyou. He was a micron from snapping.

Bran, returning, said bluntly: "Not hitting any of them is more than I would have managed. Want to start to get it out of your system in the gym? Then we can see whether my cello playing is able to keep up with you while you work through the rest."

Rin shivered, but then stopped staring at nothing, and nodded. "Yeah."

He paused, then summoned a faint smile for me and Kyou, and said: "At least we're past that," before following Bran away.

Kyou let out his breath, then hugged me. "We've been preparing to walk away for the better part of a decade, and it still feels like we were completely unready."

"Which one of them hit him?" I asked.

"Most likely his mother. She's the one with the quickest temper. His father's way more difficult to move. Rin's temper's actually a weird combination of the two: difficult to move, but then flashpoint. He'll give the sandbag a good workout."

"Want to go recover in the courtyard hammock? I'm really not in the right headspace to work."

"The...yeah, why not? We can enjoy the first touches of autumn colour."

I hadn't spent much time in the courtyard, and thought I should come down more often before autumn progressed. We hooked up the hammock and curled together, not speaking. Perhaps a quarter hour later, piano and cello notes joined the muted sound of traffic. An idle wind occasionally rattled the leaves above us, sending the shadows dancing. Only a handful had even begun to hint at changing colour, but it was still beautiful.

Kyou fell asleep. A sign, I suspected, of how much he'd put into not showing he was upset. Even I had felt shaken all out of proportion for a relatively tame scene. Part of that was my own powerlessness: I could not fix their relationships with their families, or change whether they wanted them. Nor could I simply enjoy a spectator role. Kyou obviously hated this kind of confrontation, and Rin had been beyond upset, and I had discovered an urgent need to make it better. Thankfully Bran had cut through, driving Rin's parents away without any pretence to courtesy.

I realised I didn't know any of their parents' names. Although this was obviously to be a period of separation, and Rin the only one who'd seemed at all interested in keeping in touch with his family, I shrugged off the idea of asking for more detail, and let the sky soothe me until Kyou woke up, and we returned to all the things we'd meant to do that afternoon.

Rin and Bran played for hours, and I kept my door open so I could listen to them. Piano and cello first, but then Rin switched to violin. The music became less thunderous, shifted through a piercing ache, then moved on to a calm that showed on Rin's face when we all came down for dinner.

He'd left his phone in the kitchen, and picked it up with a grimace, reading through a series of messages as Kyou and Bran began to collect together the ingredients for the basic Bolognese sauce on the recipe card Mrs Janssen had given us.

"Cut another onion," Kyou said, rolling one over to Rin, who looked at it with disgust, but then picked it up.

"At least when we do it together, cooking only takes half of forever," he commented.

We talked more about meal arrangements now that we'd had our first cooking lesson, and decided that we would each cook once a week, using the meal cards with pre-prepared ingredients option suggested by Mrs Janssen. The other three days we'd either eat out or order takeout. Helping whoever was cooking to be strongly encouraged.

"Though it's particularly useful to have someone who knows that ovens have grill settings around," Kyou added, smiling at me as we settled into the breakfast nook, which we preferred over the larger dining table.

"I admit that discovering the common knowledge you're missing is pretty entertaining," I said. "Did you literally never prepare your own meals until you left home?"

"I've managed some of my own food," Bran said, shrugging. "I wouldn't go into the main house until after meals were done, and would put together something resembling dinner. Paola really didn't like anyone messing with her kitchen, though. That's the longest-lasting live-in help. We went through quite a few of them when I was young, but Paola's obsessed with my father, so puts up with all the super-pickiness and whatever."

"I signed up for a home economics class at school once," Rin said. "I never fully understood why that upset my mother to the point she insisted I cancel. She'd be furious if anyone suggested Anthea and Jessamin weren't allowed to do woodwork, or car repair, or whatever is their latest fancy."

"Baking would threaten your overbearing CEO image," Bran said.

"We missed an opportunity to have you greet them wearing a cheery apron," Kyou added, smiling. Then he frowned down at his shirt. "Next time I cook, remind me to actually put on one of our aprons. They're not just kitchen decoration."

We'd made too much, and transferred leftovers to containers, stacked the dishwasher, and then went to the game room to review what I'd come up with so far for headquarter designs.

"I'm just going to page through them," I said, bringing up my files. "Think of them as starting points, to see if there's any concepts you like at all, or want to retain. I'm happy to draw fantasy buildings for months on end, so if there's nothing at all that works in this lot, don't hesitate to say it."

"I'm waiting to see if you've somehow incorporated a bridge into this one," Kyou said.

"Not this time," I said, then paused as his phone vibrated several times in a row.

Rin's followed suit, and then Kyou's phone buzzed some more. He picked it up, killed a call, and put it down again. To my surprise, my own phone chimed, and I paused, then read out a text from Anthea:

> *Hi Mika we've all just been in a big family sesh ultra dramatic great-grandfather more or less ex-communicated Rin and co but at the same time sounded kind of proud of them idk mum banned us from talking as predic not fun*

"Dahat must have dropped your parents an early warning, Rin," Kyou said. "Judging from my father's reaction, Great-Grandfather's summoned everyone out to The Grove and announced that we three have been adjusted out of his will." He killed another call, and said: "I think I'll put this into flight mode."

He glanced at the screen as another call came in, but this time he answered, and we listened to a one-sided conversation: "Hey Stacia. Yes, he talked to us yesterday. Gratifying to know where I stood, but this has been long planned and we won't be turning back. Google 'Kybirn'—that will give you an idea of our main focus. I can imagine. Quite good terms, really: he wants to cooperate on some property I acquired. I'll have to show you what we're planning there: you'll laugh. Drop by some time for dinner. We're learning to cook."

It seemed Stacia was one of the few cousins they were on good terms with, but my attention drifted from the conversation to Bran, whose phone had not sounded at all. Was he really so isolated in this sprawling family? Not even his brother had contacted him. He caught me watching him, seemed to effortlessly decode the reason, and shrugged.

Rin, also paying attention, said: "He's blocked almost everyone we know. The rest don't bother, since he usually doesn't respond."

After texting Anthea a neutral response, so that she could honestly say she hadn't talked to the three who'd been 'ex-communicated', I put my own phone on mute, waited until Rin and Kyou had followed suit, and then began paging through the five building concepts I'd worked up.

It would be silly to pretend I didn't want them to fall in love with something immediately, but I was prepared for none of the designs to work. More complicated would be if each of them liked a different option, and I wondered how they'd resolve it as I tried to not too obviously watch their reaction. They were keeping their expressions very neutral.

"Can you go back to four?" Kyou asked, as soon as I was done.

This was my second-favourite of the designs, one of those I'd done on a theme of 'threes'. I'd started with three rectangular buildings, each rising along their length from two to four stories. I'd joined the two-story ends to form a triangular atrium, covered by a shallowly curved clear roof, and then from that point I'd distorted each rectangle into graceful arcs, and added a slight angle to each of the otherwise flat roofs, so that the outer edge of each rising curve was a quarter story higher than the inner. It was a design full of subtle angles and lovely fluid lines, faintly inspired by the view up our Art Deco staircase.

"Is this roof all about wind physics?" Bran asked, tilting his head.

"In a way. Once I sketched the design, I couldn't escape a certain resemblance to a flat-ended propeller, and—keeping in mind the monthly windstorms—spent a while working out whether it would accidentally create the occasional vortex, or cause the building to try to, ah, take off. Though there is also a potential to use the wind for passive ventilation, or even funnel turbines." I drew some lines. "I'd have to spend way longer on the physics if you wanted to use this design, and then have it confirmed and fully realised by people considerably more experienced than me, so it's not a good choice on a timeframe basis."

"But it is beautiful," Bran commented. "And turbines—if they output a worthwhile amount outside the monthly windstorm—would be nice from an environmental point of view."

"Also maximises natural light and views for everyone," Rin said. "I suppose the roof wouldn't be this clean though. We'd be fools not to put solar up there."

"True, though you could use solar tiles rather than panels. Not currently as efficient, but more decorative. I've seen some nice hexagon-shaped ones that you could play with. You'll notice that, instead of the usual rooftop air conditioning, I've positioned the plant at ground level in these non-windowed segments."

Kyou reached for my tablet, and I handed it over, watching his absorbed expression as he added a sketching layer over the top-down view, and then rapidly began adding blue and black patterns to the roof. It only took a minute or two for me to recognise the same 'organic circuitry' look he'd used for the sketch of Rin's hand. Dense black with hints of blues around the atrium, then blues dominating, transitioning to blue and white as we reached the halfway point of each roof, and the pattern became sparser, leaving the end quarter of each roof clear.

"Makes it look like a post-singularity flower," I said, stealing the tablet back off him, and trying to work out what the pattern would look like from a ground-side view. "It's a good addition. And you could tint the windows blue shading to clear to complement it, maybe add some subtle patterning to them as well."

"It meets your criteria of being Insta-material," Rin said. "It's asking to be photographed. I don't know what you'd plant the grounds with now, though. Your autumn trees don't seem to fit with all this blue and white."

"I want it," Kyou said, very definitely. "Mika, can you do me up more concept sketches, and a rough floor plan? And some information on solar tiles, so I can prepare a better version of the roof pattern. Don't worry that this option will take longer in the design phase: the new rail line is unlikely to beat us to completion, even if we spend a year before breaking ground."

Amused to discover that Kyou's opinion was definitely the heavyweight in matters of construction, I nodded, reviewed their list of requirements, and then we finished a long day with our usual crowded shower, and bed.

Sixteen

The revised high-speed rail route was announced first thing Monday morning, and between lectures I followed the explosion of discussion about Noonerry and the opening up of the Snowshield Tableland. One news site had even titled their article "Land Rush", and Kyou sent me a screenshot of texts he'd received from his Noonerry real estate contact, Richard, thanking him for the warning against further sales. The sheep farmer who rented Fox Farm's fields had almost taken a deal that was now chicken feed compared to the new value of her property.

Our Sunday tennis games had caused far less fuss, but I read through a handful of discussion threads, most speculating that I was Rin's girlfriend, since he was my partner in the doubles game, and had danced first with me at the Seniors Ball. A little potted history of Mika Niles was produced: Corascur Dux, ex-girlfriend of movie star, dad who writes racy novels. Posted by someone fairly neutral to me, but close enough they knew most of my public details. Hopefully, with a bit of clarification via the highly-gossipy Sean, my renter status would be established and things would quiet down again.

My pre-lunch lecture was Ethics in Engineering—a mandatory course made completely fascinating by a brilliant presenter—in a room quite close to the library. It gave me plenty of time to stroll down and meet Lania and, arriving first, I snagged a table to eat the somewhat limp salad sandwich I'd packed rather than face Helios

U's formidable lunch lines. These tables were in a nice spot: set back from the entrance to the library, beneath a stand of Greenland blaze and away from the constant back-and-forth of foot traffic by the lake. It gave me an excellent view of the arrival of a small deputation from my former Art Club, with Sean as its vanguard.

He ran straight up to me, paused as if to catch his breath, then gasped: "Kybirn! Kyou! Bran! Rin!"

I grinned. "Yes, it was there in front of you all along. I have to wonder what other acronyms they came up with. Brik? Krib?"

"I like to picture the Kings running a company called Birk," Natascha said, catching up. "Do you think they could be talked into a name change?"

"They seem attached to the current one," I said. "But feel free to suggest options."

"This puts a whole new light to applying for jobs at Greenland's newest game developer," Anika said, walking up with Lania. "Though I have to ask...there's also a 'Kybirn Music'. Is Bran actually writing songs?"

"Rin is," I said. "He seems to have been at it for years. I tracked all the released ones down on YouTube. Most are pretty obscure: only the most recent seems to have taken off in any way."

That distracted everyone, and I munched my sandwich as they all focused on their phones.

"Wait, Rin wrote *You Are Not My Friend*?!" Natascha exclaimed. "Kana Tika's latest?"

"Yeah. Kyou plans to throw him a little party if it makes the top ten anywhere in the world. It's doing particularly well in Iceland for some reason."

Anika was still processing. "Rin's writing music. And I've heard tell that the people who were planning to get close to him during the MBA haven't seen...is Rin doing a Sirocco?!"

I didn't know whether to laugh or choke at the way she'd phrased it, and finally managed: "Rin's doing a Masters in Music. Kyou's signed up for a Masters in Fine Arts. Bran's starting with a Bachelor of Computer Engineering and then moving on to Computer Science, so he'll probably share a bunch of classes with you and Lania. Hey, I saw we need to form a group of four for the PHY079 labs. Want to team up?"

"Sure," Anika said. "No reason to pass up a group of top students, even if they weren't..."

"Eye candy served on a platter," Natascha said. "So, Kyou's doing Fine Arts? I thought he was just hanging with Carr."

"Well, he's Kybirn's art lead, so the degree makes sense. Do you have to paint a bunch of different versions of the same apple as well?"

"Mine's a pear," Natasha said, grimacing.

"Never mind that," Sean said, having quickly run through online resources about Kybirn. "What does all this mean for L-B Corp?"

I shrugged. "Not my business. And, more to the point, both my work and rental contracts include fearsome NDAs. I'm not about to risk my super-convenient lodgings by gossiping about their private lives."

"Isn't that what you've just been doing?" Natascha asked, puzzled.

"Kybirn's existence, and their various degrees, aren't exactly private. But things people can't find out via Google, or looking at course registration, I'm not going to touch."

"I'm really astonished they're renting to you at all," Anika said. "The Kings practically never let anyone close."

"Whatever you did for Kyou must have been one hell of a favour," Sean said, glancing from me to Lania. "No details?"

"Oh, well, I guess that's now public knowledge, more or less, or at least public record. It was pretty minor from my point of view. When those caves in the Sunneway Pass were discovered, I mentioned to Kyou that I felt sorry for the high-speed rail engineers. Once he'd clarified that I was almost certain they'd never be able to run the HSR line on the planned route, he did some urgent investigation, then galloped down to the Snowshield Tableland and bought nearly everything on the market. I have to admit, I felt lightheaded when he first told me he'd spent millions on the basis of a passing comment, but, well, you've probably seen the news this morning."

"Total Investment God," Sean said, reverentially.

"Plus, they now have an extremely convenient location to build their main headquarters," I added.

"Even for Kyou, that's an extraordinary coup," Natascha said. "And now I completely understand why he thinks he owes you a favour. I will formally declare myself jealous of your breakfast eye candy, and hereafter hold my peace."

"Next time you have a tip on a hot property deal, send it my way," Anika added.

We talked Kybirn and Noonerry during the rest of the lunch break, then went on to our next lectures. Monday was a relatively busy day for me, and so I didn't get back home until after four, putting my bag in my study and feeling the strangeness that was the result of the domestic service having swept through. After a brief rest, I went upstairs to work, since the building design was officially part of my duties. Kyou was scrupulous about not getting free labour out of me.

While I'd spent years 'studying ahead' for my degree, I was definitely not yet capable of doing a complete building design on my own, especially since my technical focus had always been bridges. Architecture and engineering might be related, but with a large amount of information I'd simply never touched. Doing the modelling for wind impact, however, was one of my stronger points, and I happily lost myself in the task, after a brief side-quest to get appropriate software installed on the work machine.

Because I'd started late, most of the staff in my area were packing up as I arrived, but there were a few holdovers, including Pip, who came in with a long box just as I was stretching for a break.

"Mika, can you do me a favour?" she asked, a little hesitantly.

"Sure," I said, glad she'd talked to me. Ever since I'd revealed myself as a resident and friend of the bosses, all the part-time staff I sat with had treated me very carefully, and I was looking for ways to ease the relationship.

"I borrowed a bunch of noisemakers, and I'm supposed to give it all back tomorrow. Come help me make fun sounds?"

"No problem," I said, and followed her toward the Team 1 side of the building, where the recording studios were. "Are we already at the point where you know what sounds we'll need?"

"There's some areas they've told me to focus on first, but I'm basically building an entire Foley library from scratch, which is an incredible task."

"Aren't there sound libraries you can buy?"

"Oh, sure, and we'll probably subscribe to one of the big Foley libraries to pick up sounds we need in a pinch, but the last thing we'd want is to fill the game with the exact same footsteps and screams as everyone else with a subscription. When people finally play *Echoes*, I'll be able to close my eyes and travel through a world I recorded."

And I'd be able to walk through my cities and buildings. Even literally, if they really did go ahead with my building concepts for Noonerry. This, I sternly reminded myself, was still a long way from becoming reality, but they did seem quite serious about the headquarters design. Something I'd thought of, done the maths for, a whole building would become an actual physical object, far ahead of the time I'd expected it to be possible.

"Money really lets you cheat and take shortcuts," I said, and smiled at Pip's confusion. "This is such a fantastic job."

Her face lit with fellow feeling. "I know! And, even better, Bran said today they've decided the head office location will be at Noonerry! You know, where the new—oh, I forgot, you probably do already know."

I grinned. "Yeah, I've been down there. The views are incredible. I can hardly wait to be able to commute."

"Bran said there'll be a dedicated Foley Effects room—much larger than what I'm working with here. I'm going to end up a total packrat, you know, hoarding things that can make fun sounds."

We reached the studios, and paused at a viewing window, discovering a girl singing. She had a sleek bob of black hair set off by a vivid red lip colour, and a bombshell figure. I was disappointed that the soundproofing of the room made it impossible for us to hear more than the faintest hint, since it looked like a spectacular performance. I could see Rin and Bran in the control room, and knew from Rin's expression that he'd finally found his elusive voice.

Pleased, I left them to it, and spent a fun hour clashing pots and bits of metal together for Pip, then went down to dinner.

Mondays, since we were all relatively busy, was a takeout night, and we decided on Thai, then sat around on the rooftop enjoying the breeze brought by an approaching storm.

"The one thing this place is missing is a view," Kyou sighed. "While I like the 'embraced by trees' aspect of this rooftop, I'd really love to be able to actually watch this storm rolling in."

"Knowing that Noonerry is a reality makes it harder to wait," Bran agreed. "When we build the house, we'll absolutely need to include stairs down to the forest, like there is at that farmhouse."

"The crest of your hill is more than twice the elevation," I pointed out, then considered the advantages and added: "If you made the stair less vertical, more a long switchback ramp, it probably wouldn't be too bad. Still quite the leg workout. Are you planning to build anything at the base of the tableland where your property boundary cuts into the forest?"

"A tiny get-away-from-it-all cabin sounds tempting," Kyou said.

"The river doesn't drain off our part of the tableland, right?" Bran said. "I didn't see any falls or anything, but we should check to see what's within our property line next time we go down there."

"I don't want to overtly upset the Parks Service, so will check their preferences when we meet," Kyou added.

"Meeting? About that donation?"

"Yes, and a general development sensitivity discussion. Richard mentioned that the Service is very negative about invasive plant types, and so I want a list of things they absolutely would hate to have planted above the forest. There's apparently some kind of flowering pear that's been giving them problems. While I'm happy to give preference to natives, there's a few foreign species I particularly want to use, so we'll see how we go."

"Have you been getting a lot of calls about Noonerry?" Bran asked, as Kyou's phone mewed for the fifth time since we sat down to eat.

"Mostly from extended family, once they realised what I have in my hands. The new receptionist, Maura's, first days have been filled with calls coming in on the Kybirn Investment contact number. There was one an hour ago from a journalist who thinks he's going to make his career on a corrupt conduct scandal. I'm thinking about talking to him, since it sounds like Kybirn's name is going to get tossed around no matter what we do, so we may as well clear a few things up from the outset."

"Going to give up on the 'just happened to buy land there' story?" Bran asked.

"No, I'll say the probability of a HSR stop on the Tableland was a factor in choosing it for our headquarters."

"The truth is likely already on the forums anyway," I said, and checked. "Yeah. Sean's post is far more interested in the degrees you're studying, but he's mentioned it. Attention has shifted thoroughly off me. Mainly about Rin. Someone ran down to the Conservatorium, and apparently was very sad not to be able to find you. Whereas you, I guess, have finally found the missing piece for *One Step*."

Rin, who had been distracted the entire conversation, turned a lazily pleased expression on us. "The exact timbre I was looking for."

"Can we firm up the release date now?" Bran asked.

"Yes. Anastasia wants a couple of days to rehearse, and then will be free to record on Thursday. Then we'll have all the musical components in place, and it's down to fine-tuning."

"Art's at about sixty percent," Kyou said. "Mainly the work I've done on it the last couple of years, but Team One is progressing quickly now they've settled in with the style. If it runs to schedule, we'll be at final corrections stage mid-January. The trailer should be ready by November."

"How long until there's a fully playable version?" Rin asked.

"Depends on how much of the art you want," Bran said. "It's playable now, just with gaps for the music components you haven't recorded yet. If you're okay with the current graphics placeholders, a couple of days after you finalise the music."

Rin leaned back in his chair; eyes curved nearly shut. "Finally."

He was happy, but his voice was also very tired. *One Step More* was a passion project so personal it hurt.

I could only hope the result would be catharsis, and not a wound that would not heal.

Seventeen

Knowing the general fascination with the Three Kings, I was not at all surprised when, on Tuesday, the comments about me began to take on a nasty edge. Rin, Kyou and Bran all had their devotees, and the Noonerry-related discussion about their clear personal wealth only increased their desirability. I'd spent enough time meandering about the archives of Helios' local forums to have seen that every girlfriend they'd ever had had come in for a spree of social media hate. Even Bran's long-time girlfriend, Meggan, had not escaped a small campaign, despite her childhood sweetheart status. So, this was something that would happen even if I'd only been decorously dating one of the three.

The fact that I was theoretically only living with them didn't seem to make any difference, and perhaps was part of the reason matters ramped up so quickly. Not being attached to one of the Kings meant I was a threat to the claimants of all three.

Although impressed by the sheer variety of nasty things being said, I only had a little time to monitor developments. Between the physics of the 'propellor' building, and anticipation for my Thursday afternoon lecture with Professor Tremaine, I wasn't going to waste my thoughts on anonymous hate.

The first couple of years of my degree were a deep dive into maths, physics and chemistry, along with the core concepts of practical structural engineering. All these were things I had been freely reading for years, but Professor Tremaine's four years of monthly lectures were not available online, and I had been looking forward to starting the series enormously.

I actually fretted about clothing, which was silly, but I still used the excuse of a cooler, somewhat damp day to revert to my usual jeans-and-t-shirt style. I wanted the Professor's first impression of me to match my own self-image. Besides, the beginning of Wednesday was a chemistry lab, and floaty summer skirts really weren't a good idea.

A distracted mind wasn't ideal either, so I forced myself to focus, didn't hurry over a fairly simple series of tests, and found a study room nearby to write up the required report while eating my lunch. That done, I stopped by a bathroom to carefully tidy myself, and finally—at last—made my way back past the midpoint of campus, towards the small lecture theatre near the Marden Institute that was to house the highlight of every month.

"Mika."

Carr's voice, accompanied by a featherlight touch on my shoulder blade. Since Carr was by no means a handsy person, this surprised me, and as I turned my head, I caught a glimpse of yellow paper in his hand, swiftly crumpled out of sight.

"Post-it note?" I guessed. "What's it say?"

Carr shook his head, so I held out my hand, and after a moment's hesitation he passed the paper to me. I smoothed it out enough to read, raised my eyebrows, then put it in my pocket.

"Do people also go so amazingly overboard when you get at all close to someone?" I asked. "I mean, I know I landed a pretty cushy rental, but the reaction is starting to feel excessive."

"My profile is thankfully not quite so high," Carr said, with a helpless grimace. "Even so, I'm very careful who I bring into the firing line. You're not...bothered?"

"I won't pretend to be completely immune, but so long as it's mainly forum nonsense, I can keep it as background noise. Are you pleased Kyou ended up enrolled in Fine Arts?"

"Yes! I only wish I'd realised long ago just why he was so impatient when I talked to him about not giving up on his art. I felt a little blind once Kyou explained."

"I don't think anyone predicted the secret game developer twist," I said. "How's your course going? Happy with the content?"

He smiled. "Absolutely. What of you, now you're a step closer to your bridges?"

"Loving it," I said. "Though in danger of being late for a major lecture. Thanks for saving me from the bonus labelling, Carr."

I waved my farewell, then walked the rest of the way at double pace. I'd planned to arrive very early, and so was in no danger of being late, easily joining the small stream of students picking out seats. I aimed for dead centre of the theatre, and came close, settling in and taking out a notepad. For things I particularly wanted to remember, I preferred to use handwritten notes since I could do the formulas quicker. Preparation done, I settled in to look around me, spotting the occasional face I vaguely recognised from other classes.

Fifty students, most of whom would surely share very similar interests to me. About thirty percent female, from a wide variety of countries judging from the range of accents. Thinking ahead to the collaborative construction assignments in the second and third year, I promptly introduced myself to a girl sitting next to me, and we exchanged backgrounds. Reiko was from Osaka, and was particularly interested in the materials of large structures. On my other side was Athaine, a somewhat gloomy local boy who, after a little prodding, said he didn't have a specific area of interest.

"I sometimes want to say 'everything'," I admitted cheerfully. "Bridges are definitely top tier for me, but I'd design whole cities given the chance." I glanced back at Reiko. "Is it materials science above and beyond everything else, or is that just the favourite of many?"

Reiko smiled, quiet and reserved, but with clear fellow feeling. "If there were but time enough in the world."

Further conversation was cut short when Professor Tremaine entered the lecture theatre, trailed by three other people. I immediately focused on the Professor, who was in her late fifties: a lean woman with short silver hair, dressed with casual elegance. She paused by the lectern to survey the rapidly quieting room, while two of her companions briskly connected a laptop and set out a pointer and some paper material on the lectern. The third crossed to sit in the front row.

He was a student, and vaguely familiar. I tried to remember where I'd seen him, then put him aside as the Professor started to speak.

"Welcome," she said, her voice marked by the mellow accent I'd learned to recognise as Northern Greenland: someone from between Lake Eclipse's northern shore, but south of the glaciers of Avannaata. "I always start this program with an instinct to introduce myself, but I know that it's not necessary. To be here, to even consider this course, I know that you are all people who ask questions, and then find the answers. My own contribution will be to save you time, to give you methodologies, to point out blind avenues. Each month, I will discuss facets of engineering, and set you a problem to solve after going through highlight solutions to the previous month's issue. Since we have no problem from the previous month today, however, I'd like to start putting names to faces. First, these are my two graduate assistants, Marika Cork and Pasquale Russo. If you have questions not covered by the course resources page, they are here to help you. Now, starting from the front left here, let's go through the room. Just your name, please, and then I'll start describing the first technical aspect we're going to explore."

We went through the room at a quick pace, and I was not the only person who had a hint of pride in their voice as they crisply pronounced their name. Professor Tremaine focused on each of our faces in turn, a brief moment of intensity. Perhaps it was only my imagination, but when she looked at me, a frown seemed to shadow her eyes. But she had moved on before I could be certain.

Once exactly fifty people had named themselves, Professor Tremaine began to introduce the day's topic. Since it was the first lecture of the first year, the problem she set us was relatively simple. Just a fun little practice puzzle to get us used to the report format.

At the close, she offered to stay for ten minutes to answer any one-on-one questions we had about the course, and I couldn't resist joining the end of a line of six other people, listening with interest to what they asked, and her patient answers.

The line was down to two when she looked over and saw only the pair of us waiting. Her expression smoothed out for a moment, then she glanced at her watch and said: "Time for one more."

One short of me. After a moment's confusion, I stepped away, frowned at my feet momentarily, then lifted my bag to one shoulder and walked out. Pausing to check my phone, I glanced over my schedule, then decided to skip my next lecture and call it a day.

"What did you do to get the Prof offside?" asked a low voice.

I paused as my seatmate caught up with me: Athaine, a tall boy with a proud nose, a wide mouth, and very blue eyes he hid beneath a mop of dark hair. A face suggesting a lot of personality.

"You saw that too?" I said, after a moment.

"Looked at you, and time suddenly ran out," he said, with a kind of dull enjoyment. "You have history?"

"Not that I'm aware of," I said, then grimaced, and took hold of myself. "Unless whatever's wrong impacts my marks, I suppose it doesn't truly matter if she has an issue with me. Meanwhile, you sound like you're not very impressed with the Professor."

"Still evaluating," he said. "Best to know early what kind of person she is. Whether she has a shit list. Or plays favourites."

He paused, looking to our left as someone came out of the lecture theatre: the third of the Professor's companions, the vaguely familiar boy who'd sat in the first row. I didn't remember him introducing himself at the beginning of the lecture, so wasn't sure if he was a classmate.

"You know him?" I asked, after the boy had walked past us.

"Her son.   Much-lauded, greatly-petted child genius."

"There's probably a few of them in this class," I said mildly. "The entry requirements are pretty steep."

"Huh. You may be right."

He made the faintest gesture of farewell and walked off, back toward the Hub and the location of my next lecture. I went in the opposite direction, and found myself following the much-lauded, greatly-petted child genius out the western gate of campus, and onto my own street. I watched him enter one of the townhouses opposite Kybirn, and belatedly realised he was the boy I'd once seen walking an Afghan. I stared at the front of the townhouse for a long moment, shook my head, and went home.

After a rest in my room, failing to keep away from the forums, I went upstairs to do some more work on the main headquarters design. I'd been researching turbines, and doing some serious calculations on the concept of funnelling wind to ground-level turbines to decide whether it would add load to the building that outweighed the benefit, particularly factoring in the monthly 'Buster' the tableland experienced. Funnel turbines weren't considered commercially viable, but I couldn't find any records of someone using an entire building for the purpose, which meant I had to anticipate and address issues I couldn't simply Google the answer to. Great fun.

But today I could not concentrate, and soon gave up. I shut my computer down, then chose a simpler task: wandering about collecting the coffee cups that had migrated from the kitchen to everyone's desks. This had already become a bugbear of Bran's, who particularly disliked foodstuff being left around the office.   Most people had quickly adapted to using containers to store any food, but somehow there were always empty coffee cups at every second desk.

The sign on the washer said it was full of clean dishes, but I didn't care, cramming all the cups in, then starting a new cycle. I'd seen Rin as I passed, entirely engrossed recording a session with Anastasia, and went to watch briefly, but moved on again through the residence door next to the kitchen, thinking about going up to the roof.

The piano caught my eye, and I changed path, sitting down. I'd had piano lessons at a handful of different schools, but it had been over five years since the last one. I could still slowly pick out *Für Elise*, which I'd once dutifully practiced every Thursday afternoon for several months, but while my memory did not fail me, I'd lost any suggestion of fluency, and made a stop-start progress. It did not feel like something I could use to release pent-up emotion.

"Planning on taking it up again?" Kyou asked, appearing behind me unexpectedly. He must have been up on the roof. He was carrying a canvas—still apples—and propped it carefully on the nearest chair, then sat beside me on the piano bench.

"Thinking about music as language," I said, as he produced an impeccable rendition of the Beethoven piece. "I speak a lot of languages. Some well enough to write bad poetry, and others where I'm just barely able to ask where the train station is. There are a few I find considerably more difficult than others, but for the most part if I spend more time, I'll become proficient, though it requires a lot of immersion to come close to the level of a native speaker. Music...music's something that I think that even if I spent years on it, I'd still always be paddling in the shallow end of the pool."

"I took it very seriously for a while," Kyou said. "Practicing bored me to hell, though, and compared to Rin and Bran I always felt inadequate." He kissed my temple lightly. "Fortunately, neither of them can draw worth a damn. We each have our talents."

His phone buzzed, and he clicked his tongue, then stood up.

"I've a couple of unskippable meetings, but thankfully short ones. Are you going to join in on Bran's attempt at lasagne?"

"Yes. It sounds a nice recipe. I've been looking forward to it."

Kyou left, and I continued to fool around with the piano, only to have Rin arrive a few minutes later. The door to the offices made a noise as it closed, so he didn't get to creep up on me. I immediately stopped playing and smiled at him. He was looking very happy.

"It's going well?" I asked.

"I think I have everything I need," he said, sitting down and curling an arm around my waist. "It's unlikely we'll need to get Anastasia in again. I'll be in post-production tomorrow."

The tone was full of reassurance, as if I'd been fretting about the pushed-back release date of *One Step*. Still, it was a well-timed hug, and I leaned into his side and enjoyed it.

"You're looking forward to other people playing it," I said. "But do you actually want to play it yourself?"

"Yes, but it won't be as rewarding as watching people react." He squeezed me tighter. "I've been very deep in it the last few days, but don't take that as anything but eagerness to move the game forward."

I blinked, and looked up at a view of his Adam's apple and jaw. "Did you see me watching you record? Or did Kyou say something?"

"He told me you were in here moping over your lack of musicality. Was he wrong?"

"No, that's true enough. Music is so integral to your being that I feel like there's a part of you that I'll never be able to satisfy. I look at Anastasia and see someone who has something I can't give you. And see her not at all hiding that it's entirely her pleasure." I smiled. "But I can also see that all those signals are being neatly deflected. Why are you so happy at the idea that I might be jealous? I thought you'd hate that kind of possessiveness."

Rin went still, then let out a soft laugh, and pulled me onto his lap, the better for proper hugging.

"I'll never get used to how well you seem able to read me. Are you never even slightly anxious about us?"

I hesitated, then said: "To tell the truth, ever since we decided to try this, I've felt the most logical outcome is that each of you in turn will meet someone you like more than me, and there would be some sort of natural attrition process, and I'd be lucky to end up with any of you. I can't begin to tell you how much I hate the idea."

He searched my eyes. "Will you fight for us tooth and claw, Mika?"

"Well..." I smiled at him helplessly. "Everything about us is a big adjustment for me, so maybe I'll turn into the kind of person who tries to keep what they've lost. I doubt I'll be able to deal with it well. I'm constantly caught off-guard by how much the last couple of weeks have felt like coming home, how being with you feels like a place I've been missing, and would definitely feel as an amputation if I lost it. And I do get caught up on the silliest things, like...do you know, when we sleep together, you always turn away from me?"

Rin's eyes widened, then he said: "Mika, if I didn't turn away from you, you'd be woken at all sorts of hours by something very hard. We're already exhausting you, so the only thing I can do is turn away."

This made me laugh. "Well, when we're in your room, I might occasionally enjoy being woken. Would you like me to pretend to be jealous of girls you're not interested in?"

"The last thing I want from you is pretence," Rin said, with unexpected solemnity.

I frowned. There was a core of genuine upset beneath all this. "Rin, I wouldn't be here..."

"I know." He'd dropped his long lashes back down to shade his eyes. "You told us that, and you're very honest, when you're not having fun lying. But it's one thing to know that, and another to see you completely unfazed by a naked woman offering herself to me." He lowered his head, rubbing his cheek against my throat. "Ever since I can remember, complete strangers have wanted to own me. One of my earliest memories is a girl marching up to me in kindergarten, grabbing my arm, and declaring that I was her boyfriend."

"Was it Sirocco?"

He chuckled. "No, Sirocco didn't become obnoxious until her teens, when she somehow started to think that I'd been hers all along. My instinctive response to these people is always impatience. Even when I started to find girls attractive, started dating, boredom would creep in if they acted as if I were their property. And then I met you, and I thought we were playing a game that would end tidily, and the problem was that so did you."

"It's very cliché to like the one that doesn't fall for your charms," I pointed out.

"But almost to the end I was perfectly glad that you seemed so sensible. And then we came to a challenge where I had an opportunity to shake your composure, which I'd been longing to do. I succeeded, and then I was overwhelmed with dread that you wouldn't want to be around me anymore. Have you noticed that Kyou, Bran and I have been very...matter-of-fact with you? Friendly, relaxed, with no undying declarations? Almost as if we were continuing our game?"

"Yes. It's made it a lot easier to adapt."

"It's because we're afraid of scaring you off. We three have had some truly fascinating conversations, once we established that we were all very serious about you, and one of the first things we agreed on is that you're, well, 'commitment-phobe' is the wrong term. You're not used to long-term people, you don't usually accept passionate pursuit, and you're used to being alone in a crowd. We're getting you completely habituated to the idea of 'us' before we spook you with flowers and romantic poetry."

"Rin..." I said, laughing, but he just looked at me, and I knew he meant it. "Well," I said, tightening my arms around him. "Since I think I'm at least equal to flowers, I'll just mention I like jonquils, gerberas and sunflowers. Tell me a few of yours, so I can decorate your room for your birthday."

"You were definitely moping, though," Kyou said, after Rin and I finally came downstairs to help with dinner, and Rin had shared some conversation highlights. "Are the forums getting to you?"

"Oh, that," I said.

I dug in my pocket and pulled out the sticky note, which read 'Cheating Slut'. I showed it to them briefly, then tossed it into the bin.

"The forums have moved on to suggesting I was exchanging blowjobs for an early look at the final exams at Corascur, which really is kind of annoying, but I was mostly upset because an idol showed signs of feet of clay."

"Your professor?" Bran asked, pausing in his measurement of spices.

I described how Professor Tremaine had snubbed me.

"It was clear enough that at least one of the other students noticed. A very minor thing to do, of course, but hardly how I wanted to start the most important of my courses. Fortunately, for the first two years the monthly assignments are all on a pass/fail basis, so her current attitude is unlikely to impact my grades. I've been working on adjusting my expectations."

"But what the hell does she have against you?" Bran asked, angrily. "Forum posts that are obvious rubbish, and have only been around a couple of days? So clearly mud thrown at a wall to see what might stick?"

"I don't know. It doesn't really matter, because what's been tarnished is my opinion of her. I'll still find her lectures useful, even if she completely avoids ever talking directly to me. And there's no guarantee that today's very minor action will ever be repeated, let alone escalate. Meanwhile, boyfriends seem fantastic for helping me forget the things I'm upset about. Just what I needed."

Bran, swathed in an apron, gave me a nutmeg-scented hug.

"I've been using the IP addresses visible in the back-end of the Sunchatter forums to identify sock puppet accounts," he said. "Then sending a few of them screenshots of posts from their public and private identities. That's shut quite a few of them up, but unfortunately a couple of the major mud throwers have sense enough to use IP masking."

"You hacked into the forums?" I asked. Sunchatter was Greenland's major local message board, and older than Bran.

"I'm an administrator," he said, cocking up one corner of his mouth. "I set up a persona there years ago, and was relentlessly obliging and helpful until they welcomed me into the backend with open arms. They think I'm a retired sysop."

"It's been occasionally useful," Kyou said. "Unfortunately, we can't do much about the rubbish on other sites. We do, however, have a plan for the impact on your career development, but I'm afraid I didn't anticipate your professor possibly freezing you out. If it does reach the point of provable bias—"

I waved my hand. "She's not that important," I said, of one of my long-standing heroes. "She'll get over it, and I'll be pleased, or she won't, and I'll swap to a civil engineering degree. The Marden Institute was only ever one route to the thing I actually want: to build big, interesting things."

Kyou smiled, and dropped the subject, turning to the novel experience of peeling sweet potatoes. The lasagne was vegetarian, and not particularly complex. We set it to bake, and went into the game room, which we also used as the tv room, and sometimes just as a place to lounge on sofas. It was also useful as a very relaxed working space, as it was now when Kyou brought up a file containing all the Kybirn logos. He began adding a new one.

"You're not tempted to rename it 'Barky'?" I asked, referring to the clear leader of Sean's poll of alternate names for Kybirn.

"We've a rebranding announcement set for April First," he said, calmly. "How's the headquarters design going?"

"I've been working on some structural shifts to deal with load and accommodate rainwater, if we do go ahead with a funnel turbine concept," I said, and showed them a reworked image that included a slight raised lip that would guide water into the same outlet as the wind. "Since it would be impossible to keep rain out, it's simpler to incorporate drainage into the funnel. I've added some complexity to the connection between the three buildings and the central atrium, using a compacted earth section incorporated into the roof-to-ground portion of the wind funnel. I'm trying to keep the outlet as smooth and straight as possible to minimise turbulence, so these are potentially quite long. I'll give you a few different options as to how the outlets and turbines could look: either aboveground, or even built into the walls of an underground carpark."

"Enjoying yourself?" Kyou asked.

"Immensely. This kind of problem-solving is what I'm all about."

He nodded. "I wanted to talk to you about the next steps with the whole project. Since we now have so much prime development land, I'd rather keep the architectural and engineering process in-house by starting a subsidiary." He nodded at the partially-completed logo on the screen. "What do you think it should be called?"

I stared at him. "You...want your own architectural firm?"

"Architecture and Engineering," he said blandly.

"The most sensible thing we could do with all that spare land at Noonerry is hang on to it for a few years, then sell it at an enormous profit," Bran explained. "Or just pump out housing developments. I'm surprised you haven't already realised just why we're instead keen on fantastic, innovative buildings."

I stared at him, then at Kyou and Rin.

"Once we realised that being with us could close the door to the kind of things you've been dreaming of half your life, we looked for solutions," Rin added. "It's stupidly easy for us to fund a small company, hire a couple of architects and senior engineers to ensure legality and mentor you, and then feed you a steady stream of projects. From bridges across that little river to the more complex, interesting and reputation-establishing structures. Up to and including a viaduct hotel, since I happen to think that would look incredible."

"When in doubt, throw money at it?" My voice wobbled.

Exactly," Kyou said, warmly. "If you're half the engineer you seem to be, by the time we're thirty the fact that you have the three of us in train will be the least interesting thing about you—well, to anyone with a particularly tricky construction project. You're actually crying."

"I'm not." I blinked a couple of times, then looked at Rin. "And you thought *flowers* would spook me?"

"I think you've settled in enough to cope with a few more of our grand plans for our future," Rin said.

"I remember talking to Lania about being able to fund my own bridges. I didn't think that could come true. It seems so self-indulgent."

"Don't worry," Bran said. "If Kyou thinks it'll be profitable, there's little chance we'll make a loss. Call it a virtuous circle, where your helpful comments led to us having land to develop, and a need for a designer, while you need an opportunity to build your reputation, one fantastic project at a time, each of which will enrich Kyou's empire."

"We've no doubt of your abilities," Rin said.

"So, a name?" Kyou prompted. "Or do you want suggestions? Kybirn Manufacturing? Kybirn Create?"

"Kybirn Worldbuilding?" Rin suggested.

"Kybirn Isambard," said Bran, and looked pleased at my slight reaction. "First search result of your gaming name is some famous engineer. Inevitable that you using it means he's one of your heroes, hopefully without the feet of clay."

"Isambard Brunel, " I said. "He built a lot of bridges." Then I laughed. "His middle name was Kingdom. Very fitting."

I was not going to refuse this gift, overwhelming as it was. Kybirn had land to develop, and would need the services of architects and engineers for quite some time. I was already giving them design ideas, so adding an internship into the mix was a minor thing. Though what any prospective mentors would think of me doing initial concepts was another matter.

"Will you wait on staffing this subsidiary before you progress any of the Noonerry projects?" I asked.

Kyou shrugged. "I've the two critical hires slated for an interview next week," he said. "I started looking when I finalised the Fox Farm purchase."

"Always ten steps ahead," Rin murmured, pulling me closer into his side. "When's the interviews? I'd like to sit in."

"Tuesday. Mika, can you produce a more polished version of our overarching Noonerry plans by then? The four of us can give a presentation so our prospects know exactly what kind of wild ride they're in for."

"No problem," I said, and leaned over to kiss him.

Vegetarian lasagne was delicious, and I tackled it with a restored enthusiasm for life, then lost myself once again in Noonerry. Professor Tremaine's assignment I left for the weekend, and spent far more time than I ordinarily would for something so simple. Meticulous work, triple-checked. The forums I ignored, because the faint, underlying worry that all that mud might eventually stick had gone.

I would always have a somewhat complicated relationship with the wealth of my three boyfriends, but it would be stupid not to allow them to solve the problems they had brought me. Amazing that they'd been planning this all along, that they'd thought ahead to probable threats to me, and began to put in place counter-measures.

They had my back.

Eighteen

"The references for this Chloe Markham are suss," Bran said, flicking a finger at the screen of his tablet. "None from the place she worked at for the last five years? Fired?"

"Victim of office politics," Kyou said, shrugging. "Did a lot of the heavy lifting, got none of the credit, and lost in her attempt to win due recognition. Addison recommended her, which is enough for me."

"Who is Addison?" I asked, flipping through Chloe Markham's resume. We had gathered in the conference room to prep for the interview.

"Consulting engineer at L-B Corp," Kyou said. "Very capable. I was trying to headhunt him, but he isn't ready to make the jump, and recommended a couple of people he knew from his university days."

"These past projects from the architect aren't bad," Rin said.

"You like anything vaguely Scandinavian," Bran said.

"I prefer that clean line and light wood look as well," Kyou said. "Anything but the heavy industrial that's in fashion. And for the residential projects, I particularly want to draw in the natural environment, which is our prospect for lead architect's strong point. Google the name, by the way. It'll give you a better idea of the person than an interview and a resume is likely to."

Curious, I searched for 'Fabian Crew', and blinked at the resulting series of images. A small blond man whose piercings had to contribute to a significant proportion of his body weight.

"Post-Goth EDM band?"

Music began emanating from Rin's tablet, and he turned up the volume. "Not bad," he said, after listening to a piece heavier on instrumental than vocals. "Whoever is producing them knows their stuff."

"Happy and gloomy at the same time," I said, impressed. "I wonder if he ever does any Gothic-inspired architecture."

"We want a few different wedding halls," Kyou said. "Perhaps we can do one up as old-world ornate, and deck it out in black drapery for the less typical weddings. Anyway, personality fit's important for senior personnel, and in this case critical for you, Mika. These hires aren't only a matter of technical expertise, but how well they mentor you. If they seem like a bad match, we'll not continue them past the trial period."

His phone buzzed and he glanced at it, then stood. "They're both here. Be right back."

"How are you at interviews, Mika?" Bran asked, as Kyou left. "Are they one of the things that make you unable to sleep?"

"Not really. I've rarely had critical interviews, though. Nor conducted any."

"Thankfully Gram..." Rin began, just as Gram opened the door. He smiled faintly, then repeated: "Thankfully Gram is on board to coordinate the majority of the hiring with the various section seniors. The number of interviews we've sat through is already far beyond my limit."

Kyou returned then, and there was a brief round of handshaking and introductions. Fabian Crew had not removed all of his piercings, but had changed many of them to tiny, barely-visible studs and loops, and was dressed very snappily in a closely-tailored suit. The lack of heavy eyeliner made his relatively youthful face look closer to his late-thirties age.

Chloe Markham was thirty-six, and wore only a touch of eyeliner, but plenty of concealer. She styled her dark blond hair in a low bun and adopted the professional, practical clothing used by people who go from offices to work sites. On other occasions she would probably seem a pleasant, reserved woman with a hint of natural grace, but currently exhaustion undermined her, lending all her interactions an air of gritted teeth. Still, she didn't so much as blink when met with a conference room full of teenagers, along with the colourful Gram and Fabian.

"You've both come to us through trusted recommendations, so we'll leave behind standard interview formats," Kyou said, sitting down and moving forward a page on the presentation he'd set to display on the wall screen. "First, we'll give you some idea about what we're inviting you to join. Since we've already been assured of your technical abilities, what we're looking to establish is whether the project interests you, and if we can work together well."

He'd brought up Kybirn's structure chart, to which Kybirn Isambard had joined Kybirn Games and Kybirn Music underneath the umbrella of Kybirn Investments. Kyou had already had the new logo professionally retouched, and I felt more than strange looking at it. A company that existed to benefit me.

"Kybirn's primary focus is game development," Kyou was saying. "But our hunt for a location for our main office led us to a significant land purchase on the

Snowshield Tableland. Since this is an investment opportunity that we're not stupid enough to pass up, we're establishing Kybirn Isambard to manage construction of our originally-planned headquarters, and a staged development of the rest of the land."

I could see from Fabian and Chloe's faces that the Noonerry purchase wasn't news to them. When they'd been contacted with an invitation to interview, they'd surely gone looking for information about Kybirn—and had dug deep enough to find the forum posts discussing Noonerry. But when Kyou brought up the slides showing Kybirn Investment's land at Noonerry and Moonmere, their expressions did flicker. Mine had too, once I'd seen how much land Kyou had purchased at Moonmere, which he'd confessed he'd thought the more likely option for the station. Kyou was definitely willing to gamble.

The Moonmere land I had simply highlighted, but for the land in Noonerry I'd added very simplified imagery to represent each of the items for development, and then added coloured overlays to indicate development stages. Kyou stopped on a slide of Noonerry's town centre.

"We're looking for expertise to establish and manage the team necessary to bring the property projects to completion, along with taking on any external commercial work that comes your way, since there's certainly going to be a rush of development on the Tableland. While Rin, Bran, Mika and I will be heavily involved in the initial concepts of some of the projects, for most of the housing we'll provide broad outlines of requirements and budget, and only expect to be brought in for concept approval and the relevant sign-offs."

Kyou paused to explain his evaluation of the Tableland's future as an expensive satellite suburb of Helios, before bringing up a photo of one the houses he'd purchased: small, run-down, surrounded by grass and bushes. It was a corner block on the western edge of the town, on the main road.

"I want this piece of land to become an advertisement for Kybirn Isambard," he said. "Between six to eight separate residences, preferably working together as a whole to become something that makes people stop and admire, balancing beauty and function. They'll eventually be used for the mid-to-upper holiday let market, but in the short term will be useful for Kybirn staff working in Noonerry while other housing is being developed. There are also three houses in Moonmere that are in considerably better condition and available for staff accommodation during the early development stage." He paused and glanced at Bran and Rin. "In terms of staff housing, we might offer Kybirn staff preferential options to purchase a house and land package from one of the undeveloped blocks at Moonmere. It's only a thirty-minute commute, and the price won't skyrocket quite so quickly as Noonerry already has."

"Local housing has already gotten stupid," Bran commented.

"In contrast to our hands-off approach for the residential parcels," Kyou went on, "we'll be extensively involved in the concept designs for our headquarters and Fox Hollow before they're handed to you for realisation."

Kyou went through a series of slides showing the plan for Fox Hollow along with photographs of the area, and then talked about his destination garden resort for the wedding market, bracketed by distinctive buildings of aesthetic or conceptual interest. I had fun watching Fabian and Chloe's faces creeping toward the same bemused expression my father had worn, but mixed with a growing excitement. They asked a handful of questions about timing, and whether the park was a destination in itself, or only used for weddings, which Kyou noted as the former.

"These are the starting conditions," Kyou said, sliding over two folders setting out salary packages and perks. "The initial contract is a two-month trial, and then will be renewed every two years. For now, do you have any other questions?"

"How is Kybirn linked to L-B Corp?" Chloe asked.

"Only insofar that we've worked there, and our extended family are majority shareholders of L-B," Kyou said. "There's a possibility we might partner with L-B Corp for some of the construction, but otherwise there's no direct link. L-B Corp doesn't fund Kybirn."

"How large a team do you want us to assemble?" Chloe asked next.

"We've included an operating budget in the documentation," Kyou said. "It's based on current market rates, but we're open to review given that we aren't asking for simple results. And we are throwing in a free intern," he added, nodding at me. "Mika will be our primary liaison for the construction projects, but is also studying engineering, and can be used for appropriate-level tasks."

The somewhat wary look Chloe turned on me was not entirely surprising, but then she was distracted as Fabian opened his document pack, glanced at the first page, then sat back dramatically and said: "I only have one last thing to ask."

"What's that?" Kyou asked.

"When can I start?"

Gram laughed. "The employment contract is in your document pack," he said, and helpfully handed over a pen. "We can start onboarding after the meeting."

Fabian signed without hesitation. Chloe scanned the clauses briefly, then followed suit. An intern of dubious origin was not a sufficient deterrent to a job of a lifetime.

"We've already scoped and begun concept work on our main headquarters building," Kyou said. "And have just signed on a rental at Gore Heights that needs to be fitted out, but otherwise everything is purely at an outline stage. I'll leave Mika to give you a more detailed overview of the Noonerry site conditions, and then she'll hand you over to Gram."

More handshaking, and then they filed out, leaving me with the two people I'd potentially spend the next decade of my working life with.

"You led them to buy all that land, right?" Chloe asked. Her air of exhaustion had vanished.

"Yes. Well, I told Kyou that there was no way the high-speed rail was going to run through Sunneway Pass without years of delay, if ever. Kyou turned that into an investigation of alternate routes."

"And yet you don't even get paid for your internship?"

There was the faintest note of disapproval. Fabian glanced at Chloe, then looked thoughtful, as if this issue hadn't occurred to him before.

"Because I'm being paid out of the Kybirn Investment's budget rather than Kybirn Isambard," I explained. "So, I'm free to you, not to them. Kyou's very

particular about proper remuneration and due credit."
I smiled. "And I'm technically a Kybirn Games
employee, since I'm doing concept art of cities for one of
their games, and that task rolled over into concept
designs for Noonerry. As for balancing out my so-called
tip..." I turned the laptop and tapped Fox Farm on the
screen. "Kyou sold my parents a few acres at the
original price, and that's become the equivalent of
giving me a rather hefty cheque. I don't think we've
even shown you why he thinks Fox Hollow will become
an unmissable destination."

I called up a video taken from the farm veranda, and
projected it onto the screen, taking in the majestic view
of Vitha Valley and the Ramparts.

After a pause for due appreciation, Fabian laughed.
"A ceremony with that as a backdrop, and no-one will
be looking at the bride."

"But combined with the ease of transport, Kyou is
very likely to make the place a success," I said. "The
hotel is a later stage, though, once Noonerry
development, not to mention the garden, is a little more
mature. Let me give you an overview of environmental
conditions."

I brought up the slides I'd prepared showing the
temperature peaks and lows, rainfall patterns, and the
wind averages and extremes.

"I've started to collect data for a more detailed wind
map, especially for the garden areas. Kyou's very keen
to get trees planted, but it doesn't make sense until we
know the exposure points, and infrastructure is in
place. But the headquarters is where their attention is
focused right now. Fortunately, the Tableland's water
and waste facilities were upgraded about a decade ago,
so it has the capacity to handle the upcoming

population surge." I paused, with a faint touch of pre-performance jitters before I went on to the next slide. "This is the current concept for the main office. I'll email you the scoping document after your accounts are set up. The main brief is to be beautiful and eye-catching, and to investigate options for wind and solar power, so I've been modelling a funnel turbine solution. That's been an interesting exercise, but it's also a useful data point for how the Executive is approaching the development. Solar power can't be overlooked, but they prefer a more attractive option than efficient panel arrays. Time can be spent on wind power solutions, but they can't detract from the appearance of the building."

Chloe surveyed the 'alien flower' for a long moment, glanced at Fabian, then said: "Can you show me the modelling?"

After a quarter hour going through the work I'd done so far, I took them both out to Gram, then went downstairs. Kyou's turn to cook, and he was going to try his hand at steak.

"How did it go?" he asked, as I began to dice the potatoes he'd peeled.

"Well, keeping in mind that they're being very formal and professional and making sure not to show their opinion of me, I liked them. They're smart and adaptable, and not so stiff in their egos they can't handle a first-year student doing preliminary work. Not to mention Chloe immediately recommended a better fail-safe for dealing with the increased winds of the Buster, and Fabian sketched out a very nice improvement for the design of the HQ windows. Once they've gone through the scoping document I've sent them, they'll start work on project plans for both the HQ and the showcase residences. Fabian will have to work out notice with his current employer, while Chloe has just finished hers. She'll take lead on setting up the office in the Noonerry storefront, and has candidates in mind for a few key roles."

"How's your parents' renovation going?"

"Still waiting on approval. They did get permission to construct a garage, at least, and that should be done by the end of next week." I smiled. "My parents are going to be Kybirn Isambard's first external customers, since they need to put in their own access road and bridge. It's not in the Cassadine Malway brief."

"You should consider a small structure on the town side of the river as well," Kyou suggested. "It won't be that short a walk from the station to the farmhouse, and you could store things like umbrellas and bikes there." He paused, then washed and dried his hands and spent a little time on his phone, texting.

"New ideas?" I asked.

"Recommended to Sigrid that the town strongly support bike paths to ease congestion, and to see what they can do about bike storage for commuters."

I laughed. We hadn't seen either Robert or the Mayor when we'd last gone down to Noonerry, but Kyou had obviously kept in touch.

"Will this new friendship hold up once your interview is published?" He'd spoken to the scandal-hunting reporter the previous Friday, and hadn't hidden his motives for buying on Snowshield Tableland.

"Probably," Kyou said, shrugging. "As you said, after the announcement they surely suspected me of everything. Though warning them against further sales turned out to be good politics. There's a difference between buying property already on the market, and convincing settled residents to sell up just before a price explosion. I earned quite a few brownie points giving locals time to withdraw from a handful of sales."

"Has Sigrid given you any feel about how development's going to be dealt with?"

"Richard's been more useful there: he's quite the gossip. Currently the feel of the locals is against any form of dense development, to not lose the 'rural' nature of the place altogether, but they're not entirely opposed to rezoning what is currently agricultural land. Fortunately, council elections were at the beginning of the year, so we can expect a period of stability. And then an outright war, right around the time the rail line opens."

"Are your plans likely to fall into their definition of dense development?"

"Hard to say: we'll see how they react to the first proposals. Richard was rather delighted when I told him we wanted to turn the centre portion of Fox Hollow into a garden and park. Incorporating green space wherever possible is likely to go down well."

Rin and Bran arrived, and helped mash potatoes and assemble a salad while Kyou struggled somewhat with the steak.

"The instructions make it seem so simple," Kyou said, turning a second time. "And yet I get anaemic beige instead of juicy darkness."

"Heat control," I said. "Not that I'm much better at steaks. It'll probably still taste okay, so long as you don't overcook it."

It was edible, at least. We concocted ice cream sundaes for dessert, and were idly discussing Fabian's band when my phone rang. I glanced at the caller ID and, a little surprised, answered on speaker.

"Hi Anthea?" I said, hoping it wasn't bad news.

"Who is this?"

I paused, recognising the voice as Rin's mother's, then said: "Who is this? Why do you have Anthea's phone?"

"This is Anthea's mother," the woman said crisply.

"Oh! Hello, um, Mrs Seagrim," I said, dredging up Anthea's surname from the useful forum posts detailing the extended Laurent-Beaulieu clan. "Let Anthea know my dad promised to sign all the books she'd like. He'll be here for the writer's festival, so we can organise it then."

"Your father?" This was obviously not the expected response.

"He writes as Blake Sevenmore," I explained. "Jessamin's a fan, and Anthea wants to give her a complete signed collection for Christmas."

"I see," Mrs Seagrim said. "I'll tell her."

She hung up, and I shook my head.

"Do you think your mother is going through all the contacts in their phones to see if they're talking to you?" I asked Rin.

"Probably," Rin said, grimacing. "Anthea must have deleted the texts she's been sending you, or you wouldn't have gotten away with that."

I nodded. Anthea had taken to sending me chatty texts, full of the latest news about her and Jessamin, which I would simply show to Rin, and then respond with some neutral news about 'my job'. "She's going to end up alienating all of you, ignoring their privacy like that."

"I know," Rin said, gloomily.

"If only they could be completely evil instead of moderately bastardish," Bran said, with an edge of sarcasm.

Rin picked an almond off his sundae and flicked it at him, but Bran caught it effortlessly, and ate it.

"Weak," he taunted, then added to me: "Can I have a complete signed collection too?"

"Sure. Mum prepped all our stuff for shipping while she was in Wales, and it'll be sent as soon as the garage is built. An absolute mass of boxes, and eighty percent full of author's copies. Dad will be glad to offload some."

"From one garage to another," Kyou observed.

"We'll put one of each edition in the new library, which will be fun. Twenty years of writing two to four books a year adds up, especially if there's foreign language editions. Admittedly, he couldn't sell everything he's written, and the Rock Hardison books are almost all ebook-only, but it's still going to be impressive to look at." I grinned. "They're so excited. If Mum hadn't already committed to a hospital restructure in Mexico, I swear they'd be here already, hovering over every step of the renovation. Well, knowing Mum, optimising Cassadine Malway's processes."

"I suspect one of my best decisions will end up being luring your mother to live close at hand," Kyou said. "There's so much we could be doing better, and I fully expect you to influence her into agreeing to kick us into shape."

"She's the smartest person I know," I said.

"We should recommend her to that mayor," Bran said. "Your mother will soon be a Noonerry local, after all."

Kyou lifted his eyebrows, picked up his phone, but then shook his head. "I'll save that for an in-person chat." As he put the phone down again, it chimed for a text message, which he only glanced at before muting his phone.

"Your dad still giving you grief?" Bran asked.

"Thinks it would only make sense if we handed over all the land at Noonerry to L-B Corp. Well, to him specifically."

Bran rolled his eyes. "Just because?"

"Since we're going to waste ourselves playing games, we should give it to someone who knows what they're doing."

"He's going to hate almost everything we do there," Rin said, lips curling.

"Is there any way he can force his way in?" I asked.

"Not legally," Kyou said. "Even if he killed us all off, the only beneficiaries would be Rin's sisters, and Rowan. But he isn't likely to go quite that far, since Great-Grandfather would crucify him."

"Not that we're immune from attack," Bran said. "The idea that someone in the Planning Commission leaked information to us, for instance, sounds more like an attempt to fuck us over than common sense. You started buying before they even decided to abandon Sunneway Pass."

"Yes, there's no legs to it," Kyou said, shrugging. "All it'll achieve is Kybirn's name becoming a little better known." He smiled suddenly. "Did you say that the full trailer for *One Step* is nearly ready? Can you get it up on the site as soon as possible?"

Bran snorted, then nodded. "Yeah. May as well ride the wave."

"Nothing like free publicity," Kyou said.

oOo

The headline of "BILLION DOLLAR CHAT" certainly brought Kybirn Games plenty of attention, with a big surge of hits on *One Step More*'s trailer as soon as the article was published. Kyou was less pleased when it was followed by a number of puff pieces on "Greenland's most eligible young bachelors". Most notably a sprawling article titled "THREE YOUNG KINGS".

Rin, Kyou and Bran had long been well known in certain circles, but the discovery that they had their own now-formidable fortune outside any expectation on L-B Corp's shares shifted them into gossip column territory. And people started to literally throw themselves into their paths.

One occasion I actually recorded and sent to my dad, because I knew he'd appreciate it. I was waiting for Bran by the library, and noticed a girl constantly looking at me, and then down the path along the lake. After about five minutes of this, I started to record her, and neatly captured her performance of spotting Bran, fiddling with the fastening of one of her sandals, and then heading toward him. She turned her foot just as she reached him, the sandal flew off, and she fell right into his arms. Bran is really the wrong person to try this on. He caught her, set her on her feet, and then walked around her and continued on to me, wearing an entirely disgusted expression and completely ignoring the rest of her carefully-rehearsed 'meet cute'. He soon grew so tired of the enthusiasm that he wore a hoodie for the rest of autumn.

Ironically, the burst of interest in the Kings added to my popularity. While I still got hate on forums, I also had a wave of strangers trying to strike up conversations, and ended up having to stop hanging out at the library tables because it made me too easy to find for people who wanted a stepping stone to my housemates.

Fully appreciating the origins of the Three Kings' reputation for being standoffish, I minimised my own time on campus. Fortunately, I was so busy that was a natural outcome. Along with my full course load, I was having a glorious time drawing concept art, and helping Kybirn Isambard become the job of my dreams.

Nineteen

"Bothered that your report didn't get highlighted?" Athaine asked, following me out of the third of Professor Tremaine's monthly lectures.

"Itching to go home and play a new game," I admitted. "And I'm entirely prepared for my reports to never get highlighted, no matter what Professor Tremaine's view of me. Remember, one of the things that's interesting about this course is there's a distinct possibility I'm not the smartest person in the room."

Athaine looked startled, then laughed, an action that lightened his usually brooding features into something vivid and brilliant.

"I mightn't be either. How lowering. Still, I refuse to believe you'd be entirely unbothered if the Prof ignores everything you do."

"So long as my reports are passed," I replied, noticing Lania and waving at her. "The highlighting doesn't gain me anything but a moment of gloss, so rather than get caught up in competing with my fellow students, I'd prefer to focus on practical things."

"But we are all competing, aren't we? At least, those who want to get into that Graduate Program."

I paused, because I'd discovered something remarkable: I had completely lost the urge to compete for a place in the Marden Institute.

"Ever since I started my internship, graduate studies haven't meant a lot to me."

"Internship?" Athaine was so astonished he almost ran into Lania. "Have I missed something? Has there been a time skip, and we're no longer in our first semester?"

Lania, hearing this, laughed. "The longer you know Mika, the greater the creeping sense of unreality."

"That sounds outright ominous," Athaine said, looking down at her. I introduced them, and then Athaine returned to the point: "Really an internship?"

"We're encouraged to get some practical experience before we graduate," I told him.

"In our third or fourth year!" Athaine protested.

I shrugged, and followed the horde into one of the larger lecture theatres.

"I remember when I thought I'd be sitting with you in half my lectures," Lania said, as we managed to grab three consecutive seats. "Instead, I'm usually lucky to be able to wave at you from across the room."

"I'm increasingly starting to only watch them online," I said. "Save my campus time for labs."

"Is everyone in the course getting internships?" Athaine asked, doggedly. "I suddenly feel like I should start job hunting."

"Have you decided what you want to go into yet?" I asked.

"That's...complicated," Athaine said. "Is it bad not to love anything?"

"Better than loving too many things," Lania said, in her mildest voice.

I grinned. Lania still fought shy of even visiting me at home again, but she was definitely growing more accustomed to my complicated private life if she was willing to tweak my nose about it.

We quieted down for the lecture, and then I said my goodbyes and walked briskly back to the house, washed up, and went down to the gaming room to discover an interior decoration committee.

"Why did we not think to install picture rails?" Rin was saying, relaxing on one of the couches as Bran and Kyou adjusted the position of a new painting. "It's very off-centre for the wall."

"Not helpful, Rin," Kyou said, without rancour.

"When," Rin asked, with a gusty sigh, "have I ever wanted to be helpful?" He saw me and smiled gently. "Mika will no doubt be able to bring to bear all the practical experience we lack."

"Living in rentals, you're not usually allowed to hang pictures," I said, glanced at their progress, and added: "You're going to want to start by buying a stud detector, and no that's not a reference to the way you three look, but is giving me ideas for another of our games."

"You in a blindfold, us just out of reach?" Kyou asked, interestedly.

"Would we call that Blind Man in the Buff?"

"I'll add it to the list," Bran said, putting the hammer on the coffee table. He sat on the floor and pulled out the keyboard to the game room PC, searched briefly for 'stud detector', and then ordered one for delivery.

"It seemed too simple to need looking up a tutorial," Kyou said. "Buy hook, nail it on the wall, hang picture."

I'd picked up his painting to admire. For Rin's birthday I'd bought him a bouquet of mixed white flowers peppered with a small number of forget-me-nots, and they'd all immediately recognised the clothing items the flowers represented. Kyou had promised to paint Rin a permanent copy, which he'd done in the same Impressionist style as his view of a summerhouse.

"We're going to end up with a house full of hidden references to me in my underwear," I said, propping the frame against the wall.

"That sounds fantastic," Kyou said. "And if you happened to occasionally make that your chosen mode of dress, even better."

"I'll match the general trend," I said, amused. "Bran, did you say Rowan's video would launch today? I searched and couldn't find it."

"His stage name's Ashen-R," Bran said, doing another quick search. "Ten thousand hits already," he said. "Not bad for a complete unknown."

He started the video playing, and we all sat down to watch. I'd only met Rowan the one time, and had to revise my impression of him as he strutted through a crowd of teens, mouth twisted with impatience, reaching Bran's level of magnetism as he snarled out a song Rin had written for him: *Don't Waste My Time.*

"It should do well," Rin said judiciously. "Stronger than what they were going to lead with."

"And I thought he was shy," I said.

"Not on stage," Bran said.

"Just don't try to get him to make small talk," Kyou said, grinning. "Speaking of music videos, a query came in from Glacier Records. Co-Motion told them about our setup and they want to rent out the capture facilities for an animated clip. Any objections?"

"Probably helpful to give the rooms an extended test run," Bran said. "So long as they don't think they're taking over the building."

"Who for?" Rin asked.

"*Easy Cat*," Kyou said. This was a Greenlander band considered to be past its peak.

"Oh, them. Sure." Rin shrugged.

"Do we only rent to bands we like?" Bran asked. I saw he'd texted his brother 'Clip looks good' and Rowan had replied 'thx'.

"It's not like we set the rooms up for commercial leasing," Rin said. "But *Easy Cat's* worth listening to. Make sure they know it's a non-smoking site."

Bran had switched to installing files on the game room pc, and glanced at Rin as the progress bar ran swiftly. "Want us to leave?"

Rin shook his head. "Stay if you can resist commentary."

He had switched from lazy to serious, and swapped seats so he was sitting with me on the left couch, while Kyou and Bran occupied the other. A title screen launched, focused around an ink and watercolour rendition of a recorder and a violin, and the words *One Step More*.

"The first full playthrough," Rin said, handing me the controller. "You can tell me your impressions, or play in silence: whatever works better for you."

"If you hit an impassable bug, we can reload from an autosave," Bran added. "Though we've stamped out most of them."

With such an attentive audience, I could only hope that it turned out to be the kind of game I enjoyed. I selected New Game, and watched a tiny pen rapidly draw a pastoral landscape: trees, small buildings, a tractor, crops, grapevines, and the beginning of rambling villa. The 'camera' zoomed in through a window of the villa and shifted to a close view of a sheet of music, and finally sound, a single, drawn-out note from a violin as our perspective shifted to the child holding the instrument—a pre-teen with long, light brown hair, rendered in pure watercolour, without any ink framing.

Rin does tend to look feminine, and if I hadn't known him, I would assume this was a young girl. A half-heard call interrupted the note, and the boy looked around, then hastily tucked the violin into a case and reached up to perch the case on top of a cupboard. Then he climbed out the window, and dropped down between a blond and a black-haired boy. The violin note returned, and then steadily grew, joined with a swirl of other instruments, and transformed into a triumphal accompaniment as the three hunted through grape vines, dodged between haystacks, and clambered onto roofs. And, just when the music reached a crescendo, leaped across a small gap between two buildings.

The music stopped. One boy fell.

I'd known that Rin had injured his back as a child, but never asked the details. Hadn't expected to watch Kyou and Bran's wordless distress, or segue through blurred moments of consciousness as the bright colours of an afternoon's play shifted through hospital scenes, and back to the original room, a drab and dreary place where a child sat lifelessly in a wheelchair, his visitors swept out with an imperative shushing, and the only sound a haze of rain.

I had shifted closer to Rin, pressing into his side, and my mouth was dry when I asked: "What's the line between 'deeply personal' and 'outright autobiographical'?"

"More a summary," Rin said, squeezing me comfortingly. "How I felt about it emotionally, rather than a strict retelling."

"We weren't allowed to visit," Kyou said. "He had a few headaches at the start, and everyone fixated on Rin needing quiet."

"They blamed us," Bran said, bluntly. "They also gave him a complete course of homework to keep him occupied."

"The doctors were very optimistic about my recovery," Rin went on. "The diagnosis was a bruised spinal cord. No tears detected, just swelling. But nothing was guaranteed, and I wasn't in a very good place mentally. Every day seemed an eternity."

On the screen, the boy in the wheelchair had not moved, and the rain outside the room poured down in a steady, numbing hush. There were no instructions, so I followed the standard controller configuration for movement and looking around, and the boy shifted away from the grey haze of window and crossed to the wardrobe to look up at his violin case.

The game played with perspective briefly, turning the wardrobe into an insurmountable cliff. The boy bowed his head, and sat unmoving as the rain faded, and left a dripping hush.

Into this came a splash-SPLASH-splash and then a tap-tap-tap. A hand waved, obviously reaching up from some point well below the window. I guided the boy over, and struggled to open the window when the latch was barely within reach. A wooden object waved in the boy's face, and he grabbed it.

A recorder, larger than the versions I remembered from a variety of early music classes. The boy, with the urging of the controller, played a few shrill notes, then began the same melody he'd been practicing on the violin. I paused.

"How long does it actually take you to learn an instrument?" I asked.

"Weeks to months for rough competency, depending on whether I've played something similar," Rin said, smiling down at me. "This is a game about composing, not learning the basics.

"He was playing that thing smoothly in less than a week," Bran said.

"We picked a recorder because it's easier to hide," Kyou added, just as the boy on-screen hastily tucked his under the blanket across his knees.

"We'd already brought him a handheld and a tablet," Bran added. "He barely used them, and then they were confiscated."

"Did you still have headaches, or were they punishing you?" I asked Rin, quietly appalled.

"They'd never term it like that," Rin said, and glanced at the screen as a parental figure swept through the room, closing the window, moving the wheelchair, shifting the table closer to hand, and then whisked out again. "Most of the books were interesting enough, once I had the energy to read them."

"Pre-reading for the next five years of literature classes," Bran muttered.

"Play the game," Kyou advised.

I played, following a simple tutorial to select different song components that eventually merged into a completed piece, accompanied by images that matched the mood of the music. It allowed me to 'compose' several brief recorder pieces, and I smiled when one of them turned out to be the lazily winding melody that had become one of my favourite pieces of thinking music. And then shot Rin a delighted glance when the resulting imagery included the towers I'd drawn in response.

"It was initially supposed to be smoke drifting between tall trees," Rin said, looking exceptionally pleased. "But I ended up liking this more. If you'll give us permission to use it."

I took time out to kiss him, because I enjoyed this discovery very much, but then controlled myself and went back to the game. It wasn't a long one, perhaps two hours, though with the potential for a lot of replayability, to choose different paths through the musical options. And, despite the rather grim start, became peaceful, then outright cheerful and even funny, as more and more instruments were smuggled into the room, and then hidden in increasingly unlikely ways: hung from the ceiling, behind coats in the now Narnia-like cupboard, miniaturized in a small fish tank, or simply sitting in plain sight, but with a lampshade on top. And ended as it had begun, with another triumphal cascade of music, as the instruments were strung together into a ramp that allowed the boy to escape his room, and join his friends to once again hurtle through the countryside, the wheelchair bouncing over small obstacles, and then rocketing with all three of them clinging, through the closing credits.

I watched these for a few moments, then looked up at Rin again.

"I had been thinking of music as almost like oxygen for you," I said, after a pause. "But is it really a release? Trapped inside you, pushing to get out?"

"Both of those," he said. "More things as well. A compulsion, a puzzle. An addiction. Sometimes outright torture." He glanced back at the screen, as the wheelchair slid down a hill of music credits. "Mostly just joy, though."

"That's what this game will give people," I said, watching as the two friends began pushing the wheelchair up a slope made of the names of the art team. "I can see people hoarding it for the days when they're at their worst."

"There's different ending sequences as well," Bran said. "And hidden instruments."

"Did you notice that you always chose the calm or upbeat options?" Rin asked.

"Well, I have to admit that in part I was trying to cheer virtual you up," I said, catching one of his hands so I could curl my fingers through his. "Are there bad endings?"

"No. Though quite different ones." He squeezed my hand, then let go and stretched, looking highly pleased with himself. "You can find them another day. It's well past time for dinner."

"Takeout," Kyou said, firmly.

It was his turn to cook, but no-one argued. We were always flexible about rostered tasks because our schedules were so packed. And today was a special day.

"I'd say let's celebrate, but I'm in the mood for something light," I said.

"We'll have a launch party on release day," Bran said. "I might try out a cake for it."

"Hopefully by then your cakes won't sag in the middle," Kyou said.

For my birthday, my Kings had surprised me with a kirsch cake, and claimed that next year they would make me one themselves. They'd bought a massive baking-for-beginners book, but Bran was really the only one who'd started working his way through it, with variable results.

"Any suggestions for improvements on the game?" Rin asked, while Kyou ordered Thai.

"Is the 'step' in the title a reference to the interval between notes in a scale?"

"Were you expecting me to be walking by the end? A rehab sequence?"

"Not once I was a little way through the game. But I don't necessarily think people will know that definition of 'step'."

"We can put definitions of musical terms on the transition screens," Bran said.

Talk became technical, and they'd settled on the change by the time dinner was over.

"We need your parents to get over themselves so that you can watch your sisters play," I said, as we packed the dishwasher.

"I'm not sure that's going to happen soon," Rin said, frowning.

Smaller deputations of Rin's parents had visited to 'talk reason' into him, on occasions when I wasn't around, but no progress had been made. Kyou had blocked all his immediate family, and received no in-person visitations, while I still wasn't sure if Bran's were even aware of his living arrangements, or that the Kybirn Music who'd provided Rowan with a last-minute song had anything to do with their other son.

Because my relationship with my parents was so good, a part of me kept wanting to find a way to help them all reconcile. But I had to trust their own views.

"We can organise an illicit visit," Bran said. "I expect they'd rather be punished than miss out on seeing the game before launch."

"We'll look into smuggling them over when we're back from our internship," Rin said. "Possibly Christmas will bring a brief thaw, and they can visit without accompanying drama."

"Let's put up a tree before we leave," Kyou said. "We'll be well into December before we're back."

Despite Kybirn continuing to gear up, Rin, Kyou and Bran were still heading off to Seattle for another two-week internship they'd arranged over a year ago. They wanted to get as much first-hand experience as possible with larger developers before Kybirn really started to ramp up.

"Are you planning to spend the whole of the time we're gone down at Noonerry, Mika?" Kyou asked.

"Most of it," I said. "I was only planning on a week, up to when the Fox Farm renovation was due to complete, but with the delay on the glass, I'm going to stay until that's installed. Probably up until the second Friday."

"I'm very interested to know how long it takes for you to adjust to our absence," he said.

"Me too," I said, smiling. "Simply not seeing you for a fortnight is going to be weird, let alone facing my sleep issues again. Don't get tempted to hang around Seattle, okay?"

We talked lightly of souvenirs, and possible future holidays, and then went up to Rin's room, because he was in the mood to duet with Bran for a while, and Kyou and I wanted to listen. We shifted Rin's divan to a convenient spot, and I enjoyed myself watching Kyou sketch Bran and Rin. Two tall boys, one standing upright with a violin tucked beneath his chin, the other cradling a cello, somehow managing to look entirely relaxed sitting on the curving bench Rin had had installed in his corner roomlet.

I used my phone to take a picture of Kyou, and one of Rin and Bran, then settled back to listen, only to shiver as a cool draft stirred the gauzy curtains. Rin's love for leaving his windows open had its issues at the end of autumn. At least, unlike the last time this had bothered me, I was wearing clothes, so I simply got up and closed them, then paused to survey the street.

On the corner, in the glow of the ornamental street light, stood a boy and a dog, listening to the free concert. Professor Tremaine's son, Greysen, and the Afghan I often saw him walking. I still wasn't entirely sure if he was a student of her course, or just came along to the lectures, and I suspect he had no idea who I was when he saw me in the window, but he still ducked his head in embarrassment and then walked back to the third townhouse opposite.

He went inside, and I started to turn away, then caught movement out of the corner of my eye, and glimpsed someone who had been standing in the gloom on the opposite corner of the side street. It was too dark for me to make out more than the figure, but even so the height and head-down posture struck a note of recognition.

Athaine?

Twenty

End-of-term came and went without difficulty, but immediately after the last exam, my Kings caught an overnight flight to Seattle, and I slept alone in a house that suddenly felt echoing and empty. My bed especially felt cold, and ridiculously large. While I am a person who appreciates a certain amount of solitude, the transition to winter was definitely the wrong time of year to test my ability to adapt to a lack of warm boy.

Fortunately, I had arranged a distraction.

"Welcome back to the lion's den," I said. "Or is it more dragon's lair? I was beginning to think you'd never come over again."

Lania stuck out her tongue as I gestured her into the foyer. "If I could figure out a way to face the three of them without going cherry-red at the idea of the four of you..." she said, manoeuvring a compact suitcase through the inner door.

"You deal well enough with Bran during our labs."

"Bran spends his time staring off into the distance, or at his feet," Lania said. "Whereas Rin would laugh at me while pretending not to, and Kyou would indulge in double entendre to see if he could make me go redder."

"I probably would too," I said, judiciously. "But only for the first couple of minutes, and then we'd all get over it. Do you want a drink or a rest before we hit the road?"

"Before a four-hour drive, bathroom break," she said, glancing admiringly at the excessively tall

Christmas tree, then pausing as she saw the staircase. Two kettle drums stood before the newel posts.

"Rin's idea of decoration?" she asked.

"More that the only other place big enough for them is the piano room, and he doesn't want them there since it's supposed to fill in as a function area." I started to reach out, then restrained myself. "Rin is going to relocate them to Noonerry because it's too difficult to resist tapping them whenever we walk by. Once, he had a spark of inspiration, and started to play them at three in the morning. Bad timing, because the rest of us had been up late. Closest I've ever seen to Kyou losing his temper."

I pointed Lania at the ground-floor bathroom, grabbed my prepared cold drinks from the fridge, and led her to the garage when she returned.

"Put your bag in the back seat of the Hummer: the rear's full already. Want to drive?"

"Can I?" Lania asked, blinking at the enormous vehicle.

"You do the first half, and I'll do the second," I suggested. "I've already racked up more driving hours than anyone could need, and am looking forward to quick trips on the high-speed rail more than I can say."

"There's no way I could afford to pay for any damage."

"That's why insurance," I said. "And Rin okayed you driving—he knows I'm not someone who enjoys it."

"Lucky I have a full license."

Much hilarity was afforded adjusting the seat and steering wheel so that Lania could actually drive Rin's behemoth. I took a photo and posted it to our Mockingbird app, but it was too early in Seattle for even

Kyou to respond. Lania was my opposite: she liked driving, but didn't have much opportunity to practice, and so wore a blend of excitement and caution as she backed the Hummer out of the garage and headed for the main street.

"Great pick up," she said, after we'd started down Gore Heights Road.

"Yeah, seems to be a strength of electric vehicles."

"I guess it can't make the whole trip there and back on a single charge?"

"No. On our first couple of trips, we had to make sure to hit a particular Power Stop in Moonmere because there's none currently in Noonerry, but the house we've had renovated on Noonerry High Street will be fine for charging. Reviewing and signing off on the work there is my first task for this trip."

"Why did this renovation complete before your parents' house?"

"The High Street house only involved paint work, and a new kitchen and bathroom. Fox Farm is a complete remodelling—not to mention the fact that the roof beams needed replacing, and, oh, all these things that came up. I'm glad we didn't start on Fox Farm without a buffer of money, because expediting the build, and all the extra costs, really..." I shook my head. "Nothing my parents couldn't handle, but outlaying such big chunks of their savings these past couple of months has been an experience. Mum says we'll eventually adjust to enjoying our money, and only hoard a bit of it."

"Helps that the property has to have tripled in value, even with an unfinished renovation."

"Yeah, in terms of investment I don't think we'll ever make as much so quickly as we did with Fox Farm. Kyou really did me a favour."

"Given how he ended up with the place, I'd call it the absolute minimum!" Lania said. "The land he's bought isn't really worth a billion, I expect, but..."

"It still made quite a headline," I said, smiling. "And a nice excuse for my room rental, but I can't really take credit for Kyou's bonanza. I started him off early, yeah, but I expect he'd have done the same thing once the first hint of problems with the original route came out. The real credit goes to Gyden Adderway, the firm he hired to analyse the most likely route. They were a good deal more accurate than those who thought it would go through Vitha Valley, and they reached that conclusion in a spectacularly short amount of time, giving him a lead on all the other people who eventually started trying to buy on the Tableland."

"How would you have felt if he'd bought all that land, and it hadn't worked out?"

"He says he wouldn't have made a loss no matter where the station ended up. And at this point, I completely believe he could turn a random pile of leaves into money, or spin straw into gold, but I'm glad not to have to feel responsible, while still ending up with a home with a matchless view."

"Speaking of views, I really like the height of this thing," Lania said. "Not that I'd want to try to squeeze it around some of the more claustrophobic parking garages. At least, now that he has a farm, having a big car..."

Lania, slowing down for traffic lights, stopped well short of front position. I followed her gaze, and saw a convertible in the next lane, occupied by three beautiful girls. The driver must have spotted the Hummer in her rear vision mirror, because she turned in her seat.

"I suppose today's warm enough for an open top," I said, as the girls all waved excitedly at the Hummer, while not apparently able to make out the driver. "I haven't seen Katerina and co since we started at Helios U. She seems awfully enthusiastic about Rin for someone apparently devoted to Carr."

"Rin is Corascur's eternal moonlight: shining but untouchable," Lania said, then shot me a quick smile. "Mine too, remember, before he got so tall, and before I worked with him on the Student Council and understood him a little better."

"You don't like tall guys?" I asked, interested.

"To a certain point, but I always feel like I'm talking to Rin's navel." Lania's attention was still on the convertible.

"You should say hi," I suggested.

Lania hesitated, then shook her head. "Irrelevant people," she said, paused, then added: "And they'll hate a complete lack of response even more than me gloating at them from the driver's seat."

The lights changed, and we left the convertible behind as we headed for the southern expressway. During the middle part of the drive, I revolted Lania by having an entirely innocuous conversation with Rin that I admit might have sounded syrupy sweet purely because of my tone of voice. What can I say? I missed him.

We swapped drivers just before the Incun-Moonmere turnoff so Lania could properly appreciate the autumn colour in Strathold Forest.

"Past its prime, but still very beautiful," I said, enjoying the great swathes of Greenland Blaze. They'd already passed the golden stage, and most of the leaves were now white and falling like confetti. "Even in Winter the walks will be gorgeous. Mum's going to love it here."

"I can see why Kyou saw this area and thought 'weddings'," Lania said. "A service under Greenland Blaze in autumn would be absolutely magical."

"Since the property actually covers the base of the tableland, we did briefly discuss having a chapel in the forest, but Kyou wants to avoid annoying the Park Service. Not that we won't have a forest venue, but one we grow ourselves. The garden designer is starting on Monday, and will be faced with coming up with something functional that includes Kyou's laundry list of garden features. One of which is a 'ripped from Tolkien' venue. For small services only, tree branches woven together overhead, hand carved wooden benches, art piece lighting." I shook my head. "Kyou wanting to turn the place into a destination wedding resort seemed totally out of left field when he first mentioned the idea, but Fox Hollow probably really will end up a world-famous 'must see' location."

"What a fun thing to put together," Lania said, sighing. "No wonder you say 'loving it' every time I ask about your job."

"It's bliss. For KG I get paid for something I usually do for fun, and at KI I've leapfrogged about five years ahead in my lifelong goals."

"You've started calling where you work by initials now? But don't you have two companies with the same letters?"

"When we talk about Kybirn Investment, we tend to just call it 'Kybirn'," I explained. "Almost all employees belong to one of the sub-companies. Kybirn Isambard now has eight people. Ten from next week."

Lania lowered her window to take a photo, then said: "You need that many architects? Engineers?"

"Chloe and Fabian have headhunted a whole team of specialists, to handle everything from drainage to interior decoration. Not only to tackle the decade's worth of construction projects Kyou has lined up, but because there's plenty of people on the tableland who want to subdivide, sell some of their land, and use the proceeds to develop the remainder. We already have two external jobs, both remodels of big old houses to turn them into B&Bs. There's a desperate need for accommodation across the whole of the eastern half of the tableland, for HSR project staff, construction crews, and just this flood of businesses trying to get in on the action."

"Where are all the Kybirn Isambard staff staying?"

"Moonmere, in the half-dozen houses Kyou bought there. Currently rent-free, to make the move to the tableland easier, and then transitioning to rental in six months, after some staged remodelling. Two of the bigger houses will be long-term share accommodation, because staff numbers here are going to go up long before any of the construction projects are finished."

"Moonmere's the nearest place to Noonerry? What's it like as a town?"

"Semi-rural, population of eight thousand. A lot of unemployment, some issues with kids stealing cars and racing around the hilly curvy roads to the west. A couple of really lovely late 1800s manor houses. Some suburbs that are basically a collection of tin shacks.

Quite a few big personalities and old feuds, which is going to matter because zoning changes have to go through the Shire Council rather than the Town Council, and there's only one person from Noonerry on the Shire Council."

"Politics," Lania said, with a lack of enthusiasm that matched my own. "How's it working out with your boss? Bosses? Mentors?"

"Bosses and mentors," I said. "Chloe and Fabian are both very good at what they do, of course, or they'd never have been recommended to Kyou in the first place. Thankfully, they're also the kind of people who are interested in getting a job done well, with the least amount of fuss. Chloe in particular is superbly organised and methodical, with a lot of deep experience. She anticipates so many things that I've never encountered."

"You like her more than your Professor Tremaine?"

"Interesting question. Even though she doesn't have a fraction of Professor Tremaine's reputation, I think Chloe is going to end up teaching me more. And Chloe, at least, waited to see what I was like before forming an opinion about me. I'm deeply curious about how she ended up sidelined in her previous job since, while she's quiet, she's not a shrinking violet or anything. Fabian's background is more straightforward: he loves Goth styling, and things like live-action roleplay, and his piercings scare off the more conservative customers, so he's struggled to attract business. Noonerry is going to end up being a reputation-setting showpiece for him."

"No wonder they were willing to relocate. Are their families coming too, or waiting for the rail line?"

"Chloe's single. Fabian's family was easy to relocate, since his kids are young and his wife works from home. Danika makes custom clothing: gorgeous dresses and brocade suits and things like that. She showed me this awesome photo of their two kids done up as Edwardian vampires."

"They're not bothered by you being both an intern and, what, lead designer?"

"Almost certainly the most awkward part of the job for them," I said. "I do everything I can to make sure I'm very much an intern when I'm being an intern, and keep my weird extra role to the background. It helps a lot that the headquarters is the only active project that's based on my concepts. Kyou wants Fabian and Chloe to be lead on all the residential buildings, and any external jobs that come in, and has straightforwardly signed off on everything they've given him so far. The only exception has been when Chloe handheld me through the entire process of designing the bridge for my parents' access road, just so that I could truly call it mine, even if it was officially under her name. It and the new road will be ready just before Mum and Dad are due to arrive."

After the long drone of the expressway, the trip through the forest and up onto the tableland always seemed to go by in a flash. The drive back east along Noonerry Road had on previous weekends featured straying sheep, one mass crossing of cows, a small cavalcade of tractors, and a carful of teens who had mooned us. Today, we were stuck in a line behind a pair of dump trucks, but I didn't mind this particularly, since driving slow gave me a chance to consider a proliferation of signs touting upcoming auctions. The land rush was still in full swing.

Noonerry High Street was the one north of Noonerry Main Street, and featured most of the town's larger houses. I pulled smoothly into the driveway of the renovated house, appreciating the outer transformation from shabby genteel to neat renewal. Sang-Hoon Park, the coordinator from Cassadine Malway for this project, had arrived early, and so I decided to postpone lunch, introduced Lania, and briskly went over the house with him. This was problem-free. The place looked immaculate, and didn't even smell too much of varnish and fresh paint.

"It's weird," Lania said, as we waved Sang-Hoon off. "He seemed vaguely disappointed the entire time."

I laughed. "Yeah, so far we're two for two on Cassadine Malway staff falling for Rin. Let's bring our stuff in, then walk over to get lunch while the car's charging. Even with all the snacking I did on the drive, my stomach's pretending to be neglected."

Kyou had arranged for another 'final touch' service from Cassadine Malway, so the house was already stocked with linen, staple foods, and other basics, but I'd also brought down a few boxes of extras, including an array of laptops and tablets properly set up for Kybirn connectivity.

"Leave the rest of the boxes in the car," I told Lania, after separating out the items for the house. "That's for the office on Monday."

"More computers?"

"No, part of this display idea Kyou came up with. The local residents are very worried that the tableland will be covered in skyscrapers and housing blocks, so he asked us to put something together to show our upcoming projects. He figures it might also work as free advertising, drawing people in for a look. Kyou has a pet hatred for advertising costs."

We dumped boxes and bags in the loungeroom, locked up, and headed down the short flight of stairs at the front of the house. I admired the colourful sandstone of the walkway, and searched out a few photos on my phone to show Lania what it had looked like before the recent power washing.

"Really fun to watch them clean: attracted quite a few of the neighbourhood kids too. Kyou's even considering starting a garden maintenance business, since Fox Hollow will need a ton of care, not to mention all the other properties Kybirn will own."

"Does he have some sort of addiction to starting businesses?" Lania asked.

"I think it's more that if he sees a really good opportunity, he can't resist following it up. Especially if it's something that represents an ongoing cost. He's also being a bit political: he'll have more influence if he employs locals, and there's only a limited number he can use for Kybirn Games."

We reached *Madison's*—the combined bakery/café that was one of the very few choices for food in Noonerry.

"Hey Mika," said Shona, the lead on *Madison's* afternoon shift, coming across from the café section to the bakery counter. "Not much left, I'm afraid."

"Give me a half-dozen mixed," I said, eyeing the meagre scatter of tarts and pastries philosophically. It was past three, after all. "And then we'll look at what's available in the café. We're going to go have a picnic dinner on a hill."

"Enjoy it while the weather's still fine," Shona said agreeably, as she glanced past me. "No eye candy today?"

"They're off for two weeks to check out the operations of another game company," I explained, sharing her grin. "We're all going to come down here for Christmas after my parents arrive, though."

"The farmhouse is nearly finished? What is it you're building down by the river?"

"A gazebo. Somewhere to sit and enjoy the water. Dad says he's going to write down there when the weather's nice, and be a local sight for the people passing on the train."

"Don't joke: a real published writer is definitely going to be an attraction around here," Shona said, laughing. "He can set up a stall and sell his books to the gawkers."

"Now there's an idea," I said, entertained. "My mother shipped about a thousand boxes of old author's copies, which are going to fill up way too much of the new garage. Once we've sorted them out, we'll definitely have to hold some kind of sale. Or...there's not currently a bookstore in town, but there might be eventually."

"Simon at the grocery might put out a little table for him," Shona suggested.

"Feels like you're practically one of the locals already," Lania said, as we headed back, snacking on hot chips. "Does everyone know all about your family?"

"It's more I can't resist that bakery, and Shona met Dad when we came down the first time. I've only spread the Rock Hardison and Blake Sevenmore pen names, so far." I smiled. "It's really interesting how I behave differently about long-term things, since I actually thought about holding off on Rock Hardison until Dad's had a chance to charm everyone. But old Rock has fed us for too long for Dad to start denying him now."

"On the subject of charm offensives, how did the Kings manage to swing themselves internships at a rival game company? I can't imagine it's standard practice to let the competition visit for a couple of weeks."

"A combination of Bran and Rin. Bran often helps people out on the more esoteric technical forums, and has managed to rack up quite a few favours. Rin, as Kybirn Music, did a few pieces for *Crimson After*, and asked for, not exactly an internship, more a session to understand development processes. They won't be exposed to anything juicy. Plus, NDAs and all that."

We returned to the house, and finished our chips before driving east out of town.

The scene here had changed considerably, with a chunk of the public reserve fenced off and occupied by temporary buildings. Not too far away a cluster of workers were centred around a machine busily digging a trench.

"You can tell the government's planning to make the completion of the line part of its election campaign," Lania joked, watching the swarm of activity. "I bet public construction on a Saturday is expensive."

I nodded. "It's also a priority to get the line up to the tableland underway as soon as possible, as it's by far the most complex part of the project left. The land acquisition here is already complete, including the chunk it takes out of Fox Farm. Even though they valued the land at a scandalously low rate, Kyou didn't try to bargain." I laughed. "Instead, he used the negotiation discussion to propose a pedestrian footbridge across the boundary road to the small strip of buildings he wants to use as an entrance to Fox Hollow. The idea is to save people from having to leave the station and cross the road to enter the park. And, of course, to channel them past expensive retail."

The sheep had long been moved off the farmland, so the farm gates stood open, and I drove through, crossed the bridge, and paused.

"This was all milking sheds and flimsy housing," I said, looking over the flat stretch of raw earth. "The asbestos jungle, as Kyou ended up calling it. So far, Fox Farm has been a mess of old problems needing fixing." I turned the Hummer toward the farmhouse. "Not just the problems with demolition here, but the windbreak for the farmhouse had a bug infestation that meant they wouldn't last much longer, so I had to have a half-dozen massive evergreens removed. And then there were the cracks in the roofing beams. Fortunately, that was discovered on the first deep inspection, so we were able to factor it into the submitted plan. The architect even came up with an elegant way of including the new conservatory into the main structure by extending the new beams out. We were doing amazingly well to get it ready for December, but there's been a manufacturing delay in the glass, and everything's ground to a halt. I'm hoping hard that it will be in next week, but they can't guarantee it."

"Didn't you say this area gets regular gale-force winds?" Lania asked, surveying the swathes of plastic and tarp currently protecting the new conservatory.

"Yes. And with the wind break gone...let's just say I'm crossing my fingers."

I drove past the new three-door garage at the foot of the hill, and parked beneath the carport next to the steps, but then led Lania around the side of the house rather than try to go inside.

"Best not to go into construction zones unescorted, even if you own the place," I explained. "I just wanted to show you my new favourite spot."

The hill behind the farmhouse descended in a few undulations before dropping dramatically to the forest, and I took Lania down a new path to a semi-circular stone seat set into the hillside, with a full moon's circle of slate before it. I'd spent a lot of thought on this seat, which was large enough to fit a half-dozen people, carefully sculpted for comfortable sitting, with the ends bracketed by two stone fire pits. But the main feature was the smooth platform.

"My new yoga spot," I said, happily.

Lania's attention was not on garden features, but on the view. Mid-afternoon in winter, and the patchwork of towns and fields was already mixed with shadows cast by the twin mountain ranges, though there was still a glimmer of light on the distant lake. Below, a breeze tossed up a drift of gold and white confetti.

"The pictures you sent didn't begin to capture the...the vastness," Lania said.

"I know," I said, sitting down and starting to set out our picnic. "Mum and Dad wanted a view, and this is absolutely A View."

Even though we were facing east, we could still watch a spectacular sunset dyeing the Ramparts and Lake Dorsey: an entire palette of reds and golds. While we ate, dramatic shadows swept over the landscape, and then the sky paled, and began to hint at stars.

"Do these hills have names?" Lania asked idly, nibbling on the last of the pastries.

"The locals call them The Windbreak," I said. "They do have formal names. This one is Hirth. The big one is Borger. The middle three are Herra, Skeldder, and Vetter."

"Remnants of Greenland's Norse period? With Kyou's plans, it's a pity they're not called something more romantic."

"Kyou fights clear of anything too sappy. And was thoroughly entertained when we discovered the far side of the fence between Skeldder and Vetter is used as an illicit make out location, judging from the large number of discarded condoms and cigarette butts. One of the many minor discoveries we made when putting out my anemometers."

Lania snorted, but then said: "Don't you think Kyou building a wedding resort is seriously ironic?"

"Because, if we stay together, we can't get married? Plenty of people spend their lives together and never get married. My parents weren't married for ages, because for the first couple of years Mum couldn't get married without her parents' permission, and my grandmother wouldn't even talk to her. It's like she was determined to make everything as difficult as possible." I shrugged. "I guess if we stick with each other long enough, we could hold a commitment ceremony or something. I never really thought long-term relationships were something I'd do."

"You mean because you've always been travelling about?"

"No, because I'm not very..." I struggled for a moment. "Emotional? No, that's the wrong word. Romantic? I never thought I'd be that deeply into anyone that I'd be willing to risk the things I care about to be with them. I'm a thoroughly selfish person, in my own way, and yet I couldn't bring myself to walk away from seeing if this could work. I keep being astonished that it has, so far, and that was before Kyou effortlessly overcame my biggest difficulty. I never would have thought of simply hiring a bunch of people to make sure my career wasn't impacted."

"Money," Lania said, looking out at the glimmer of lights in the vast valley.

"Yeah. So much of how they're approaching Noonerry is about me, and I'd be a complete hypocrite not to be glad about that, but nothing could make me more aware of the immense imbalance between us. I find it highly ironic that I came to Corascur thinking I was a freshly-minted little rich girl. Kyou can earn more in a week than my parents have in their lifetime, and my salary is definitely never going to match up. I think I'll end up paying rent to Kyou for the rest of our...together, just so I feel I'm not completely leaching off them."

"Do Bran and Rin feel like Kyou's supporting them?" she asked.

"I doubt it. A lot of Kyou's initial capital came from them, especially in the very early days when they'd give him half of their allowances and any money they got for Christmas and birthdays. I can thoroughly understand why he came close to melting down when he thought he'd lost most of it. He must have felt he'd betrayed their trust. Whereas they'd choose him over the money no matter the consequences." I smiled. "I love the bond between them. It's incredible."

Lania was quiet on the drive back, and I wondered if I'd been insensitive being so obviously happy with my excess of boys when I knew she'd been eating her heart out over Carr for years. Or perhaps she was reflecting on relative wealth, and where she and her family sat on that scale.

"You said your family weren't sure what they were doing for Christmas?" I asked, unlocking the door to the house.

"It's settled now—and exciting. Usually, it's just staying in at home avoiding the weather, with a few family visits," Lania said. "This year, Mum and Dad are going on a working holiday to meet Evelyn and one of her major clients. On his private island. In the Bahamas. And we're go with them."

I laughed. "You'll probably get to meet some of Evelyn's assistants then. Is it Teodore you're visiting? Mum did some work for him."

"Yeah, Teodore Vossen. What's he like?" Lania asked. "Will we need to be very quiet and polite?"

"No, he's extremely social. Always has a ton of guests around, loves meeting new people. Been married to a guy he met in college ever since it was legal for them to be married, and they're constantly throwing surprise parties for each other. He won't work with people he doesn't like, so the visit will be a kind of job interview for your parents. He's apparently a dangerous person to cross in the shipping industry, but treats those who work for him as family. Admittedly, the more dramatic type of family, and their kids are...challenging. I recommend going for a walk on the beach whenever the conversation reaches a certain decibel level."

"A rowdy, noisy Christmas, huh? I like it."

"Does this mean you're going to miss the Book Festival?"

"No, I can still meet up for the first day. We're flying out the day after."

Despite sensible layers, we were thoroughly chilled after sitting on a hill on the cusp of winter. Lania went to take a shower, and I started to unpack, realised the house was so cold because we'd left the windows open to try to air out the paint and adhesive, and ran around to close them.

Lania had chosen a front corner room with lots of windows, and the curtains stirred idly as I shut them all. On her bed, the pages of a sketch pad flipped in the breeze, and I paused to stare at a series of sketches of a boy. Laughing, face vivid. Gazing thoughtfully into the distance. Walking, hands in pockets, head down.

Athaine.

Twenty-One

On the subject of being careful what you wish for, I'd been hoping Lania would meet someone who would help her get past Carr. I didn't know Athaine well enough to guess what kind of romantic prospect he'd be, but I'd certainly noticed he had a strange attitude toward Professor Tremaine and her son. The fact that he seemed to be lurking near their home brought up all my vigilance.

Of course, just because Athaine had been hanging out on a particular street corner didn't necessarily mean he'd been stalking the Tremaines. For all I knew, Athaine was another neighbour. Or had been just passing by. Or really was being a bit suss, but Reasons. I still wished I hadn't introduced him to Lania.

However, since Athaine wouldn't be an issue until classes started up again, I simply closed the sketch book, worked out how to start the living room heater, and spent a couple of hours playing a co-op adventure game with Lania before we both settled down with our laptops. The coursework wasn't giving me any issues, but some of it involved a hefty time investment, and so I planned my boy-free fortnight to be days working at Kybirn Isambard, and evenings getting ahead on my assignments.

Plus, outings, of course. We filled Sunday morning with a stroll through the 'confetti' of Strathold Forest, stopped in Moonmere for lunch and groceries, and spent a less than virtuous afternoon on another gaming stint before settling down to grind out some theoretical reading.

"I'll normally walk this," I said, as we drove the short distance to the office on Monday. "If there's a day you want to get away from your assignments for a tour of the Tableland, I won't need the car most of the time."

"I'll stick at the house working: I'm desperate to get ahead of the pile. But on the weekend, do you want to go all the way west to Mount Marah?"

That was a long drive, right to the rim of mountains that wrapped the coast of Greenland. But Mount Marah was a hot springs resort, and in winter featured steaming pools surrounded by snow.

"We can overnight there," I said. "See if there's any available bookings once we're done setting up here."

Spotting a parking place, I grabbed it immediately. Parking in the centre of Noonerry had become an early bird game, so I'd set out well before nine, and had managed to grab a spot one building down from the corner store that had become Kybirn Isambard's office.

There were a half-dozen kids hanging out on the benches out front, and they jumped up as I got out of the Hummer. Recognising the mayor's children, Arne and Marit, among them, I waved and was a little surprised when they all rushed forward eagerly.

"Are you going to put out the buildings today?" Marit asked. "Chessy said you were going to."

Laughing, I nodded, and said: "You can help bring them inside," as I opened the rear of the Hummer.

"I think I've guessed Kyou's clever advertising campaign," Lania said, as we unloaded a few interestingly-labelled boxes.

"It seems it's already effective," I said, leading a procession to Kybirn Isambard's door, and finding it unlocked. "Hey, Chessy," I said, smiling at the curly-haired blond woman who'd been hired as receptionist.

"Hey Mika. Sorry about the welcome committee."

"All part of the plan, really," I said, nodding a greeting to Chloe, as usual bright and early at work.

"We missed an opportunity not selling tickets," she commented. "And almost certainly will have half the town through here by the end of the day, given the interest they've shown in the base model. Chessy, when Jacob gets in, can you move the coffee table and anything else that's likely to be a trip hazard out of here? You can leave those chairs in the corner."

I introduced Lania, and took time out to check in with Chloe about my schedule for the day: morning with the model, a lunch break, then survey work with Torsten and Cassidy, two of the engineering team.

KI's office, previously a corner convenience store with attached residence, had been very simply fitted out, but not restructured significantly. Most of the workstations were upstairs in the converted living quarters, and there were a couple of consulting rooms behind the reception desk, while the storeroom now housed a simple kitchen. A full third of the former main area of the store was given over to the visitor waiting area. And most of that devoted to the advertising display Kyou had requested: a model of the whole of Noonerry.

Both enormous fun to put together, and simply enormous, I'd invested my fair share of evenings carving out the entire eastern portion of the Snowshield Tableland from blocks of Styrofoam. Kyou had gone over it with spray-paint for an initial coat, and then touched up details with his brushes, until it had transformed into a creditable replica of the local landscape, with the river and streets carefully rendered. We'd sourced the Styrofoam direct from a manufacturer who could provide it in a matching size to the ten knee-high tables currently taking up the main chunk of the visitor area, and assembled it the previous weekend. Today it was finally time to add the buildings.

"Let's start with Main Street," I said, gently tugging the whole model apart. The Styrofoam was fastened to the tables, but none of the blocks were connected to each other, so it was easy to unlock the table wheels and pull them away from each other.

The correct box was found and the kids crowded close. I glanced at them, then said: "Okay, line up one foot back. You can each take turns being my able assistant. And, hm, Lania, when we put the rope barrier up later, remind me to find something that younger kids can stand on to see."

"I'll go borrow a step from *Meggie's*," said Chessy. "She has a couple that she uses when doing the hair of the taller clientele. I'm sure she'll spare one until you can get something permanent."

"Can we put our own houses on?" asked Marit, excitedly taking the place of 'first assistant'.

"If you can decide between you who does the honours," I said, opening the box and picking out the first section of 'Main Street': very recognisably a chunk of shopfronts including the building we were standing in. These had been a small project for Kybirn Games' art team: modelling all the existing buildings in Noonerry, outputting them to a 3D printer, and painting the result. Given the scale, most of them were the size of Monopoly houses, but shape and colouring still made them very recognisable, and I was pleased with the result as the town grew piece by piece.

Once all the existing structures were in place, I opened up the 'Projects' box, and carefully set out several parts of Noonerry's future that had been designed but not yet built. First the railway station, and Kyou's strip of stores and galleries set between the rail line and the river—currently without the connection between the two that Kyou was negotiating. Next, the five houses Fabian had designed to replace the old Main Street house we'd already had torn down. He'd taken inspiration from the shapes of Kybirn's headquarters and transformed what was essentially a line of townhouses into a rising spiral curved around a central pool, with a water feature that connected to the rooftop drainage. The rest of the sprawling plot was divided into small gardens, entertaining areas, and a discreet line of carports tucked against the rear property line.

Finally, I put out the main headquarters building, which Kyou had painted personally, spending the better part of an hour on a minute rendition of the bio-circuitry pattern. The headquarters design had been refined considerably thanks to Chloe and Fabian's input, and the shapes of the three conjoined buildings were sleeker and more beautiful, and now included three outflung walls that supported the funnel turbine outlets. On a model that could fit in my palm, they looked like threads between the main blades of the pinwheel, but at full size they would present as a line of decorative arches.

"You're going to build a giant fidget spinner?" Marit asked, producing a gust of laughter from the audience that had slipped in while we were laying everything out:

already enough people that things were getting cramped. Lucky we'd started early.

"Sadly, we weren't ambitious enough to make one that spins," I said, a little regretfully. "Just some labels to go now, and then we can put all the tables back together to make more room."

I was brisk with the labels, which didn't have to be quite so precisely placed, and simply noted what Kybirn intended to build. Then my bevy of assistants pushed the tables back together, with the wasteland west of town oriented to the wall, and 'The Windbreak' aimed directly at the door.

"Use these extra stanchions to make clear where this step stool is, or someone will fall over it," Lania suggested, as we set up the rope barrier.

"Good thought," I said, arranged a prime viewing spot for the kids, then let the crowd close in.

"Very effective way to get people through the door," Fabian said, propping an elbow on the reception desk. "I've always wanted to be a tourist attraction."

"The wall displays look great too," I said, glancing around at the renderings and info summaries of Kybirn's plans that had been mounted since my last visit. "Now the challenge is to get any of this approved."

"I doubt it'll happen this year," he said, grimacing. "The Shire Council meets next week and then is off until late January. I still have hopes for the Main Street houses, since there's no rezoning involved, but what little scuttlebutt I've gotten hold of suggests even the Town Council plans to sit on everything until some of these major property sales have been finalised."

"The only thing that Kyou really cares about getting underway in the next six months is the tree planting, and you don't need council approval to plant trees."

"Not that you'd plant in winter," said a very tall man who'd found his way to my elbow. He smiled as we looked at him, then added: "I'm a little late: distracted by the excitement." His accent was RP British, and he almost looked like he'd strayed out of a May Brunsfield period production.

"Well, so were we," Fabian said. "Mika, this is Aaron Ryne, our Landscape Designer. We should also have our graduate engineer starting..."

"Right here," said a small woman with a stylish silver-blond crop, poking her head around from behind Aaron. "Meredith Conrad."

"There," Fabian said, smiling. "And this is Mika, our engineering intern. Mika will set you up with accounts and IDs, and start you off on Kybirn's online training, before handing you over to Chloe and I."

I greeted them, enjoying the contrast between the pale pixie-like Meredith and the tanned Aaron, who was even taller than Rin. After letting Lania know I'd be about twenty minutes, I took them into the back room, gave them the very brief mandatory safety tour, got their accounts set up and ID photos taken, and then left them listening to the code of conduct training on headphones.

The crowd had actually grown by the time I returned, and I found Lania and Cassidy managing a line outside and only letting newcomers in when others left.

"It's slackening off," Cassidy said, rubbing a hand over the stubble that matched the seemingly-permanent dark circles under his eyes. "Unless a new batch turns up, we can probably stop playing door guard before lunch."

"Sorry Lania, I didn't mean to get you drafted," I said.

"Lania?" Cassidy looked startled. "I thought this was the new starter, uh, Meredith."

"No, Meredith's inside. Lania's my friend from high school—though she probably will end up working for Kybirn, just on the KG side of things."

"Sorry for dragging you out here, then," Cassidy said.

"It's all good," Lania said. "Today's my day for checking out what Mika's job's like."

"Oh? Are you going to come out on survey with us?" Cassidy asked.

"Sure, if I can."

After we changed another batch of gawkers, Cassidy chatted idly with Lania, asking what she was studying, and what she might be doing at Kybirn Games. It was a fairly flirtatious conversation on his end, but I don't think Lania caught it at all. Or simply thought a man closing in on thirty out of her age range.

When the line faded away, I went inside and got Chloe's permission to show Lania the rest of the office, and then Fabian sent me on a lunch run, picking up drinks and sandwiches.

"They really do treat you just as an intern," Lania said, as we waited in line at *Madison's*.

"Most of them only know of me as an intern," I said. "They're aware I went to high school with the owners, but that just makes them think I got the job through nepotism, and as a return favour for the tip-off. Which is true. Besides, even if certain buildings are based on my design ideas, it's incredibly valuable for me to properly act as an intern here, especially when Chloe and Fabian have sourced some great subject-specific experts. I'm learning so much."

Since the office was crowded today, we dropped off purchases, then went to eat on the benches outside in the sun.

"Put on some sun block if you're going to come out on survey with us," I warned Lania.

"Already done," Lania said, with the satisfaction of the well-prepared. "Though remind me to reapply in a couple of hours: I need to keep a good layer or by sunset I'll be in matching colours."

By the time we were back from lunch, the crowd had died down to a return attendance of the kids we'd started out with.

"I'm going to take a few photos to send to the guys," I said, and worked to get a shot that didn't just look like coloured specks on formless green.

Some newcomers arrived while I was taking a close up of main street, and I have to admit my hand shook a little when I heard a certain voice. I glanced up, but then managed to pretend not to pay attention to them.

The majority of the Laurent-Beaulieus I'd encountered conformed to a certain type: long-boned, on the paler side, with hair in shades from brown to blond, and similarities about the eye shape in particular. All three of the people now surveying the model met that template, but it had been the voice—Kyou's dipped in cream and honey voice, but with Rin's faint French accent—that had startled me.

I'd now read enough online gossip about the L-B clan to recognise Kyou's father, and even know his name was Marcus Westhaven. I also recognised the young woman with him as Damasque Beaumont, one of the prime possibilities for Heir now that Kyou was out of the running. She was, as Bran had commented, very beautiful, and had Rin's champagne colouring and innate elegance. The third in the group, a boy about seventeen, was one I didn't recognise, but was certainly an L-B. Perhaps the son of Kyou's aunt who liked to call him to try to upset him?

Naturally, they came across to inspect the model, their focus on the labels outlining proposed development, so I stepped away, pretending to be texting on my phone.

After a frowning moment, Marcus Westhaven clicked his tongue and said in French:

"*A park! Of all the fool things he could do with the place.*"

"*Not a park, a garden resort,*" Damasque commented, discovering the information display about Fox Hollow.

"*Concert Hall,*" read the boy. "*Artists' Retreat. A positive for us. If he manages to turn it into a real attraction, everything we do goes up in value.*"

"*How big of an attraction can a park be?*" Marcus Westhaven asked, disgustedly.

"*Many are world-wide draws,*" Damasque said, reading carefully through the limited detail Kyou had chosen to release about Fox Hollow. "*The hotel should have spectacular views, as well, and this suggests it'll be aimed at the wedding market. Gabriel is right—Kyou's plans are very good for us. We should adjust to treat this as a destination, rather than an outlying suburb. Hotels, a different approach to retail."*

They turned as another newcomer approached them: a man in his thirties, his hair a tumble of dark curls setting off even darker eyes and a copper skin tone. He brought an air of energy and humour as, hands in pockets, he swooped down to peer at the Main Street model, and then shifted to an up-close inspection of Kybirn headquarters.

"Now this is fun," he said. "What is...are they drains?" He stood up as quickly as he'd bent over, looked around, then called: "Chloe! What in the world are you doing with this rooftop?"

Chloe, who had emerged from the back office in time to hear this, looked at him calmly and said: "Funnel wind turbines." She glanced at me, then added: "It's a refinement of a design that came down from the exec. It seems a feasible solution for anyone who wants to cut down the power bill for a very specific large structure, at any rate."

"When Kyou said he wanted to do interesting buildings, he wasn't joking!" the man said, striding around the reception desk and giving Chloe a hug.

She looked faintly startled, but smiled and said: "Good to see you, Addison."

"It must be nearly ten years," the man, Addison, said. "Are you free for dinner tonight? But before that, let me introduce Marcus and Gabriel Westhaven, and Damasque Beaumont. RailCorp still hasn't released the RFT for the station and surrounds, but we've come down early to look over the situation. Do you have time for a general discussion?"

As Chloe took the unexpected L-B Corp visitation into one of the consulting rooms, I shut down the recording function on my phone, and went to check if Cassidy and Torsten were ready to head out.

Torsten was a roads and drainage specialist, while Cassidy was KI's survey lead. I'd only had a limited opportunity to help out with the survey work already done on the sites of the main headquarters and the entry galleria, and so was very happy to be able to spend a good chunk of a week refining my practical skills. I was particularly interested in Torsten's work, since he would design the infrastructure plan for Fox Hollow, and this was an area where my understanding was shallow. Since he'd only started two weeks ago, the most I knew of the man was that he was small, blond and very reserved.

"Meredith and Aaron will be coming with us," Cassidy told me. "Show them where the gear is kept, and we'll set out when everyone's kitted up."

Even though only paddocks were involved, Chloe was very particular about safety, and we were required to wear our hard hats and hi-vis vests while working. I issued Meredith and Aaron a set from supply, gave them a marker to add their names, then made a 'visitor' set for Lania.

"Are you parked anywhere time-sensitive?" I asked, leading them outside. "The Town Council's been having a field day ticketing people."

"Next street over," Aaron said. "I didn't see any time limits."

"Same," Meredith said.

"I hear they're going to add restrictions outside Main Street, so be wary. Since you don't have to move, ride over with us: my spot's about to expire."

"How long does it take to walk?" Meredith asked.

"Around ten minutes to the rail line," I said, unlocking the Hummer.

"What an over-the-top car," Meredith said, with a faint change to the tone of her voice.

"Filched it from one of the bosses while they're overseas," I said, with a quick grin. "I'd want one of my own, but then I think about parking it in the city."

The trip from Main Street to the entrance of Fox Hollow was a bare couple of minutes by car, and once through the gate I immediately turned right, and followed Cassidy's pickup to a section of boundary markers between the fence and the river.

"This spot is where the main pedestrian entrance to Fox Hollow will be," I explained, as we got out of the Hummer. "We're doing a preliminary site survey on this section of the river today."

"For a bridge?" Aaron asked, then paused and gazed across the vista of grass, lake, hills and mountains. "A well-chosen starting point. If you ignore the outermost hills, the major features are lined up almost symmetrically. Though that might work against us, since the imperfections will draw the eye. Do you know what the hotel on the centre hill is going to look like? If it's spectacular enough, it'll be the focal point of the whole scene."

Cassidy, coming up in time to hear this, snorted: "No hotel is going to beat the access road. Do you have that concept drawing, Mika?"

"There's no current design for the hotel, beyond that it'll mostly be on the far side of the hill," I said, grabbing my tablet from my day bag. "But, yeah, the viaduct will dominate over everything else."

I showed Aaron and Meredith the sketches I'd done, which had taken the slightly different heights of the three central hills into account, and carefully cut across a point a little lower than their peaks.

"Good lord!" Aaron said. "They're not thinking small!"

He held up the tablet against the backdrop of the hills, and shook his head. "A very literal way to add structure to an outlook. This is several years down the track, yes?"

I nodded. "The upper portion is stage 4 to 5, but the lower ring road and light rail will be stage 2. The ring road won't cross the river, but the main stopping point will be just on the far side of the entry bridge. Here's the current concept for this bridge—we needed something that could take a solid crowd, and not be completely exposed on wet days."

I showed him a sketch of a broad, very gently curved pedestrian bridge, with covered walkways on either side, and a clear centre that didn't interrupt the view to the hills.

"And do you know how much of this grab bag of garden features is set in stone?"

"The Sakura walk along the river," I said. "Everything else is 'desirable' rather than absolute. You've got the list of plants the Parks Service would really prefer we don't use?"

He nodded. "Nothing surprising there." Aaron gave me back the tablet, took a deep breath, then said: "I think I'll tramp about for a while, let the shape of the place settle in, and get down to soil samples tomorrow."

Aaron and Torsten left, and I worked with Cassidy and Meredith—with extra assistance from Lania—for the rest of the afternoon. The good weather held until around four, when clouds crept up on us and offered an annoying drizzle. Since the visibility dropped considerably, Cassidy called it a day.

"Torsten's at the lake," Cassidy said. "But I didn't have the forethought to get Aaron's phone number. Hopefully he hasn't fallen off anything."

"I saw him up on the big hill," Lania said. "About quarter of an hour ago."

"Cassidy, if you take Meredith back, I'll go pick up our strays," I volunteered.

Torsten was easy to locate, but Aaron not immediately apparent as I drove up the long western face of Borger. Visibility wasn't too bad, though, and when we stopped at the crest and got out to look around, we spotted him labouring back up the southern slope, slipping a little on the damp grass.

"AWOL," he said, apologetically. "An excursion that seemed harmless before the weather changed."

"I'm told it's common for big changes in the late afternoon," I said, climbing back into the Hummer.

"I spotted a few recent posts and ropes down there. Plans for a stair?"

"Yeah. There's already one over on Hirth, but this side is more difficult."

"What about the central hills?"

"The Park Service was very unkeen: they don't want floods of people in what was previously a secluded part of the forest. They're also worried about litter falling from the hotel. All things we'll need to take into account when we start on that area."

"Is this the biggest garden you've designed?" Lania asked, as I turned the Hummer. "Or...it looks enormous to me, but I don't know how big they usually are."

Aaron chuckled. "I asked the acreage early on in the interview process, and when I realised it would be larger than Kew, I have to admit to feeling I wasn't ready for such a challenge. But thankfully the briefing makes clear the aim is primarily a parklike woodland, with a core of garden rooms within it, rather than the whole area structured into formal gardens. To be honest, the biggest challenge now will be to make it not appear to be some kind of soulless wedding production line."

I failed to suppress my grin. "Turn the ring road into a conveyer belt, feed in a mess of satin and cake, and try to not overload the whole thing with drama? It definitely has the potential to be that appalling. Fortunately, I think Kyou wants the hotel to be the primary focus of the weddings. Every second day of the park is supposed to be general admission, and have open-air performances and other activities. Bike paths and a sculpture trail are definitely not what comes to mind for a marriage ceremony, at any rate, though it would be kind of fun if someone worked them in."

"Would make great photos," Lania said. "Bride and groom on a tandem, page boys on tricycles, and a trail of bridesmaids sitting on the luggage racks of the groomsmen."

We occupied the short drive back constructing a fantastical wheeled wedding parade, found parking right out front, and stopped briefly to drop off our gear and check in with Chloe, and then home for dinner.

I texted Kyou while eating, and he rang just as we were packing the dishwasher.

"*Enjoying yourself?*" he asked.

"Immensely. I'm getting so much practical experience, the weather has mostly held up, and Lania fills my evenings nicely." I smirked at her expression. "I'm distracted enough I only remember to miss you every hour or so."

"*Would French poetry bring up the frequency?*"

"Probably," I said, heading to my bedroom and switching to speakerphone while I searched through my phone files. "I'm going to send you a video. Not as fun as poetry, but in French."

"*You need to start with the important point. What will I do with these suddenly quickened pulses?*"

"Save them for when we get back. We absolutely have to do something fun."

"*Some chasing you around the house in the dark is definitely in order,*" Kyou said, judiciously. "*I also like that pass the parcel idea. Now, what is this video?*"

He paused to play it, and I knew from his prolonged silence that I'd guessed right.

"*So, he's called Gabriel.*"

"The resemblance to your father is striking, but I wasn't sure if that was just a Laurent-Beaulieu feature. What I can't understand is that I'd parked Rin's Hummer practically at the door. Unless they're really keeping track of your movements, they must have thought at least one of you was inside."

"*Now that I'm firmly not playing along, and Great-Grandfather has made clear that he's fishing in our generation for a new heir, my father has fewer reason to hide old scandals, and might even hope Great-Grandfather will accept a talented addition.*" He chuckled. "*At least the kid spotted the impact of what I'm doing with Fox Hollow. Prices on the tableland were always going to skyrocket, but a Destination brings the situation to a new level. Thank you for getting that display up so quickly, by the way. I wanted it in place before the first wave of big sales later this week."*

"Are you planning on buying anything?"

"Depends on the price. Land only if it comes in far under what I currently estimate. I'll try for the houses that have been listed because we need the ready accommodation."

"You sound tired," I said, catching a croaky note to his voice.

"Still haven't adjusted to the time zone. It's been a fun couple of days here, though. Weekend induction, when the offices are quieter."

We talked for a while, then I went and worked on assignments, pushing my concern into a box for later delectation. The boy called Gabriel was probably only three or four years younger than Kyou. An old scandal, hardly worth hiding.

Before I went to bed, I sent the video to Rin and Bran, glad Kyou was at least with people who loved him far better than his immediate family.

Twenty-Two

Snowshield Tableland was not immune to the sleety rain that plagued Helios in winter, but it had far less of it during the ten days Lania and I worked and played in Noonerry. While it was too early in the year for snow in the town, we could see it on the peaks of the Ramparts, and were very happy to encounter a light fall when we journeyed to the western mountains to sample the hot springs.

Lania, a far better photographer than I, helped me with an early Christmas present for my Kings that involved steaming water, falling specks of ice, and an excess of wet skin. It was more suggestive than graphic, but still represented something of a milestone for our relationship, since I'm generally too cautious to do something like send a nude. I uploaded it to our Mockingbird app late on the night I got back to the big empty house in Hutton Forest, and filled in some of the drear hours until dawn in a four-way chat full of inconsequentialities and longing.

Without whatever chemical or psychological trigger sex provided, I'd been struggling to control my sleep patterns, but had managed well enough until the return to the university district. After a difficult night, and with three more days until my Kings returned, I decided to abandon normal hours, throw myself into concept art and gaming, and sleep when sleep happened.

It was a great opportunity to tackle the most difficult location for my concept art task: the central city where the majority of *Echoes* would play out. The brief was for something completely fantastical, both beautiful and grand, but with a mind for the rendering load. I played with a few different layouts, toying with cities of helixes, spirals, stacked bowls, and even something like a maypole, all streaming ribbon roads around a central support. And then a set of comma-shaped aerial islands, with some graceful ribbon roads arching out, but without the solidity of a supporting pole. Then I switched to a series of columns, dark with crystal insets, giving an Art Deco feel.

I didn't spend more than an hour on each concept, since I'd want feedback before developing any of them further, and wasn't truly satisfied with any of them. I decided to take a break to have dinner and try to work out a direction. Instead of designing a fantastical city, I needed to start with a fantastical landscape: a central lake and surrounding mountains that were only possible thanks to the future tech equivalent of magic.

This reflection inspired me, and I turned to shaping the mountains, and played with options for a couple of hours, until a stiff back sent me to shower and curl up in bed to play a few games.

I was deep in a round of *Tyranny* when the doorbell chimed through Castellan's speakers. I hesitated to completely abandon my randomly matched teammates, so tried to keep playing while wriggling across the bed and reaching for the house control tablet.

"Hello?" I said, trying to divide my vision between the game field and the video feed of the front door.

There was no response, beyond the shush of yet another sleety rainfall, and I looked properly, then let my hero die.

The automatic outdoor lights gave me a clear and useless view of a figure in a hoodie. Even though I could barely make out a jawline, the outline was completely familiar, and yet not possible. I'd spoken to all three of my Kings when I stopped for dinner, and no plane could get them to Helios in a few short hours.

"Rowan?" I said, and the boy looked up, making enough of his face visible to confirm that Bran's kid brother was standing at the door, soaked. "Come in," I said. "I'll bring some towels down."

I triggered the foyer doors, but not the interior, just in case there was someone unexpected with him, and trotted quickly downstairs with an armful of towels and the tablet, watching on the internal camera as he came slowly inside. He was definitely not behaving normally, but the doors closed behind him without any sign of a second person. They wouldn't open again unless triggered internally, so I put that concern aside and opened the residence door.

"The guys are all in Seattle," I told him, stepping back to let him in. "Hang your jacket on one of the coat hooks and start to dry off, and I'll go find some of Bran's clothes for you."

He was barefoot, and smelled faintly of alcohol. The lack of waterproof clothes had already told me something was very wrong, but it wasn't until he— seemingly on autopilot—pulled down the zip of the hoodie that I understood just how bad it was. No shirt underneath, and a zigzag of lines crossed his chest: some vivid red, some deeper but white and faintly puckered in the rain. Fingernail marks.

"Rowan..." I said, searching for the right reaction and coming up short. "Do—do you need me to call the police? Or take you to a hospital?"

The question pierced through the numb state, and he glanced up at me and then flushed, looking painfully young.

"No," he said, in a voice that sounded unused. "I left before anything, before..."

He'd gone scarlet, and I quickly handed him a towel so he could hide behind it.

"Then let me point you in the direction of the nearest shower," I said, getting a better hold of myself, and indicating the ground floor bathroom. "That's the quickest way you can warm yourself up. I'll go get those clothes, and will put them just outside the door, and then make something hot for you to drink."

He escaped, and it wasn't until I heard the lock of the bathroom door engage that I managed to push away my own paralysis. I transferred the dripping hoodie to the rack in the laundry, then went up to my room and grabbed my phone, calling Bran as I crossed to his bedroom. He didn't answer, so I swapped to Kyou, and then Rin.

Thankfully, this third call got through. "*Not gone to bed yet?*" he asked, sounding a little surprised.

"Rowan just showed up here," I explained. "Half-frozen, missing clothing, scratches on his chest. Says he doesn't need a doctor because he 'left before'. Do you think his parents are likely to come here? And should I let them in?"

Silence, then: "*No, best to appear that no-one is home. We'll catch the next flight. Bran will call you back once I find him.*"

"Okay," I said. "The kid's pretty shocky, but I think I believe him about the 'before' part. Whatever 'before' actually means. Talk to you soon."

I hung up and collected together several layers of clothing, both for warmth and hopefully a sense of security, and parked them outside the ground floor bathroom before heading to the kitchen. Not sure if Rowan would be hungry, I made a couple of sandwiches in addition to the drinks, and set out some snacks.

When Rowan emerged, I pushed a cup toward him and said: "Anti-cold brew: grated ginger, lemon juice and lots of honey. If it's something you can't drink, there's hot chocolate, or some malted stuff Bran likes."

He hesitated, then picked up the honey-lemon: as a singer who loved performing, I figured he'd be protective of his throat. The food didn't interest him much. He bit one corner of a sandwich, put it down, and sat cupping the warm mug. As a near stranger, I wasn't going to push conversation on him, so I tried to foster a peaceable mood, and was very glad when my phone rang.

"Your brother," I said, and answered it simply to say: "He's right here." I passed the phone over and left to tidy the bathroom and transfer a pair of sopping jeans and the towels to the laundry. I was mopping up the puddles in the foyer, when Rowan found me and handed me back the phone.

"Hi," I said, briskly. "Did you manage to get a flight?"

"*Yeah,*" Bran said, his voice a little croaky, as if he was the one in danger of catching a cold. "*Have to go through a couple of connections, but we'll be there mid-morning your time.*"

"Okay, we'll bunker down and see you soon."

"*Mika...thanks for being there.*"

"I'm glad I was." The idea of Rowan turning up to a locked and empty house was less than pleasant. "Safe flight."

Rowan had gone back to the kitchen, and I looked at him restlessly turning the mug in his hands. Leaving him alone seemed a bad idea. Giving him a hug would probably be worse.

"Want to play the game they've been making?" I suggested, and saw his expression finally lighten.

"Sure."

The game room was a good place to lay low and pretend not to be home, so I set Rowan up with an install of the latest version of *One Step*, transferred a sufficiency of snacks and a flask of warm water, gave him one of the plush blankets, and curled up on the other couch with my own. After briefly checking the news for any alerts about rising young musicians gone missing, I returned to *Tyranny*, this time with accompanying music.

oOo

"Mika."

I blinked awake, smiled up at Kyou and Rin, then glanced at Bran, who was sitting next to a sleeping Rowan.

"What's the time?" I murmured.

"Ten," Kyou said, helping me up.

"He was on his third play-through when I fell asleep," I said, rubbing my eyes. I glanced at the screen, which proclaimed 'Fin', then joined Kyou and Rin in a tactful withdrawal.

We were at the door when Bran lightly shook Rowan's foot to wake him up, and the kid recoiled like he'd been scalded. We closed the door.

"Did he say anything on the phone about what happened?" I asked.

"Industry party," Rin said, voice edged with ice. "His parents were networking, Rowan was strictly only drinking coke, but woke up alone in a room with a producer. Beyond that, he'd only say he 'just left'."

"I caught whiffs of rum," I said. "But he did seem more shocked than drunk or drugged. Have his parents, uh, noticed? That's he's missing?"

"Bran started getting calls during our first flight," Kyou said. "He answered when we landed, told them he was in Montreal, and when he asked them what happened they hung up on him. If Bran hadn't known Rowan was with you, he'd have been through the roof."

"It still looks like it was a rough flight," I said, surveying their shadowed eyes.

"Travelling with a lit powder keg is not recommended," Kyou said.

"Want some breakfast?" I suggested. "Go have a shower and I'll start putting something together."

I'd had enough sleep to get by, and so changed briskly and made crêpe batter, and a variety of quick fillings for them, sweet and savoury. Kyou and then Rin came down and helped me, and everything was ready to cook by the time Bran and Rowan emerged. I gave a quick demonstration on basic crêpe production, and then let everyone fry their own, which was a learning experience that provided free entertainment. Luckily, I'd made plenty of batter.

Both Rowan and Bran's eyes were red, possibly for different reasons, but they seemed calm enough, if less than inclined to chat.

"I've been wondering for ages why you were hunting for a singer for *One Step*," I told Rin. "And then on Rowan's second playthrough he turns up those puppets! What am I doing wrong that I've never gotten puppets?"

"Not wrong," Rin said. "It's mood choices, rather than 'correct' ways to play the game. It will take players quite a few sessions to get all the hidden instruments, as they explore the various tonal shifts."

The little singing mice puppets had been unbearably cute, and brought out a collector urge in me that I firmly suppressed.

"Is the playable demo nearly done?"

"Yeah," Bran said, his voice still a little croaky. "We'll make it available for pre-order by the end of the month, but won't begin the real marketing process until mid-January."

"Kezia is lining up demo play-throughs with streamers, but we'll submit to the usual big reviewers and are trying to get it into a March game showcase," Kyou added. "Player word of mouth is what's going to sell the game, though, and the storefront did pick up a reasonable smattering of followers after all those puff pieces about Noonerry."

Kezia, KG's new part-time marketing hire, was a fresh graduate, and an enthusiastic cosplayer, with an inexhaustible love for the *Kingdom Hearts* series. She'd been a surprise to me, since Kyou had taken a top-down approach to building Kybirn's personnel: usually starting out with a heavy-hitter who could control the division. He'd explained that by the time *Echoes* was at a stage to be marketed, Kezia would either have proven the potential he'd seen in her, or be onboarding a supervisor.

"Are you going to have an entirely separate marketing unit for Fox Hollow?" I asked now.

"Too early to decide," Kyou said.

"The whole concept is Kyou's pet hatred and personal kryptonite," Rin said, smiling faintly.

"I see the value in it," Kyou said, shrugging. "But it's a tricky form of art. My only failed project involved an advertising campaign as effective as starting a fire during a downpour, using cash for tinder."

We chatted about the mid-February release date, and the posters and collectibles the art team were developing.

"Can I have one of everything?" Rowan asked, speaking for the first time.

"Sure," Kyou said. "That reminds me, Mika, do we have space to add a collectibles archive to the HQ?"

"Depends on how big you want it," I said, smiling wryly. "Additions are why we left those 'general purpose' rooms, but you've already used two of them. A proper archive also has various heat and moisture controls, so you might want to consider a collectibles display room, with a true archive off-site."

"Or just make the building bigger," Rin suggested, with a faint smile to show he understood that 'bigger' was not exactly simple with what we'd inevitably started calling 'the fidget spinner'.

"I suppose it's fortunate we're delayed by the zoning issue," Kyou mused. "Hopefully we'll have completed the requirements list by the time we're able to submit a planning application."

"Try to finalise it when we're down there for Christmas," Bran said. "We also need to get a housewarming gift for your parents, Mika. Any suggestions?"

"Something for the conservatory?" I suggested. "The house is going to look absolutely bare because they didn't want anything except basic furniture added, so they can have fun shopping for themselves—not to mention rediscovering the contents of all the boxes Mum shipped over. Most of the places we've lived were already furnished, and we've just made do with whatever's provided, and anything that we've ever bought that didn't fit in our suitcases was given away or shipped to Wales. We've long forgotten what most of it is. Thankfully the boxes turned up safely at the beginning of the week, just before the glass was installed, so one of the first things I guess we'll do is see what we have already. A plant's a pretty safe bet for not being something we would pack."

"Would they like a pet?" Rin asked. "I know someone with a new litter of border collies."

"I...don't know," I said. "They both love dogs, but while Dad said they're going to be spending the majority of their time here for the next couple of years, that doesn't mean not travelling at all. Though, of course, I can look after a pup while they're away. But..." I looked at them.

"I have no objection to occasional pup sitting," Kyou said. "I just don't think we have the time to properly train one or keep it entertained."

"Once we're living down there, animals will be easier than dealing with one here," Bran said.

I had to agree with that: I didn't want to leave a dog stuck in a small yard wishing we cared more. But a dog for visits...

"It can't hurt to ask," I said. "We've never had a pet. I've only done occasional pet-sitting and dog-walking and things."

"I'll ask for one to be reserved in case," Rin said, equably. He surveyed the remains of our breakfast, then looked at Bran. "But first things first. What now?"

Rowan, who had relaxed in the midst of our conversation, immediately hunched his shoulders.

"Three points," Bran said. "First, this producer. Kyou and I will take care of that problem quietly."

"Gone by the end of the week," Kyou murmured.

"Next..." Bran looked at his brother's bowed head. "You want this career, so the least dumb thing to do is to make it safer for you. You need an assistant and bodyguards, and yeah, it'll feel stuffy having people on your ass all the time, but you need to start taking control of what's happening around you. Without a team that follows your orders, instead of Their whims, it's too easy for you to get played. We'll try for them not to be too much older than you, and you can swap out any you don't like. They'll officially be your employees, but we'll fund them for you until you're ready. Okay with that?"

Rowan, just barely, nodded.

"Last point: how much do you want Them to suffer?"

'Them' could only refer to Bran and Rowan's parents: nothing else brought out that tone of contempt. Since Rowan clearly didn't know how to respond, Bran simply went on.

"We can wait a few days, until there's a nationwide manhunt, and She's crying on TV. We can spread it all out as ugly as possible, how careless they were with you. Or we can just wait a couple of hours, or until tomorrow, then say we found you, that you came here because you felt weird after that drink, couldn't find Them, and left to clear your head, then passed out. You decide."

Silence. But then Rowan lifted his head. "Find me today. I've got rehearsals tomorrow."

Firm, decisive. Until now, I really hadn't been able to see at all the kid who'd strutted confidently through a crowd of dancers, telling people not to waste his time.

"Okay, we'll tell them after lunch. Want to stay here a few days until we have your staff lined up?" Bran asked.

"Can I?"

The note of relief confused me, since I'd understood Rowan to have a much better relationship with his parents than Bran. Bran just nodded, then pulled out his phone and made a call.

"Hey Toby. We just flew in. Have they found him? U-huh. What do the police say? What? Why not? That's idiotic. Call them or I will."

He hung up, and said: "They haven't even brought the police in yet." He glanced at Rowan, who had clenched his fists, then said: "They're idiots thinking they can fix this without rocking any boats. Forget them. Bunk down in my room a while—sleep, read, or use the guest account on my laptop, whatever."

As Rowan went upstairs, we moved on to packing the dishwasher. It wasn't until we heard the distant click of the door closing that Kyou spoke up.

"Bran...your parents weren't *involved*, were they?"

"They're not quite that stupid," Bran said, disgustedly. "But whatever they actually *did* do, it's obviously left Rowan second-guessing them."

"Probably told him to make nice, without being fully aware where that might lead," Rin said. "You remember that time with Uncle Claude? Same kind of concept, though we had it milder."

"Not actually our uncle," Kyou explained to me. "Very influential, we were expected to keep on his good side. And he just loved hugs."

"Rot in hell," Bran muttered.

"There we were, six years old, working out how to get him to fall off a cliff," Rin said, smiling faintly. "He obligingly had a heart attack before we could etch a major notch on our juvenile record."

"What are you going to do about this producer?"

Kyou shrugged. "See what's there. Make use of it. Taxes are usually the easiest way to bring someone down."

"But not enough for this," Bran said hoarsely, then touched my shoulder, perhaps in response to my worried expression. "Before anything else, we'll look for any password vulnerabilities, see if we can get access to any digital cloud in case..." He grimaced. "In case there's photos. Protecting Rowan is the most important thing."

I hugged him. "You're a great big brother."

He made a sound that was nine parts denial, but squeezed me hard, and seemed a little less keyed up when he let me go. "Let me know soonest what you can find out," he said to Kyou, then followed Rowan upstairs.

"I'll start making calls," Kyou said. "And I'll order in something for lunch—a late one, around two?"

"Make it an early dinner instead," Rin said. "Aim for four o'clock, hopefully after the drama has departed."

Kyou nodded and left, and Rin took the opportunity to collect me, sat us down on the edge of the breakfast nook bench and, giving in to a deep weariness, rested his cheek on my shoulder.

"We had to stuff him over by the window because he was making the flight attendants nervous," he said, after a long pause. "Just sitting there with his eyes shut and his fists clenched. Bran's usually very good at managing himself: he heads straight to the gym when something really gets to him, but there wasn't time." Rin touched my hair. "Same for me. I'm rarely truly angry, but when I am, I need to work it off. I frightened you a little, didn't I? When my parents were here."

"Not frightened," I said. "I was definitely hesitant to stress you further, and flailed a little privately about not being able to do anything about your families except support your decisions. I'm a problem-solver by nature, so struggle to sit on my hands."

Rin laughed softly. "You want to fix us?"

"Despite all the pressure, you're far from broken," I said. "Chipped around the edges, maybe, but firm at the core. Have I mentioned that I really love the way you support each other?"

"We wouldn't be here otherwise," he said, sighing.

"How...how is Kyou dealing with becoming an older brother?"

"Pretending it doesn't matter. Not sleeping well. I sometimes wish Kyou found hitting things an outlet."

Rin lifted his head and smirked down at me. "Of course, there is something he does like doing that will help."

I laughed. "I know. I've been wondering how having Rowan stay over will impact our sleeping arrangements."

"Not to mention your parents in a few days. Are you still planning on telling them?"

"I think it's time. Probably they'll be a bit unsettled, but they...well, everything I know of them tells me that they'll accept it as long as they see I'm happy."

He kissed me then, a quick peck.

"Happy," he affirmed, and then he, too, left to make some calls.

oOo

Around two, we all came downstairs again, and I made everyone more ginger, lemon and honey, since being tired and stressed was a sure recipe for a lowered immune system. While we sipped, Bran sent a text, and immediately received a call back, again from his mother's secretary, Toby.

With typical curtness, Bran told the story he and Rowan had agreed on: Rowan had felt strange after drinking a soda, couldn't find his parents, and went outside to try to clear his head. He'd been confused, started walking, and found himself near Bran's house, so he'd let himself in with the emergency code we'd given him, and crashed in a spare room, emerging only now.

He didn't mention that while the emergency code would allow us to get into the house without the passkey on our phones, it also sent an alert to all of us so that we'd know it had been used.

After telling Toby to bring Rowan a few days of clothes so he could stay for a visit, Bran hung up. "They still hadn't called the police," he said, gloomily.

"Image control," Rin suggested. "They're positioning him as a kind of untouchable musical prodigy. Going missing at a party, spiked drink or not, messes with the message."

This produced an unhappy silence. Kyou looked helpless, Rowan bit his lip, and Bran tried to strangle his phone.

"How do you manage interviews, Rowan?" I asked, with an unapologetically direct change of subject. "Are they difficult for you to get through?"

Rowan looked startled, but then shook his head.

"Ashen-R isn't me," he said, softly. "He's like Ziggy Stardust, but without all the cool bits."

"A persona?" I said, surprised.

Rowan nodded. "He's a caricature of an auteur. To Ashen-R, everything except music is inconsequential. He makes interviews easy."

Shy or not, Rowan obviously took after Bran in the brains department. A very smart kid.

"Did you write any of your songs?" I asked.

"Four," he said. "But they got reworked a lot. I prefer them the way they were before."

"Taking control of your output is another big step to work toward," Bran said. "Unfortunately, it'll be a year and half before you really have a say."

"There's a few soft techniques you can use to get your way without blowing up into a confrontation," Kyou added. "I know a great personal coach—I'll see if he has time while you're here."

"Do you have any recordings of what your songs were like originally?" Rin asked.

Rowan had lost his phone, but a trip upstairs to the piano room gave him a chance to show us instead. The kid completely bloomed, no longer pitching his voice low or ducking his head as he, Rin and Bran dissected a few songs.

"Ashen-R doesn't seem so much a persona as a core self," I said to Kyou, as we faithfully played audience.

"Hard to say," he said, taking the opportunity of Rowan's distraction to snag my hand. "To be honest, we haven't had a lot to do with the kid for quite a while. He's always either been at training or being home schooled, and tends to hide in the background during clan gatherings. Paradoxically, he loves performance as much as Bran hates it, and because of that he's always been...in the wrong camp, I suppose you could say. Not understanding why Bran hates their parents so much, why Bran wasn't grateful for all the opportunities. Uncomfortable about the way the Ashtens pretend Bran doesn't exist, but otherwise not at all close. It was a surprise when he turned up with the girls."

"Maybe yesterday wasn't the first time he'd suspected that his career wasn't actually about him. In any case, it doesn't hurt for Bran and Rowan to be a little closer." I rubbed my thumb against Kyou's palm. "If your newly-discovered family member wants to be closer to you, do you think you'd like that?"

"I think it'd be hard not to be suspicious of his motives," Kyou said. "I'm not going to hate on him just because he's the product of an affair, but..." He shrugged. "I'll try to judge him by his actions."

"I don't know how I'd go being an affair child," I mused. "He'd have to have a lot of opinions about you, if only because people are sure to compare."

"If only I'd been weak and ineffectual," Kyou said, with a chuckle. "But unless someone officially introduces us, I'm trying not to spend too much thought on him. We separated so clearly from L-B Corp precisely so we wouldn't need to waste mental energy on our extended family."

Bran's parents arrived and, giving in to curiosity, I followed a little behind the group going downstairs and witnessed a touching scene of reunion, as Kyou led in a man who had Bran's colouring, but not his general looks, and a woman who was clearly a Laurent-Beaulieu. She ran past Kyou and flung her arms around Rowan, then broke down crying.

It wasn't performative. She seemed genuinely distressed, sobbing painfully as she squeezed the kid. He patted her awkwardly in return, until his father bent to embrace the pair of them. Without context, it was very touching, but these were still the people who treated Bran like he didn't exist.

And, really, truly, seemed to plan to continue doing so, as they recovered themselves, straightened, then said: "Let's go home," and started toward the door.

Rin laughed, amazingly cold, then said: "I think we should call Department of Families on them for child endangerment."

"Taking your teen to a clearly unsafe party and then not bothering with even minimal supervision definitely calls for some official response," Kyou said. "But I'd recommend going directly to the press for a few nice headlines. 'Parents Party While Teen Wanders Street'.

There's nothing like the court of public opinion to really get an effect."

"What the hell?" Bran's father said. "We're not here for this."

"No," Bran said, maintaining a flat tone. "But if you walk out that door, it's what you'll get."

The older man's face turned an ugly puce, while his wife clutched Rowan to her, as if he were in danger of being stolen.

"Why are you so selfish?" she asked. "Jealous of your little brother, only thinking of yourself. You were too weak, so now you want to ruin his chances?"

"I'm not the one who took him to a nightclub and let him get roofied," Bran snapped.

"Let's sit down," Kyou said, walking quickly between them. "And discuss terms."

They went into the same room where they'd received 'Great-Grandfather'. Since 'tenant' wasn't a role with any place in this scene, I retreated upstairs to catch up my parents on the progress of the renovation, and to run through our plans for their arrival.

Solid progress had been made since the glass had finally arrived, but the completion date had blown out until after my parents were due to fly in. Not a big issue, since they'd be staying with us, and then at the Book Festival hotel, for much of next week. While we were then supposed to head down to Noonerry for a Christmas and New Year break, we could all stay in the High Street house if Fox Farm wasn't ready.

"*And what about you?*" my mother asked, once we'd settled our timetable. "*You sound tired.*"

"Stayed up most of the night watching playthroughs of Kybirn's upcoming game," I said, honestly.

She chuckled. *"And will you follow your usual Christmas tradition of parking yourself on the couch playing new releases?"*

"I expect you to be with me part of the time. Isn't there anything that interests you?"

"Only that space station management sim," she said. *"Do you think I'd be able to play your new game?"*

"Definitely. Though I hope you have a tolerance for being cross-examined on player experience."

"I hope I like it then," she said, with the voice of someone who has been paid very well for a blunt opinion. *"I'm really looking forward to some quality time home with you."*

"Miss you, Mum," I said. "See you soon."

Ringing off, I actually felt a little choked up. I'd always thought my parents were the best, but lately I'd been given a lot of reasons to doubly appreciate them. I couldn't be happier that they'd decided to settle in Greenland.

A tap on my door brought me back to the present. I turned to see Bran, and immediately crossed to squeeze him hard. He leaned into the embrace: a long stretch of silence full of unspoken hurt. No kid starts out not loving their parents, and Bran had been so unlucky with his.

"They called our bluff," he said at last, voice exhausted. "They know we can't attack them without hurting Rowan as well."

"He—?" I was a little shocked. My Kings worked so well together; it was rare to see them fail. "I'm sorry."

"It's fine." He relaxed a fraction, the faintest smile creeping into his tone. "We already knew we didn't have enough to corner them. But Rowan pulled off a strategy

Kyou came up with, and insisted single-mindedly that he and Rin were in the process of workshopping something special, and he absolutely had to spend more time getting a new single together. My parents want nothing more than a big hit, so they'll be dropping Rowan back tomorrow. We'll keep him until it's time to head down to Noonerry."

"Carrot and stick treatment, huh?" I leaned back so I could look at his face, then went in for another squeeze. "Drama aside, I'm glad you came home early. I've been missing you."

I'd gone from never having a real home, to having two. Next would be the biggest step I'd taken so far: bringing those two clearly together. I could only hope my parents would live up to my trust.

Twenty-Three

"You seem distracted," Rin said, as we hunted for airport parking. "Are you picturing your father coming after us with an axe when you tell all?"

I laughed. "Are you? I can't remember the last time my parents chose violence...oh, wait, I do. I was around ten, and there was a young couple living next door to us. He was enormous, never spoke, and she was this tiny very chatty girl named Eva who always wore these oversized jumpers, and startled easily. We'd occasionally hear the sound of things breaking, but never any yelling, and of course were on high alert and very worried about the dynamic. The curtains of their unit were always drawn, but one day there was a chink, and I couldn't resist peering inside to investigate the weird sounds. And Eva was laying into him. He was sitting on the couch with his arms up to cover his face and she was hitting and kicking him, spitting out something in a voice too low for me to make out the words. I must have made a sound, because she suddenly looked up, and then rushed out onto the balcony and just...ran at me, and slammed me right against the railing. I've never seen anyone so furious."

"Okay, didn't expect that. But where were your parents?"

"Still coming up the stairs with the groceries. Half a flight down, and too far away. I think Eva might actually have been trying to push me over the railing, but fortunately the big guy ran out after her and just picked her up and held her away from me. She started flailing, kicking back at him, and trying to hit him in the face with her elbows. And then my mother came up, and slapped her. Super hard. I'd never seen my mother hit *anything* before."

"I expect your mother had never seen anyone try to push her daughter over a railing, either," Rin said, finally spotting an empty space and reversing into it. "What happened next?"

"Dad called the police. Eva calmed down like a switch had been flipped and started to try to talk her way out of it. The big guy—his name was Marcel—put her down, and she immediately ran away. We waited for the police, made a report, and then my parents took me and Marcel to hospital. I had an amazing horizontal bruise below my shoulder blades. Marcel was covered in them—he was an islander, and they didn't show up well, so we'd never noticed—and he had a hairline skull fracture. Eva apparently liked to wake him up by breaking crockery over his head."

"Okay, I'm going to assume there was some kind of mental illness involved here. Did she get treated?"

"People who only fly off the handle when there are no witnesses are more in control than they'd like you to believe. I don't know where Eva fell in terms of diagnosis, since she took her stuff while we were at the hospital and left town, presumably because she didn't want to be arrested for assaulting a minor. Two minors, as it turned out. Marcel was only seventeen. Eva had latched onto him, been very affectionate to him most of the time, but had a lightning temper. He was so confused, and too embarrassed to even go to his family for help. He could have squashed her like a bug, but even if he could bring himself to use force against her, she'd convinced him no-one would believe he wasn't the abusive one. Which may well have been true, since he was so inarticulate. I learned a lot about not being fooled by appearances from Marcel and Eva."

"And also a lesson to not peer through the cracks in the curtains?"

I laughed. "No, I'd probably still do that, at least in terms of wanting to rescue people who seem to need help. Mum still keeps in touch with Marcel. He makes gourmet ice cream, and has just opened his second store."

Rin locked the Hummer and arced an eyebrow at me. "Entertaining side story, but we still haven't established whether you're worried about your parents' reaction."

"While I'm fairly confident they'll respect my choices, I've not quite worked out when and how to tell them. And, well, there's a difference between acceptance and enthusiasm."

The parking space hunt and a long line at security had us running a little late, so my parents' plane was already taxiing in when we arrived at the gate.

"It really does feel like half the city flies out this time of year," I said, eyeing the crowd. Three adjoining gates due to leave made for near-chaos.

"You either escape Helios in winter, or you find something to do indoors," Rin said. "We've only been here for Christmas a handful of times."

"I guess the rest of your family must be opting for 'indoors' if your sisters are going to the Book Festival."

"My parents are all heavily involved in the Winter Solstice Fashion Gala. It's sponsored by L-B Corp, in an attempt to increase off-season use of the Mymassi Convention Centre."

"Doomed to fail," said a familiar voice.

I turned to see Sean with a handsome mid-twenties man.

"Unless it's winter woollies, no-one wants to think clothes right now," Sean said, with a cheeky grin. "You should do a film festival with juicy prize money instead. The movie theatres are always packed in this weather, and a big enclosed convention centre with lots of movies and hot food is infinitely more tempting than fashion right now."

"You may be right," Rin said, judiciously. "I'll suggest it for next year."

Sean lit up, and skipped in a circle around Rin. "If it happens, I'm totally taking credit," he said. "All the little local directors will line up to thank me, and cast me in their sexiest roles."

I laughed, and Sean circled around me for good measure, then glanced about before producing a sly smile. "Not our full complement of Kings today? Are you two...flying out alone?"

"Waiting for my parents to arrive," I said.

"Oh? Rock Hardison himself? Can I get an autograph?"

"We're going to miss our flight," Sean's companion said, giving us an impatient glance.

"Right, right. This is Damon, by the way," Sean said. "Light of my soul, this is Mika, the most fortunate, and Rin, King of Kings."

"Hi," Damon said. "Your Dad is called Rock Hardison?"

"His favourite pen name," I said, smiling in the face of faint derision. "Where are you heading, Sean?"

"Brazil! Watching fireworks and eating ice cream on the beach. Even your esteemed father can't tempt me to turn back, but I am sorry to miss him. I've caught up on all his books now."

"He'll still be here when you're back," I said, as Damon hooked Sean's arm and began hauling him unceremoniously toward a dwindling boarding line. "My parents bought a house in Noonerry, remember?"

"Of course! I absolutely want to pester him about where he gets his ideas from...say hi for me!"

"There's a dynamic," Rin said, as the crowd swelled to block them.

"I haven't heard a lot of enthusiasm about Damon from Sean's usual friend group, but most of them are adopting a wait-and-see attitude. Sean's too far up in the clouds of early romance to hear any criticism anyway."

"Since this Damon failed your little test, I know where you stand." Rin looked down at me, a hint of a smile hovering. "Do you ever approach the clouds, Mika?"

I pretended nonchalance, focusing on a trickle of arrivals from the gate. "I'll let you know once I catch my footing."

He paused to parse this, and from the corner of my eye I saw his habitual smile shift to a smirk.

"No way Sean would believe I was just a renter if he saw you now," I murmured.

"Does my face say 'going to make you mewl'?"

Before I could return more than a derisive snort, I spotted a familiar profile, and waved.

My mother and I clearly came off the same assembly line, but we're not identical. Her hair is a little darker, never grows to my length, and she prefers to keep it short. Her eyes are a blue-hazel, her jawline enviably chiselled. We're more than similar enough to get a lot of 'sisters' comments, and she's a fair prediction of what I'll look like in my late thirties.

I hugged her hard, since it felt like more than a few months since I'd seen her, but then paused, frowning a little.

"Pure exodus," my dad said, ambling over to squeeze us both. "I feel like we're heading the wrong way on the *Titanic*."

"Helios in winter doesn't have much in the way of attractions except sleet," I said, letting go of my mother and then examining her closely. She'd felt different in a way that I didn't fully process until the open front of her favourite coat made it clear. "Wow," I said, shocked out of any more meaningful expression, then pulled myself together enough to attempt a smile, and ask: "How far are you along?"

"Seventeen weeks," she said, patting my back gently. "We decided to start trying when we made the decision to look for a house here. You've gone pale."

"Axis of my world just tilted," I said, as Rin came up to us. My smile felt less shaky on the second attempt, though I suspected it was rather rueful. "Sadly, my love of springing surprise information on people means I don't get to complain about the lack of forewarning, but I am going to need a little adjustment time. So, am I getting a brother or a sister?"

"We don't know. Possibly both: fraternals run in the McAllister line, you know."

I hadn't. After another long moment of staring at my mother's abdomen, imagining not one, but two surprise siblings, I pulled myself together and said: "Mum, meet Rin, who volunteered to be transport."

"And a trip well worth it, to see Mika caught off guard," Rin said, briefly touching my shoulder as he nodded to my mother. "Welcome to the worst-named city in Greenland."

"With weather as Mika's described it, I'm not surprised there was such a prolonged period of sun worship here," Mum said. "Given the latitude, I'd originally pictured the place to be carpeted in snow."

"As I understand it, a heat pocket gets trapped above the city by some trick of conflicting air currents," Rin said. "Plenty of snow north, east, and west, quite a lot to the south and of course in all the mountains, but the southern lakeshore only gets snow in the coldest winters."

"It's nice enough on the sunny days," I said. "And I think there were more sunny days than sleety ones last year. It's just the bad days are so...drear." I shook my head, then took my mother's cabin bag. "Today's one of the sunny ones, fortunately, so the only problem is that the days are also short. Let's get your luggage and get home while you can still enjoy the sights."

The walk to the baggage carousels gave me time to recover from my surprise, and by the time we reached the Hummer, I'd adjusted enough to pull Mum into the back seat and ask if there were any ultrasound pictures.

"The first ultrasound was later than normal," she said, searching through her phone. "Thanks to some mixed physical signals, I didn't even take a test until I was nine weeks along. But then I was suddenly so big weeks ahead of expectation, and we went in for checks." She handed me her phone. "We were holding off telling you to avoid emotional rollercoasters, and then when we were so close to flying over, we held off a couple of weeks more."

"Not strictly for the entertainment value," my father added, smiling at me from the front seat. "But the doctor said everything looks stable now, so we can relax and start sharing the news."

"This does make some of your decisions in the house remodel much more understandable," I said. "The 'reading room' next to your bedroom, with just a rug and that big comfy upright chair..."

"I will use that as a quiet room eventually," Mum said. "But, yes, the nursery for now. We particularly want to pick everything out ourselves."

"We should hit a few of the baby supply stores tomorrow when we're car shopping," I said. "I need to start my spoiling campaign early."

"We're definitely facing a different set of baby-raising challenges this time around," my dad said frankly. "The temptation will be to overload them with everything we couldn't give you, and produce our very own pair of hell-demons."

"There's always a balance," my mother said, comfortably.

"Not to mention the challenges we'll face if we're dealing with Mika-levels of curiosity, but in duplicate." My dad laughed. "Do you remember when you disassembled all the appliances in that rental?"

"Made them run better, too," I said, unperturbed. "Rin might have suggestions for handling twins. He has two sets of younger sisters."

Anecdotes of Marcelline, Evgenie, Anthea and Jessamin took us most of the way home, and it wasn't until we drew into the garage that Rin said: "A relative of mine has a new litter of puppies—I asked her to reserve a couple in case you'd like a dog to go with your farm, but I don't know if that's an attractive thought given your new development."

"What kind of dog?" my mother asked.

"Border collies. The longer-hair type." From the way her face lit up, my mother didn't even need to say anything, so Rin smiled and said: "I can arrange for you to visit on the way down to Noonerry, to see if you want to take one—and whether you pass muster as potential owners. The pups are just on eight weeks old now. There's a couple of boys and one girl available: the remainder of a massive litter."

"Is there a good spot at Noonerry to set up one of those pet obstacle courses?" Mum asked. "I always wanted to do that. We had a spaniel when I was a kid, and he was far too fat and lazy to race about on command, no matter how many treats I gave him."

"Sounds like the treats might have been the problem," my dad said.

"There's plenty of flat stretches," I said. "The lot is nearly six full acres, after all, and the hill sits on the back two acres. It does occur to me that we're going to need to make very sure not to aim any dogs—or siblings—at some of the edges of Fox Farm when throwing balls."

"No fences?" my mother asked, frowning.

"There's drystone all around, but not so tall a collie couldn't hurl themselves over. There's also some internal fencing sectioning off two paddocks, one with that cow byre I sent you a photo of."

"Maybe we could get some sheep to go with the dog," Dad said. "I was wondering how to keep the grass down."

"Things to explore," my mother said, looking cheerful. "Just remember that they all come with a time investment. While we can easily hire some home help, babies and a puppy are a big load."

"Chickens," Dad murmured. "At least one cat, surely..."

"Buying a farm doesn't mean you have to stock it," I said, as we tried to fit people and suitcases into the elevator.

"But it's super tempting," Dad said, lifting one suitcase to sit on another to make room. "Nearly there."

"Go ahead," Rin said, rather than cram in with us. "I'll see you in the kitchen."

"Very convenient to have an internal elevator," Mum said, as we were wafted up two floors.

My mind was on babies, and adjustments that should be made to Fox Farm. "Even though we cleaned up those slippy front steps at Fox Farm, and put in a railing, they're still far from ideal for the mobility challenged. Plus, Noonerry doesn't have a hospital, and it's twenty minutes to Moonmere. You should come stay with us when you're near due."

"We were planning on renting an apartment for the last month," Dad said. "Since twins often turn up early. We weren't anticipating an energy-filled puppy, though, so maybe we'll try for a small house near a useful hospital instead."

I took over hoisting her suitcase into the larger guest room.

"Are you going to fret?" Mum asked. "I'm quite stable now."

"You still need to let us do the heavy lifting," I said, knowing my mother's independent streak. "What did you mean by 'mixed physical signals' delaying your tests?"

"Spotting," she said, shrugging. "I thought it was just my period adjusting back in after going off birth control, and had no idea we'd succeeded almost immediately. In retrospect, we saved ourselves a lot of stress."

"And a little extra care will save us unnecessary worry now," my dad said, no doubt having had a few conversations on the subject of lifting suitcases.

Trying to push my mother never got anyone anywhere, so I smiled, hugged her, and said: "You probably want to wash up after the flight. We were aiming for an early dinner, around five-thirty, but come down any time to enjoy watching relative newbies try to cook."

Downstairs, I found the main meal prep complete, and the cooks indulging in cupcake production. Kyou would readily attempt icing art, so long as Bran prepared all the ingredients, and was currently following a YouTube video, while Bran was injecting some sort of filling into uniced cakes. They both were wearing somewhat sour expressions, while Rin looked particularly smug.

Since I knew that Rin occasionally indulged in a weakness for pranks, I paused, then said: "He came in here and announced 'She's pregnant!', didn't he?"

"Almost had cupcakes all over the floor," Kyou said. "It only took us a moment, but it was quite a moment."

"We'd decided it'd be a few years before we could try to talk you into kids," Bran said.

"That...is definitely not a discussion for now," I said, blinking a few times.

"I think I saw the whites of your eyes there," Rin murmured, entertained.

"I need to learn how to be a big sister first. And graduate."

Rin kissed my cheek, then drew me into his side. "I couldn't tell if you were truly upset about these babies," he said. "You really did go pale at the airport."

"I think I'll enjoy siblings," I said, relaxing against him. "But today brought home to me something I'd kind of realised when I was showing Fox Farm to Lania. She asked how much use I'd get out of that paved area I planned for yoga. And the answer was 'hardly any', because I'm going to be a visitor to Fox Farm. I'll never experience it the way Mum, Dad, and the upcoming additions will."

"'Home' can be both us and your parents," Bran said firmly, as he and Kyou abandoned cupcakes to make it a group hug. "You don't have to choose one over the other."

"We'll be babysitting, and staying over, and living in each other's pockets in no time," Kyou added. "Depending on your parents' tolerance for, uh, news, we or just you could directly stay at Fox Farm for Christmas, if you prefer, rather than at the High Street house. From what Rin said, a few spare helping hands would probably be timely."

"It's going to be a challenge to keep my Mum in rest mode," I agreed. "First thing I need to do is get someone out to build a path from the carport to the side entrance, because I don't want her risking those stairs when she's big. And for later on, for prams and things. Actually, I might try and arrange it for before we go down there."

I squeezed them gratefully, then let go, and sat down to make a list of safety concerns. Sharp corners. Child locks. Some kind of protective fence to keep toddler fingers away from the double-sided fireplace. Rin joined Kyou in decorating cupcakes, and all three of them gently teased me about reining in my over-protective older sister mode at least until my new siblings were born.

My Kings are so nice.

Twenty-Four

"Rowan not back from rehearsal?" I asked, once I'd settled my emotions with a good action plan.

"Delayed start," Bran said, offering me a cupcake. "The group due to be on stage before him was having a meltdown."

I happily devoured a chocolate-mint treat. Bran's baking had really improved.

"Looking back over all the cakes given to us on Bake Sale Day, or Valentine's, I feel I should have appreciated them more," Kyou said, attempting another rose. "I truly underestimated the sheer amount of labour involved."

"When you're giving cakes to someone with twenty piled on their desk already, the act is more about how you feel than how they feel," Rin said, abandoning an attempt at a rose and just adding random swirls. "Though my sisters did a lot of appreciating on my behalf." He frowned then, and asked me: "Have you heard anything from Anthea?"

"Nothing, but I doubt she'd risk texting me unless something important came up."

Rin's mother had installed a monitoring app on Anthea and Jessamin's phones, and so now Rin only occasionally received calls or texts via the phones of friends, or talked to them via chat in an online game. It seemed like the longer he was out of their control, the more tightly Rin's parents wanted to manage his sisters.

"Do you think, when *One Step* is released, they'll calm down a little? When they see how important music is to you?"

"At this stage, I suspect they'll just take it as an attack on them," he said, with a dispassionate air. "As I understand it, I've made them look bad by choosing music over L-B Corp."

Rin no longer sounded so tired when he talked about his parents, but I was still glad when voices from the central hall drew our attention. I followed them out to see Mum and Dad talking to Rowan and one of his new bodyguards.

"No, not a ghost story," Dad said. "It's somewhere between magic realism and outright science fiction. But it will feel rather like a ghost story at first."

"Are you past the research stage?" I asked, a little surprised. Dad hadn't mentioned his new book for a while.

"First draft done," he said, happily. "One of those books that put itself together in the subconscious while I was reading up on the background, and then poured out in a space of weeks. I'll let it rest for a while, then do revisions after I've finished with the outline of the expansion pack script."

"Expansion?" I looked between Dad and Bran. "You took on the DLC as well?"

"Talked him into the sequel, too," Bran said. "It's good to see you again Mr Teyrn. And nice to meet you, Ms Niles."

"Sorenson," my mum said. "Is Gareth really making you call him Mr Teyrn?"

"When balancing parent status and colleague, we've erred on the side of formality," Kyou said, smiling.

"I just wanted to see how long they'd keep it up," Dad said. "I'm fine with being called any of my myriad names. Speaking of which, I've already guessed that this is your brother, Bran, but is this another relative?"

"My new bodyguard, Eden," Rowan said, ducking his head as if at a faintly embarrassing admission.

The younger of the two bodyguards Bran had arranged, Eden was twenty-one, very pale of skin beneath close-cropped dark hair, but otherwise entirely unremarkable, unless you counted a quietly alert air. He gave my parents a brief smile and a nod.

"Really?" Dad asked, lighting up the way he does whenever he comes across a new perspective. "Are you staying for dinner? I hope you're staying. I promise to be nosy for only ten minutes or so."

Eden laughed, then shook his head. "I'm sorry, I'm due to go to training. Another time?"

My dad happily agreed, and then Eden left, Rowan went upstairs to wash, and the rest of us relocated to the kitchen for some less chaotic introductions for my mother, and a survey of what still needed to be done for dinner.

"We've made the things that worked the best from previous attempts," Kyou said, transferring cupcakes to a three-tiered server I didn't even know we had. "Vegetarian lasagne, chicken pesto pasta, and a Thai beef salad. We, ah, had picked out a few choice bottles of wine to go with it all, but I'm not sure how wide our range of other options is currently."

"I'm fine for anything except alcohol and caffeine," my mum said, pausing to admire the kitchen. "What a smart set-up. Enough for a crowd in here without getting in each other's way. Have you been enjoying learning how to cook?"

"Yes," Kyou and Bran said.

Rin shrugged with lazy grace and said: "On the whole it bores me, but it's useful to understand it better. I like more that we get together and chat about the day."

"Annoyingly, Rin's dishes almost always seem to turn out well, without any sign of effort," Kyou said.

The dining room table had already been set, so we transferred there, and were just cutting portions when Rowan arrived, hair wet from a shower.

"What happened at rehearsal?" Bran asked, pushing the lasagne dish toward him.

"*Sun Chillin'* all hate each other," Rowan said, to his plate. "Two of them were shoving back and forth, part of the set got knocked over, bits went flying everywhere. I wasn't close, but a few people ended up with bruises, some cuts." He paused. "Eden could tell they were about to pop off. He got me to move before they even started up."

Dad, as usual, started asking questions about how all of this would work: having bodyguards, and how one goes about building a career as a musician.

"Are you thinking of writing a book set in the biz?" Kyou asked, as we started on the cupcakes.

"Not currently, but who knows what will percolate in the background while my attention is on the fun things we can do with *Echoes*."

"What does Devine think about all the gaming work?" I asked, and added as an aside to the rest of the table: "Dad's agent."

"He hasn't told her yet," Mum said.

"For serious?"

"Devine only represents me for traditionally published books, and any related media linked to those books," Dad explained. "She originally approached me for the Rock Hardison work, you know. Bad timing, since I'd just started to self-publish them, after finally ending the contract with that terrible house Donna stuck me with. Since I had a few manuscripts I hadn't managed to sell, I offered Devine the unpublished books under all my other names, to see what she would do with them, which was one of my better decisions. And she's understanding about my love of different genres, and urge to go off to try out exciting new things, instead of churning out my most profitable lines." He laughed. "Though it does help that I have *Yesterday, Upon the Stair* to distract her when I 'fess up."

"Is that what you're calling the new book?" I asked, curious about my mother's wry expression.

"Working name. I've rarely had a title survive the publication process. Devine tells me I have no feel for marketing. Probably because I hate it."

"A fellow sufferer!" Kyou said. "Our marketing lead has been waiting on my response to her draft plans for *One Step's* release, and all I have for her is an overwhelming 'meh'. The options seem suitable enough, but because I have no feel for it, I'm struggling to decide."

"Just let them go with their favourite," my mother advised. "When all your choices seem equally good, pick the one at least someone's passionate about."

"Or draw one from a hat," Dad added. "Saves ever so much agonising."

Once the discussion had turned to *One Step*, it was inevitable for Rin to propose a playthrough. Dad settled down for music-and-inquisition, while I took Mum off for a tour of the house, ending up with my bedroom.

"I really love this study," I said, stepping back so she could explore it. "Something about it being relatively small is great for focusing. It's the quietest corner of the house."

Mum touched the curving desk, mouth curving faintly. "Your dad said not taking a photo of your face when you saw it is a major regret. You've always been a positive person, but it's rare to see you overwhelmed. 'Lit from within', Gareth said. I'm glad you've found friends who give you that." She paused, looking at me, and said with very deliberate emphasis: "'*Friends*'."

"I knew you'd spot something," I said, smiling.

"Gareth said he'd give it four weeks before at least one of your landlords asked you out. He planned to have enormous fun today trying to guess what the progress had been, but to me it's clear all three of those boys are more than interested in you. Are you heading toward an unpleasant situation?"

"No. They did briefly suggest I date one of them, but we all knew it wouldn't work."

I drew Mum back into my bedroom and sat with her on my couch to try to begin to approach why three was better than one.

"Would you date someone who lived in the pockets of his two best friends?" I asked.

"I suppose it would depend on the friends."

"Oh, they're great friends. Smart, talented, generally considerate, protective of those in their inner circle, but out of necessity keeping at a distance the jostling crowd of people wanting some part of them. They spend a large part of every day with each other. They plan every holiday together. They share the same house. They share their finances, have started a company together, and work together. They've made *wills* in each other's favour." I shook my head. "Bran had a long-term childhood sweetheart. Meggan. She seemed like a really nice, warm-hearted person, and they shared an enjoyment of dancing, though from my impression she didn't match him that well on other interests.

"She'd grown up with Rin and Kyou as well, of course, and they considered her a close friend. Until she gave Bran a me or them ultimatum. Not to maybe at least reconsider the living together part, but to cut Rin and Kyou off altogether, or she'd walk away."

"No need for me to guess which one he chose."

"And by doing so, he proved her point. The sheer intensity of the bond between them would always make her—any girlfriend—an outside decoration on a rock-solid fortress. Secondary and non-essential."

"Something I can't imagine you'd find acceptable in a relationship."

"No. They asked me to pick one of them to date, and I turned them down because it might strain their friendship, and I would have hated that. But perhaps I was thinking too much of myself, and instead I'd have ended up a limpet clinging to a fortress tower." I looked at my mother, trying to gauge her reaction, then said: "After that, they asked me to date all three of them, and that was a way more interesting idea."

Even though she must have suspected, my mum's eyes still widened. Then she turned her head and looked at the oversized bed. Her eyebrows went up, then she looked back at me and said: "Aren't you *tired*?"

I burst out laughing. I should have expected Mum to look at it from an unusual angle.

"Sometimes. I sleep very well though. They're an unbeatable insomnia treatment, and got me through my exams."

"This has been going on for a while?"

"We were meeting up over the school year, but it wasn't until the end of classes that we started thinking in terms of something more...tangible."

"And that's what this is?" My mother continued to look dubious. "A committed relationship? You care deeply enough about all three of them?"

"How much is deeply?" I asked. "This is a whole new set of emotions for me. There's a lot of feeling really comfortable, and plenty of excitement, and an undercurrent of anxiety that it will fall apart. How did you know with Dad? He always says he fell in love with you at first sight, but you once said that you fell in love with him over time. How long did that take?"

"Hard question to answer," she said, leaning back— and eyeing the super-king bed again. "Obviously I liked him a lot at first meeting. Cute, funny, smart. We chatted up a storm during that protest march, and I more or less seduced him. But with an attitude of 'this will be a first time I'm happy to remember' rather than as a 'start of the rest of my life' moment. I did want to continue seeing him afterwards, and both appreciated and was mildly disappointed when he found out my age, and chose to dial back our relationship to 'formal courting' rather than more trips to his dorm room."

"I'm not sure I'm old enough to know you just wanted to use Dad for sex," I said. "And...am not going to comment on how similar we are. Do...do you think you'd still be with Dad if you hadn't gotten pregnant?"

"Equally hard to say. My parents would certainly have done everything to break us up, since they couldn't stomach him being openly bisexual. But I had you, and no plans to give you up, so they broke up with me instead. Gareth wasn't my only option for what to do next, but circumstances certainly forced us together. And I didn't think I was in love with him at that point. We felt more like partners in adversity. But he was a great partner, and I knew both of us were the type to make the best of things, and we...grew together, step by step.

"The first time I realised how far we'd come, you were almost four. We were in a terrible little apartment somewhere treacle-humid. My last employer was stringing me along about payment, meaning we didn't have the funds to get to my next job, and we all had a stomach bug. When the toilet stopped up, even Gareth couldn't maintain a smile. We were lying on the bed because we didn't have any other furniture, listening to a fly beating against one of the windows. It was the most squalid moment of my entire life. Then Gareth took my hand, and made a little speech. Let's see if I can remember it word for word..."

Mum paused, so I reached out and took her hand. She squeezed mine back.

"'*At some point in the future we'll look back on this day and...shudder, probably,*'" she quoted. "'*But it is my honour and joy to be on this adventure with you. The path ahead will inevitably have other hurdles, hopefully less smelly, but we'll make our way over them. And on that day years from now, the place we will be looking back from is the castle I build for you in the clouds, Sorenson. I promise you."*

Her voice cracked a fraction on the last sentence, and she let out a long breath.

"He was so earnest. And sure. And I found that I could imagine no future that didn't involve him. No happy one, at least."

I hugged her. Mum's always been very honest with me, but she's far less chatty than my dad, at least about emotional things.

"I want you to have someone who brings you joy in the same way," she told me. "And while I have to admit to being very dubious, I'll trust your judgment that this might be possible with your 'fortress' of friends. Just remember that we are here for you if you're not sure, want to chat, or need help in any way."

"Do you think Dad will, uh, be able to cope?"

"Maybe with a dose of brain bleach. We've met a few people in poly relationships, but it hits rather different when it's three boys and your daughter. I'll talk to him later, to give him a night to adapt to the idea."

"Is he having problems with Devine, by the way? You were kind of weird when he was talking about her."

Mum rolled her eyes. "Your friends' game isn't the only thing he hasn't mentioned to Devine. You remember *In the Ashes*? That fantasy novel he couldn't sell, back when Donna was his agent?"

"Sure. I really liked that one."

"He's self-published it. New pen name, cover bought off a pre-made site. It's sold six copies so far."

"And he hasn't even told Devine? Why? He's not thinking of getting a different agent, is he? Devine's been so good for him."

"No, nothing like that. He's just developed a bugbear about his books now being more about the name they're published under than their actual content."

"Well..." I said, thinking back over the evolution of my dad's career. "That's true. He's put out more than enough that it's his name selling the books—even if he's divvied up the impact. Isn't that the whole point?" I opened up my e-reader app and began searching.

"He's always been sensitive about *In the Ashes*. He thinks it's one of his best works, and not being able to sell it on its own merits bothers him enormously. He doesn't want Devine to leverage his other pen names to make the sale."

"Broderick Snow, huh?" I said, finding *In the Ashes*. "Super-generic cover, no reviews." I began happily gifting copies. One for each King, one for Lania, one for Anthea, one for Millie, one for Sean, one for Anika, one for Sue. "I've run out of email addresses of people I know who read fantasy," I said. "But I've doubled his sales. Is he not planning to tell Devine at all?"

"I've suggested he 'fess up when we meet at the convention centre hotel. It's good timing, because he can present her with *Yesterday, Upon the Stair*, and then get all his sins out of the way while she's in the mood to absolve. Not to mention that fantasy and science fiction have never been Devine's strong area, which is one of the reasons he never gave her the manuscript in the first place."

"Has he picked which pen name to use for *Yesterday*?   Devine won't be all that pleased if it's another Blake Sevenmore. Or did they end up deciding to go ahead with 'crossing the streams'?"

"You haven't looked at the convention schedule yet, have you?" Mum asked, with a wry smile.

I raised my eyebrows, then fetched my laptop to look up the convention schedule.   "Oh.   Wow.   Dad's planning to have fun on the first day, isn't he? Devine and Caitlin are both okay with this?"

"From Devine's point of view, it means all Gareth's books will have publicity across a much wider audience. Caitlin's long been reluctant, but with the super-strong early reviews for *Six Copper Coins*, she finally agreed."

"I'm surprised," I said, after a pause to recollect that *A Tranquil Death* had been renamed *Six Copper Coins*. "Caitlin's been so firmly against 'making things messy'."

"She's caught wind of some low-level gossip about authors with hidden identities, and thinks it might be about Gareth, so decided the convention is a good opportunity for a semi-controlled 'exposure'. His other publishers are a combination of pleasantly surprised, and counting money in advance.   The only really reluctant party is Rashelle, from *Minor Morrissey*. The L K Moorehouse books have really picked up the last couple of years, and Rashelle thinks there might be a fan backlash, since there's been a strong assumption that 'Elkie' is a female writer."

"Dad just loves his romantic suspense," I said. "What happened to that film option for *The High Trail* that's been dragging on forever?"

"They didn't renew it last year. That yearly five thousand has come in more than handy, so I feel a little sentimental to see the option lapse, even though it's not a major thing for us anymore."

"Does mixing together all Dad's readers mean he's finally going to take a break while they catch up?"

"I think the flood of output has become ingrained. He gets itchy if he hasn't produced at least a couple of pages every day."

Because he travels, works wherever he's living, and takes breaks to go for walks, a lot of people think my dad has a holiday-style life. But writing thousands of words a day requires a level of discipline that not many people possess. Admittedly, he loves it. The only time I'd seen him stressed was when my Nan nearly lost her house, and Dad tried to write five books in one year in order to get together the funds to save it.

"I hope he can adjust to my boyfriends," I said, after a pause. "I really want to spend Christmas with you all." I looked at her stomach. "And I really want you to stay with us when you're due. I'm going to need to be able to keep a good eye on you in order not to fret."

Mum laughed. "If you want to baby me, let's go downstairs and find Gareth. Time zones mean it's been rather a long day for both of us, and the next few days are going to be busy."

"Yeah."

I could barely wait to show my parents their castle.

Twenty-Five

Even if my parents were so inclined, I knew there wouldn't be a dramatic scene at breakfast, since Dad would be on autopilot. By the time the morning's coffee had worked its magic, Rin had whisked Mum off for a feedback session with *One Step*, and Kyou and Bran had gone upstairs to check the set-up of the motion capture room.

"Go for a walk?" Dad asked, after he'd come back to himself enough to start frowning at me.

"Sure," I said. "Campus, river, or suburban meander?"

"River."

It had rained overnight, but thin sunlight alleviated the chill rising from the still-damp ground, and there was only a hint of wind, so—with the secret weapon of my thermals—we had a pleasant stroll down to the esplanade, where a few hardy souls were setting up their regular stalls.

"They have entire market days down here in other seasons," I said, after Dad had bought himself a top-up coffee. "I've grabbed some great snacks on the loop back from morning jogs."

We found the sunniest bench, and talked about attractions to see in Helios, and the stages of the immigration process my parents would spend the next few years stepping through. Dad tossed his empty coffee cup neatly into a nearby bin, sighed, and leaned back on the bench.

"I googled your name last night," he said.

"That must have been exciting," I said. "And all that just from renting a room. It's going to be a circus if I ever publicly admit to dating them."

"I can certainly see the reason you're officially 'just friends'. But major secrets can be hard to live with long-term, kiddo. Do you really want a life being...unacknowledged?"

"My sleeping arrangements have never been something I'd announce," I said. "There's only a handful of people whose opinion I care about anyway." I smiled at him. "I went in knowing there'd be a price for all this. It's more than balanced by how they make me feel, Dad."

"Bah. And humbug, for that matter. Just because you know your own mind doesn't mean I can't be extraordinarily uncomfortable about the whole set-up."

"Absolutely," I said, encouragingly.

"Fine, fine, be all shiny and happy," he said. "But I reserve the right to glower at them in a stereotypical threatening manner. Even if they're all rather taller and fitter than me."

I laughed, then turned the talk to his new 'Broderick Snow' persona, and his plans to mix together his various identities.

"After the car purchase today, we'll not have so much ready cash, so the more talk about me the better," he said as we started walking back. "Fox Farm is a delight, but it's been quite the money pit. Besides, I've never believed that I would lose that many fans just because of the Rock Hardison name. Twenty or thirty years ago that might have been a juicy scandal, but now it's just another question to ask in interviews. I'll gain more than I lose, anyway."

"Do you need me to hold off on more spending?" I asked, feeling vaguely guilty. Because I knew my parents had taken to channelling a good portion of their income into investment, I'd been very free making payments from their general account. "While the Cassadine Malway team is still onsite, I was going to put in a pathway for unwieldy mums. And some dog-related stuff in the garage."

"So long as it's not in the order of another new roof, spend away. Particularly anything pet-related: Sorenson is very excited about this puppy. We had briefly discussed animals to go with the farm when we signed off on the purchase, but this is the first I've heard of her passion for border collies. She stayed up last night watching training videos, and then competitions of something called 'flyball', which I'd never encountered before, but have a suspicion I'll see a lot of in the future."

He was describing exciting fetch-a-ball races when we turned into Sycamore Street and found a tangle of vehicles blocking the street.

"You're having an event?" Dad asked, tilting his head, as people attempted to unload three white vans at once.

"We rented out the motion capture facilities to a local band," I explained. "I'd take you up to gawk, but we've already asked as many people as possible to work from home today to cut down on the strain on office space."

We dodged through the crowd, and snuck into the game room as Mum neared the end of her playthrough of *One Step*.

"Do you think you'll ever get tired of watching people play this?" I asked Rin, after he'd finished his cross-examination, and let Mum and Dad go get ready for our car-buying expedition.

He stretched lazily, then pulled me into his arms. "Right now, every playthrough is cathartic, but I assume the effect will weaken over time. Ask me in a few years." He squeezed me lightly. "Your mother made many of the same choices as yours."

"We're pretty similar. She's smarter; I'm a bit more sporty, and have my dad's sense of humour."

"Were the faces your father was making at me humour or serious?"

"Humour. Mostly."

Rin pretended to be relieved, then said: "They treat you like you're their friend, not their child."

I thought about that. "No, they definitely treat me as their daughter, but an adult one. If I was sixteen and decided it was a good idea to have three guys on my string, there would be a lot less 'respecting my opinion' and plenty more 'this isn't acceptable'."

Kyou, who had walked into the room in time to hear this, chuckled. "'On your string'? That's quite the term. A criss-crossed red thread of fate, perhaps?"

"Cleverly-laid snare," I said, with an air of complacence. "Ready to head out?"

"I told your parents ten minutes. Let's watch the news first."

He settled down beside Rin and wielded the remote, bringing up the ten o'clock news. This was in the middle of a piece about the high-speed rail, and the imminent opening of the intra-city part of the track. I was wondering if the brief mention of the rocketing land prices on the Snowshield Tableland was the point of the viewing session when the presenter moved on to the dramatic fall of a local big-name producer, whose entire back catalogue of dirty secrets had spilled out overnight. 'Arrest imminent'.

"Were there photographs?" I asked.

"Not of Rowan. Others, yes." Kyou's matter-of-fact tone faltered momentarily, then he went on: "In the end, we decided not to delete all of them, but we removed a chunk of the more recent. Then changed passwords and sent the new password in an anonymous tip-off."

The fact that my Kings made for dangerous enemies might, in the long run, be a positive point for my parents, but I decided it was an item that didn't currently need to be discussed, and instead went upstairs to quickly get ready for a day's shopping.

Kyou was our driver for the morning, since I'd passed up the opportunity to rack up a few more hours driving practice, and while I browsed the news on my phone, he cheerfully talked cars, and tips for getting about Helios with my parents. Dad had told Kyou that, "Presuming it's not a known lemon, our focus is mainly comfort of driving, ability to negotiate the occasional mud track, but not too big a clamber to get in and out of," and Kyou had found a suitable dealer out by the airport that had vehicles without a wait time for delivery. Two test-drives later we were able to free Kyou and head off in something 'large but still parkable' to tour a nearby big box mall with an impressive pet supply store.

It was mid-afternoon by the time we returned, me having purchased a toy for each of my upcoming siblings, and Mum with everything a puppy could need. When we got back, my Mum lay down for a rest, while

Dad and I sorted out excess packaging and took it down to the recycling bins.

"Mum is actually willing to take afternoon naps," I said, not hiding my worry. My mother is usually indefatigable.

"She needs to be mindful of her energy levels," Dad admitted. "We had a few very worrying days a month ago, and Sorenson isn't going to risk fatigue again. She only has one job lined up for the whole of next year, and that one something she can do at her own pace at home." He grimaced. "She's sure to fill her time with other projects—like this puppy—but the important part is that she stops as soon as she's feeling the least bit worn."

"I hope you're not thinking of picking up the slack," I said.

"Realistically, despite the bank account looking a little sparse right now, Sorenson and I could live comfortably off my existing work for quite some time— especially if the current run of translation deals continues. Now I officially write because I love it, rather than to cover the rent." He gave me a teasing smile. "Thank you for your contribution yesterday. Quite doubled my income for that pen name."

"Bad timing on my part," I said. "Bran was going to shadow the motion capture work today so that he got a feel for the issues, but he stayed up all night reading *In the Ashes*."

"I knew I liked that boy," Dad said.

"Let's go see how they're faring."

About half the usual staff had stayed at home in order to leave space for visitors, but I took the opportunity to introduce *Echoes'* lead writer to whoever was in. *Echoes'* development was ramping up, and we admired the storyboards already completed. Dad was delighted to discover the leader of the Graphics Team, Imani, had worked on a few games he particularly liked, and chatted with her about the difference between movie production and development of the kind of cutscene-heavy game *Echoes* would become.

"You sound like you've been involved in a production or two yourself," Imani said.

"I explored script work for a little while," Dad said. "Not really for me, but very interesting."

"No?" Imani looked surprised. "Your dialogue work is so good, though. I would have thought film would be a natural avenue."

"I always miss stopping to describe the roses, so to speak," Dad said. "I'm happy enough to go dialogue-heavy occasionally, such as with this game, but novels are my natural medium." He smiled at her. "Are games yours, or would you prefer something less integrated?"

They were deep into the unique attractions of art in an action-focused game when the door of the mocap room opened, and a stream of people flooded out. I'm not at all familiar with *Easy Cat*, but spotted the band members simply because they were the ones wearing the mocap suits. They disappeared off to the bathrooms to change, while Rin chatted lightly with what I presumed was the clip's director. Rowan and Bran, apparently both tired and energised at the same time, emerged last, along with a new Kybirn staff member, Daria, whose speciality was motion capture. Bran, who was a very matter-of-fact and organised boss, gave her a few instructions, and then saw me and came over, smiling.

"Wasn't terrible," he said. "Minor hitches in the system, but only took a minute or two to fix."

"It was fun," Rowan murmured.

"Did you stay up half the night as well?" I asked, discovering shadows beneath the boy's eyes, then added to Bran: "Do you want to change tonight's dinner to takeaway rather than eating out?"

He shook his head. "I'll take a nap, and be ready by six." He gave my dad an embarrassed smile. "I was only going to read the start of *In the Ashes* yesterday, and then it was morning."

"Music to my ears," Dad said, gleefully. "Be warned, I have an insatiable appetite for hearing which bits readers liked the most."

"He stalks the reviews of every release," I said. "Then dismisses the good ones and obsesses over everything negative."

"Only for the first week or so," Dad said. "Then I get distracted by the next book."

"Go get a little rest," I urged Bran. "You can finish *In the Ashes* tomorrow."

Bran, after a pause to bid goodbye to returning band members, took Rowan off, and Dad decided he wanted to get a start on fleshing out the outline for the DLC for *Echoes*. Not unusually for this kind of post-release mini-expansion, the DLC was meant to show a different perspective on the story, and other than some points they wanted to particularly cover, my Kings had asked Dad to take the world they'd created and run with it. Dad had plans for "bittersweet tragedy", which is a style he liked to wallow in occasionally, between his more optimistic work.

We'd decided on a nearby steak house for dinner, and risked walking over, since we could easily send someone to play driver if it started sleeting. There was a bitter edge to the wind that made it seem likely, and I had to restrain an impulse to hover over Mum, who was sensibly dressed for the weather, and happily chatting with Rin about his cousin Stacia's mother, Nadia: the owner of a horse stud with a sideline breeding and showing border collies.

I had only met Stacia once: between working on her thesis, taking on a managerial role with L-B Corp, and maintaining a hectic social whirl, she seemed to have very little time. I'd liked her, as best as I could judge from a brief conversation when she, Kyou and I had crossed paths at Helios U.

The steak house was noisy and overheated, and we shrugged coats as soon as we were through the door, then thankfully escaped to the private room Bran had reserved, which at least would let us hear our own voices.

"Popular," my mother murmured as Kyou tucked her coat over the back of her chair.

"Good rep," Bran said. "We've meant to come here before, but haven't eaten out much lately."

Mum began to ask about motion capture, and led Bran deep into technical detail, as was her habit. She'd probably read up on it when she had a chance, because my mother liked to know things thoroughly when she found them interesting.

We'd ordered dessert and moved onto a discussion of one of the first major milestones of game development, called a vertical slice, when Rowan, who had been silently playing with his phone next to me, handed it to me, opened to an Instagram page belonging to *Easy Cat*. They'd taken a number of entertaining photos of their day's adventure in silly suits, mixed in with shots of various Kybirn staff members. There was a spectacularly beautiful one of Rin, presumably during a lunch break, sitting at the rooftop table, chin propped on one hand, chatting to the lead singer.

Rin deep-down happy is an amazingly beautiful creature, and it was no surprise that the image had attracted a soaring swarm of likes, but its popularity was dwarfed by a brief clip of Rowan duetting a song he told me was *Easy Cat's* first hit. The contrast between the quiet, almost repressed boy beside me, and the brilliant performer when on a stage, would never cease to amaze me.

"How are the reworks of your own songs going?" I asked, giving him back his phone.

He shrugged and said: "Okay," but added a shy little smile that suggested they were going well.

"We're going to drop the strongest on YouTube, probably the day after tomorrow," Rin said. "See how the reaction is."

My own phone vibrated then, so I handed Rowan's back, and found a message from Lania: *Say hi to your Mum.* This innocuous sentence was accompanied by a link, and I followed it, blinked a few times, then turned on the photo mode of my phone and handed it to Rowan.

"Take a pic for me?" I said, and drew Mum to her feet.

We posed, got Dad up for a couple more pics, then I took a photo of everyone at the table. I then sent Lania a couple of shots, told her to have fun with them, and promised to see her bright and early tomorrow at the book festival.

It wasn't until we were walking back home that Kyou and Rin's phones began blowing up. Rin only checked his screen before putting his phone away, while Kyou paged through some messages, then laughed.

"Is this why you suddenly wanted photos?" he asked, tilting the phone so I could see the same forum post Lania had sent me.

"Yeah. I guess Lania's response hasn't gotten enough attention yet. Or people just prefer rumours."

"Rumours? What rumours?" my dad asked.

Kyou handed him his phone, and I watched Dad's face as he saw the photo of Rin, Kyou, Bran and Mum, just after we'd entered the steak house, and Kyou had politely taken her coat. You could only see my Mum in partial profile, but couldn't miss the outward curve of her stomach.

Dad scrolled through several pages of foaming guesswork on which of the Kings was the father, briefly showed the thread to my Mum, then returned Kyou's phone. "Always said you look like sisters," he commented.

Rowan, who had also received a small flood of texts, showed one to Bran. "Should I answer this?"

Bran snorted. "Ignore it. It's not like the truth will stop them jumping." He glanced at my parents, and added in a milder tone: "This is part of our lives. Pandas in a zoo."

"One of the reasons we've been eating out less is because the interest in us has grown exponentially in the past few months," Kyou said.

"Thanks to your excursion into real estate," Rin pointed out.

"In part," Kyou agreed. "Noonerry is far too much fun for me to regret buying there, but it certainly brought a larger spotlight. Just as your venture into the music world will." He, too, was addressing his remarks to my parents: "We are, for want of a better word, coveted, and those around us are drawn into the whirlpool of attention. Which is why we have a broad acquaintance, but are slow to consider people close friends."

"One of the things we've never been able to control is gossip," Rin added. 'But we are extremely protective of those who are important to us."

I had to wonder what Rowan made of this conversation, which to me read as a series of statements amounting to "we promise to take good care of your daughter". From my dad's faint smile, I could tell he was starting to find it extremely funny.

As I'd guessed, neither of my parents really liked my romantic situation. But they were willing to support my choice. In the parental department, I was the wealthiest person in the room.

Twenty-Six

My parents left after dinner, since they'd booked a room at the convention centre hotel to make it easier for my dad to attend an authorial get-together breakfast. Rather than face parking challenges, my Kings and I—with Rowan tagging along last-minute—took the Sunrise Line tram early, aiming to get through registration with time to spare to reach my dad's first session at ten.

"So, Atherton Mullahy, Blake Sevenmore and Rock Hardison are all having a signing session together?" Kyou asked, chuckling over the day's program. "You and your father have some distinct similarities."

"Dad's going to have so much fun today," I said, grinning. "So am I."

"How many pen names does your father have?" Rowan asked, curiously.

"Fourteen," I said. "No, wait, fifteen with this new one. But some have been one-offs. Julius Rule, for instance, which he used for this super bleak post-modernist novel. He says he's never been in a bad enough mood to write another, which is probably a good thing since it barely sold anything. And K J Frost is a pen name he uses exclusively for the syrupy Christmas short story he writes every year. Most of them are pretty obscure."

"Do you have a favourite?" Bran asked.

"To read? Either the fantasy he just released, or the hard SF novels. On a sentimental side, Rock, of course." I smiled. "I don't lead with the Rock Hardison pen name just to enjoy the reaction. Until four or five years ago, old Rock was the mainstay of Dad's income. Each book always brought a little celebration: a nice takeout, or a cake, or a new release game. Silly as the name is, it's still what I think of first when I talk about my dad the author."

"How old were you when your father let you actually read a Rock Hardison?" Kyou asked.

"Fourteen. Officially. I'd sneaked looks at them on and off, though, and have a distinct memory of thinking them very boring, and then later understanding why I needed to be grown up to read them and being uncomfortable about the whole subject. I don't think it was until I was sixteen that I made it all the way through one, but now I really like them. Part of the reason Rock's so popular is they're all solid romances, along with being erotica."

We took our day passes and while we meandered toward the room where Dad had his ten o'clock signing session, I asked my Kings if there were any stand-out features of the book festival that we should make sure not to miss.

"Other than specific authors?" Rin said. "Depends on whether you like media tie-ins."

"The festival started off very literary," Kyou explained. "But now includes anything even vaguely related to books. And cosplay has grown massively. I don't remember even seeing a costume when I first went to a festival—"

"When he was ten," Bran noted.

"But now it's a major attraction, with a parade and photo sessions," Kyou continued. "The parade's on Day

Three but there's a few gathering points that have become cosplay hubs. We're supposed to be meeting the girls near one of them."

Rin's sisters had been carefully silent the past few weeks, out of fear they'd alert their parents to their plans. From the way he kept checking his phone, I'd assumed Rin was worrying they'd not be able to make it, but the expression of faint disgust didn't seem to match that possibility.

"What is it?" I asked.

After a pause, he showed me a group chat that mainly involved his parents' reaction to last night's entertaining photographs of my mother, along with a lot of questions about me, and warnings to not 'get trapped' by 'people with an agenda'.

"What's next on your agenda, Mika?" Kyou asked, after peering over my shoulder.

"House design," I said. "Or, at least, firming up your list of requirements. But I want to spend more time at Fox Farm to see what hilltop life is like before I start giving you options."

Talking about the planned house on Borger Hill always pleased Kyou, and we debated whether we'd give it a name to go with Fox Farm and Fox Hollow. While calling it Fox Castle was very tempting, we didn't want a castle-like house, but neither 'Fox View' nor 'Fox Heights' sparked any interest.

Abandoning the discussion when we reached the room for my dad's signing, I poked my head inside and saw my parents, along with a short, muscular woman in exquisitely tailored Chanel.

"Devine! Long time."

Dad's agent turned and waved, faltered momentarily at the sheer aesthetic value of my companions, then said: "Glad to see you with hair again."

The last time I'd talked to Devine, I'd just shaved my head for a charity appeal. "Short hair sure was easier," I said, then played a round of introductions before asking: "Are you looking forward to the big reveal?"

"It'll be something," Devine said, dryly. "It would have helped if Gareth had mentioned all his various side projects before I'd written up the press release."

"When were you planning to send it? How long will it take to add a couple of names?"

"Don't be logical at me," Devine commanded.

I grinned, then asked Kyou: "Do you want a copy of the release? It'll probably bring *Echoes* a bit of buzz."

"Sure," he said. "I'll pass it on to Kezia, and we'll see if we can attract a few more followers."

"So, is this game a class project?" Devine asked, clearly having taken in the "Mika's friends from school" part of Dad's explanation, but not any real understanding of Kybirn's scope.

"No, just something we've always wanted to do," Kyou said. "I'm responsible for coordinating the art, Rin composes the music, and Bran manages the programmers. We were extremely lucky to connect with Gareth through Mika."

Devine laughed and nodded, then asked Dad: "Which name are you using for it? Though I suppose it'll be a moot point after today."

"My own," Dad said. "Using one of the pen names seemed redundant. Besides, strictly speaking I've only been doing a dialogue pass, despite being generously called lead writer. While I'm taking on a larger role in the later development, games are really a collaborative effort, and a pen name doesn't fit the situation." He gave Kyou, Rin and Bran an impish smile. "Of course, today's merging of identity means you gain all the benefit of my various names. Some of old Rock's fans are particularly devoted. And impatient. Be prepared for five years of questions about the release date."

"We're already getting those," Rin said, then his expression changed to surprised delight and he turned and strode to the door.

I hadn't heard whatever had caught his attention, but I wasn't at all shocked when he was almost barrelled over by four excited girls. Much hugging occurred, interspersed with an explanation that they knew we'd be here when they saw Blake Sevenmore on the festival program, and hadn't wanted to wait for the meeting time we'd arranged.

"I'm surprised you're allowed out without an escort," Kyou said, when they'd finally separated. "Given Rin usually takes you to the festival, weren't they suspicious that you'd meet him here?"

"We got around that by insisting one of them had to take us in his place," Evgenie explained, looking from me to where my parents had gone to inspect the three author's tables at the front of the room. "Mother was supposed to, since she had books she wanted signed, but we knew she'd bail last moment for the fashion show."

"Then we insisted our father take us," Marcelline added, smiling faintly. "Because he was sure to tell us we're old enough to get on a tram by ourselves. Which we did."

"Not that they aren't keeping an eye on all their spy software," Anthea said, wearily.

"Can you introduce me to your dad, Mika?" Jessamin asked, pulling a couple of Sevenmore classics out of her packed tote bag.

"Good idea to get in early, before the line gets too long," I said, cheerfully.

Since my dad hardly ever goes to conventions, I didn't have a real idea how many fans would show up for these three pen names, but I was pleased to see a few people peeking in the door. Dad had taken all three authorial name cards and stuck them into one holder at an angle. He gave up trying to make them stay in place, and smiled as I brought Rin's sisters over.

"No need for me to guess the relationship," he said. "And a refined taste for horror, I see: you've picked my favourites of the Sevenmores."

I left Dad in author mode with Jessamin, and followed the other three girls, who had made a beeline to my mother.

"I wanted to say congratulations," Evgenie said, then added forthrightly: "Your baby caused our extended family group chat to melt down this morning. It was the most fun I've had all year."

After a disconcerted moment, my mother smiled slowly, then said: "What I fail to understand is how whoever took that photo didn't see Mika. She was standing right next to me."

"Most likely they did see her," Marcelline said. "Sometimes the truth is the less entertaining option."

"I'm glad you didn't fall for it," Rin said.

"We knew you'd tell us," Marcelline said, gave me a wry look, and added: "Not necessarily about dating, but babies. You would never let us find out about babies third-hand."

I smiled blandly. Rin's sisters definitely suspected I wasn't just a housemate, but I'd leave it to him to manage their curiosity.

Dad's fans had started to form a line, though more than a little distracted by the collection of stunners to one side of the author table. Rowan had sensibly worn a mask and hat, but my Kings were busy lighting up the room, and Rin's sisters, while only fourteen, were already show-stoppers. Another drift of fans walked in, then paused in confusion, nearly leading further arrivals into a collision. I saw Lania at the back and raised a hand to wave, then checked momentarily as Athaine followed her in.

After a moment to manage my expression, I crossed over to say Hi.

"Did you bring your Mullahy's?" I asked.

Lania nodded, and slid her backpack off one shoulder to pull out the slightly worn copies. "Athaine's a fan too, did you know?"

"Well, I've read them," Athaine corrected. "Good science. I'm not a signature collector, though."

"I read almost exclusively electronically myself," I admitted. "Next time you come down to Noonerry, Lania, you can have fun picking out any first editions you want."

"Deal," Lania said, then noticed another little cluster of new arrivals, and hastily got in line.

"I have an impression I'm suddenly in your bad books," Athaine said, propping himself against the rear wall of the room. "Or..." He smiled, slowly. "I just met her at the registration desk, honest. Though she is adorable."

"She is," I said, agreeably. "And a good friend. Your habit of skulking around in front of Professor Tremaine's house makes me want to keep her away from you."

I hadn't planned on the blunt approach, but saw him suitably disconcerted before he recovered, shrugging ruefully. "I wouldn't call that skulking. You have me curious how you know I've been in the area."

"I live in the big white building across the road."

Athaine laughed. "Truly? And spend your time peering out the windows? Maybe that's why the Professor has an opinion on you."

"Unlikely, but possible I suppose."

He clearly wasn't planning to explain. If anything, he seemed less gloomy than usual, enjoying my discomfort. I'd had a reasonably good impression of Athaine before I'd discovered the skulking. He obviously had some kind of chip on his shoulder, but seemed self-aware, and able to moderate himself.

"Everyone in that corner is staring at us," he said, almost sunnily. "What do you think they'd do if I leaned a little closer?"

"What I'd do would probably be more relevant," I said. "You wouldn't gain much from it. Any more than I guess you're doing yourself any good hanging around watching Professor Tremaine and her son."

"I'm too clever to only do the smart thing."

I shook my head, but smiled. "Okay Clever. Let me introduce you to some more of my friends."

Taking him over to our interested audience, I said: "This is Athaine, who is also in the Engineering Physics course. These are my housemates, Rin, Kyou and Bran, along with Rowan, Anthea, Jessamin, Evgenie and Marcelline. And my mother, Sorenson."

Athaine clearly didn't follow gossip forums, and simply made polite sounds.

"Do you share Mika's passion for bridges?" Rin asked, secretly touching my back. All three of my Kings had gone hyper-alert, which I found strange, given they didn't usually react to potential competition.

"Nope," Athaine said, with a hooked smile. "Though I know it will disgust Mika to hear it, Engineering Physics is simply where I ended up, for various reasons. It's interesting enough, but I might go on from it to something more theoretical." He shrugged. "I like many things, but I wouldn't say I'm passionate about any of them."

"Do you do any acting?" Kyou asked, unexpectedly.

"Acting? Wouldn't have thought I had the face for it."

I didn't know about that—Athaine wasn't traditionally handsome, but he certainly was striking.

"Don't you think he sounds like Vaughn would?" Kyou asked, then turned and called out: "Gareth!". When my dad looked over, Kyou pointed to Athaine and said: "Vaughn?"

Dad blinked, then told Athaine: "Say 'Why in the Three Names would I do that?'"

"Why in the Three Names would I do that?" Athaine repeated, quizzically.

"Sounds like Vaughn to me," Dad said, and went back to signing.

"This isn't how I expected you to go about auditioning for *Echoes*," I commented. Though I had to admit that Athaine's edge of black humour really did fit the image of Vaughn, one of the major characters in *Echoes*.

"Always seize an opportunity," Kyou said, hefting his phone and adding to Athaine: "Give me a contact number and I'll send you an outline of the role, and you can think about whether you want a future filled with recording booths and mocap suits."

Athaine laughed, reported his number, and said: "I'd recommend a longer audition. Completely new area for me."

Kyou just shrugged and said: "Try it out and see."

Lania was still in line, so I took the opportunity to duck to the bathroom, suggesting that everyone work out where they wanted to wander while I was gone. I had quite a few authors I liked, but no physical books for them to sign, so I was happy to fall in with whatever everyone else wanted to do.

Though I could buy a few books. I had a study, with a bookshelf, and could buy things I particularly liked and put them on it, and not ever worry about them fitting in my suitcase. Such a nice thing. I'd never exchange the experiences I'd had in my nomad life, but I was only beginning to understand what a difference it made to have a home.

The author of some of my favourite space adventures had a signing in the afternoon, so I decided I should swing by the trade hall and see if there were any copies I could pick up. The only thing better than a comfort read would be a signed comfort read.

"Are you done running about?"

A hand hooked my elbow, and I found myself being hauled away from the room of my dad's signing.

Astonished, I tried to pull free, only to be told: "Don't be so selfish. This was supposed to be a relaxing trip for Dad, and you pulling a vanishing act isn't helping."

"Hold up."

Bran was suddenly there to steady me while Athaine, who had apparently just left the signing, turned to get in front of the boy pulling at me. I found firmer footing and freed myself, and the boy, who seemed to be a couple of years my junior, glared at me in exasperation, and then froze.

"Who are you?" he asked.

"That should be my line," I said, rubbing my arm pointedly, though he hadn't really hurt me.

"You..."

"Are you Mikaela?" asked a new voice.

Turning, I found a mirror. Well, no more a mirror than my mother, but it explained the confusion. The fact that this girl knew my name brought its own explanation.

"I'm guessing your surname is Niles," I said.

Twenty-Seven

"I'm Isla and this is Brodie," the girl said. "We're your—your Uncle Calum is our dad."

"My mother's older brother," I told Bran, who was clearly restraining a need to be bristlingly protective. He gave me a look, then shifted so he wasn't half between me and Brodie.

I regarded my two newly discovered cousins. While Isla completely looked like a cheerful younger sister, Brodie was less obviously related: paler, with pleasant, gentle features that didn't match his attempt to haul me off so abruptly. Currently, he seemed torn between embarrassment and anxiety.

"Did you know they were here?" he asked Isla. "Is that why you were so set on coming? Don't you care about what springing this on him might do to Dad?"

"Make him happy?" Isla retorted. "Get him to stop moping over old family photos?"

"You saw Dad's pen name on the festival program?" I guessed.

Isla nodded. "We were thinking about coming to the festival anyway, but when I saw 'Rock Hardison' would be here, I made sure we'd arrive in time for the signing session." She paused, and gave a wry little shrug. "I've read all his books. They're really good."

"Seriously?" Brodie asked. "Isla, what the hell are you thinking? You know Dad can't take any shocks, let alone another blow up with Gran."

Gathering that my Uncle Calum was ill in some way, I hefted my mobile. "Take my number and go talk to your dad. I'll let my Mum know you're here, and they can decide between them whether they want to chat."

"Even if they decide not to talk, it doesn't mean we can't," Isla said firmly, as we exchanged numbers. "It's stupid acting like you're some dirty little secret."

I laughed. "Well, I can't argue with that," I said, and lifted my hand in farewell as Brodie resumed hauling his—this time correct—sister away.

"You're very calm," Athaine said, clearly enjoying watching the show. "For someone's dirty little secret."

"I don't really see how I qualify as a secret," I said, lifting my eyebrows. "I don't know how my grandmother could have hidden that she kicked my mum out when Mum was sixteen."

Though I supposed it was possible. I wondered what they might have said, and how Mum would feel about hearing it.

"Thinking about not telling her?" Bran asked.

"Tempted, but not silly enough to try," I said. "Mum's super-observant. I just need to get my over-protective urges under control."

"Not easy," Bran said, laconically.

I smiled at him, then looked at Athaine. "No more quips from the peanut gallery?"

Athaine's expression seemed a little complicated, but then he laughed and held up his hands. "I'll get out of your hair. Good luck with the family drama."

"Chasing Lania?" Bran asked, as we watched him walk away.

"Not sure," I said.

"Don't want him to?"

My mother wasn't the only observant person around. I shrugged.

"Smart and funny, but I don't know him well enough to understand his faults. Still, Lania—like my mother—is old enough to make her own choices."

After all, the simplest thing for me to do was mention the lurking to Lania, and leave the rest to her. I looked at Bran, thinking back over a certain reluctance on my part to ask him about the things I knew had to hurt him, and eventually said: "If your parents ever came to their senses and apologised to you, would you want to reconcile with them?"

He sneered. "There's some things you don't get to come back from."

Not that Bran's parents seemed the least bit interested in returning. I hated them a little for that, and had to resist the urge to hug him, only letting the back of my hand brush against his.

We returned to Dad's signing. There weren't any people left in line, but Dad was happily explaining today's 'crossing of the streams' to an interested half-dozen.

"There'll be a full list in the press release," he was saying. "And I'll possibly be adding to it, since I haven't a good fit for my latest. It'll read like a Sevenmore for the first third of the book, but since there's no actual ghosts involved, I don't think it's a good idea to publish under that name."

Crossing to the corner where Rin's sisters were now asking my mother for details of her most interesting jobs, I listened for a while, then said: "I'm going to drag Mum off for a chat, and then check out the trade hall. Have you all decided on an itinerary?"

"Jessamin has an elaborate schedule of signings and panels," Anthea said. "I'd rather go look at the costumes. Evgenie wants to go to some craft workshop. Marcelline won't admit it, but she mainly wants to get a photo with one of the voice actors for *Skyship Sectara*. Our problem is dividing Rin between us, but we think we've worked out a plan. Bran, you really need to put on a mask as well."

Rowan, while far from internationally recognisable, had edged into being locally recognisable, and I'd noticed some very particular glances heading Bran's, and then Rowan's way. Although they weren't identical, Bran was more than similar enough to negate Rowan's attempts at disguise when standing next to him.

"Starting to look like leaving the bodyguards behind was the wrong call," Kyou said. "Swing by the trade hall and you might find a more effective disguise."

We agreed on a meet-up time for lunch, and then Rin and Bran dispersed with various siblings, leaving me, Kyou and Lania behind. Kyou cast me a thoughtful glance and said he'd join the disguise-buying expedition.

"I have a small family tangle to clear up," I told Lania. "Do you mind waiting a half hour or so? Or, we could catch up in a bit?"

"Trade hall," she said, and departed in Kyou's wake, no doubt having picked up on the somewhat unusual note to the arrangements.

As did my mother, who said: "Sit down and tell me about it?"

Shifting to seats at the back of the room, I said: "Just wanted to warn you to reconsider Isla or Brodie if you have them on your list of baby names, unless you want to name the twins for my cousins. Who are at the book festival with their dad."

Mum looked down at her hands, frowning. Her family was never a subject she enjoyed.

"Isla saw Rock Hardison on the program and manoeuvred her father and brother to come to the festival, but didn't tell them. He—Uncle Calum—is apparently not able to take shocks very well, so I suggested Isla tell him her plans before actually showing up with him. Meanwhile, we have the perfect opportunity to make ourselves scarce, should you deem it necessary."

This eased the frown, and she raised an eyebrow at me, saying: "I don't have anything to run away from."

"Isla talked about her dad as if he was wracked by guilt," I said. "Did he do something awful?"

"He was only nineteen when I left, and contributed not much more than a couple of pointless lectures about not wasting my life." She grimaced. "I'm not petty enough to say no if he does want to talk, but not if my mother is anywhere in the vicinity."

"Okay," I said, and sent a text to Isla.

We settled back to watch Dad being self-effacing at his small collection of fans, and by the time his hour-long room booking was up, we had arranged to meet my uncle and cousins at the nearest convention centre café.

"Calum? Really?" my dad said, after we explained our change of plans. "I wonder if he's thought up any more names to call me."

"Predictable or interesting names?" I asked.

"Oh, quite inventive. He was in his first year of a literature degree at the time, and had clearly been wallowing in the Renaissance. Didn't quite call me a varlet, but lapsed into iambic pentameter once or twice."

"I seem to recall a couple of his phrases showing up in your books," Mum said. "Usually from sneering henchmen types."

"Few things more satisfying than to pillory one's enemies in prose," Dad murmured. "Maybe today will give me new material."

This was possibly not the correct attitude to go into a family reunion, but it made my mother smile, and she maintained that when we located my cousins and their father at one of the tables. Calum Niles didn't at all resemble his son, and I was surprised to find someone who needed only a cravat or some lace cuffs to be the model of a Romantic poet, though with a layer of ill-health that gave him an air of not just burning the candle at both ends, but tossing it in the oven.

"Sorenson." Uncle Calum stood up, and looked like he was thinking over attempting to hug her, but then just awkwardly sat down again. "Thank you for coming."

I don't think Mum had anticipated how ill he'd seem. I saw her expression shift, then she sat down, and there was a brief exchange of names.

"How did Isla manage to convince you to come all the way to Greenland for a book festival?" Mum asked. "I know it's a large one, but hardly notable."

"Oh, we live here," Isla said.

"I teach Modern Literature at Sunderry University," Uncle Calum explained. "Helios isn't exactly where I'd usually want to visit in winter, but after this we're going to head up north of Lake Helios. Cabin in the snow kind of thing. Are you here just for the festival?"

"No, we've started the process of immigrating," Mum said. "Mika's studying Engineering at the local university, and seems to have lined up a decade's worth of work after she graduates, so we bought an old farmhouse and renovated it. It'll also be difficult to be mobile for a while, which made the decision to settle down easy." She made a vague indication toward her stomach.

"Congratulations," Uncle Calum said. "And small world. I never thought I'd see—" He broke off, then said in a choked voice: "I thought perhaps I'd never see you again Sorenson. I'm so sorry for not supporting you more. I should have stood up for you."

"That would have only ended with you excommunicated as well," Mum said.

"Maybe." Uncle Calum studied his hands. "I could have at least sent you money. Or not been so stupidly self-righteous."

"...you didn't tell me when Gran died." I had never heard my mother's voice so small. I guessed her throat was stiff.

Uncle Calum was looking thoroughly confused. "But...you refused to come to the funeral. Told us never to contact you again."

Mum looked at him. I think she simply couldn't speak.

Taking Mum's hand, Dad said lightly: "Never happened. Found out about a month after the fact."

"Oh." Uncle Calum looked shocked, but then not that surprised. "Ah."

"We stopped trying to maintain contact after that," Dad said.

"I owe you an apology, too, Gareth," Uncle Calum said, looking desperately uncomfortable. "I said a lot of rubbish. And, ah, scoffed about your writing a great deal. But you stepped up in a tough situation. I wish I had half your courage."

As big confrontation scenes go, this one was turning out very restrained, but my mother's silence made clear a hurt that I absolutely hated. She's usually so strong, so unflappable, and her loss of voice only made clear how deep the wound went.

My dad continued to step into the breach, asking a little about Uncle Calum's health, and how long he'd been in Greenland.

"Do you have to be so horrible about Gran?" Brodie asked, in a muffled voice.

Mum's mother hadn't so much as been mentioned, but I guess there'd been a strong undercurrent about just why my uncle rarely took his family back to Scotland.

"Brodie is Gran's favourite of favourites," Isla said. "He doesn't get why no-one likes her."

"How has she ever been bad to you?" Brodie snapped. "You just like to be dramatic."

Before this could develop, my father's phone buzzed a timely interruption.

"Sorry, I'm running late for a meet-up with one of my publishers," Dad said, after glancing at a text. "I'm having an event later today, and a couple of them want their hands held."

"How many publishers do you have?" Isla asked.

"That's a technically complex question," Dad said, with a slight laugh. "This one is a rep for the imprint that published my Eirich Mailer books. They didn't pick up my last effort, but are now eager to negotiate a contract, while very happily organising reprints." He turned to Mum. "Do you want me to push the meeting back?"

"I'm fine," Mum said. "Let's meet back at the room this afternoon." She'd clearly recovered her equilibrium, and patted my hand in response to my questioning look. "Why don't you explore the convention with your cousins?"

"Sure," I said, and turned to Isla. "Was there anything you particularly wanted to see? I was heading to the trade hall."

"I'm not fussy," Isla said, with a shrug. "Brodie has a couple of books to get signed, but I don't think that starts until later."

"I'll stay here," Brodie said, glaring at me as if I'd done him wrong.

"Don't pout," Isla said, tweaking his ear. "Come on, let's give Dad a chance to catch up with Aunt Sorenson." She hauled Brodie unceremoniously out of his chair, and out of the café seating area.

"Asshole," Brodie snapped, pulling his arm free, but appearing to accept his fate after a few glances back at his father, and joined Isla in catching up with my father.

"You don't only write as Rock Hardison, Uncle Gareth?" Isla asked, ignoring her brother.

"He likes a different pen name for every genre," I said, a little wryly. "Do you have a favourite genre?"

Isla was a keen *Star Wars* fan. Brodie didn't admit to a genre for a while, and then said he read literature, not rubbish. Hopefully 'prat' was a phase Brodie would recover from, just like Uncle Calum apparently had.

The trade hall was massive, and I gauged the milling crowds, messaged my Kings and Lania that I'd be in the book-focused section, then took Isla off to introduce her to a few space fantasy series that a *Star Wars* fan might like. I lucked into grabbing copies of a couple of my favourite re-reads, then double-checked the schedule to see what I could do about getting them signed.

"What now?" Brodie asked, grumpy to a fault.

I glanced about, and spotted a familiar face beside a pair of boys wearing head-covering masks: Spider-Man and Deadpool. While waving, I told Brodie: "There's a signing I want to get to at twelve, and then I guess lunch? Are there any authors here you'd like to see?"

He shrugged. "Thanks to Isla, I missed mine. There's some panels that might be okay to watch this afternoon."

"Oh, which ones? My dad's on a panel, but not until tomorrow."

"They have a program stream for trashy romance?" Brodie asked, not suppressing a sneer.

"If not, they should definitely add one," I said. "I wonder if they take suggestions?"

Kyou, Bran and Rowan had reached me by then, and I took a breath to make introductions, only to let it out in awed appreciation.

"What?" Kyou asked, turned, then chuckled.

Lania and Athaine. Lania in a corset. It was cosplay from a pirate anime, I think, and transformed her from 'adorable' to 'pocket bombshell'. She was moving through the crowd like a head-turning parting of the Red Sea and, typically, was too caught up looking for us to have noticed her wider audience. Athaine, in matching gear, prowled along behind her wearing a faint, self-satisfied smile.

"You said you weren't planning to buy anything," I commented, as Lania reached us.

"Athaine talked me into it," she said, a little pink, but obviously happy.

"You look fabulous," Kyou said, warmly. "Though I feel it might be a little uncomfortable."

"It's not too bad," Lania said. "Wouldn't want to have to escape a zombie invasion, or pick something up off the ground for that matter, but otherwise I feel like I've developed a magnificent...posture."

Making some belated introductions, I suggested we ditch the trade hall in favour of an early lunch, and relocated to a buffet-style eatery that was just starting to fill up.

"I feel this thing is also going to be excellent for portion control," Lania commented, making very careful additions to her plate.

"Tell me if you want me to undo your laces," I said. "How did you even put this thing on?" I'd noticed that Brodie's grinch had foundered in the face of Lania's cleavage. Fortunately, he primarily expressed the change by staring at his feet, ears pink.

"They had assistant dressers," Lania told me. "Thinking of getting one?"

"I'm not sure I've even watched a whole episode of the show," I said, and settled back as Lania, Athaine and—to my faint surprise—Rowan, began happily talking about a space pirate cartoon that had been big in Greenland when they were much younger. Rowan seemed to have blossomed behind Spider-Man's mask, though he'd had to fold it halfway up in order to eat.

"I get a weird feeling I've seen your friend somewhere," Isla commented to me, as we went to refill our plates.

"Rowan's a singer," I said, eyeing the dessert selection. "New, but getting a bit popular."

She frowned. "Is he? I meant the cute Asian one. Is he in the band?"

I laughed. "No, but if you've read anything about the development on the Snowshield Tableland, you might have seen a picture. He bought a bunch of land there."

"Oh? Wait, Three Young Kings? Seriously?"

"Yeah. Mum and Dad bought their farmhouse from Kyou. I'd say it's right next to the high-speed rail, but the house is way to the rear of the property, so it's not at all a short walk. Even if you start from the farm entrance, you're about ten minutes away from where the station entrance will be."

"We're about a half hour drive away from the rail line in Sunderry," she said. "Hopefully, after today, we could even think about visiting some time. I think it'd do Dad the world of good."

My view on this would depend on how my mother was later.

"What did you mean about the family acting like I'm a secret?" I asked, deciding on the tiramisu. "Surely our grandmother didn't manage to hide that Mum had a baby."

"Oh, more than that," Isla said, with a grimace. "She told everyone Aunt Sorenson died."

Twenty-Eight

Secret relationships mean sometimes not getting a hug when you want one. Being with Kyou and Bran, however, meant a few long looks at my subdued air, an adeptly-created diversion soon after we left the restaurant, and separation off into an empty conference room. Then, hugs.

"I find that I have a very low tolerance for seeing you upset," Kyou said. "You're usually so unphased by everything."

"Funny, I'm feeling the exact same way about my mother," I said, leaning further into their arms. "I'm not ordinarily so protective of her, because I've never seen her as needing protection, but today made me see she's never really recovered from being kicked out."

"Cutting relatives off doesn't mean you can make yourself not care," Bran said, with full awareness that he would probably never reconcile with his own parents. "What did your cousin tell you?"

"When my grandmother kicked my mother out, she told everyone Mum had gone away on a school exchange program. And later claimed Mum had died in a car accident."

"Extreme," Kyou commented, after a moment.

"The McAllister side of Mum's family isn't very large, and while there's more on the Niles side, Mum was never close to them growing up, since her dad died when she was pretty young. But I'd always found it strange that *everyone* cut Mum off, and were never interested in meeting me. It turns out I really am a family secret. Isla and Brodie only know because their dad got drunk and had an argument with my grandmother."

"You're thinking your mother will be particularly upset by this?" Bran asked.

"I..." I paused. "Probably not that much. I think the person she's been most upset with is Uncle Calum." Taking a steadying breath, I straightened. "Sorry. I'm a bit over-the-top about Mum at the moment."

"I expect she appreciates the cotton wool treatment, even if it isn't necessary," Kyou said. "Let's take today as a happy accident, rather than an unfortunate encounter."

"And give anyone who tries to screw that up a big serving of regret," Bran added.

As we returned to the group, I entertained myself thinking up petty revenges I could inflict, but decided I preferred not to spend any of my energy on such an irrelevant person as my grandmother. Today was supposed to be the day I thoroughly enjoyed the fallout from my dad crossing his authorial streams, and I damn well was going to wring every drop of fun out of it.

After managing to get my newly-purchased books signed, I had no particular goals, and followed Kyou to the art show, laughing when he handed out business cards to the artists he particularly liked. We managed to meet up with two of Rin's sisters, and headed toward one of the central halls, where a couple of big-name authors were due to start signing.

"I can't decide between Margaret Marriman and Simon Courtney," Lania said, sorting through her book bag. "I think I like Marriman more, but Courtney almost never does signings, and I'm really loving his latest. New country, different era, and incredibly suspenseful."

"Go with whichever one has the shorter line," Jessamin advised. "Or give us the Courtneys."

"But there's a limited number of books per person," Lania said.

"Don't we know it," Evgenie said. "Our Mums both want copies signed. But we've got more than enough people here to manage."

Copies of Marrimans and Courtneys were shared around, and we worked our way through the throng, only to be met by two "Queue full" signs.

"Filled up half an hour ago," one of the staff members managing the queues said, shrugging. "Try again tomorrow."

Disappointed, Lania and Jessamin retreated.

"We could probably come back tomorrow," Evgenie said, though a little dubiously. "And line up earlier."

"Give me your books and I'll give them to Dad," I said. "He's here for the whole festival, and will definitely be able to get them signed for you."

Brodie snorted. "Yeah, I'm sure 'Rock Hardison' wakes up every day with Booker prize winners like Margaret Marriman."

"Well, he did have breakfast with her," I said. "But I think there was, like, forty other authors there."

"He'd really be able to get them signed?" Jessamin asked. "I'd absolutely love that."

A pile of Marrimans and Courtneys were handed over to me. I transferred them to my backpack—and the overflow to Bran's—and then we turned over where to go next, now that we weren't going to spend an hour in a queue.

"Let's go up to the mezzanine," Lania suggested. "We can get a photo of the authors and the crowd. It won't be the same as getting the books signed ourselves, but it'll be a step closer."

No-one had any objection, so we began to make our way out of the press. I couldn't fail to spot Lania's happy glance when Athaine followed us. And he obviously didn't miss my faint frown, but only looked amused.

"Should we hunt down a guard dog costume for you?" he murmured, after we'd climbed to the mezzanine level, and were looking for the main hall gallery doors.

"Tell me the story behind your stalking tendencies, and I'll tell you whether you need to leg it over the nearest fence."

He cocked a corner of his mouth, then laughed outright when Bran, who was nearest to us in front, dropped back to keep in step with me. The Deadpool mask made it impossible to gauge Bran's expression, but I'm sure Athaine could feel a chill. Athaine only shrugged.

"Turns out you and I have more in common than I thought," he said.

"You're someone's dirty little secret?" I said, after a pause.

"My mother was, technically. A closed adoption. Had a happy childhood, but a combination of divorce and faulty brakes left her in the foster system in her mid-teens." He shoved his hands into his pockets. "She died a few years ago, never knowing who her mother was. I found out thanks to a cousin using one of those family tree DNA sites, which gave me a starting point."

To stalking Professor Tremaine. A moment's calculation told me the Professor may have been even younger than my mother when she had her daughter.

"So, are you, um, planning to introduce yourself?"

"No."

"Just taking the course to make yourself feel bad, then?"

He snorted. "I guess. To give myself a better idea of the personalities, perhaps, to decide if I ever wanted to make myself known. You helped with that, with the way she shut you out. Bet you can't guess why that happened."

"You know?" I asked, remembering him tweaking me about it earlier. "How?"

"Cornered my uncle after the last class and asked outright."

The much-lauded, greatly-cosseted child genius. Greysen, from my observation, was a quiet, maths-focused kid that I'd probably get along with.

"Okay, so why the snub?"

"You made some model of the Sunseeker Bridge? Apparently enough people talked it up to the Professor that she's had enough of the subject of one Mikaela Niles."

I almost staggered. "That's it? That's all?"

"It's possible she's also read the interesting things the internet says about you and your...circle of friends, but if so, I don't think my little uncle has noticed."

"How petty," I said, mourning the clay at the feet of a former personal hero.

Bran took my hand, and I smiled at him, squeezed lightly, then let go.

"Well, I'm still learning interesting things. And, thankfully, Kybirn Isambard more than succeeds in giving me a personal mentor."

"That's the place you're interning? Or the game company?"

"Part of Kyou's ever-expanding corporate conglomerate," I said, watched him turn at his name, then murmured: "I'm very fortunate."

"We bring each other luck," Kyou said, adding with a quizzical smile: "Any guesses why Rin just messaged to say we're going to owe you several million in marketing savings?"

"Dad's press release must have gone out," I said, pulling out my phone. "With that many identities, *Echoes* will surely get a bit of notice."

While searching, I followed Lania out onto the gallery overlooking the main hall, and did a quick scan of the massed crowd below. A pair of author tables at the front, and an entire cavernous room filled with two snaking lines following rope-line bollards. I watched Lania complete the same quick survey I'd made, then return her attention to the authors.

"Ah!"

Several hundred people fell silent all at once, and turned in the same direction. I'm not sure Lania noticed, being caught up in gaping.

Among those gazing up was Simon Courtney, who adjusted his glasses to better see up to the mezzanine, then said: "Hi, Lania."

Dad wears a certain get-up when appearing as Simon Courtney: tweedy jacket and thick-rimmed glasses, with his hair combed neatly back. It does take a second glance to recognise him, but then he's unmistakeably my dad, a fact that Lania still couldn't process.

"Sorry for the interruption," I told the crowd. "If you're looking for something to read, Mr 'Courtney' here just put out a press release outing his fourteen other pen names."

"You've finally come clean, Gareth?" asked Margaret Marriman, looking highly entertained.

"Well, people keep asking for more books," Dad said, with a bashful smile. "This should stave everyone off until I put out another Courtney. I gather I'll have a consolidated website from now on, to make it easier for people to track my releases."

There're few things more fun than finding bonus books from a favourite author, and the crowd responded with suitable delight. As we moved back from the balcony edge, I could hear a few exclamations of 'Rock Hardison?!' that had me smiling. Dad had insisted it be first on the list.

Last was 'Lead Writer: *Echoes of Samerkel*, Kybirn Games', as Kyou soon discovered.

"Cheshire," he said. Nothing else, but the tone covered everything.

It's amazing how happy you can be, just by making someone else happy. "An early Christmas present," I told him.

"Your dad," Lania suddenly said.

I turned, saw that she didn't seem inclined to strangle me, and repeated: "My dad."

"Is Simon Courtney."

"Yep.   Glad to see your internal processes are resuming their function."

Lania covered her mouth and nose, then made a noise that sounded decidedly like a snort. Eyes welling up with tears of suppressed emotion, she ducked quickly back out to the corridor, and then began to laugh—considerably hampered by her corset.

"Awesome," Isla said. "Maybe my dad will end up teaching your dad's books. He said the latest one is really something."

"I don't get why it's funny," Evgenie said, eyeing Lania dubiously.

"Do you get why it's funny, Brodie?" Isla asked, grinning hugely.

"Oh, shut up," Brodie said.

"I never guessed," Jessamin said. "Even having seen author pictures of Simon Courtney. Clark Kent level glasses."

"Most of Dad's books don't come with author photos, and when he started needing to do them, he decided he wanted to avoid getting stopped in the street, and wore some clear lens glasses. Dad's not exactly shy, but he'd find it a bit weird to have people come up to him when we're out shopping." I smiled at Lania, who was now wheezing. "Before, I never bothered to mention the Courtney pen name because it was one of his worst sellers. After May Brunsfield decided to option *Pool of Glass*, I definitely avoided mentioning it because everyone had suddenly become his biggest fan all their lives."

Lania started laughing again, clutched her sides, gulped, then said: "When we went to see *Sky of*

Diamond, and you told Sirocco that Simon Courtney books were too samey, and—and—"

She began laughing again, started to tilt, and was propped up by Athaine.

"When Katerina told me my father would be proud?" I recalled. "Dad knows I don't like tragedies. And the latest Courtney is far more my taste. I don't know if May will be interested in it, though."

Evgenie had answered a call, and said: "Marcelline has a scheme."

"Marcelline usually does," Kyou commented.

"The mums really are Simon Courtney fans," Evgenie said. "More to the point, they're competitive about...everything. Marcelline says we should tell them that the line was full and we didn't get our copies signed, but that we discovered that you were Simon Courtney's daughter."

"Will that move me out of the people with an agenda grouping?"

"It will give Mum an agenda," Evgenie said. "Especially if Marcelline tells her that Jessamin is going to ask her mum if she can ask you to get them signed."

I liked the way Marcelline operated. "Mention our garage full of first editions out at Noonerry," I recommended. "Those print runs were so small that they're super rare."

"Maybe we'll eventually have a chance to see this town you're trying to take over, Koo-Koo," Jessamin sighed.

"Now that Marcelline finally has an angle of attack, you'll probably be visiting before the New Year," Kyou said. "I don't say the Cold War is over, but chances are there'll be a détente."

From my point of view, this wasn't necessarily a good thing, since Rin's parents brought him a lot of stress. Hopefully, being able to talk to his sisters again would balance matters out.

"Well," I said. "Let's work out which books you actually want to get signed, then find somewhere we can sit down and coordinate our stories."

Twenty-Nine

"Be careful on the ride down."

Bran murmured agreement, squeezed me tightly, then donned jacket, gloves and helmet before heading out into the chill. It had rained around dawn, and the streets were icy. I watched him go, then triggered the garage door mechanism, and transferred my own jacket and helmet to Kyou's car.

"Worried?" Kyou asked.

"Always a little," I said. "Bikes are fun, but dangerous."

"We did a lot of defensive driving courses," Kyou said, tucking travel bags into the back seat. "And Bran, thankfully, drives to the conditions. At least when he's not at a low ebb, which he hasn't been at all lately." He smiled at me. "You're a rising tide, Cheshire."

"What's sparked this reversion to the nickname?" I asked.

"Does it bother you? We tried not to use the name out of fear of exposing you, but that doesn't seem to have made any difference to the amount of forum hate slung your way. I think I'll always think of you as Cheshire, but I'll try to only use it in private."

"I like it," I admitted. "Brings back so many fun memories."

Kyou reached out and lifted the hood of the jacket I was wearing. "So does this."

The jacket was his, an official Corascur piece that he'd lent me after we'd fallen asleep on school grounds. It was a little large for me, but I loved to wear it, and inevitably had to kiss Kyou in proper acknowledgement of how fun it had been to wake up with him for the first time.

"What time's the handover?" Rin asked, watching us from the top of the garage stairs.

"Two," I said, reluctantly sliding out of Kyou's arms. "We planned to grab lunch and groceries in Moonmere."

"Then you better get going before I'm tempted to put you over the hood of Kyou's car," Rin said. "See you Christmas eve."

Rin was in a complex mood: hopeful that Marcelline would succeed in manoeuvring his parents into contacting him, but still angry with them. Fortunately, work would take up a lot of his attention, as he made tiny refinements to *One Step's* score. He'd only head down to Noonerry two days from now, after helping collect a puppy.

I trotted over to hug him goodbye, then double-checked I had stowed everything, and climbed into the passenger seat of Kyou's car. Then I read various fluff articles about my father while we navigated out of the cramped university district. An author having multiple pen names was hardly front-page news, but was giving the literary columns some fun.

"We had our biggest surge in hits to the site yesterday," Kyou said, when we finally reached the expressway. "And an increase in wish list additions for *One Step* as a bonus."

"Dad's a gift that keeps on giving," I said.

"Has he met any backlash?"

"I've seen some griping about Rock, but nothing major. The impact has been much as we'd predicted: Devine has been flooded with rights queries, particularly for the Sevenmore books. Sales of all Dad's various pen names have spiked. That Broderick Snow fantasy is sitting at the top of a few charts, which is quite the turn-around. Caitlin is probably the only person who isn't entirely happy—Caitlin's the editor for his Simon Courtney books—because the Courtney name doesn't gain all that much. But *Three Copper Coins* has been received super well, so it's hard for her to be unhappy with him at the moment."

"You think it might really have a chance at the Booker?"

I shrugged. "From the reviews, it's sure to be nominated for some awards, somewhere. Whether it satisfies the criteria of the Booker is another question. I really want to read *Yesterday, Upon the Stair*, since Mum said she thinks it's even better. Dad's still fussing with it, and won't give me a copy."

"That would be the ideal one to be shortlisted," Kyou said. "We could take photos of our staircase."

I laughed, because he was so pleased by the knock-on impact of my dad's fame. "You really do dislike spending money on advertising."

"Everyone deserves at least one pet hate." He gave me a swift glance, lips curling. "And just think about when we open up Fox Hollow, with views of your father in the distance."

"He'll think that's hilarious," I said. "Unless his fans turn up at the front door, of course. Good thing it's such a hike to the house."

"We'll consolidate security for the headquarters and Fox Hollow with the residences," Kyou said. "I'm aiming to have something in place before construction starts up. Noonerry doesn't even have a local police station."

"Services really aren't likely to keep up with the sudden population explosion. I'm glad Mum's planning on staying in the city for her last month, and I think she's coming around to the idea of staying with us instead of renting. You're really okay with them staying?"

He laughed. "Since we all took you suggesting that as progress toward you considering the place your home, instead of somewhere you're staying as a guest yourself, we're very happy to have them."

"Do I seem like I haven't settled in?" I tried to decide. "We've always avoided being guests at places for an extended period—I think in part because of my Aunt Nia's attitude whenever we'd visit with Gran—but I don't really think..."

I paused. I am, after all, only renting from my Kings. It wasn't my house, even if it was my home.

"It feels homelike," I said, after a while.

Kyou, who would tease but never push me about my feelings, changed the topic to the progress of the office refit in Gore Heights, and we chatted lightly about the upcoming expansion of Kybirn.

"Do you think you can put down your workaholic nature long enough take a proper break over Christmas?" I asked. "Don't think I haven't noticed how little sleep you've been getting."

"Some of what you call work are the things I consider fun," he pointed out. "Just as doing all those calculations seems to relax you. I have some coursework to catch up on, but otherwise am planning a lot of naps, games, reading, and over-indulgence in delicious food. I wouldn't have agreed to a complete holiday shutdown for Kybirn, otherwise."

After meeting Bran at one of Moonmere's café's, we hit the larger of the town's two supermarkets, and filled multiple trolleys. With luggage already taking up part of the space, there was barely room in Kyou's car for everything we wanted, so we had to sacrifice my passenger seat, and I swapped to Bran's bike for the ride into Noonerry, and found myself very glad of my leather jacket—and of Bran's, as I shamelessly tucked my hands beneath his shirt to warm them. Tableland winters really were much nicer than Helios, though, and when we weren't travelling at speed it was quite pleasant outdoors.

"Do Kyou and Rin have bike licences?" I asked, as we relaxed on the front steps of the High Street house, waiting for Kyou to catch up.

"Never been their thing," Bran said. "I like the rush, but even I don't care for riding in city traffic, for all you can slip through the clogs. What about you? Want to go for a licence?"

"I'm always happy to pick up a new skill," I said. "Though not having this one means I get the benefits of a bike while watching the view, zoning out to think about my latest projects, and also hugging you. So, no hurry."

He laughed, and actually went a little pink. Bran is such a mess of contradictions. But he is, as he once told me, a very considerate and attentive boyfriend, and very honest, as he proved now by meeting my eyes and saying: "Meggan emailed me."

The little shock that ran through me wasn't pleasant. Bran had found it enormously difficult to put his feelings for Meggan down, and no matter how distant their relationship was now, there was an immense amount of history between them.

"Is she enjoying Oxford?" I asked, after a moment's pause.

"Seems to be. A little lonely, since she went in without knowing anyone. But I'm not going to reply to her. Wouldn't do either of us any good."

Did this mean he thought he would be tempted? "I'd be uncomfortable if you did," I admitted. "I don't think I'm a naturally jealous person, and I can let myself be entertained by the stream of hopefuls that hit on you three, but, well, Meggan and you were close for a long time."

"Until she kicked everything apart," Bran said, studying the toe of his boot. "I think Meggan tried to break me away from Rin and Kyou not necessarily because they consumed too much of my attention, but because she could feel something off about our relationship. Because around her I was always trying to be an idealised version of myself, and she could feel there was a gap."

"Whereas you started out rude and surly with me, so don't have to hide it?" I asked, laughing, but then could not help but try to match his steady gaze, feeling a little pink myself. "Do you know, I think the thing I like most about you is the way you cut through a lot of social niceties. Blunt and forthright seems to work wonders when polite invention fails."

He smiled: the beautiful and rare smile that only came out when something had made him particularly happy. "Next you'll be saying you find Rin's general disinterest in 99% of humanity appealing."

"Well," I said, judiciously. "The...superlative disdain that seems to be his resting state is kind of compelling, but I can say that because he's never directed it toward me. His sisters balance him."

"Wrapped around their collective fingers," Bran agreed. "What about Kyou? Do you find his bad traits adorable?"

"No," I said as Kyou, in a show of perfect timing, turned into the driveway. "Kyou's greatest fault is he hides when he's hurting. He spends his energy supporting everyone else, but doesn't let us help in return."

"He's always been one to lick his wounds alone," Bran said. "Don't think any of us are going to get him to change that, though."

"No," I agreed.

Not easily, anyway, so I could only keep an eye out for signs of upset, such as Kyou's recent tendency to work himself into the ground. He did enjoy his burgeoning business empire, but the hours he put in seemed to be growing out of control.

After transferring the contents of Kyou's car indoors, we headed directly to Fox Farm with only ten minutes to spare, and once again disappointed our Cassadine Malway liaison by not being Rin.

"We should hire them a few more times," I said, after we had completed the inspection and handover, and Sang-Hoon had departed. "Just to see if all the consultants fall for Rin."

"Tempting, but we may as well keep the work in-house from now on," Kyou said, pausing to look across the vast reach of Fox Hollow to Borger Hill. "I gather the external work at KI has increased again?"

"Our first request for a new build came in, yeah. Future holiday lets a little way along the river. Currently zoned as rural use only, though."

"Next year is going to be exciting," Kyou said, sounding as if he was looking forward to the zoning disputes.

We'd designated one of the rooms at the High Street house to be a shared home office, and spent what little remained of the afternoon setting it up, before making a very simple pasta dinner, and starting on a busy schedule of gaming, cuddling, and teasing Rin over the messaging app.

I made sure to thoroughly exhaust Kyou, and the three of us slept in a comfortable tangle, but next morning as we walked down to the office, I caught a strange flicker of expression and, looking ahead, found what I suspected to be a major source of his current unease.

A teen sat on one of the benches out front of the office, playing with his phone. If he'd been a little taller, I'd have almost mistaken him for Rin. He didn't quite have Rin's innate elegance, but he was long-limbed and attractive, and unmistakably a Laurent-Beaulieu.

"You must be Gabriel," Kyou said, as we reached speaking distance.

The boy looked up, clearly recognised Kyou, and said: "I prefer Gabe."

His voice wasn't as deep as Kyou's, but still had the mellow note that made you want to listen.

"This is Bran, and I think you've met Mika," Kyou said, very calm. "Are you here with Damasque again?"

"No, they dumped me on Addison to follow his design process," Gabe said. "He and I have an agreement to not waste each other's time when the overseers aren't around."

Kyou's eyebrows went up. "Not interested in construction?"

"Couldn't care less," Gabe said. "But I've got fourteen months before I can leave this shitty family in the dust, so I pretend I'm listening." He glanced from Bran to Kyou. "Keep that to yourself. I only say it so you won't waste time thinking you need to deal with me."

"What you looking at instead?" Kyou asked.

"Futures trading."

"Exciting stuff," Kyou said. "I spent a while with futures, but don't have the time for it right now."

"I'll move into angel investment when I've built a large enough stake," Gabe said. "Won't be getting hands-on like you seem to want to."

"You might find what Addison does useful in the long run," Kyou advised.

"Yeah, he said so too. I take some of it in."

The two newly-met brothers gave each other a long look, then Kyou pulled out a business card and handed it over. "Call me if you need anything," he said, and headed inside.

"For a lot of parents, having kids who are smarter than them is a good thing," I murmured to Bran as we followed. "But I don't think it's really worked out for Kyou's dad."

"Most parents at least introduce their children to each other," Bran replied.

Kyou's mood showed no more wavering during a busy day of meeting new staff, sitting down with Addison to discuss the rail overpass/mall access proposal they intended to raise, and then heading down to Fox Hollow to make decisions about drainage and garden placement with Torsten and Aaron.

While it didn't change that he'd finally met living confirmation that his father had cheated on his mother, I suspect Kyou found considerable pleasure in the discovery that his half-brother shared his hatred for their less-than-stellar father. I don't know if he'd ever have a relationship with Gabe, but it would be good if they could at least be neutral with each other.

Thirty

With the farmhouse sitting at the back of a six-acre property, I'd spent some thought on how to deal with visitors to Fox Farm, and eventually put in something similar to a bus shelter by the gate, with a security camera and video doorbell. It would also be a good spot for parcel deliveries when it was raining, and had a concealed nook behind it where we could store our wheeled rubbish bins somewhere out of the wind. Getting the rubbish to the bins was going to be a trek, but hopefully easier than hauling the bins from the house each week.

On Christmas Eve, Bran, Kyou and I set up a small welcome at Fox Farm, then they dropped me at the new entry gate and returned to the High Street house to finish some last-minute Kybirn business with Rin, who would be driving down separately from my parents after the meet-up at Stacia's family home.

While I waited, I skimmed through the logs of the newly activated security cameras, and discovered Fox Farm's first visitors: a pair of actual vitha foxes, who trotted up the repaired stairway from the forest to explore.

A protected endangered species would complicate my dad's plans for a chicken coop. I was pondering the addition of gates, and maybe even a 'Private Property' sign to deter human wanderers, when my parents' silvery new car slowed and started the turn into our driveway. Waving, I stood up, triggering the gate to open.

"Going our way?" Dad asked, smiling down at me.

"Absolutely," I said.

"We'll stop just inside so we can look at your bridge," Mum said.

"And my gazebo," Dad added, and drove on through.

I closed the gate and followed along behind them, quickening my pace so I could properly see their expressions as they got out the car and looked around. They both stopped and stared at the hill ahead, with the farmhouse at its crest.

"Let's let the pups out so they can do their business before we get to the house," Dad suggested.

"Pups?" I repeated. "Plural?"

"Yes, male and female," Mum said. "They're very attached, and Nadia decided that rather than break them up, she'd let us have both."

I sent Dad a dubious glance. Border collies require a lot of entertaining, and I would have hesitated to give one to a couple who would be wrangling twins, let alone two. But, as Dad's shrug reminded me, my mum was Sorenson Niles, who made almost everything seem effortless. And who had reached the point in her career where she could take a few years off, then work without needing to leave the comfort of her new home, with its views and large fields and probably, inevitably, a small herd of sheep.

The entire rear compartment was taken up by two pet crates, which Mum opened after checking that the entry gate was firmly closed. The two pups had the classic border collie markings: one black and white with beautiful brown eyes, and the other a chocolate and white with heterochromatic eyes of blue and black.

"This is Shy," Mum said, lifting the smaller, black puppy from the crate. "He was the runt of the litter, but the vet says he's healthy. His sister is Dash."

"A name she's had picked out for twenty years," Dad commented. "She has no idea of what wants to call the twins."

The pups were knee-high fluffballs in matching red harnesses, and immediately romped into the grass beside the drive. Shy was noticeably shorter than Dash, but gambolled without any issue in her wake, then returned at a word from Mum, who bent to reward him with a treat. Dad produced a small bag containing kibble from his pocket, and called Dash back.

"Extremely food oriented," he said. "To avoid confusion, I'm keeping an eye on Dash, and your mother is managing Shy. We'll swap between us over the next couple of days, until we've reinforced their names."

"Let's get some photos of us on your bridge," Mum said.

I had a lot of feelings about my first bridge, though it had hardly been technically complex. The newly-added drive crossed the river close to the long drywall fence that divided Fox Farm from Fox Hollow. The banks were lower but further apart here, with a hint of sandy beach where the river started to curve west. Mum and Dad clipped leads to the harnesses to prevent cold baths, and I snapped pictures, then freely filmed as we walked from the bridge along the path to the gazebo. This was painted creamy-white, had lighting and power, a built-in curve that could be used as a desk, and storage underneath.

"Big as a bandstand," Dad said approvingly, gazing up the short flight of stairs. "I could hold concerts."

"I figure we can put a couple of bikes or scooters in here," I said, pointing out the chest-high locked doors to the rear of the gazebo's base. "It really is a hike to the house."

"What's the chances that we'll be able to bike all over town?" Dad asked, starting up the stairs, then pausing as Dash fumbled this new challenge.

"Depends on whether town planning manages to avoid traffic hell," I said. "It's fine at the moment, but once the rail line's open..."

"Next year, let's do it up in Christmas lights," Dad said, as we walked back to the car. "I almost wish Halloween were bigger here, so we could make it a haunted cave in October."

"Nothing stopping you," I said, then paused to eye the contents of the car. "Do you think we could both cram into the front passenger seat, Mum? No, wait, I'll ride on the bonnet if you go slow."

"Get in front and I'll sit on your lap," Mum said, and we made short work of the drive to the house, slowing down to appreciate the three-door garage.

"I had them put a kind of doggy spa into the workshop portion," I said. "For all the bathing and brushing you've signed up for. Could even hose off toddlers, if they get particularly muddy."

"How much of the garage is filled with boxes at the moment?" Dad asked.

"Enough you'd only be able to park one car," I said, grinning. "I sorted it into types when I was stacking them, so all the things that aren't books are easy to find."

I'd lost their attention, which had shifted firmly to the house. The simple outline had changed considerably from the A-line with ageing veranda that Dad had first viewed. The angle of the roof had been adjusted, dormer windows added, along with an arch of glass above the veranda. The veranda itself had been refurbished and partially enclosed, and a red brick wall now extended into the area that had once been a dark mass of evergreens. On the right I'd added an extensive conservatory that would allow us to enjoy the southern and western views without venturing out into the cold.

Dad parked in the carport, and I helped Mum out of the car, pointing out the curving path I'd had added last-minute, when I'd learned of my upcoming siblings. It was a relatively tight spiral that joined with the northern edge of the veranda, just before the enclosed section.

"For when you're wrangling prams and things," I said. "Though we should go up the front steps today. But, first..."

I pulled two small boxes from my jacket pockets and handed each of them one. Dad opened his immediately, and laughed. Holding up a keyring of a vitha fox hunched over a typewriter, he said: "What's yours, Sorenson?"

She showed him the fox riding a border collie, and said to me: "Custom made? It's only been a handful of days since we decided to get a dog."

"Kybirn's marketing unit—well, person—has been putting together some promotional bits and pieces for *One Step*, so we knew where we could get something quickly. Kyou did the design."

"Speaking of dogs..." Dad said.

We fetched the pups once again from their crates, and then I recorded Mum and Dad walking slowly up the stairs together and unlocking the front door. Their home, the castle in the clouds they'd earned together.

Since they'd both been consulted on every step of the design process, the spacious interior would come as no surprise to my parents. Even with the addition of the rooftop level, the large farmhouse had been converted from six bedrooms to four. The colours were all light and neutral, with a certain air of being under-decorated that I knew had frustrated our Cassadine Malway consultants. But my parents wanted to add all the finishing touches themselves. In parts it looked thoroughly barren, particularly the walled garden I'd had added to the north side of the house. After working out the places that would get the most sun, I'd had raised garden beds added, but not any plants beyond a patch of grass.

"I wasn't thinking puppies or infants when putting this in," I commented. "It'll be more useful than I expected."

"And it helps to have a place to hang out laundry without risking it being strewn across a forest," Dad said.

"The conservatory's even safer for that," I said, leading them back across the house. "It'll get a lot of sun in winter."

Again, this was an almost empty room, the shelves bare, but with a wonderful view of the green swathe of Fox Hollow. The south-east corner was the exception: slightly separated from the rest of the conservatory by four standard citrus trees in heavy pots, and furnished with a large tiled café table, complete with plates, cups, and chairs in matching colours.

"A breakfast spot," I said. "Perfect for watching the dawn. The trees are housewarming gifts from us: there's an orange, a lemon, a kumquat and a lime."

A potted standard orange tree had proven to be the single-most expensive present I'd bought my parents. Large trees are not cheap. Though now that I was earning a reasonable sum, I had many ideas for future gifts.

"Is this just for show, or are we having afternoon tea?" Dad asked, nodding at the table setting.

"Afternoon tea," I said. "Our treat should be ready by the time we've finished our tour."

I'd turned the oven on as we came through the kitchen, and as we returned, I uncovered a tray of uncooked pumpkin scones that Bran had left rising in the pantry. Sliding them into the oven, I set a timer, started the kettle boiling, and then said: "And now, the view."

Again, in the shared office, I'd held back on final touches. In addition to the central sealed fireplace and the two desk areas with double monitors, there were only some bookshelves along the inner wall, a comfortable twin-seat chair set close to the rear wall of the fireplace and nothing else to get in way of the view.

"How do we go out?" my mother asked, discovering there was no way onto the deck.

"Through the enclosed veranda," I said, pointing to a door on the left. "I didn't want you to be bugged by rattling doors or the possibility of the seals loosening and letting in a draft."

We headed back onto the veranda, and then out to the broad deck that had replaced the area where the former owners had kept a collection of sagging chairs.

The deck, again, I'd left clear of any obstruction, but the designers had suggested some seating incorporated into the broad steps down to the grass, which meant you could still come out here to sit and watch the view. Even better was the view from my yoga spot, where we inevitably gravitated to just *gaze.* Snow-tipped crags, shaded water, green horizons, and naked forest.

"Overwhelming," Mum said at last. "It really is..." She trailed off, and blinked.

My phone beeped a timely reminder that the scones were nearly ready, so I said: "I'll go set up afternoon tea. Come in in about ten minutes. Tea or coffee or both?"

"Tea's fine," Dad said, a little distractedly.

He was smiling at Mum in a way I don't think I could ever capture. I left them alone, busying myself whipping cream and opening jam jars, and musing over my relationship with my Kings, and whether we could really achieve something like that absolute togetherness. But it was stupid to compare twenty years to our first official six months.

Though it had been a very happy six months. And a whole lot easier than what my parents had gone through. Comfortable and fulfilling and just...fitting. Surely it wasn't bad that it hadn't been a struggle?

The scones were plentiful and perfectly fluffy. I sealed some away for my Kings, laid out the jam, cream and tea, and took a couple of photos. Then I couldn't resist eating just one scone before my parents came in, sending Bran a few compliments because they'd turned out so well.

Mum and Dad ate almost in silence. Not subdued, but with that quiet satisfaction that doesn't require filling the air with noise. Even Shy and Dash had quieted down, resting on the slate tiles beneath the table.

"Well," Dad said, at last. "We'd better start moving things in. Unpacking."

"No more suitcases for a while," I said.

"That'll take some getting used to," Dad said, nodding. He tilted his head, looking at me. "Whereabouts are your friends?"

"They'll stay at the High Street house if you're not comfortable with having them here," I said. "I'd much rather spend Christmas all together, but I can swap back and forth if you'd prefer."

"Are you being considerate of my delicate sensibilities?" Dad asked, smiling wryly. "No, have them over by all means. I can glare at them better."

But there was no sign of glaring when my Kings arrived in response to my text, perhaps because Rin's Hummer was half-hidden under an enormous freshly-cut Christmas tree.

"We measured the height," Kyou said, following with a heavy stand as Bran and Rin manoeuvred the tree up the stairs. "It'll fit nicely in your study—or we could set it out in that walled garden, if you prefer."

"The study," Mum said, and decided on the northern side of the central fireplace.

After much back and forth, we had the tree firmly upright, a special collar beneath it to catch falling needles, and I followed my Kings out to the Hummer to help unload decorations, all the food we'd bought, and various bits of luggage.

Rin did all this in silence, and I guessed from his subdued air that our attempt to lure his parents with a case of author envy had failed.

"Will this be your first Christmas away from your sisters?" I asked, after he'd finally moved the Hummer into the one free space in the garage.

"No, we went on a trip once before, but I could call them that time." He shrugged. "I'll try not to get too caught up on it. I expected not to be able to talk to them this year."

"You can't just call? What could your parents do?"

"Make Christmas all about the feud with me," he said, sighing. "At least I managed to give the girls gifts when we went to the book festival. You remembered to pass on that set of signed Sevenmores?"

"Duly delivered."

Once everything had been brought inside, we decided to postpone decorating the tree until after dinner. We'd crated the pups, and were discussing what to cook when Kyou received a text.

Lifting an eyebrow, he told my parents: "Addison is asking if you're settled in enough for visitors."

"Addison is a Senior Engineer at L-B Corp, working on a proposal for the station-adjacent buildings," I added. "You'll probably like him."

Dad shrugged. "If he doesn't mind watching us cut vegetables, visit away."

Our doorbell passed its first test, and I triggered the gate. Two cars drove through.

"A deputation," Dad commented. "I hope they're not going to propose buying our paddocks or something."

But when the two cars drew up in the turning circle opposite the garages, property negotiation didn't seem likely, as Addison stepped out of one car, and Mayor Thornley and her children, Arne and Marit, emerged from the other.

"I think it's a welcoming committee," I said, eyeing the enormous fruit...bouquet Addison was negotiating out of his back seat.

The mayor also had offerings, but more prosaic ones, in the form of two pies—one sweet, one savory—and a tray of cookies.

"A housewarming gift from the town," Mayor Thornley said, after depositing the dishes on the kitchen island.

"And this monstrosity is from L-B Corp," Addison added, carefully lowering a massive plate holding an explosion of cut fruit, and covered by a clear dome. He stepped back, put his hands in pockets, and shook his head in mild disgust.

"Why thank you," Dad said politely, obviously a little nonplussed. "It's very...very."

"Is it meant to be a Christmas tree?" Bran asked, tilting his head.

"I think you're right," I said, making out a roughly conical shape beneath 'baubles' of cherries, strawberries and pineapple chunks suspended on skewers.

"Dare we ask why L-B Corp is showering Fox Farm with fruit?" Kyou asked, though from his repressed smile I suspect he had some guesses.

"Is your boss a fan of Mr Courtney?" Marit asked, distracted from peeking around her mother at Rin.

"Who's Mr Courtney?" Addison asked.

Dad waved. "Pen name," he said.

"Okay. Anything's possible, I'm not sure." Hands still in pockets, Addison turned, and bowed deeply to my mother. "I do, however, know that he is a fan of money, and the talents who can make or save it for him.

And when I put together a Mikaela Niles with a mother called Sorenson, I was so excited I couldn't resist telling all sorts of people, for which I apologise, since I should have asked first if you minded. Be prepared for some sustained wooing."

"Are you famous too, Ms Niles?" Marit asked interestedly.

"Not really," Mum said, looking amused.

"Sorenson figures out solutions to tricky problems," Dad explained. "She's very good at it, so there's a lot of people who want to hire her."

"What kind of problems?" Arne asked. "We have a big problem now. Can you help us?"

"Arne," Mayor Thornley said, sternly, adding apologetically to my Mum: "Don't mind him. We've been dealing with a lot of political drama, not a technical issue."

"Are the zoning wars flaring up already?" Kyou asked.

"A skirmish during early positioning of troops," Mayor Thornley said.

"The Shire Council controls zoning for the Tableland," I told my parents. "And sound like a real mix of extreme characters and vested interests."

"They're not going to do anything we want unless we agree to all these stupid things," Arne said. "They want this massive car park."

"Traffic is already becoming a real problem," Mayor Thornley said. "The Town Council doesn't begin to have enough public land to deal with the probable parking needs."

"I suspect I also have a vested interest here," my Mum said, smiling.

"We were just saying we hoped we'd be able to bike around town," Dad added.

"Or even ride horses," Kyou put in.

"Why don't you all stay for dinner and give me a little more detail," Mum suggested. "I can't say I'd be much use for political wrangling, but perhaps there's a workaround that doesn't involve converting the town to a parking lot."

"Though a parking lot accompanied by astronomical prices would be a nice piece of malicious compliance," Dad put in.

We divided forces, with Mum taking our guests off for a brief tour and a review of maps of the Snowshield Tableland, while my Kings and I offered ourselves to Dad as kitchen hands. He set us peeling and chopping vegetables, then went to the pantry to consider spices.

"What impact do you see from L-B Corp pursuing Mika's mother?" Rin asked Kyou, in an undertone.

"If it's come direct from Great-Grandfather?" Kyou smiled slowly. "Addison, of course, will report back on the response to his 'wooing'. I'm sure he won't mind mentioning that we're staying with the illustrious Ms Niles because we're all at odds with those who'd usually suffer us."

Rin let out a breath, then looked at Kyou. "You knew this would happen."

"After I'd properly looked into Mika's mother's reputation, it seemed a logical progression," Kyou said, clearly pleased with himself.

"Hoping to keep her to himself," Bran put in.

"I also like saving money," Kyou admitted, unabashed.

"Hmph." Rin's eyes narrowed dangerously a moment, then he shrugged it off. "What's Addison still doing hanging around the Tableland? The RFT isn't even out yet, and he's usually anywhere but Greenland this time of year."

"Chasing Mika's favourite mentor," Kyou said.

"What?" I said.

"Why did you think he's been permanently parked at KI? There's nothing he gains by being in Noonerry except company."

"Should I be protective?" I asked.

"I expect Chloe understands Addison's eccentricities well enough to know whether she'd like to take them on long-term," Kyou said, comfortably.

His smile was meaningful. I looked at him, then handed him some onions to cut.

We supplemented the fruit arrangement and pies with cauliflower cheese, ribs, and kebabs, deciding to keep the roast for Christmas dinner. By the time everything was assembled, the pups attended to, and all hands washed, the sun was well and truly setting, and thoroughly distracted us as we sat down for a meal. Floating glass doors opened from the combined kitchen/dining room to the conservatory, and through it we had an oblique view of the sunset, and enjoyed all the glass dyed crimson and gold.

"I think I'll add some west-facing seats out there," Dad said, contemplatively.

"It could make a great winter entertaining area," I agreed.

"Are you going to have a new year's party?" Arne asked, hopefully. "You'll have the best view of the fireworks."

"There's fireworks?" Dad asked, surprised.

"The Reisford lakeside fireworks," Mayor Thornley explained. "They're distant, but very lovely above the lake."

"They reflect off the snow on the mountains, too," Marit said.

"I should warn you," the mayor added to Kyou. "There's a spot between Hera and Skeldder that local teens tend to visit—and on New Year's Eve whole families have been known to sneak up there to watch the fireworks. I've warned everyone that they shouldn't trespass, but I don't know how practical it is to police it."

Kyou tilted his head, then shrugged. "There's liability issues, of course, but instead of fighting against human nature, it'll probably be simpler to put a viewing platform in that spot, make sure the path is even and well-lit, and turn it into an event. Not sure I can get that done in time this year, but I'll see what can be managed to at least minimise the chance of someone breaking an ankle crossing the paddocks."

"Cool!" Arne said, happily. "Can we go then, Mum?"

"Well...we'll talk about it closer to the day," Mayor Thornley said, then smiled gratefully at Kyou. "We quickly realised the rail line isn't an entirely positive development for Noonerry, and there's more than a few residents who are very worried about being cut off from things they're used to. A gesture like allowing the firework viewing to continue will also go a long way."

"Did you find a way to stave off the parking lot?" Rin asked, curiously.

My mother had spent the meal wearing the abstracted air she used when puzzling through issues, so I knew she was still thinking it through. But she half-nodded, and smiled when Addison made a small cheering gesture.

"You won't entirely overcome the zoning roadblock without replacing the parties involved," Mum said. "But larger vested interests will be moving onto the Tableland and will very likely take care of that."

"L-B Corp isn't the only group rushing to develop up here," Kyou put in.

"The very obvious solution to traffic issues is public transport," Mum went on. "Park-and-ride is a solution many established tourist locations utilise: that at least shifts the location of the parking lots to less high-cost areas. But having gone over what public land is currently available, the best course seems to be to aggressively promote an east-west rail line, either to the next town, or all the way to the western mountains. With the exception of two properties that would need to be partially acquired, there's already a pre-existing corridor of land between the main body of the town and that cheese factory."

Mayor Thornley developed a very tangled expression, but only said: "While the Shire Council would probably enjoy a western rail line, that would just give them one more thing to hold over us zoning-wise."

"Rail is federal," Addison said.

Mum nodded. "You're facing a big fish in a small pond issue, but they're minnows when you start expanding the scope of your planning. Noonerry is now a major stop on a national north-south artery, and parking is only the beginning of your issues. Water and power capacity need to be reviewed. Locations for hospital, fire, police, ambulance and school facilities all need to be reserved. The main road isn't adequate to the current amount of traffic, let alone what it will be in ten years. You need a twenty-year roadmap for the whole of the Tableland, and you need to make it an election issue."

"But I wouldn't even know where to begin..." Mayor Thornley said.

"Begin with the vested interests around the table," Mum said, smiling. "Mika and I can certainly devise a town layout that balances transporting a lot of people while still including bike paths. You've a newly local investor ready-made to do cooperative development, and a representative of a major international construction firm that will not only be anxious to be in early on the opportunities going west will offer, but no doubt has the federal political connections to get the proposal onto the right desks."

"And," Kyou said, "like the model we have at Kybirn Isambard, creating a plan and showing it to residents both in Noonerry and further west will be both a reassurance and an opportunity to draw in supporters. The proposed path of the line west, and exactly where stops will be, can be used very judiciously, even if we have no actual control over the final result."

"The important point is to be proactive, not reactive," Mum went on. "You know there's an ideal result for Noonerry's development. Lay it out so everyone can see, and you'll find that others will start pushing for it."

After seeing off the visitors and stacking the dishwasher, we decorated the tree while chatting about things we'd like to see in Noonerry. Mum began a rough layout, and also pointed to a spot between the Kybirn headquarters site and the cheese factory that the mayor had said had long been discussed for either an access road or at least a walking path down off the Tableland.

Since it would lead to back-end farming land bordering on the national park, there'd never been a reason to justify the cost.

"I'll try to acquire the adjacent land down there before spreading the idea any further," Kyou said.

"This increasing tendency to buy any old farm you see..." Rin murmured.

"We could put a warehouse for your instruments down there," Kyou replied blandly.

"What were you thinking of using it for?" Dad asked, regaining his bemused expression.

"Nothing as yet. I'd primarily be looking at ensuring we don't face access issues driving out, if we do go to the trouble of putting in a road down. Since horse riding is permitted in the national park, I'm really more interested in being able to ride down off the Tableland to explore, without having to go all the way to Moonmere."

"Just remember our main funding goals," Bran said, with a shrug. "We can't risk a shortfall on *Echoes*."

"I've set aside half the Moonmere land purchase as a reserve fund. We'll have no problems making a sale if we encounter cashflow issues."

"I'm going to take a shower and have an early night," I said. "Do you all have any preferences for time for breakfast? I'm going to try out that waffle maker."

"Eight should be doable," Dad said, as the one person who had real trouble with mornings. "I don't suppose there's a forecast for snow tomorrow?"

I laughed. "No, wind! If they've predicted right, we finally get to meet the Buster."

"Want company?" Rin asked in a low voice, when I was a safe distance from my parents. He loved showering with me.

"No, I'm going to wrap a present," I said. "Come up in half an hour."

Upstairs had its own bathroom, two bedrooms, a storage room, and a shared living area at the western end of the house, where we'd installed an arched window that looked toward the town, and would again give beautiful sunset views. Eventually, this area would be a shared playroom for my siblings, but for now it was a nice sitting room away from the rest of the house.

Since it was night, I drew the curtains, tried out the shower, and then carefully chose a new camisole set before moving on to wrapping.

"What are you doing?"

My mother stood staring at me from the sitting room entrance as I laboured to pull on another layer. I felt myself blush, but then grinned, twirled to display the extra-curvy shape all my clothing—and some of my Kings'—had given me, and said:

"We've always been talking about playing pass the parcel."

I think I almost made *her* blush, but my mother is nothing if not adaptable, so she only said: "I'll make sure your father doesn't come upstairs." Then she gave me a hug—somewhat impeded by my many layers—and said: "Thank you, sweetheart. The house is everything I hoped it would be."

"I'm glad," I said, hugging her back. "Though it's probably lucky it's winter and we don't have to worry about mowing the lawn."

Mum laughed. "I talked to Sigrid about sheep, and herding. Having a connection with the town mayor is very useful: she knows someone who'd be willing to sell us a few of the local sheep, and who has experience with training dogs. That will nicely take care of both keeping the grass under control, and entertaining Shy and Dash."

"The more animals you acquire, the less you'll be able to travel."

"I'm willing to ruthlessly exploit you when I need to be out of town," Mum said, comfortably.

"Thanks!"

"Even when the twins are older, I'll probably only take short work trips from now on, for particularly interesting jobs or locales. I'll never regret all our adventures, but I have such...burning delight at the idea of putting down roots in this place. The journey's what matters, but it's nice when the destination has views in every direction."

"Tomorrow—no, the day after, since tomorrow's going to be windy—we'll have to drive up to the top of Borger. All these views, plus this magnificent southern aspect. I'm going to love trying to design a house that sits well in the environment, and maximises the outlook." I paused. "Well, I'll come up with the structural concept, and Fabian will add the parts I'm missing. What I'm really looking forward to is the viaduct, but we won't be able to start that for years."

My mother, who I knew was still very dubious about the long-term health of my four-way romance, glanced at me, then said: "Well, I hope you get to build it."

Thirty-One

Pass the parcel worked my Kings up to a fever pitch, and we ended exhausted, collapsed in a post-shower tangle on a smaller than usual bed. Despite all the exercise, I still woke early, and for once before Kyou. He was on my right, and I enjoyed his profile for a while. He seemed younger and more vulnerable asleep.

"Do you ever look at me that way?"

Rin, who I hadn't even realised was propped up against the bed head on Kyou's far side. It was rare that any of them approached the touchy subject of whether I liked one of them more, but the tone was only curious.

"I've spent quality time admiring your beauty and trying to work out a way to solve your problems," I told him. "I hate how upset you've been, and keep wishing I'd at least yelled back at your parents when they came over to be awful at you."

He laughed. "I'm glad you restrained yourself. While Bran's probably right that I need to take a harder line with my parents, I do want to keep some sort of relationship with them. And I want them to like you...well, not completely hate you."

From what I'd seen of them, Rin's parents would not take well to the idea of a four-way relationship, and would actively campaign to break us up.

"What would you do if they tried to make you choose between me and your sisters?" I asked quietly.

"They have no power to impose that choice," he said, seriously, holding out a hand to help me out of bed across Kyou. "Though it's convenient that we're flying under the radar. I know they won't react nearly so well as your parents."

"Who are poised to snatch you away as soon as they see anything amiss," Kyou added, having inevitably woken up. "Let's not talk about that today."

"Yeah," Bran murmured, shifting to look at us.

"There are more interesting topics," Rin agreed, and dropped his pitch a notch. "Are you sore, Mika?"

"Yes!" I said. "I need a good rest today."

"Worth it," Bran said, sitting up. "We should make that a Christmas Eve tradition."

"Some sort of game, anyway," I said. "Too much fun not to. What time is it?"

"A bit after seven," Bran said, snagging his phone from the bedside table.

"Presents, then we'll all go make breakfast," Kyou declared.

"Get dressed first," I said, wandering out into the shared lounge area, and looking wryly around at my scattered clothing.

"My present involves you getting dressed," Rin said.

"Is it something white and delicate?" I asked, but this only made him look deeply pleased with himself.

"Rin's present, and then we'll all clean up and get dressed," Kyou said.

Rin went into the second bedroom and returned with a very large box. I had to chuckle when the four of us, all very naked, gathered around for gift unwrapping, and then laughed aloud because the contents of the box were indeed white, white, cream, beige and white.

It was a complete outfit, from dainty underwear embroidered with dandelions, all the way to a pair of thigh-high sheepskin boots with chocolate-brown laces. These matched with white corduroy trousers and snug top, along with a bleached sheepskin jacket. Rin had even included accessories like gloves, scarf, and a pompom beanie.

After much assistance lacing up the boots, I had to admit that I looked amazing: Rin's interest in clothing me was fortunately accompanied by an excellent fashion sense.

"I'd say make this a Christmas tradition as well," I said, after kissing him. "But my entire wardrobe would end up white and off-white."

"You say that like it's a bad thing," Rin said, and let me go to open the curtains, then took a photo of me.

I shook my head, then said: "My presents to you three next."

Shopping for 'Three Young Kings' was no easy task, so I'd given up and made them models instead. I'd built the circular nook from each of their bedrooms, and added touches like a finger-sized violin, an open book on Bran's window seat, and canvasses propped against the wall by Kyou's easel.

"Where did you find the time?" Kyou asked, holding his up to admire. "Is this real glass?"

"Here and there, and yes."

"Did you do one of yours as well?" Bran asked, lifting his gift and passing it to me.

"No, though I might start on it when we get back to the city, to complete the set. Not having to think about how to fit things into suitcases is so nice."

The gift Bran handed me next was obviously a framed picture, and as I eased the paper back, I tried to guess what Bran might have chosen, then caught my breath in recognition. Brunel's design for the roof of Paddington Station.

"I couldn't find any original plans of his for sale," Bran said, almost apologetically.

"I'd be astonished if you had!" I said, hugging him. "I think this is exactly what I would have bought, if I'd thought to buy myself a print. I'll put it on the wall by the bed, so I can see it whenever I wake up."

"I feel that's symbolic in a way I don't quite like," Rin said. "Wouldn't you rather see us?"

"This, on the other hand," Kyou continued, "is conditional that you hang it somewhere I don't usually go."

He also handed me a wrapped picture frame, and I paused, suddenly hopeful, then quickly tore the paper away.

A painting of me. Me in my study, head propped on one hand, completely immersed in drawing a city in the world we were all working on creating. There was a coffee cup with a wolf, a fox and cat design, and an actual cat, visible in the branches of the tree through the window.

"Put it away for now," Kyou said. "If I look at it, I'll need to fix errors."

I remembered Rin telling me that Kyou's non-digital paintings were deeply personal to him, that he painted the things he felt strongly about, which is why he kept most of them turned to the walls. Since he had no problem displaying the non-figurative work he'd been assigned for classes, I hadn't been sure whether it was his mother's perfectionism, or simply the emotions tied up in particular paintings that he struggled with. This at least seemed to be perfectionism.

"I have to show Mum and Dad," I said, setting it down carefully so I could hug Kyou. "Would it work for you if I kept it here, but somewhere central? I really don't want to hide it."

"So long as you don't put it up until we're about to leave."

Agreeing on this, we tidied up and went down to make waffles and a variety of toppings. With two new puppies my parents had, of course, been up during the night, but were currently in their bedroom. Our Christmas gifts for my parents were an ice cream maker, and another excessive coffee machine, which soon lured my dad into the open. I swear I could seal a cup of coffee in a locked box and bury it, and so long as it was within a certain range, my dad would still emerge, eyes half shut, and gravitate in its general direction.

By the time Mum came out, caffeine had worked enough magic on Dad that he could follow her outside without apparent danger of falling off the hillside, and he was fully conscious when they returned.

"All the best breakfasts could be mistaken for dessert," he said, rubbing his hands at the lavish range of toppings. "How about French toast for New Year's Day?"

"Sure, but let's work on Christmas first," I said. "Shall we have a late lunch/dinner so that we're properly hungry after all these waffles?"

"I'd like to go down to the forest for a walk before this wind storm arrives," my mum said, firmly.

"That's a lot of stairs," Dad said.

"I'll stop and rest coming back up. The pups won't be able to walk very far, so it could only be a short walk anyway."

I hesitated, knowing I should trust my mum to gauge her own limits, but still feeling this was risky. Her low tolerance for cossetting did not mix well with high-risk pregnancies.

"There's a trail entrance about fifteen minutes' walk north," Kyou said. "Why don't you three head down, and one of us will drive around with the cars to collect you? Do you think the pups can make it?"

"We can carry them, if not," my dad said, giving Kyou an approving nod. "I'll have a look at what ingredients we have and decide on a cooking plan while we walk. Anyone have anything special they'd like to do?"

"I'm making those candied pecans," I said.

"I brought the ingredients for cassata," Bran said. "I'll have to start the first ice cream flavour mixing, so I'll catch up."

"And, given the roundabout route, we'd better leave sooner rather than later to play pickup," Rin said. "Should I put the pups' crates in the Hummer?"

Within a couple of minutes, they had our outing organised, and Kyou and Rin set off on the drive down to the trail head. In the meantime, Bran had tucked a couple of flasks of water into my day bag, along with a few snacks, leaving Mum, Dad and me little more to do than move our feet.

"They make it so hard to find fault with them," Dad griped, as we followed the new path along the outside of the garden wall to the top of our stairs down.

"I'm sure once we all stop being on our best behaviour, we'll find something to annoy you," I said, smiling. "But this is very much who they are. At least for the people they like."

"What about those they don't like?" Mum asked.

"Well, Kyou genuinely enjoys helping people, unless they're awful people. Bran doesn't mind helping, but only if it doesn't encourage the horde who want a piece of him. Rin would put a stranger out if they were on fire, but otherwise reserves his energy for the very small group he cares about deeply."

Dad laughed, but said: "Okay, I'll stop picking on them for now. They're great company for Christmas, at any rate."

"Oh, I forgot to tell you about some uninvited guests," I said. "I'll show you when we get downstairs."

The stairs had been fully refurbished, and had a solid railing, but I still fretted watching my mother going down them. We chose to carry the pups, though they were already agile and inclined to try to race off when we reached the overgrown path that connected our property to one of the official trails. After admiring my video of vitha foxes, Mum and Dad spent some time using treats to continue training Shy and Dash to walk to heel and not pull on their leads. The pups had already learned some basics before meeting my parents, and were quick to obey after a little reinforcement.

They slowed us down, though, so we weren't even halfway when Bran caught us up. He glanced at my parents, whose focus was on the pups, and then took my hand to walk with me, clearly in a very good mood indeed.

We were nearly at the trail head when Kyou and Rin met us, and Dad, who was also in a good mood, proclaimed that he'd always wanted to drive a Hummer, accepted the keys, and let me and my Kings enjoy the walk back. I liked that none of us felt the need to fill the air with chat, that we could wander together just enjoying the stark branches and exposed views of winter.

The stairs back up weren't that taxing, but I was glad my mother had been able to have her walk without taking on the climb. In her shoes, I'd probably have wanted to do much the same, since it would niggle at me to have a forest stair at my doorstep, and not be able to go down it for months. Halfway up, I was especially glad we'd sent my parents back by car, since the Buster chose to rise just when we could appreciate it most.

Windstorms are exciting, and brought a touch of hilarity to everything we did, especially when my parents arrived, and we all had to go out to help them in with the crates and pups. While preparing dinner, we had enormous fun talking about windborne patio tables, pets, and the occasional bride.

It wasn't until late afternoon that the blast began to fade, and we four decided to take a stroll along the drive to help digest some of our excess intake of food. It was still quite breezy, and I was glad of my coat, but on the walk back up our little hill, Rin and I amused ourselves by letting our hair out to stream behind us. Fun is worth a little chill.

"Having witnessed this Buster in person, I find myself very interested in the data from your anemometers," Kyou said. "Will our park be stripped bare multiple times a year?"

"The hills deserve their nickname," I said. "An effective windbreak. There's a lot of safety features we'll need for a hotel on top of them, though."

We circled around the conservatory to where, inevitably, the pups were again out to exercise their obedience and their bladders. My Kings and I sat on the patio and watched as my parents let Shy and Dash romp, then called them to heel, and rewarded them with kibble. The sun was starting to set, and the whole scene took on a burnished tinge. We took a lot of photos.

"I want this so badly," Kyou said, looking down at a gorgeous shot of Mum and Dad.

"Puppies, babies, or Mika's parents?" Rin asked, amused.

"Their relationship," Bran said, almost flatly. "A family full of support and joy."

"But we have that," Rin said. "Don't we Mika?"

They all looked at me, with a weight of expectation almost as powerful as the Buster. I hadn't been prepared to be put on the spot, but could at least answer Rin's question.

"To be honest, I never thought I'd make good girlfriend material," I said, slowly. "But I decided I'd give us a try, and have, I guess you could say, been expecting a major turning point. Either we'd find there simply wasn't enough of me to share between you all, or we'd be reforged by adversity until I found a whole new definition of love. But all the while we've gone along simply and comfortably. It's just been so...easy."

Rin, who was sitting a little behind me, laughed. "I hope you're not saying you want a few arguments?"

"No." I leaned back against his legs, curled my arm together with Bran's, and took Kyou's hand. "I'm just saying I discovered I like being your girlfriend. Instead of ever finding you a distraction, or too demanding, it bothers me not to see you. Even if it sometime involves juggling my energy, I never feel like you're too much. I want to walk through a thousand forests with you. I want to be the first to hear every piece of music you compose. And be someone you're willing to talk about your pictures with. Because, however I define it, I am completely in love with you."

This was the first time I'd put it into words: my big step from 'trying it out' to 'official'.

"Don't even think about taking that back," Rin commanded.

Kyou's hand gripped mine tightly, then he let go and hugged me instead, murmuring: "Cheshire"

"We're not trying anything out," Bran said. "You're a part of us."

Most certainly not a limpet clinging to the outside of a fortress of three, trying to become Queen, but a fourth in a relationship that only grew deeper because of my addition. I had really been so lucky to meet my Kings, and couldn't help but try to kiss them all at once.

"Do I need to turn the hose on you four?" my dad asked, sometime later.

I laughed as my Kings let me go, and grinned unashamedly at my parents.

"We're going to build a castle in the clouds," I told them, finally confident that what had first been a game, and then something of an addiction, could be my happily ever after.

Epilogue

Beneath a rain of white-gold leaves, and to the accompaniment of swooning violin, tender cello and gentle piano, I walked down the aisle. My dress was not new: I'd chosen to wear the green and white gown I'd had custom-made for my high school Seniors' Ball, with the addition of a narrow chiffon shawl in a matching shade. I doubt I'll ever have another dress I love as much, and I don't have nearly enough opportunities to wear it.

Adjusting my grip on a trailing bouquet in matching colours, I smiled at my dad, then glanced at my Kings as I reached the head of the aisle, and resolutely turned left.

My Kings continued to play, the music shifting, becoming unusually fast for a processional, because Rin had composed it, and knew well the girl of four who came next, bursting into view at a pace far greater than we'd rehearsed. Hair a riot of blond curls threaded with flowers, her dress pale green with trailing dark green ribbons, Carys gleefully threw flower petals at the sky, the seated attendants, and at Shy, who trotted patiently after her, wearing a flower crown of green and white.

The music calmed, became almost staid, and brought Dash, herding Carys' twin, Elis, who looked like he was walking to his execution. Elis was dark-haired with vivid blue eyes—taking after the Niles side of the family—and would surely grow to be a chisel-cheeked heartbreaker. His reserve was almost palpable, and he focused all his attention on carrying a small cushion holding two golden rings.

Once Elis was in place, my Kings allowed complete silence for a full count of ten, while the wind stirred through the braided branches of the Greenland blaze. As white-gold leaves rained down, a single violin note rose, joined by cello and piano to fill the air with a sense of anticipation, of joy, and then of triumph as my mother appeared, wearing a gown of ivory with a barely visible embroidery of green leaves, unutterably beautiful.

Evelyn officiated. Still indomitable, she had been happy to preside over my latest gift to my parents: a very-belated 'proper' wedding, nearly a quarter century after they'd signed papers in a registry office, with no friends or family present, and two strangers for witnesses.

"I hear some reporters tried to sneak in," Lania told me, much later. She, too, had been unable to resist wearing her favourite gown.

"Yeah – between Dad, May Brunsfield, and a few of the other guests, I guess it's newsworthy. Even the first official wedding at Fox Hollow would make a nice puff piece."

"If you put out photos of that ceremony, you'll have the venue booked through to the next century," Lania said. She started to say something else, hesitated, then fell silent.

"You and Athaine should have your ceremony here," I said, helpfully.

"How did you—?" Lania began, but followed my gaze to her hand, and laughed. "Yeah, should have known you'd notice."

"When did he propose?"

"Yesterday, when we went on that river walk in the forest."

I hugged her. Athaine, while a little complicated, had also been a terrific partner for Lania. He had a geek side just as strong as hers, loved to tease, but also treated her as if it was his greatest fortune to have met her.

"Send me a save the date, and I'll reserve you a spot," I said. "Send it soon-ish, though. We're planning to open bookings next week." I smiled at her. "And there's no need to avoid the topic of weddings around me. This might be the first official ceremony here, but Kyou, Rin, Bran and I held our own little commitment ritual a few days ago, just between us." I smiled wryly. "After having quite the argument about rent."

"Rent?"

"Rin has long hated that I pay them rent," I said, shrugging. "He says it implies that everything is temporary. But I would never be comfortable just living with them and not contributing."

"Yeah, I can see both sides of that argument."

"Doubly complicated because we decided to try for kids now that I'm graduated, and *Echoes* is in its final release stages. Kyou ended the argument by saying he wanted us to go through some formal preparation if we really plan on having children, and yesterday we sat down with their lawyer, doing up wills and powers of attorney and all that to factor me in. And to redistribute shares." I smiled at Lania's little gasp. "I was all set to argue about that, but Kyou pointed out that technically I'm coming up short, because if they were one person and we married, half of everything would be mine. But instead, I'll have to settle for a quarter of Kybirn."

"Wow. Just wow."

"Then they had a hilarious discussion about what to rename Kybirn to add an 'M', but since there's an 'M' in all the longer company names, I feel like I've been there all along. I quite like the idea of being the hidden king."

I glanced up toward Borger, and the only part of the house inevitably known as 'Fox Castle' that was visible on this side of the hill. My house, every inch of it. The home we'd built together, one step at a time.

END